DUEL

IAN DUNCAN MACDONALD

Other Books By

IAN DUNCAN
MACDONALD

BEWARE THE ABANDONED

USING DROUGHT USA

For more information
on these two novels
go to
www.informus.ca

TABLE OF CONTENTS

ACKNOWLEDGMENTS, DISCLAIMER & FOREWORD

DUEL

Copyright © 2018 by Informus Inc.

INFORMUS INC
Publishing division
2 Vista Humber Drive
Toronto, Ontario
Canada
M9P 3R7

There is no island called Saint Matts in the Caribbean. While this book is one of fiction, set in the future, it could happen.

A special acknowledgement to my friend, Peter King, who went carefully through the book looking for errors. He provided many excellent suggestions for improving the story.

For more information contact Informus Inc at telephone 929-800-2397 or admin@informus.ca or visit www.informus.ca

MASSIVE RETALIATION

"Massive Retaliation, also known as a massive response, or massive deterrence, is a military doctrine and nuclear strategy in which a state commits itself to retaliate in much greater force in the event of an attack."

DUEL explores the possibility of a massive retaliation.

Ever since the first nuclear bomb was detonated by the United States in 1945, we have lived with the fear of nuclear annihilation of the world. That fear has tempered confrontations between powerful countries and given us more than 70 years without a world war. Automobiles kill more people every year than armed conflicts.

This novel considers at a transfer of world domination from the United States to the People's Republic of China without a world war and nuclear annihilation.

Ian Duncan MacDonald
October 2018

CHAPTER 1

STATE

Floating, he was lost in the rhythm, breathing easily, oblivious to the smooth movement of his body. Suddenly, his five-mile treadmill run was rudely interrupted. One of Russel Horsemont's officious assistants, looking totally out of place in his dark blue suit and tie, had invaded the Foreign Affairs Recreation Association Gym.

The officious assistant was shouting at him over the noise of the music and the machines. All Rob Lyons caught was, "Hurry.... an emergency meeting upstairs at 8:15 ... you have to be ..." Rob looked at the clock on the gym wall. It said 7:40 A.M. He slowed the machine down to a slow walk, to lower his pounding heart. The assistant impatiently paced and fidgeted, waiting for Rob to get off the treadmill. Everyone in the gym was staring at them. Drenched in good honest sweat, Rob headed for the showers. The assistant marched along behind him.

As he was drying himself off after a quick shower, Rob glanced at the television suspended from the ceiling of the dressing room. It was perpetually set on CNN. They were interviewing Senator Rick Wilcox. A picture of the island of Saint Matt's flashed on the screen. That got Rob's immediate attention. He moved closer to the television, so he could read the close caption. Now, he understood why he was being summoned to an unscheduled meeting.

Horsemont's assistant escorted him to a closed door of a meeting room on the top floor. He had never been there before. He was told to sit and wait on a couch in the hallway until he was summoned.

Inside that meeting room, the Secretary of State, Coleen MacSween, slowly sipped her black coffee and scrutinized her top advisors. The big guns had finally arrived: the Deputy Secretary of State, the Chief of Staff, the Director of the Office of Global Intergovernmental Affairs and the Assistant Secretary in charge of the Bureau of Western Hemisphere Affairs. For an 8:15 Monday morning crisis meeting, it was a good turnout.

She twirled and whirled her white bead necklace, oblivious to all the eyes that were riveted on her nervous habit. On her command, these aging civil servants had quickly assembled around the elaborately carved antique table of her top floor meeting room in the Harry S. Truman Building in Washington's Foggy Bottom neighborhood. They werea dignified, up tight bunch.

President Willie Brown, during breakfast, had been watching Senator Wilcox's press conference on CNN. He had almost choked on his cereal when Senator Wilcox dramatically said the Chinese were developing a naval base on an Eastern Caribbean island.

An agitated President had immediately phoned the Secretary of State to find out what she was doing about this intrusion into America's sphere of influence. Fortunately, Coleen had also been watching CNN. She, at least, knew what the president was excited about.

When the director of the Central Intelligence Agency, who watched FOX in the morning, was contacted by the president, he had a hard time explaining why he had never heard of an island called Saint Matts. He also had a difficult time explaining why he had not been informed of the Senator's press conference on CNN. His protests, that it was only minutes after Senator Wilcox's appearance on CNN, were ignored

Those sitting around the table were trying to judge what kind of mood MacSween was in and whether she would buy their rapidly drafted action plan. Her reputation for sarcasm and ability to pick holes in their elaborate, clever plans was legendary.

A large monitor filled almost the entire south wall of the meeting room. It displayed a satellite image of an island. The island was almost round. It had a narrow channel at the south end leading into a large circular harbor. The shadows in the photograph showed that the ring of mountains around the harbor were high and would provide protection from whatever the Atlantic Ocean could hurl at that island.

The dark mahogany table was polished to a rich sheen. It reflected the early morning's winter sun, annoyingly, right into Coleen's steely blue eyes. She put her coffee gently down on a deep blue embossed leather coaster. She motioned to the hovering white jacketed waiter to close the blinds. As soon as the blinds closed, the murmuring undertones and the tapping of personal communication devices ceased. All eyes focused on her.

"Is that the island that Senator Wilcox says we should nuke into oblivion?" she sarcastically murmured. There were a few quiet chuckles from the more insecure brownnosers at the table.

The very dignified, tall, thin, white haired, Russell Horsemont, Assistant Secretary of Western Hemisphere Affairs, (under whose mandate Saint Matts fell - as did everything in the Americas) slowly stood and in quiet modulated tones responded, "Madam Secretary that is Saint Matt's". He took himself and his responsibilities very seriously. He had failed to hear any humor in the Secretary of State's sarcastic comment. If any of his subordinates had been in the meeting and had chuckled, they would have received a severe frown for their lack of dignity. He was fond of saying, "There is nothing funny at State".

Not intimidated by Horsemont's professorial air, Coleen MacSween fixed her gaze on him and tossed out another seemingly off hand question, just to establish who was boss," What's its claim to fame - beside the rumors of it being the People's Republic of China's favorite Caribbean island?"

Given his chance to shine, Horsemont was quick to responded, "Discovered on September 21st in 1494 by Christopher Columbus, on his second voyage. The patron saint for that day is the apostle, Saint Mathew. Over the years Saint Mathew has been corrupted down to Saint Matts."

Russel coughed, looked around the room to see if anyone was impressed with that obscure gem of knowledge. He continued, "It is an island nation of about sixty-five square miles. The most easterly of the Caribbean islands, about 80 miles east of the better-known island of Antigua."

"Originally a French colony, it was awarded to the British in the 1713 Treaty of Utrecht. It remained a British Colony until it became independent in 1981. Its democratically elected parliamentary form of government is modeled on the British system. The British monarch is the nominal head of government. A governor general is the king's official representative on the island although it is largely a ceremonial role.

He paused, and took a staged, slow, sip of his coffee and scanned the room to see if there were any of his peers who dared to interrupt and make some brownie points with the boss lady. There were none this morning. He continued, "For centuries great wealth was realized on the island from the growing of sugar cane. Until the late 19th century it was the richest colony, per capita, in the British Empire. Riches deserted Saint Matts when Britain outlawed slavery in 1834.

This made sugar cane cultivation unprofitable. Slavery continued in Cuba and Brazil for several more decades and these countries became rich from sugar. When Europeans started to grow sugar beets to meet their sugar needs, sugar cane cultivation in the Caribbean became unprofitable. The descendants of those African slaves that were brought in to work the cane fields are still there. Saint Matts has a population that is about ninety-five percent black."

He paused again to see if there were any challenges to his historical interpretation. Seeing no challengers, he took another sip of his coffee and continued.

"These days they have a tourist-based economy. It makes good money for only a few months in the winter and struggles for the rest of the year. About half the tourists come from the US. There are also two American medical schools there. They cater to a few thousand foreign students, mostly Americans. These are students whose marks weren't good enough to get into U.S. medical schools. Housing and feeding these students is important in an economy where $10,000 a year is a good salary.

The locals, by our standards, are poor. The life span, for men is about 72 years and about 79 years for women. The population of about 40,000 has been shrinking steadily for the last forty years. Their biggest export is their citizens who leave for better opportunities in the United States, Canada and Britain. I should also not fail to mention that it also has an estimated population of 80,000 vervet African monkeys. It is believed this population grew from a few pets that the French settlers set free when they abandoned the island."

With this kernel of critical intelligence, Coleen MacSween stopped twirling her beads and looked up. She wondered what the hell monkeys had to do with this morning's meeting. Perhaps Russel Horsemont was getting a bit senile. She looked at her watch and wondered where he was going with his monologue.

Russel Horsemont did not seem to notice that he had got her attention. He droned on, "Their education system is based on the British system and is quite good with a level of literacy, according to international testing, better than the U.S. There is one giant seven hundred room hotel casino on the island. With 1,200 employees it is the island's largest employer. The hotel's hidden ownership is believed to be the New York mob. They appear to be using the operation to launder money from various illegal foreign operations. There is a high murder rate on the island which arises out of turf wars to control the transportation of drugs, up the Caribbean island chain from South America, to the United States." The Assistant Secretary paused, took another sip of his coffee, and checked the room to make sure no one had nodded off. The Secretary of State started to impatiently tap her beads on the table. Russel took the hint and got to the point.

"What is unique about Saint Matts is its excellent harbor, probably one of the best in the world" the Assistant Secretary used a laser pointer to project a small, bright red arrow on the monitor. He pointed to the slit in the donut shaped island. "It has a narrow entrance, about eight hundred feet wide, which opens up into a basin about six miles in diameter. Both the channel and the harbor are deep. The harbor is the flooded cone of an extinct volcano and is protected on all sides by a ring of mountains. That basin could easily protect a whole fleet from any hurricane. Until independence, it was the British Navy's South Atlantic headquarters. Although abandoned for decades, the fortifications on both sides of the channel entrance and naval infrastructure were built to last and could be easily activated."

For dramatic effect, he took another long, sip of coffee before getting to the essence of why they were all gathered around this table, "The signing of a secret agreement between the government of Saint Matts and the People's Republic of China would benefit both parties. It would bring jobs and much needed capital to the island while giving the Chinese an opportunity to counter America's military bases in Korea, Japan and the Philippines. We, of course, see their proposed interjection, into what has been our private lake, as a direct strategic threat against the national security of the United States. Our objective should be this direct threat by whatever means it takes". Russel Horsemont shot a quick glance over at the Secretary of State to see if he had overstepped his authority in concluding what their policy should be. She nodded her agreement. Horsemont sat, feeling pleased that the information his assistants had quickly cobbled together had made him appear to be the truly professional, wise, elder statesman that, in his mind, he knew he was.

Ralph Pasha, the Assistant Secretary of Military Affairs, a large round man, fattened by many fine meals hosted by military hardware lobbyists, earnestly interjected, "Does this include dropping a nuclear bomb on the island as Senator Wilcox has proposed?"

Peering at Pasha with his face a mask of disdain and disbelief, Russel replied in his most patrician voice, "Although such a response lies within our capabilities, obliterating any sovereign state, even one as small and defenseless as this one, would have horrible diplomatic repercussions. Honey usually works a lot better than vinegar. We need to see why St. Matts feels that snubbing us is to their benefit. Next, we must do our best to change their mind. If we can't change their mind, then perhaps an invasion, like we carried out in Grenada, in 1983, might make sense. However, initially, sanctions, a blockade and even a suspension of relationships with this government may be all that is required to bring them in line. We really don't know what they are thinking. Our first step is to investigate what Senator Wilcox states is their intention. Are they really going to provide a Western Hemisphere naval base for the Chinese or are we just having our chain yanked to test our response?"

There was silence while this was considered, then the Secretary of State threw out the question, "Russel, do you have any idea who leaked this supposedly secret agreement to Wilcox?"

The Assistant Secretary of Western Hemisphere Affairs responded, "No Madam Secretary but it is my understanding that our friends at the Central Intelligence Agency are looking into it."

The Secretary of State turned to her right, "Is that true Mister Cassels?"

Neil Cassels, a slim grey weasel, with a comb over, was the liaison with the State Department. He wore a wrinkled, dated, grey suit that he had bought off the bargain rack for two hundred dollars. He nervously cleared his throat. This was a new appointment for him and he hoped it would be a stepping stone to a higher salary grade. His voice was unusually high pitched, nasal and irritating, "That's right Madam Secretary, it is under investigation. At this stage we have not confirmed that such an agreement is even being considered by these two nations. For several years, ever since the Chinese opened an embassy there, we have been tracking their involvement in Saint Matts. It seemed to be just grants and loans for building new roads, schools and a hospital. These goodies were in exchange for St. Matts declaration that the P.R.C. was the only legitimate Chinese government. If you remember back in 1971 the People's Republic of China was able to oust Taiwan as China's legitimate spokesperson at the United Nations. Until a few years ago Saint Matts had been a supporter of Taiwan's claim to being China's legitimate government. As I am sure you know, the People's Republic of China has always regarded Taiwan as their twenty-third province. In view of the aid that other Caribbean islands were getting, from the P.R.C., Saint Matts switched their support. The P.R.C.'s policy is to deny foreign aid to supporters of Taiwan. Over the last three decades the Chinese have poured billions of dollars into the Caribbean."

"We can confirm that there are now a thousand Chinese nationals on the island fixing the roads and building schools. With our distractions in Iran, Iraq and Afghanistan, and with Cuba no longer a concern after the withdrawal of the Russians from Cuba at the end of the Cold War, the Caribbean has really been on our back burner. In our absence, the Chinese have moved in. Madam Secretary, be assured as soon as we nail down some hard information, we will be advising the State Department." He paused and then continued, "Perhaps all this is a figment of Senator Wilcox's very active imagination, after all he is facing an election in November and any free publicity helps him generate donations to his campaign."

Coleen MacSween, in a very quiet voice, but in a tone that left no doubt that this was a top priority for everyone at the table said, "President Brown is very concerned about the situation and needs our recommendations on how it can be quickly resolved. The fact that the he too is facing re-election in November means he wants to put a lid on this."

The Russel Horsemont responded equally quietly, "Since this is such a foggy situation, I believe we need a skilled State Department analyst on the ground in St Matts as soon as possible. He would of course be there unofficially. We wouldn't want them to think that the only super power in the world is at all concerned about what goes on in this tropical pimple".

"We don't have representation on the island?" the Secretary incredulously enquired.

"No, the closest embassy is Barbados. They handle most of these small Caribbean nations. However, we do have an honorary American consulate there, an elderly judge in his seventies, who retired there several years ago. I talked to him just before I came to the meeting, but he seems to have only a superficial understanding of what is going on in the Island."

Neil Cassels looked like he was going to object to this infringement upon the CIA's fact gathering turf, but thought better of it, after, all it was a State Department meeting and there was a fine line between spying and gathering of information for diplomatic decisions.

The Secretary of State enquired, "Do we not have anyone that we could parachute in there today to find out what is going on? Someone, who won't stand out like a sore thumb and be able to give us some credible feedback?"

Horsemont smiled smugly and mentally patted himself on the back for his own intelligence and foresight. He had skillfully manipulated the Secretary to where he wanted her to be. With his usual smug air of superiority, he responded "We may have caught a bit of a break here. We have an analyst in the Policy Planning Staff, a smart, young, fellow, Doctor Rob Lyons, who may be able to assist us. He has a doctorate in history and has had some success in predicting Chinese government trends." He flashed a picture of Rob Lyons on to the Monitor and continued. "Doctor Lyons is an American, born in New Jersey. His mother, Monique Bishop, was born in St Matts, to one of the islands leading families." He flashed a picture of an older but still beautiful black woman on the monitor and continued.

"She was sent to Canada for her secondary and post- secondary education. She married a schoolmate there, a Canadian, Colin Lyons. He joined Bull & Goring in Toronto after graduating from University. He was subsequently transferred to an executive position in their head office in New York while still in his early thirties." He flashed a picture of a heavy set, blue eyed, white, tough looking businessman on the screen. He did not look seventy years old.

"He went back to Canada as the president of their subsidiary and then eventually ended up back in New York as B&G's Senior Vice President in charge of all their international operations. I have met with him many times over the years.

Some of you may not know this, but when the Central Intelligence Agency was being set up after the Second World War, it was staffed by many ex- Bull & Goring people. They were one of a few large international organizations that had any expertise in gathering huge volumes of strategic data from every corner of the world through their branch offices and correspondents. Although B&G is a public company, traded on the New York Stock Exchange, they have always had a close working relationship with us, the CIA and many of other departments. Their ability to quickly supply credible risk reports on every business in the world, for almost two centuries, has proven to be an invaluable resource to not only our government but many governments around the world."

"Rob Lyons, not only has a good pedigree but he has legitimate passports for the USA, Canada and most importantly, St. Matts. His parents are now retired. They spend the winters in St Matts and are down there right now. I am sure they would not object to a visit from their son. He is waiting outside, if you would like him to join the meeting."

The Secretary of State nodded and said, "By all means, bring him in. Let's get a look at him."

Russell went out of the meeting room and returned in a few minutes with Rob Lyons. He was six foot five inches tall, with amazing green eyes. Going prematurely bald, he had recently started shaving his entire head. Some people, like Rob, look good bald. He was wearing an expensive Yves St. Laurent suit that hugged his body. It made him look extremely fit and strong. Like many children of mixed-race marriages, it was difficult to visually peg his ancestry. He liked to put on an exaggerated Spanish accent, when he was asked what he was, and say, "Duh-min-i- khan". He thought it was funny.

Bigger, stronger and more coordinated than the other kids, he had excelled at sports. He was always the first chosen for any team- when he wasn't doing the choosing. His mother had gotten him into martial arts at a very young age to strengthen his lungs to help counter juvenile asthma attacks. She had almost fainted when he came back all bruised and bloody after his first kick boxing match. He persisted and was soon winning martial arts tournaments. A natural leader, he was laid back, funny, creative and quietly competitive. He made friends easily and they stayed friends.

While his parents were able to afford him every opportunity, much of his education had been paid for by scholarships and grants. He had been an outstanding student. Having Canadian citizenship, through his father, he was able to study at the University of Toronto, Canada's largest and most prestigious university, for a fraction of what it would have cost him if he had been a "foreign student". U of T was his parent's alma mater. That is where they had met and where he had wanted to go to school.

While still a graduate student, Rob had married a Chinese medical student from Singapore, Poh Gek Fan. She was ten years older than Rob and had recently been divorced. Her wealthy parents had engineered her first marriage into one of Singapore's best families. They were embarrassed socially when she walked out on her first husband and left for medical school in Canada. They were horrified when she chose to marry some foreign, mixed race, near penniless student who was almost ten years younger than herself. They had threatened to sever all connections with her. When that did not bring her into line, they reluctantly tolerated her unorthodox behavior.

Her parents' disapproval had cast a black cloud over Rob's marriage. Festering away, just beneath the surface, it was never a big issue but always an irritant. For two years, they lived the carefree, Bohemian existence of graduate students in their small one bedroom flat, a few blocks from the university.

Upon graduation, career opportunities arose in two different countries. Both were stubborn and ambitious. Unable to abandon the attractive job offers, they reached the conclusion that divorce was the only logical solution. They parted as friends, wished each other well, and set forth to meet their new challenges.

When Rob thought back over the two years they had had together, he thought of the fun times and all that Poh Gek had taught him about Chinese culture; the unusual, but great food, she had cooked for him, like winkles in a brown bean sauce which they had eaten with tooth picks. He remembered how hard it had been training his fingers to use chop sticks. At night, he thought about her amazing sexual energy.

Rob had accepted a position at the U.S. State Department in Washington. The last he had heard, Poh Gek was practicing medicine in Australia.

The Secretary of State motioned for a chair to be placed next to her. Those around the table shifted to accommodate his inclusion. She stood and shook Rob's hand.

"Doctor Lyons, thanks for joining us. I believe you are aware of Senator Wilcox's press conference in which he announced an agreement between Saint Matts and China."

"Yes, I watched it on CNN this morning."

"What is your assessment of what is going in Saint Matts?"

"I've spent a lot of time in Saint Matts and I am always interested in what is going on there, probably, because I know the issues and most of the politicians. I read their daily newspaper on the internet just to keep on top of things. Prime Minister Chumley is brilliant, in his own way, but he sometimes lets his emotions overcome his common sense. He is a skilled, greedy, ruthless politician. Although he comes from a poor family, he has become very wealthy and there are many rumors and conjectures as to how he has acquired his fortune. Many of the old moneyed families on the island are appalled by the changes he has made but afraid to show any opposition. Those, who have spoken up against him, have been harassed until they felt compelled to either sell out and leave the island or face having everything, they owned on the island confiscated through questionable legal means. "

He paused and then continued, "This agreement with the Chinese doesn't surprise me. He will love the political reward that snubbing the US gets him at home and abroad. In the islands and in most places in the world, America is usually seen as an insensitive, arrogant, bully that pushes foreign governments around and denigrates anything that is not American. I am also sure that Chumley would make sure that he was well rewarded by the Chinese for his assistance. I would not be surprised to learn that he is the one who is leaking Saint Matts secret negotiations with the Chinese to Senator Wilcox."

The room was quiet. It was unusual for a State Department employee to be so bluntly disparaging of America's image abroad. The Secretary of State realized that this was someone who would tell her the truth without sugar coating it. She turned to him and said, "Can you fly down and give us a quick assessment of what is going on."

"Of course, there is a daily American Airline afternoon flight out of Miami that I could catch."

"Are you sure you want to take this on. It is potentially dangerous. Neither the Chinese, nor Chumley, are going to appreciate any obstruction to their plans. We will do everything we can to shield you from any harm, but we want you to be sure you have an understanding of all the dangers inherent in it."

"I could get hit by a taxi crossing Pennsylvania Avenue this afternoon. Every day is potentially dangerous. Don't worry, I can take care of myself and I am not without resources in St. Matts. As well, I, more than anyone in this room, really care about what happens to Saint Matts. I fear what could happen if Chumley has got them into something that could destroy the island."

Colleen MacSween looked at Rob Lyons, long and hard. She saw the commitment shining in his eyes. She had warned him. He was an adult working for the State Department. She now took the steps that were available to protect him, "A communication technician will meet you at your apartment within the next two hours to link you into our satellite system and give you instruction in how to use our new experimental X200 communication device." He quickly responded, "O.K, I had better get going if I am going to pack and catch that flight from Miami."

Ralph Pasha, the Assistant Secretary of Military Affairs interjected, "In view of the importance of your assignment and the necessity for you to make that flight, I'll arrange for the Air Force to fly you to Miami International. We will send a car over to drive you to the Dulles. If you need any further military assistance, just call me at this private number". He handed Rob his card. "We'll also make sure you get a seat on that flight to Saint Matts. That flight is bound to be overbooked as the world's media descend on Saint Matts looking for the next hot story - thanks to Senator Wilcox's impetuous remarks. I considered having the Air Force flying you all the way to Saint Matts, but I think that might get a little too much attention from Chumley and the Chinese intelligence operatives on the island. As much as it is possible, I think we want your trip to appear to be, just a normal family visit. Using your Saint Mattitian passport should help hide you from scrutiny and keep you under their radar.

The Secretary of State nodded her agreement.

Making points for the CIA, Cassels, the CIA liaison interjected, "We have field staff on the island. They will contact you after you arrive."

Rob, stood up, shook the Secretary of State's hand, nodded to rest of the room full of suits and left.

The Secretary of State, waited for him to leave before addressing the CIA liaison, "Can you arrange for unmanned drones to be circling Saint Matts twenty-four hours a day. Make sure they are fully armed. I want them to keep a close eye on Rob Lyons in case he needs immediate assistance. We also need to keep a close eye on Chumley and the Chinese.

She then added viciously, "If possible, see that Chumley becomes aware of the armed drone so he can consider the possibility that at any minute the United States could zap him off the face of this earth if he should step too far over the line".

Cassels nodded his agreement and raised a question, ``While I am sure that Doctor Lyons is an outstanding employee, it concerns me that his training in gathering and delivering relevant strategic intelligence data is lacking. ``

``With the communication technology that the X200 will equip Doctor Lyons with, all he needs to do is get us in front of the right people. The gathering and delivering of the data will take care of itself. I think with his connections on the island that he will be able to do this better than any CIA operative. ``

With that, the Secretary of State stood up, gathered her papers together and walked out of the conference room. The others took this as their cue that the meeting was over.

Colleen often wondered about the wisdom of having accepted this appointment. The president had once been one of her star graduate students.

Even before he had been elected, he had sounded her out on the possibility of her appointment to Secretary of State in his administration. She had been flattered.
Now, she no longer slept well at night. The flood of disturbing information she was bombarded with never stopped. It was impossible to ignore the fact that there really were forces loose in the world intent upon destroying the privileged way of life that she had grown up with and cherished. She had come to accept that only through the luck of being born to a wealthy family, in post-World War II United States, had she avoided the harsh realities of the daily life struggle that billions of women in the world faced. To these women, to just get enough food and water to survive to the next day was something they did not take for granted. Whatever pain and

discomfort she now experienced, she knew was minor by comparison. Knowing of her privileged lot in life did little to ease the stress she was required to cope with, day in, day out.

To- day she felt every one of her sixty-three years. It was very sobering to wake up each morning and realize that if a disaster were to occur that you were fourth in line of succession to the President. Only the Vice President, the Speaker of the House and the President of the Senate were ahead of her. She knew that no matter how well she and the others in the government did their job in protecting the nation, there were equally dedicated, resourceful individuals, out there with such a hatred for the United States that they would make any sacrifice to destroy its leadership.

Although recognized as a brilliant thinker, the sheltered academic life of a Harvard international law professor had not prepared her for the problems of administering and leading twelve thousand Foreign Service employees in 265 diplomatic missions. Focusing these employees on the safety and the wellbeing of the nation instead of their personal ambitions and problems was the most difficult challenge she had ever faced. At times, she felt like a total failure, but all she could do at such times was to suck it up and try not to make the same mistake again. The press was always quick to publicize her errors and usually mute when it came to her wins.

She understood her personal life was being overwhelmed by her public responsibilities. Her husband, a proud, kind, loving man, had been reduced to playing a secondary support role and he resented it. Days went by when their only contact was maybe a few minutes on the phone. She knew her marriage was hanging by a thread, but she was unable to turn her back on what she saw as her primary responsibilities to the president and to the country.

A perfectionist, her intellectual arrogance would not accept that her subordinates could do as good a job as she could do. She was unable to see that she was running herself ragged by being involved in too many situations that should have been delegated. She did not understand that if you are unable to prioritize, then everything becomes a priority. Thus, situations either had to wait until she eventually got to them or they got resolved with snap decisions when she was forced into a corner and had to immediately make a decision. Without sufficient research and analysis, mistakes were being made by these snap decisions.

The career diplomats had seen Secretaries of State come and go. They saw her drowning under the work load she had piled on herself. They wondered how long she could keep it up. Either her physical or mental health would bring it to a stop, or some traumatic point would be reached where she would finally have to accept her limitations and let them do their jobs. They knew ten years from now people would have a hard time remembering her name.

The strain showed in her face. The makeup could no longer hide the puffy, dark circles under her eyes and the faint grey cast to her skin. The lines around her eyes and mouth had deepened each month. Slowly, because she thought she no longer had time to go to the gym, her weight had gone up. It was inevitable with a daily schedule of official luncheons, dinners and receptions.

Not having time to shop for new clothes, the extra fifteen pounds were not fitting well into her old clothes. The weight of the nation's problems fell on her shoulders and she was convinced, if she failed to carry that load, that the country would be destroyed. Once a beautiful, attractive woman, she now looked faded, tired, worn and much older than her sixty-three years. She walked swiftly down the hall to her large, suitably impressive, office ready to put out the next fire. She had always seen herself as a super star and was unable to accept the reality that she was only human.

CHAPTER 2

Senator

"WOOOOYEEEEE. That ought to piss off those commie pinko Democrats. We'll blast Saint Matts to smithereens," Rick Wilcox, the junior senator from Texas, broke off into peals of laughter as he watched a television rerun of his early morning news conference. He ran around his very substantial office on the second floor of the hundred-year-old Russell Senate Office Building, high fiving and slapping his entourage on the back. His lackeys joined in a chorus of support laughter, like a pack of hyenas.

"We got coverage on every network. That should get their attention back home? I thought I was just great. What did you guys think?"

The chorus echoed back, "Oh, you were great Ricky. You knocked them dead. You sucker punched them, cowboy. Way to go, Ricky."

"What are they saying in Armarillo?"

"Ricky, they love you in Armarillo."

"What about Houston?"

"They love you in Houston too."

"Are the donations pouring in?"

"Like a waterfall Ricky, like a waterfall."

"How many people, we got working the phones?"

"A hundred Ricky, they are just dialing for dollars. The election is in the bag".

A grinning Rick Wilcox smiled ear-to-ear and shifted one cowboy booted leg over the other one on his desk. He leaned way back in his swivel chair and considered lighting up a cigar. Screw the Senate and their no smoking rules. The two flags behind his desk, framed him like the true patriot he was.

"Ricky a crew from Fox News is in the reception room. They want to do an interview."

"Great, show them in."

Rick took his boots off the desk and put on his serious politician's face as the crew was led into his office. "Welcome, it's always a pleasure to meet with Fox News"

"Senator Wilcox, my name is Tom Brogden, we just want a few minutes of your time, so we can get an update on the News at Noon."

"By all means, it is important that this threat to our national security gets full coverage."

The light and the camera came on. Brogden threw out his first question. "Since your news conference early this morning, questions have arisen as to whether this news, that the People's Republic of China is establishing a naval base on the Caribbean island of Saint Matts, is just an election publicity stunt on your part?"

Looking as serious as hound with a cornered raccoon, Wilcox replied in his sonorous Texas twang (that sold well back home in Texas)," How typical of this weak-kneed administration to attack the messenger instead of responding to a threat to national security that is greater than the Cuban Missile crisis in 1963. We've got the nation teetering on the brink of an abyss. This administration's intelligence service is so inept that they were not even aware of what the Chinese were doing in their own backyard".

"Senator Wilcox, who was the source of your information?"

Not about to demean himself by saying he had no idea who his source was. It had been an anonymous, digitally altered voice that had somehow acquired his private cell phone number. He had presumed it was some weasel of a lobbyist who had been paid to hunt down a senator who needed a national publicity vehicle that would play well in their home state. Senator Wilcox responded with, "The source was a patriot involved in the negotiations with the Chinese. My research staff carefully and thoroughly vetted this information before bringing it to my attention. I knew immediately that it was critical to the national security of our great republic that its citizens be informed of this clear and present danger."

"Senator, can you not give us any information about this source?"

"Unfortunately, I am unable, at this time, to supply any details that could identify this information. It could put that person's life in great danger. Once I know that this person's safety is secure, I will be more than pleased to provide their name."

"Senator, are you aware that there are several thousand American medical students residing on the island? Your recommendation that the island be immediately bombed with a nuclear device would kill every one of these innocent young Americans."

"The safety of all-American citizens is my primary concern. It is critical that there be an immediate government airlift to get e v e r y American off that island in the next twenty-four hours. Only, when every American is removed would a bomb be dropped."

"Aren't you now worried that American citizens could be held hostage on the island to prevent it from being bombed?"

"If they were held for ransom then that would be a reason to call in the marines to invade and free them."

"What about other nationalities on the island and the poor innocent citizens of Saint Matts, thousands of innocent women and children. Are you saying you condone America killing them?"

"Unfortunately to protect the lives of millions of American citizens, we may well have to sacrifice a few foreigners. These are the strategic casualties of war. All American citizens are urged to immediately get off that island. It is an unfortunate reflection of our current incompetent administration that our citizens must face such threats. There was a time under presidents, like Ronald Reagan, where the

United States was feared, and these small foreign nations would have done everything they could to show their allegiance to the United States. When they thumb their noses at us, then they must be prepared to suffer the consequences. "

"Thanks Senator, we appreciate your candid assessment of this situation."
"

"The pleasure was all mine. I am always open to a frank and open exchange with the public. God Bless America, the Best Country in the World."

The camera crew scurried out of his office anxious to get Rick Wilcox's inflammatory statements on the air. As soon as they were out of the door, the cowboy boots went back on the desk. Rick Wilcox basked in the warmth of his publicity and his genius.

When this interview appeared on the News at Noon, politicians and civil servants in Washington and many countries around the world, shook their heads in disbelief at Senator Rick Wilcox's irresponsible aggressiveness. It reminded the world that the United States was the only country to have ever used nuclear weapons in war. When they had dropped the bombs on Nagasaki and Hiroshima in 1945, they had thought it strategically logical that hundreds of thousands of innocent civilians should die to send a strong message to the Japanese government that it was now time to surrender. The alleged objective was to avoid having America troops wage a bloody invasion of Japan. Some believe it was done to send a message to the world as to who was now "the boss". Other governments might have considered a lesser target to demonstrate to the Japanese government their newly acquired super weapon. However, it was payback time for the sneak attack on Pearl Harbor, and the American government believed their own propaganda that the Japanese were sub humans and thus expendable. Since the citizens of Saint Matts were almost all black, it would be easy for the propaganda machines to convince the majority of American voters that Mattitians were also disposable.

The senator would have been surprised to find that people really took his flip statements seriously. To him it was just how the political game was played. The only thing he really believed in was saying and doing whatever it took to get re-elected in Texas. He didn't really give a damn what they thought of him in Washington or the rest of America. He was totally oblivious to any foreign concerns. He knew the more he was attacked by Washington and the rest of America for his aggressive statements, the more popular he would become in Texas.

Senator Wilcox had the strong masculine features, thin athletic body and good hair that appealed to Texas voters. There was a carefully chosen western cut to his suits and his collection of fancy cowboy boots was legendary. His blond-haired wife, Wilma, with her perfect teeth and the best hair that money could buy, was his trophy to be flaunted at appropriate times along with their three young, very photogenic, children. They were a legend that attracted crowds of Texans when they attended the World Champion Ranch Rodeo at Amarillo's Tri State Exposition Grounds every November, to press the flesh and show what a great Texan they had sent to Washington.

To the constituents, the Wilcox's were exactly the kind of God fearing, good Christian folk that they wanted representing them. The fact that the Wilcox children never missed Sunday school was an important message that was fed to the electorate. A devout faith had become important in Texas politics ever since the Christian, right wing, fundamentalists had wrestled the Texas Republican party away from the "country club" Republican's in the early nineteen-nineties. Only those who played to the Christian right could now get a Republican nomination in Texas. Ricky had long ago seen the light and had come to Jesus.

Politics had been good to him. His very generous corporate backers made sure that he had enough financial incentives to stay focused on their issues. Their main issue was, "What was good for "business" was good for Texas". Thus, he was expected to fight any attempts by legislators to impose pollution controls on Texas oil and gas refineries or to interfere with the selling of prime beef. He was to fully support any tort legislation that would limit the liabilities that might be imposed on Texas health, insurance and oil businesses by unfortunate judgments. It was a given that he would do his best to privatize every possible public institution from prisons to welfare departments and to make sure his backers got first crack at acquiring them. Business came first because big corporations with their multimillion-dollar war chests would make sure those political candidates, who danced to their tune, got elected.

To get the money for advertising and running your campaign, you danced to the tune of the Texas' Christians. You kept right on dancing to get the nomination and their subsequent votes. This tune included making abortions illegal, promoting private charter school funding with public money, executing as many murderers on death row as quickly as possible (no matter what the circumstances), imprisoning any man, woman or child found in the presence of marijuana or cocaine, making homosexuality illegal and, of course, preventing same sex marriages.

20

Is it any wonder that, per capita, there were more people incarcerated in Texas then just about anywhere else in the world or that it was the most polluted state in the United States. For such a rich state their treatment of the poor was worse than any other state. Texas is the home of rugged individualism where the settlers, on an empty prairie, had to survive on their own resources or perish. The fact that eighty percent of the population now lived in large cities had not changed this attitude. True Texans regretted that their independent country had joined the union of the United States of America.

His fans and backers would have been surprised to find out that Rick Wilcox had a master's degree in English literature and that his graduate thesis had been "Moby Dick as a Reaction Against Emersonian Transcendentalism". His private office, at home, was walled with fine literature. When he got drunk and let his guard down, which was rare, he could quote from the plays and sonnets of Shakespeare and discuss the impact of Charles Dickens nineteenth century writings upon English social welfare laws.

Texans only knew him as good old "Ricky Wilcox Chevrolet and Cadillac" from Amarillo, Texas. At first, he had not been pleased when he had been yanked away from his doctoral studies at West Texas A&M University in Canyon, Texas. He had been intent upon a career of teaching and writing. While his father's death had permanently side tracked his ambitions, he had felt at the time that he had had no choice, when pressed by the family, in taking over the dealership. At twenty-five he had been one of the youngest chief executives of a major car dealership in the USA. It is only in looking back that he realized just how young he had been.

Convinced he would hate it; much to his surprise, he found he loved it. He was a natural executive and salesman. He loved selling cars. Being smart and inclined to laziness, he had had no problem in finding great managers, treating them generously and leaving them to manage their departments while he oversaw the business and wisely invested the profits.

His exposure to amateur theatre in university and with the Amarillo Little Theatre group had let him pour his creativity and acting skills into television ads and promotional stunts that brought in car buyers from all over Texas. When, the power brokers came calling, he found the transition into politics, was easy. It was no different than selling cars. It was just a matter of telling Texans what they wanted to hear.

He had met his wife in his undergraduate years when they were both students at the A&M's satellite campus in the Chase tower in downtown Amarillo. She knew the real Richard E. Wilcox. She knew what he really thought and believed. She could play the game as well as he could.

CHAPTER 3

Flight

Rob left the meeting and walked back to his apartment to pack. His apartment was in the infamous Watergate at 700 New Hampshire Avenue. The 1,280 square foot apartment included a large master bedroom and an office. From every window he could look out over the Potomac River. He had chosen it because of the view and because it was close enough to the Harry S. Truman building that he could walk to work in a few minutes. Those State Department employees living in the suburbs spent an hour or more each day commuting to work through the traffic clogged freeways.

Within an hour Rob was ready to go. He had phoned his parents in Saint Matts to tell them that he would be on that days American Airline flight. They were delighted but not surprised. They watched CNN in Saint Matts too. He figured his father would put two and two together as to why their son was showing up unexpectedly.

As he waited for the technician to arrive, he turned the television on and started flipping through the channels. St. Matts was obviously the hot news item in a dull news day. Commentators debated the morality of bombing a country into oblivion, the threat of the Chinese ascension to being the next world power, as well as hysterical interviews by CNN with parents of students in St. Matts convinced the bombing was going to take place within hours. The BBC, in its dry analytical way, analyzed which way a radiation cloud would drift from St. Matts and how long it would take to circle the globe and increase cancer in Great Britain. Fox television wondered whether bombing St. Matts might result in a war between China and the USA and lead to retaliatory bombings of San Francisco or perhaps Anchorage, Alaska.

There was a knock at his apartment door. Rob wondered, if it was the NSA technician. He also wondered if it was, how he had got by the lobby security and avoided being buzzed up. He opened the door to find what looked like a college student who was dressed in jeans, hiking boots, flannel shirt, bomber jacket and back pack.

"Doctor Lyons?"
"Yes?"

"I'm Les Prince from the National Security, here to hook you up with X200"

Rob ushered him in. He took Prince's jacket and hung it across a chair. He had been expecting a suit with a briefcase. Agent Prince took a blue plastic case out of his back pack. He opened it. Inside were a dozen gold rings. The rings were large but not unusually so. They had what looked like a shiny, black, domed, oval stone rising above their setting.

Agent prince, asked, "Can I see your right hand."

Rob held out his right hand. Prince examined it and then selected one of the rings from the case. He grasped the pointing finger next to Rob's thumb and fitted the ring on to it. He twisted it back and forth to make sure it fit snugly. Satisfied, he let Rob's hand go free.

"This is the X200. I am going to activate it and link it to our satellite network. Can you please say your full name, what day of the week it is and my name"?

Rob could hardly feel the smoothness of the ring on his finger. It did not weigh enough to be gold. He figured it must be titanium. He then spoke the initiation code that agent Prince had told him to speak.

"Robert Lyons, Thursday, Les Prince"

Prince looked away from Rob and addressed the wall or some unknown mysterious authority and said, "Got that?" He nodded his head and smiled to whom-ever the hidden participant was that he was somehow communicating with.

"Great, this device allows us to record your unique biorhythms and voice pattern. If this ring should be worn by anyone else but you, it will shut down. To reactivate it all you must do is to repeat, "Robert Lyons, Thursday, Les Prince." It has a battery that is constantly being recharged by the heat from your body. It will also be doing some neat things like constantly monitoring your heart beats per minute and respiratory functions.

"The ring will pass through a metal detector undetected. It is constantly on. This means it is transmitting all the time. It allows us to know exactly where you are within six inches. As well, within the black dome of the ring are dozens of microscopic cameras that are transmitting images in a 240-degree range that our computers are able to blend into one picture that allows us to see actually more than what you are able to see. It operates very much like an insect's compound eyes. When using its infrared technology option, it even allows us to see in the dark. Not only can we see more than you can see, it also allows us to hear very clearly every conversation plus ultra-high frequency and low frequency noises that you are not able to hear. At Control there will be a team of people constantly monitoring your environment 24 hours a day. I will be one of those people. If someone is speaking a foreign language, we will be able to provide you with an instant translation. We are also able to match the conversations of those speaking to you to a voice record library of over twenty-five million records. This will usually allow us to tell you who you are speaking to and give you background information on them and warnings. It is constantly keeping a video and audio record of everything you see and hear."

He then took out second very small black box. He opened it for Rob to see. In it was what appeared to be a small, shiny, flesh colored, rod shaped, piece of plastic.

"This part of the X200, it is how we communicate with you. If you could please lie down on your left side on the couch, then I am going to place this lightly in your ear. It is going to be activated by Control and will slowly start to crawl into your ear far enough that it cannot be detected. Loading it is a bit creepy and initially it feels a bit irritating, but you will quickly get used to it and forget it is even there. In addition to allowing us to communicate with you it also functions as a hearing aid. You can ask for the volume to be increased if you want to listen to a distant conversation. To get it out of your ear, you ask control to remove it and it will crawl out. It is always on. Like the ring, it also has an internal battery that is constantly being recharged by your body heat. As a backup, the ring has a speaker and a vibrator. They would only be used to communicate with you if for some reason the hearing device was removed from your ear."

Rob lay down on the couch with his one ear up. The speaker was placed in his ear. Like a real, live, slimy, squirmy, bug, he could feel it contracting and expanding, as it wiggled its way into his ear canal. He had to restrain himself from tearing at his ear or asking them to remove it. He could feel sweat break out on his forehead.

Control then did a sound test, **"DR LYONS WE ARE NOW GOING TO REPEAT NUMBERS. PLEASE TELL US WHICH NUMBER IS THE MOST COMFORTABLE FOR YOU TO HEAR. TEST ONE. TEST TWO. TEST THREE. TEST FOUR. TEST FIVE. "**

Rob responded, "Test Three was the most comfortable."

He then sat up. Prince continued, "For your own safety, you will wear the ring at all times. When you go for a shower, the X200 goes with you. It is waterproof and virtually indestructible. If there is a device picking up and transmitting your conversations, Control can detect it, warn you and tell you where that device is. Any document you are reading is automatically being photographed, indexed and stored for future reference just by pointing your finger at it. Summaries on your activities are going to be prepared by Control and posted every ten minutes for the Secretary of State and to any others that she gives access to your file.

"Now, the final feature which we hope you will never have to use. You will notice what looks like a very small hole at the top of the oval pointing down towards your fingernail. If you are ever in a life and death situation, you will point your ring finger at the attacker and tell Control to, "Activate Laser". They will instantly reply, "Laser Activated". When you now bring your thumb against the edge of the ring it will trigger a laser beam that will stop the heart of any living thing within twenty feet of you. Up to sixty feet from you, it will permanently blind an attacker. Since, you are constantly being monitored in real time; Control will probably have activated the laser long before you ask for it."

"Since we know exactly where you are, we will be able to position drones and satellites to monitor your environment and warn you of any hazards or send others to assist you. Ok, you are all set up. Any further questions address them to Control."

Rob saw Prince to the door. As the door closed, he received an update from Control.

"DOCTOR LYONS, THIS IS CONTROL. ARE YOU PACKED AND READY TO GO?"

He had not expected this bodiless voice. It took him by surprise. He stood there disorientated for a few seconds before he got his wits about him. He had gasped with surprise and had felt his pulse accelerate. He wondered if this is how schizophrenics hear voices in their head. He replied to the voice in his head, "Yes, I am all packed"

"SORRY, WE DID NOT MEAN TO STARTLE YOU. THE CAR IS ON ITS WAY. WE ESTIMATE IT'S TIME OF ARRIVAL IN THREE MINUTES. YOU CAN PROCEED TO THE LOBBY AT ANY TIME. IT WILL BE WAITING FOR YOU. WE HAVE DONE A SWEEP OF YOUR APARTMENT AND HAVE NOT DETECTED ANY TRANSMITTING OR LISTENING DEVICES."

He took the elevator down and strode through the lobby with his small carryon bag. A black Chevy Suburban with deeply tinted windows and its engine running was waiting by the door. The driver had received a picture of Rob on his personal communication device. He got out and opened the rear passenger door for him. Rob hoisted himself up into the large, plush black leather rear seat. He was surprised at the comfortable ride. It wasn't like riding in a truck.

Since it was between rush hours and the traffic was light, they made good time to Prince George's County, Maryland. Rob was driven through base security and onto the tarmac at Andrews Air Force Base. He was deposited beside an unmarked C-37A Gulfstream executive jet. Since, he was the only passenger, it started to taxi as soon as his bottom hit the seat. Within two hours they had landed at Miami International.

Waiting for him for him on the tarmac was an airport security official in a dark blue blazer and conservative striped tie, with the prerequisite identification tag hanging around his neck. He took Rob's carry-on bag and handed Rob an envelope with his first class, American Airline boarding pass for the afternoon flight to Saint Matts and an identical identification tag. It identified Rob as an airport security official. Rob put the security tag around his neck. They took a golf cart with a flashing yellow light to an innocuous, unmarked door on the side of the terminal building. His guide inserted his finger into a scanner and the door automatically swung open. He then led Rob along a series of long, empty confusing passage ways that took them past all the normal security checks. They climbed some long, narrow steps and stopped at a door. The guide, who never identified who he worked for, took Rob's security tag from him, and removed his own, and put both into his jacket pocket. He then opened the door and Rob found they were next to the entrance to the airline's First-Class Lounge.

"Show them your boarding pass. Your flight should be boarding in about an hour. They'll take care of you from here. Have a drink. Relax". He smiled and handed Rob back his carry-on bag. He nodded and disappeared back through the door they had just come through.

The first-class lounge was large and bright with floor to ceiling glass walls overlooking the planes and ground traffic coming and going. Miami International is a very big, very busy airport. Rob found a comfortable chair and put his bag down on it. He then got himself some juice and a fancy cut salmon sandwich. Having satisfied his hunger, he took out his personal communication device and checked for messages – nothing important or urgent appeared.

He felt someone staring at him. He looked up. Across from him was a beautiful blonde with the sort of flawless skin that usually turned out to be professionally created. Her hair was thick and carefully cut to show off her high cheek bones. The full lush lips made her look soft and sensual. The big Sophia Loren cat eyes flashed a message of "don't mess with me". The form fitting dress she was wearing was understatedly expensive and failed to hide her full beasts and shapely hips. As soon as he looked up, she had looked down at her own personal communication device and pretended she was deeply absorbed in her work.

Suddenly his lecherous thoughts were interrupted, **"HI DOCTOR LYONS, THIS IS LES PRINCE HERE. MY SHIFT IS JUST BEGINNING. WOW, SHE'S A REAL LOOKER. I BET YOU ARE WONDERING WHO SHE IS. HER NAME IS BARBARA WALL; SHE IS WITH PNP NEWS, THIRTY YEARS OLD, UNMARRIED, NOT GOING OUT WITH ANYONE AND HAS BEEN AT PNP FOR TWO YEARS. HER FAVORITE DRINK IS A VODKA MARTINI. HER FATHER WAS PRESIDENT OF A MAJOR REINSURANCE COMPANY IN NEW YORK. HE AND HER MOTHER WERE KILLED LAST YEAR WHEN A SMALL PLANE HE WAS PILOTING HIT A FLOCK OF CANADA GEESE IN UPSTATE NEW YORK. I HAVE QUITE AN EXTENSIVE FILE ON HER AND WILL PASS INFORMATION TO YOU AS NEEDED."**

Rob hoped he didn't look startled. He wasn't sure what he was going to do with this information when Prince again interrupted, **"MISS WALL IS ON THE SAME FLIGHT YOU ARE ON TO SAINT MATTS. SHE IS ON ASSIGNMENT."**

As Robrolled over in his mind several scenarios that he could use to get close to Miss Wall, they announced that the flight for Saint Matts was now ready for boarding. He waited to see if Barbara Wall was going to get up. She did. He picked up his carryon bag and followed her out of the first-class lounge, down the long hall all the way to the gate. Her rear view was as good as the front.

A large, noisy, crowd had gathered around the desk at the gate. As expected, the flight was over booked. Dozens of news teams were trying to get to the small, remote island, while the story was still hot, and this was the only direct scheduled flight for the day. Any other flight would require connections and they would not arrive until the following day. The airline was begging passengers to give up their seats. News people were bribing the most vulnerable. Rob walked around this crowd, showed his boarding pass and was allowed to immediately board. He had lost sight of Barbara Wall who had passed through ahead of him. He checked his boarding pass. They had got him seat 1B. It was an aisle seat; obviously they wanted him to be the first one off the plane. Passengers with young children or needing assistance were also being loaded ahead of the herd. As he entered the cabin, the stewardess gave him her professional fake smile, glanced at his boarding pass and pointed towards the first aisle. He didn't look like a media person or a vacationer or an islander. She wondered what his story was. Who was paying for his first-class ticket?

In seat, IA, the window seat, sat Barbara Wall. She ignored Rob Lyons, as he threw his carryon bag in the overhead bin above his seat. He sat down and buckled himself in. Barbara continued to ignore him, as much as it is possible to ignore someone who is sitting a few inches away from you. Rob kept glancing at her out of the corner of his eye. He thought she was one of the most beautiful women he had ever seen. Once in a while he would catch a sideways glance from her.

Soon the noisy herd of one hundred forty-eight passengers had all funneled on to the plane. The plane was ready to go. It slowly backed out from the terminal and waddled towards the runway to join the long line that was taking off. Finally, it was their turn. There was that sudden acceleration that knocked them back in their seats and the aircraft climbed at a steep angle until they achieved cruising altitude. As soon as the seat belt sign was turned off, the stewardess appeared at Rob's elbow.

"Can I get you a beverage?"

Rob paused and then thought, what the hell, "Yes, can I please have a vodka martini." He then turned to Barbara Wall and said, "I think Miss Wall would like one too."

Barbara Wall's eyes opened wide in surprise. She paused and then she said,

"Yes, I will have one too." Rob smiled at her. She did not smile back. He felt a bit awkward. Maybe he had been too much of a smart ass. It was going to be a long, uncomfortable trip. Finally, after looking at him long and hard, she finally said, "I can see how you might know who I am but how did you know I would drink a vodka martini?"

"You looked like the type."

"And, what type is that?"

"Trapeze artist in the Ringling Brothers Circus, married to the wolf man."

"What?" she said, her eyes opened in surprise and then she started to laugh, "Really, how did you know I drank vodka martinis."

"I am a magician, a mentalist; I can read people's minds. As soon as the stewardess mentioned the word drink, immediately vodka martini popped into your mind and I was able to read it."

She looked at him quizzically, knowing it was ridiculous, but having just a bit of doubt, could it be possible. "OK, if you are so smart what am I thinking now?"

Rob looked in those beautiful eyes and said, "Well you don't believe me, and you think I am trying to pick you up."

"You're right about that."
"
I can prove that I can read your mind. Ask me a question about yourself."

"What's my phone number?"

Prince, in control immediately replied, **"HER PHONE NUMBER IS 301-298-3223 AND IT IS AN UNLISTED NUMBER."**

Rob made a big show of trying to retrieve the information from some mysterious source. He rubbed his temples, closed his eyes, rubbed his forehead and then replied,

"Your unlisted phone number at home is 301-298-3223".

Barbara's eyes again opened in surprise. She stared at him and then asked, "What is the name of my pet dog?"

Rob went into his retrieval act again.

Prince responded, **"SHE LIVES IN AN APARTMENT BUILDING IN WHICH DOGS ARE NOT ALLOWED. THE LAST DOG SHE OWNED WAS AS A CHILD AND THE DOG'S NAME WAS TARZAN."**

Rob opened his eyes and looked at her, "You don't own a dog. The last dog you owned was when you were young, and that dog's name was...wait a minute, its coming to me ...Target? No, it is Tarzan."

Barbara looked startled. "This is creeping me out."

Rob realizing, he had hammed it up a bit too much said, "Sorry, you realize it is a trick. I can't really read your mind."

"Well, how would you know something about me that only three or four people in the world would know?"

"Magicians never disclose their secrets. I apologize if I've upset you."

"No, that's OK. It intrigues me. I won't be satisfied until I can figure out how you are able to do it."

The stewardess arrived with their drinks. They toasted each other.

"Are you travelling on business," she asked?

"No, I am on vacation. My parents spend the winter in St. Matts and I am going down to see them."

"Did you hear about the senator who wants to drop a nuclear bomb on the island because the Chinese want to establish a naval base there?"

"You're kidding."

"No, I'm not kidding. I've been sent down with a camera man to do some feeds back to my network." She paused and then said," But I suppose you already know that?"

Rob laughed.

She continued, "Do you have any contacts on the island that you think would be good interviews about the situation?

"No, not really, I'm just a tourist. Where are you staying?"

"At the Saint Matts Hotel and Casino. Do you know it?"

"Yes, it is the biggest employer on the island. It is a typical five-star American hotel: expensive, comfortable, clean, good beach, lots of restaurants. If you never left their compound, you would swear you were in Florida, California or Texas."

"Are you staying with your parents?"

"Yes, I'm sure they will find a couch for me to sleep on."

They talked most of the flight. Rob heard about her struggle from a small station in the Mid-West to a network position in New York. She asked what he did. He said he was a Washington civil servant doing accounting- type-work. They laughed. They drank some more vodka martinis. They talked some more. Rob fell in love with her. As the plane was beginning its descent into Saint Matts, Rob asked if she would be available for dinner tomorrow night. She said that she was not sure what free time she would have, if any, but she was sure with his magical abilities that he would soon know if she was going to be free for dinner and how to reach her. He laughed and said to her, "This may sound like a pickup line, but I have never met anyone before where I immediately felt it was predestined that I would meet them and that I would then spend the rest of my life with them."

She looked at him long and hard, not saying anything. Rob wondered whether he had just blown to bits what he felt had become the most important relationship in his life. Finally, she whispered, "You too. I thought it was just me." She then quickly looked out the window, afraid that her distress would be mirrored on her face. She had never felt this way before. She said nothing more to him and continued to stare out the window as they taxied towards the terminal.

They had taken off at five. The winter sun was just beginning to set. Their course was South East. With a one hour's time difference plus two and half hours of travelling time it was almost nine o'clock when they landed. The island's ring of mountains, which soared thousands of feet into the night sky, was just a dark backdrop. Rob could not see their permanently cloud covered peaks. The peaks squeezed rain from those clouds which irrigated the island's thick jungle vegetation and fed the crystal-clear streams. The volcanic soil was rich. Almost anything could grow in it. Fruits and vegetables were exported to the neighboring islands.

The airport terminal was located on the North Shore, close to the best beaches and the St. Matts Hotel and Casino. Like many terminals in the Caribbean, it had been built by Canadian engineers with Canadian government grants. These Caribbean terminals all shared the same poured concrete, low profile, modern institutional look. No gates projected out from the terminals like elephant trunks to suck the passengers into the terminal. Motorized steps were wheeled up to the airplane's door

The passengers descended and walked to the terminal. Rob was carrying the coat he had worn in Washington. He now took off his shirt and folded it into his coat. He had worn a black T shirt under his shirt anticipating it would be warm when they reached Saint Matts. It showed off his narrow waist, muscular arms and chest.

The two of them walked together across the tarmac to customs and immigration. They didn't make more than a few safe comments about the humidity and heat. Dark uniformed security personnel with florescent orange vests stood like traffic cones, forming a security corridor that herded the passengers to the correct entrance. The soft, warm, humidity had hit him as soon as he stepped out of the airplane. It brought back a flood of memories of arriving on this welcoming island. He could smell the richness of the jungle that fringed the landing strip.

Rob smiled when he entered the immigration room. There was the same sign that he had seen every year since the airport was built, apologizing to passengers because the air conditioning was temporarily out of service. Two large standing floor fans were doing a poor job of keeping the one hundred and forty-eight passengers cool.

Rob took out his Saint Matts passport. He moved towards the line for locals who were returning to the island. He saw the tourist line for Barbara. He pointed it out to Barbara and said, "Well I guess this is where we part until supper tomorrow."

Barbara laughed and said, "I think that is called a presumptive close. Who knows what the future holds?" She gave him a quick affectionate peck on his cheek. He figured it would take Barbara and her camera man good half hour to get through the line. His line was short and fast. He considered waiting for her but now that both he and she had returned to the real world, he suspected it would be awkward, especially now that she had linked up with her colleague. He could wait until tomorrow.

His passport was casually scanned and stamped by a bored customs officer. Rob proceeded down the frozen steps of the perennially malfunctioning escalator to the baggage carrousel and exit. Since he had checked no bag, he immediately headed towards the exit. The customs officers seeing his one carry-on bag just waved him through. He stepped out into the usual chaos of car horns honking, people shouting, porters pushing their carts, travelers waiting for taxis, taxis leaving and arriving and families waiting behind a metal rail calling out to arriving family members. His mother was the first in line to give him a fierce hug. His young, pretty, cousin, Chloe, gave a less fierce hug but a kiss on the cheek. His father squeezed his shoulder and grabbed his bag. Canadians aren't into hugging and kissing.

They proceeded down the steps to the open-air parking lot. His father limped along and threw the bag into the back of his ancient giant Hummer that he had bought fifteen years ago. A rugged Hummer had seemed to make sense on an island where there the roads had almost as many potholes as pavement. Rob buckled himself in for the forty-five-minute drive through the mountains to the family compound. It was on a ridge, high above the capital, overlooking the Georgetown harbor.

As they circled the parking lot, Rob noticed a large crowd of people standing outside the Departure level. If there were that many lined up outside, how many were inside? There must be more than a thousand. On an island of 40,000 people, a thousand people in a small space are noticeable. Rob turned to his father who was driving and asked, "What's going on at Departures?"

His father chuckled and said, "Those are the pessimists. They think that the island is going to be bombed by the U.S. tomorrow or the day after. They started lining up shortly after that interview with that senator ended on CNN. If they couldn't get on a scheduled airline flights, then they've been paying outrageous amounts to charter small propeller aircraft to fly them to the main Caribbean hubs in Saint Martin, Antigua, Barbados and San Juan. Those charter companies have been running a regular shuttle service all day. They've made a fortune. I hear that the parents of the kids at the medical school are trying to charter a large plane to get their kids out of here as quickly as possible."

"You and mom don't look like you are getting ready to leave?"

"At my age you can't get too excited because some Texan windbag in Washington makes a stupid comment."

Rob heard his mother sucking her teeth in disapproval of his father's explanation. As they exited the airport parking lot and drove into the first traffic circle (driving on the left-hand side, a reminder of British colonial times) he noticed a new highway had been built.

"What's this? A new road, I don't believe it."

"Oh, you're going to see many improvements since you were here five years ago. This new road to the capital was just finished two months ago. It now only takes about thirty minutes to get home. Your mother used to refuse to drive it at night. It was so dangerous."

Through the thick jungle of massive trees, vines and underbrush, the road climbed up a thousand feet into the rain forest only to descend a thousand feet before climbing the next ridge. As they approached Georgetown, they were suddenly drowned in light from what looked like a small city of tents with wooden walls and other portable buildings. Large yellow trucks, of a make that Rob did not recognize, were parked neatly in rows. Expensive earth moving equipment of all sorts was also parked off in another area. Rob put his hand on the dashboard, so Control could see what he was seeing.

"What's this?" he asked.

"It's a tent city for the Chinese construction crews who are doing all this new work. There was a lot of complaining about the Chinese not hiring any local people; however, the government is getting this work done for free with no strings attached, so the complaints didn't get very far. They've just about finished the new hospital and have already completed two new schools plus this new road. They are also repaving many of the old ones."

He turned off the main road onto a private road and started up the final hill to the ridge where the family compound lay like an eagle's nest. They went through a narrow rock cut for several hundred feet that then opened up on a plateau with half a dozen large houses in a semicircle. The houses were brightly lit. In the middle of the semicircle, a large patio area around a turquoise swimming pool was full of cousins, aunts, uncles and close family friends, all gathered to welcome Rob home. They did not need much of an excuse for a party. A long table groaned under the weight of peas and rice, BBQ chicken, roast pig, pork ribs, yams, cooked local greens, fish chowder, christophine in a cheese sauce, okra, curried lobster, mustard greens with bacon, boiled corn, broccoli, steamed fish, turned corn meal and numerous salads. Off to the side, in tubs of ice were beer, wine and soft drinks. Bottles of rum from the Bishop's own distillery were also in evidence. His cousins had not waited for him to arrive before starting his welcome home party.

Rob made his grand entrance to many hugs, kisses and handshakes. As a boy he had spent most of his summer, Christmas and spring vacations here with his grandparents. His uncles had been his substitute father. His aunts had been his substitute mother. His cousins were the brothers and sisters that he had never had. Most of the cousins now worked in the family businesses. His mother had inherited the main house after his grandmother died.

A century ago his great grandfather had started a small dry goods store in Georgetown. Over the years it had grown into a large department store. The profits from it were used to diversify into wholesale dry goods, a rum distillery, a car dealership, car rentals and a lumber mill. The Bishops were thought to be the richest family on the island. They had learned a long time ago to keep a low profile.

At the South edge of the compound patio area was a stone wall. He walked over to it and looked down several hundred feet to the street lights of Georgetown that lay below. A jumble of poorly constructed, small, wooden houses, with rusty tin roofs, stacked like so many cubes thrown down in a pile at random. They stretched from the bottom of the cliff a half mile to the harbors edge. Communal water pipes, on each street, served dozens of houses. Trash and battered, rusty cars dotted the streets. He could see a man selling cold green coconuts from an old abandoned electric refrigerator filled with ice to which he had added wheels. Flames and smoke from the charcoal barbeques of street vendors were flaring on every corner as the fat from the pork, the chicken and the fish fell onto the coals. People filled the streets. The sound of laughter, dogs barking, noisy car exhausts and the steady beat of Caribbean reggae music filled the night. These weren't pessimists. They were too busy enjoying life to bother watching Washington Texans on CNN.

He looked out over the harbor; a large, brightly lit ship with red crosses on it was at the main dock. He turned to his cousin Malcolm, who was standing beside him drinking a Saint Matts beer.

"What's the ship?"

"It's the Chinese People's Liberation Army hospital ship. It cruises the islands servicing their construction crews, sailors and other Chinese nationals. They give free medical care to anyone who asks for it. A lot of the poor have been going to them. I heard they have three-hundred and fifty nurses and doctors and a cleaning staff of over one hundred and fifty. Doctor Smith said it is better equipped than any hospital in the Caribbean."

Rob rested his hand on the railing that ran along the top of the cliff, so that Control could easily see the ship. As he watched, a large helicopter ambulance lifted off from the rear of the ship with lights blinking and headed off into the night.

"What are those large grey military looking ships with all the cranes on them?"

"You saw all those bulldozers, graders and trucks parked at the Chinese construction work camp?"

"Yeah."

"Well, all that came off those three ships. It was incredible how quickly they unloaded that equipment, set up their tent city and organized the thousand people that to do the work. They had it all done in a day. They were already starting to work within hours of arriving."

Not seeing his father in the gathering, he went into what had been his grandmother's house to look for him. He found him in the study bent over his computer, writing. He stopped when Rob came into the room. Folded down his laptop and swung around. Rob slumped into one of the leather wing back chairs across from him.

"Not hungry, Dad?"

"Not really, I ate earlier. What about you?"

"I ate on the pane."

"Well don't tell your mother that. She wants to feed you. She thinks you're wasting away up there. How are they treating you in Washington?"

"I'm enjoying the job. It is challenging, a bit too much bureaucracy but that is to be expected. After all it is the civil service."

"I gather", he paused then continued, "That more than a desire to see your mother and me has brought you to St. Matts?"

Rob smiled and said, "Officially, as far as the State Department is concerned, I am on vacation but as you know I am always curious as to what is going on in the island?"

Control whispered in Rob's ear, **"WE HAVE DETECTED LISTENING DEVICES IN THIS ROOM, TWENTY FEET TO YOUR RIGHT."**

"Dad, why don't we go for a little walk in the garden?"

His father stood, grabbed a file folder off his desk and motioned for Rob to accompany him through the French doors on to the deck that circled the house. They went outside. The tree frogs were peeping away. It was almost deafening. They walked down the steps, across the lawn to a large white, screened, gazebo in the middle of the garden with a picnic table in it. His father switched on an overhead light.

Once again, Control whispered in his ear, **"WE HAVE YOU ON VISUAL. WE HAVE SCANNED A 100 FOOT PERIMETER AND CAN DETECT NO ONE IN THAT AREA OTHER THAN YOU. THERE ARE NO TRANSMITTING DEVICES WITHIN THIS PERIMETER."**

Rob's father sighed and sat down slowly with a groan on the bench. Rob sat beside him.

"My arthritis bothers me. Maybe I've seen too many spy movies but lately I've been worrying about bugs – not cockroaches, the electronic kind. Your phone call this morning did not surprise me. I had been watching CNN and if I were someone of authority in the State Department, the first thing I would do is look for someone I could trust, who knew the island to assess what is going on. I suspect no one else working for the State Department has citizenship in an island nation which only has 40,000 citizens. Be that as it may, your mother and I are more than pleased to see our pride and joy."

Rob looked at him and smiled. His father continued as if he had been thinking all day about how to best describe the island's situation to the State Department, "In regard to the Chinese building a naval station on this island, to me it would make a lot of sense for both them and for St. Matts. The island is basically bankrupt. By bankrupt I mean the classic definition of bankruptcy, which is failing to meet your obligations as they come due. They have defaulted on paying their bonds that came due at the beginning of the year. They are trying to do some voodoo by claiming that they are negotiating a compromise with their lenders. The World Bank has stepped in and is keeping a close watch on them to make sure they get back the money they have loaned. The island government recently introduced a 15% value added tax on all purchases. It is adding to the poor people's hardships."

Rob leaned forward, and interjected, "How did they get themselves into such a mess".

"Yes, it is a mess. Every man, woman and child on this island is responsible for a debt of $900,000,000. The government is running the island on $250,000,000 in revenue which includes interest payments on their operating loans. Unfortunately, they are only collecting $249,000,000 and there is no reserve. They have nothing to pay off their long-term bonds. They just go deeper into debt.

You obviously get into this mess by spending money that you don't have. If you don't watch it you go deeper and deeper into debt. Politicians tend to be born optimists, always hoping the clouds will go away and the sun will shine again tomorrow. The national budget was being balanced up until 9/11. After that hit, tourism was slow in recovering. It picked up and then got hammered again by the US downturn in 2008. They've never recovered. It may end up like Japan, who never recovered from their downturn. Unemployment is high. A lot of people have reached the desperate stage and have voted with their feet. We've been losing about five percent of the population each year to emigration. The more that leave, for greener pastures, the fewer the sources of tax revenue."

Rob asked, "What is the government doing about it?"

"What can they do? They've got no money, so the infrastructure of the island is slowly deteriorating. This means more electricity black outs, roads full of potholes and fewer policemen. Health care has deteriorated. The island is starting to look shabby and unattractive to tourists.

"Then along comes a life line. The People's Republic of China has bags of money which they have been spending freely throughout the Caribbean. To get a piece of it, all you must do is recognize them in the United Nations as the true representatives of the Chinese people, instead of Taiwan, which isn't much of stretch, considering they have a population of one and a third billion people compared to only 23 million in Taiwan. This was easily passed by the legislature. Since then, things have started to improve. As a bonus it turns out that Saint Matts has something they want. They want that old British naval yard. This abandoned ghost from the past has not been utilized in decades. If someone is willing to pay to use it then let them write the check."

Rob interrupted again, "Is anyone objecting to the Chinese taking it over".

"Why would anyone object? The opposition party would only be shooting themselves in the foot if they did. There isn't anyone else offering to bail poor old St. Matts out of the hole they are in. Even if the opposition did object, what can they do about it? This isn't a ridiculously complicated system like the US government where each state can directly influence its senators, where presidents can veto legislation and the House of Representatives can throw a monkey wrench into things. Not to mention the phantom government, the lobbyists, who protect their corporation's special interests. The lobbyists are the real power in Washington. I was part of it. If I saw any legislation that was going to interfere with our profits, you better believe that we were willing to spend millions to get that legislation blocked or changed to our liking. Here in Saint Matts, like any British parliamentary system, if you hold a majority of the seats in the parliament, then for the five years of your mandate, you can behave like a dictator of a banana republic. All you need to do, to keep your party's members of parliament in line, is to throw some of them sweet carrots and beat others with a big stick. Doctor Chumley has a majority and he is not about to relinquish   it. Even if he did, I doubt if the opposition would behave any differently, unless they had some significant incentive to do so."

Colin Lyons got up and slowly paced around the gazebo as he continued his rant, "Which brings me to this morning, as I see it; there is only one reason that the Chinese naval dockyard was leaked to that senator. I suspect that Chumley is playing a bit of poker here. He is trying to see if he can get the US to bid against the

Chinese. Perhaps he is trying to get one of them to pay down the country's massive debt but more likely he is looking for a big deposit in his Cayman bank account. It is a dangerous game for him to play. One or both might arrange for him to disappear if he pushes them too far with his greedy little games. I remember when he arrived on this island after medical school. He didn't have two cents to rub together. Now, it is believed he has close to a hundred million stashed away in Cayman. Before I forget it, I thought you would be interested in seeing this document that I obtained from my sources."

He slid the file fold across to his son. Rob opened it and started to read,

"In 2005, Foreign ministry spokesman Qin Gang made a statement about the eight-point diplomatic philosophy of the People's Republic of China: [11]

1. China will not seek hegemony. China is still a developing country and has no resources to seek hegemony. Even if China becomes a developed country, it will not seek hegemony.

2. China will not play power politics and will not interfere with other countries' internal affairs. China will not impose its own ideology on other countries.

3. China maintains all countries, big or small, should be treated equally and respect each other. All affairs should be consulted and resolved by all countries on the basis of equal participation. No country should bully others on the basis of strength.

4. China will make judgment on each case in international affairs, each matter on the merit of the matter itself and it will not have double standards. China will not have two policies: one for itself and one for others. China believes that it cannot do unto others what they do not wish others do unto them.

5. China advocates that all countries handle their relations on the basis of the United Nations Charter and norms governing international relations. China advocates stepping up international cooperation and is against unilateral politics. China should not undermine the dignity and the authority of the U.N. China should not impose and set its own wishes above the U.N. Charter, international law and norms.

6. China advocates peaceful negotiation and consultation so as to resolve its international disputes. China does not resort to force, or threat of force, in resolving international disputes. China maintains a reasonable national military buildup to defend its own sovereignty and territorial integrity. It is not made to expand, nor does it seek invasion or aggression.

7. China is firmly opposed to terrorism and the proliferation of weapons of mass destruction. China is a responsible member of the international community, and as for international treaties, China abides by all them in a faithful way. China never plays by a double standard, selecting and discarding treaties it does not need.

8. China respects the diversity of civilization and the whole world. China advocates different cultures make exchanges, learn from each other, and complement one another with their own strengths. China is opposed to clashes and confrontations between civilizations, and China does not link any particular ethnic group or religion with terrorism"

Rob finished reading. Surreptitiously, he made sure his ring was positioned so that Control could get a photo of the document and record it.

Control softly whispered in his ear, **"GOT IT."**

His father looked at him and said, "What do you think about that?

"Interesting," Rob replied. "The argument that the Chinese are making to these governments is that unlike the US, China is still a developing country and because of this they have a much greater empathy with small developing nations. Their pitch is that they are willing to assist developing countries without any expectation of a quid pro quo. It sounds good, but I worry that it is a bit like feeding biscuits to a dog to get him to learn new tricks. Once these governments start to get use to these dog biscuits it is going to be very hard to give them up. I recognize that it is one thing to distribute such a document and it is quite another thing to live up to it. Call it propaganda, but ever since this was first distributed in 2005, I am not aware of the Chinese ever violating these policies. On the other hand, the US has come across as a super bully of the world and has increasingly alienated both small and large governments. I have heard more than one arrogant senator call for a return to the days when the US was feared, and nations fell in line with their wishes. What kind of attitude is that? Fear? Is that the only thing left for America to be good at? They seem to forget that the U.S. is only 5% of the world's population and they don't need to add to their problems by pushing countries around and constantly meddling in their sovereign affairs. The days of the U.S. doing good, unselfishly with poor nations, seem to have disappeared. A mean, nasty, selfish philosophy, of each man for himself and let the other poor bastards freeze in the dark, seems to have ta ken over."

Colin Lyons shook his head and looked sad.

"Rob, I got a car out of the rental pool for you". He took car keys out of his pants pocket and tossed them over to Rob.

"Thanks. I think tomorrow I will take a ride around the island."

Control whispered in his ear, **"TWO CARS HAVE PARKED ON EACH SIDE OF THE ROCK CUT INTO THE COMPOUND. FOUR MEN GOT OUT AND HAVE TAKEN UP POSITION IN THE FOLIAGE ON EACH SIDE OF THE ENTRANCE. WE WILL KEEP AN EYE ON THEM."**

Rob wondered if they were the local security force sent by Chumley or the CIA men sent to back him up.

"Rob, I guess we better get back to the party or your mother will be upset. You want this Chinese propaganda sheet?"

"No, that's all right, I've memorized it."

"Bull. I don't believe it."

"OK, you owe me $10 if I make a mistake. Where do you want me to start?"

"OK, what's point number four?

Rob looked off into space.

Control read it to him slowly, so he could repeat it, *"CHINA WILL MAKE JUDGMENT ON EACH CASE IN INTERNATIONAL AFFAIRS, EACH MATTER ON THE MERIT OF THE MATTER ITSELF AND IT WILL NOT HAVE DOUBLE STANDARDS. CHINA WILL NOT HAVE TWO POLICIES: ONE FOR ITSELF AND ONE FOR OTHERS. CHINA BELIEVES THAT IT CANNOT DO UNTO OTHERS WHAT THEY DO NOT WISH OTHERS DO ONTO THEM."*

His father looked at him incredulously and said, "I don't believe it. How did you do that?"

Rob started to laugh and sang,

"Its magic."

His father shook his head and went into his wallet to give Rob his ten dollars. Rob laughing and waved his ten dollars away.

Colin switched off the gazebo light and they walked back across the lawn to the house. When Rob got into the house, he went to the bathroom for some privacy. He felt a bit foolish whispering and realized that if anyone could see him, they would think that he had lost it and was babbling to himself.

"Control, the men who are positioned at the driveway into the compound. Do you know who they are? Are they the CIA agents that were supposed to make contact with me?"

"THEY ARE NOT CIA AGENTS. WE ARE NOT ABLE TO IDENTIFY WHO THEY ARE AT THIS TIME. WE WILL KEEP AN EYE ON THEM."

"Is it possible to get the CIA agents on the island to find out who they are?"

"WE WILL FORWARD YOUR REQUEST AND GET BACK TO YOU."

Rob flushed the toilet in case anyone was waiting outside. He left to join the party and make his mother happy.

CHAPTER 4

Intrigue

The Customs and Immigration supervisor's telephone rang just about the same time Rob was exiting the Saint Matt's airport.

"Mister Gumbs, are the passengers on the American Airline flight still not processed? Why do I not see the passenger list in the system?"

Austin Gumbs recognized that pompous voice - so full of reflected self-importance. It was the Prime Minister's, Chief of Staff, Winston Clark.

"Good evening, Mister Clark, I am just reviewing the list now. It will be released it in a few minutes."

"The Prime minister is waiting. He has heard about the near riot at the Miami airport between the various news people trying to get seats on the flight. He wants to see which ones made it."

"No problem, it'll be there in a couple of minutes."

He took one final look at the list of passengers and the information picked up from their passports. It was gathered from the scanning system as they had passed through immigration. Gumbs hit the enter key to send the information to a central file where the prime minister's office could read it, if they so wished.

The foreign media held zero interest to him. What he was curious about, was which locals had been away and were returning to the island. It gave him something to gossip about with his wife. St. Matts was a small island. There was no such thing as privacy. Through marriage everyone seemed to be related to everyone else. His wife's sister was married to a Bishop. He noticed that Monique Bishop's son Rob Lyons had arrived. He liked Rob. He must get over to see him. He thought it had been three or four years since Rob had been in St. Matts. He was surprised that Monique had not informed him Rob was coming. He would have met him at the bottom of the steps as he came off the plane and escorted him through immigration.

As soon as the passenger list appeared in the central file, Winston Clark printed it and brought it into the Prime Minister, since looking at a computer screen was considered, by Chumley, to be beneath him. The Prime Minister had been fielding phone calls all day from other country leaders, mainly those in the Caribbean. They were concerned about getting caught up in any regional retaliation from the US. There seemed to be a fifty-fifty split between those congratulating him for standing up to the world's bully and those suggesting that he was a fool for pulling the Yankee's chain. He never lacked for free advice. Victor Chumley picked up and started to read the passenger report as he continued to carry on a conversation with the Prime Minister of Barbados.

He was pleased. The media had sent in some of their first line people. He looked at his schedule on his computer terminal for the next few days to see how many interviews could be scheduled. He also checked the list of locals who were returning. He too, out of idle curiosity, liked to see who was coming and going. His finger, as it went down the list, stopped at Rob Lyons. He quickly ended the phone call with the Barbados prime minister and called out for his Chief of Staff.

"I see Monique Bishop's son arrived on that American Airline flight. He was flying first class. Didn't I hear her bragging at the Chinese Embassy cocktail party that her son was now working for the Secretary of State in Washington? "

"I don't know Prime Minister. Do you want me to find out who his employer is?"

"Yes, see if you can confirm it. I don't believe in coincidences. The same day the Chinese naval base agreement is leaked, a representative of the US Secretary of State happens to land on the island? Really!"

"It could be just a family visit. His parents are down here every winter."

"Maybe, but let's get Island Security involved. I want them shadowing him from tonight until he leaves the island but please remind them to be discreet, Mister Clark. We don't want to aggravate the Bishop's. Tell those usually incompetent bumblers to keep a very low profile. They are not to harass him. He could be very useful to us. Put a tap on the phone lines and internet traffic into their compound.

If we can get bugs into his parent's house that would be a good idea, but they must do it without being detected."

Victor Chumley leaned back against the fine red Spanish leather cushions in his high-backed executive chair, behind his magnificent mahogany desk. It was designed to intimidate insecure minions. He was a large black man, not tall, but large. His shaved bald head was like a round brown pumpkin, fused to a thick bull neck. His shoulders were wide and thick. His stomach looked like a beach ball that was about to burst. His hands were like baseball gloves with thick, garish, gold rings on almost every finger. Bulging brown eyes that could intimidate friends and enemies alike completed his domineering, not to be toyed with, persona. He reeked of strength, arrogance and hubris - packaged inside a $3,000 Armani suit.

"Winston, tomorrow, I want you to get hold of Rob Lyons first thing in the morning and invite him to lunch. If he is here, reconnoitering for the Secretary of State, we might as well, as they say, get that skunk out on the table. Arrange lunch at the Beach House. I haven't seen him since he was a boy. Do you know his mother and I started at the Nelson Street Primary school together? We went all the way through school together until she left the island. I can remember those childhood birthday parties at the Bishop compound. Now, I am going home. Call my car."

The Prime Minister stood, yawned loudly, leaned over and turned off his gold-plated desk lamp. Picking up some papers, he placed them in his brief case and headed for his office door. As he passed by the Chief of Staff's office, he called out." Winston also tell the security force to cancel all leave and to put the island on a high alert. That idiot of a US senator has called for them to bomb the island. Those war mongers in Washington are capable of anything. Also tell Sinclair to double the size of my personal security team. The Yanks may see assassinating me as the most expedient way to remove my challenge to their world dominance." His laughter faded as he ambled down the hall.

His shiny Rolls Royce limousine with its bullet proof windows and armored walls and undercarriage, was gently purring on the circular driveway. Security vehicles in front and behind the limousine were ready to accompany the Rolls to the Prime Minister's official residence, Government House, a mile away. Armed security staff were always patrolling the beautiful landscaped grounds.

A nine-foot-high concrete wall with razor wire on top surrounded the Prime Minister's residence. There was only one entrance into the grounds. Armed security staff opened and closed the high iron gates. On one side of the Government House security wall was poverty and crumbling wooden shacks. On the other side of the wall, was opulence and privilege.

The Rolls Royce's driver was waved through the official residence's gate without stopping. It drove up the wide circular driveway which was rimmed by giant royal palms all appropriately standing at attention. The procession stopped under the residence's portico. As the Prime Minister floated from the Rolls into his residence, he looked up into the night sky. He could hear a distinct and unusual buzzing noise from on high, an unusual new sound. He could not see anything in the night sky. He wondered if it was an armed American drone aircraft

At 40,000 feet the unmanned RQ -170 Sentinel drone, circled round and round the island of St. Matts. It would do this for twenty- four hours until a second would relieve it. The drone's remote pilot was sitting inside a cubicle, buried within a bunker built within a mountain in Colorado. The infrared telescopic, camera on the drone allowed him to see the war engine of the Rolls and pick out the Prime Minister as he moved into the house. The drone pilot yelled out to another pilot sitting in the adjoining cubicle, "If they give me the word, I can send a 100-pound Hellfire missile right up his ass". The other drone pilot just grinned and snickered. It was boring flying in big circles, hour after hour, with no action.

Drones were not the reliable weapon that the U.S. military wanted their enemies to think they were. If the wind was higher than sixteen miles an hour, it was almost impossible to safely launch them, or land them.   They were also prone to mechanical failure. Over forty percent of drones crashed because of engine problems. While the military might lose seventy-five million dollars every time a drone crashed, it was a lot less than the two hundred million dollars they lost when a jet fighter crashed. Of course, being unmanned, no pilot was ever lost in a drone crash. Conventional fighter pilots were expensive to train and maintain while good video game players were easier to find and train as drone pilots.

The President had just approved a budget of over twenty billion dollars to produce more drones. This would almost double the number of drones in the Pentagon's arsenal. They had proved to be a very cost-efficient way to eliminate and contain enemies. There was zero human risk and little chance of grieving American parents appearing on television to call for an end to armed initiatives. The only problem was one of supply and demand. The generals liked the drones and had created a demand for them. The aircraft manufacturers liked building them and did everything they could to push the price up to meet the demand. They were no longer the disposable cheap airplane substitute they had once been.

CHAPTER 5

Monkeys

The first thing Barbara Wall did when she got to her room in the Saint Matts Hotel and Casino, even before she unpacked, was to get out her personal communication device and build upon the sketchy research she had already done on Saint Matts. She was looking for an interesting hook that would grab the attention of her network's viewers. Pictures of these attractive, slim, long tailed monkeys with a greenish, tan, grey fur with dark black fur around their face kept popping up. She learned that they were vervet monkeys also known as guenons. Guenons were a wiry, thin, African monkey that lived in forested areas. She read that she would hear them chattering high up in the trees to each other long before she would see them.

The monkeys were brought from Africa to Saint Matts as pets three centuries ago. They had no natural predators in Saint Matts - except human beings. At one time eating monkey meat, especially at Christmas, in Saint Matts was a special treat. Since they were no longer hunted, the monkeys had lost much of their fear of human beings and their numbers had subsequently multiplied to the point that they were now a major pest. A troop of monkeys could eat all the mangoes in a garden orchard within hours. They were messy eaters. They would take a bite out of a mango and then throw the rest on the ground. Their secret to survival was their ability to eat almost anything. Their diet consisted of insects, birds, eggs, leaves and fruit.

She also learned the monkeys were usually seen in the morning and evening when it was coolest. They spent the hot midday times sleeping. Saint Matts with its extensive forests, rugged terrain and rushing streams was an ideal environment for vervets. While they spent a lot of time on the ground, they never moved too far from the safety of trees which were their source of food and where they established their sleeping sites.

A typical monkey troop might consist of five adult males, eight adult females and twenty juveniles and infants. There would always be one alpha male who was the recognized leader. He would be the biggest and strongest in the troop. He would eat first and then while the rest of the troop grazed, he would stand guard. Any threatening behavior by humans or other animals would be met with either aggressiveness or flight. The males could weigh as much as 18 pounds and females 12 pounds.

There were estimated to be 80,000 of them on the island. Barbara made a note that she should get her cameraman up early in the morning to see if they could get some candid monkey pictures to broadcast. She knew Americans were suckers for small cute animals.

On her way to supper she asked the concierge where they could find monkeys to shoot. She explained shoot, as in camera, not with a gun. He suggested a small pond at the edge of the forest, a ten-minute walk from the hotel. He circled the pond on a map that he gave her.

Early the next morning Barbara and her camera man were at the pool waiting for the monkeys. The pool of crystal-clear water was about the size of eight bath tubs. They could hear the gurgle of creek water draining into and out of the pool. Trees and vines hung like green curtains over the pool, shading it from the rising sun. Barbara had stuffed a shopping bag with apples and bananas at the buffet breakfast. They placed the fruit on a grassy space seductively close to the pool and withdrew about 30 feet. They sat on a fallen log and quietly waited.

The cameraman was ready. In about five minutes a brave, young vervet monkey approached the fruit, grabbed a banana and disappeared back into the bushes. The rest of the troop waited to see if there was a trap. After a few minutes the large alpha male of the troop approached the fruit, sat down to eat, carefully peeling a banana and casting the skin aside. Every now and then he stared at them, letting them know that he was aware of their presence and showing them that he was not afraid of them. The warning was clear. He was not to be trifled with. After he had had his fill, he stood guard while the entire troop, of about twenty monkeys, descended on the remaining fruit, making quick work of it. Wide eyed babies clung tightly to their mother's long underbody hair as the mothers leaped effortlessly from the trees. Juveniles teased and played with each other. The adults looked wise and very human as they walked on their hind legs, clutching the fruit in their front paws. For Barbara this contact with these seemingly intelligent primates, in their home environment, was a profound life changing experience.

Back at the hotel, Barbara did a voice over, drawing a comparison between loving human families and these innocent, wild creatures in their Garden of Eden. They transmitted the video back to their network where the clip was immediately posted on the internet. Within hours it was linked into hundreds of the stories being posted around the world about the threatened destruction of Saint Matts by America. A tidal wave of horror at the senseless destruction of innocent creatures was the expected and immediate result. Barbara Wall vowed she would do whatever was necessary to save this island and these creatures, even if it meant she had to sacrifice her own life to do it.

CHAPTER 6

Game

"**G**eneral Lee, the Central Military Commission is very disappointed that there has been a premature announcement of our anticipated agreement with St. Matts".

General Lee stood beside his desk. He was tall and elegant. With his telephone pressed to his ear, he pondered a reply to his superiors in Beijing. He too was disappointed with the premature announcement, but he accepted that once a secret is no longer a secret, it is like a genie out of the bottle and there is no way it can be returned. The challenge was in responding appropriately to the new reality.

They could vehemently deny that such an agreement had ever existed and abandon their plans to develop the naval base in St. Matts. There were alternatives. However, this pained General Lee because he had fallen in love with this sheltered, deep water harbor. It was a magnificent harbor. He wanted to possess this harbor.

They could also neither confirm nor deny that such an agreement existed and proceed with their plans. The element of surprise would be gone. The Americans would then be watching them like a hawk and might even aggressively step up their presence in the China Sea to distract them from developing St. Matts. China had always feared blockades that could disrupt the flow of raw materials into their factories and the export of their finished goods to the world's markets. The Americans could even covertly sabotage the project.

They could confirm that the agreement existed and immediately confront the United States. He was sure this would be seen as such an aggressive threat that the Americans, to save face, would have to respond too aggressively. If the purpose of their development of St. Matts was to show that they were no longer intimidated by the United States, then confirmation of their plans to develop this naval base might make the actual development of the base unnecessary. Their newest aircraft carrier wouldn't need to make the long 8,000-mile voyage to bless their new Western Hemisphere base with its presence. Although he was an engineer, by training, General Lee was secretly an artist at heart. He wanted to see this naval base created and functioning. Thus, confirming their intentions was never going to be his recommendation.

In the few seconds that General Lee took to take all this into consideration, he decided the only logical course of action was to proceed with their plan and ignore this tempest in a teapot that Senator Wilcox had stirred up. If asked, the Chinese would respond that no lease had been signed with the government of St. Matts.

They had presumptively started their preliminary design work on the naval base without having one in place. There were still a few minor points in the agreement to be resolved. The General expected Chumley would now start to push to have the agreement signed so he could get his greedy paws on his substantial commission. Lee decided he would punish Chumley for leaking the proposed lease agreement to the senator. He would make himself unavailable to Chumley for a few days. There was no doubt in his mind that Chumley had leaked the information, as only a few under his command and Chumley had ever been party to the discussions.

He now responded to Beijing, "Comrade, tell the Central Military Commission not to be concerned, everything will proceed as per our plan. Any requests from the Americans, for a formal response, should be ignored until a time of our choosing. Refer them to the embassy in St. Matts. We will not make ourselves available."

General Lee could hear a murmured discussion in the background. He then received a response, "We leave this in your very capable hands General Lee.""

Lee put the phone down and went back to poring over the preliminary plans for greatly expanding the submarine caverns that the British had built into mountains. The caverns would hide their greatest technological achievement from the American spy satellites until they were ready to let the world know of their strategic technical advantage.

Although Kwan Lee, was a general in the People's Liberation Army (Navy), he was officially only the military attaché to the Chinese embassy in St. Matts. All People's Republic of China personnel in the Caribbean fell under his authority. This included the ambassador in Saint Matts.

There were a thousand Chinese construction workers in Saint Matts. All were soldiers in the People's Liberation Army who were assigned to construction platoons. They were busily upgrading the infrastructure on the island. Unlike other foreign governments who provided aid, the Chinese did not just send money; they sent the best of equipment, skilled engineers, trained labor and support personnel. Projects that would have taken years to be completed, with local Caribbean labor, could be done efficiently in months at a fraction of the local cost.

His engineers were completing the plans for the refitting of the former Royal Navy dockyard. They had already started to use it in a limited way, primarily to store construction materials. The general was anxious to start the total refit. Development of the old naval base had always been their long-term objective, long before he had been sent to Saint Matts to execute the plan.

To soften Chumley up, they had first tackled the projects that the Prime Minister had considered to be a priority – the roads, the schools and the hospital. Quickly showing tangible, rapid improvements to the island, it had then been easy to propose a ninety- nine-year lease of the long abandoned naval dockyard. The financial rewards to the island (and covertly to Chumley) were generous and would not only insure Chumley's re-election but put the island back on a firm financial platform. The General thought it ironic that the British had signed a similar ninety-nine-year lease with the Chinese for the harbor of Hong Kong in 1898.

Like the all-powerful British navy in 1898, the Chinese now felt they had the power to establish a naval base in the Caribbean to protect their financial interests in the Western Hemisphere. It would also protect their long trade routes to the Americas and Europe.

General Lee mulled over in his mind their strategic advantage. He knew they were ready to confront the Americans. They had created a weapon for which the Americans had no defense. It was a drone submarine propelled by magnetohydrodynamic propulsors.

Chinese technicians had explained to General Lee that research on this propulsion system had been abandoned by the Americans in the nineteen sixties. They had mistakenly concluded that it was impossible to make a generator small enough in size to produce enough electric current to propel a submarine.

In their lab the technicians had demonstrated to General Lee how the propulsion system worked. They had sent an electric current through a propulsion tube where it interacted with the magnetic field in seawater. The interaction pushed water out the back of the tube. This reaction allowed them to accelerate submarines to greater speeds than had ever been previously realized.

The General knew that the fastest American nuclear submarines were able to travel at twenty-five miles an hour. He saw the new Chinese drone submarines with this propulsion system traveling at close to one hundred miles an hour.

It was explained to him that these drone submarines were the perfect stealth weapon. They had no moving mechanical parts. They were silent, reliable, efficient, inexpensive and almost impossible to detect. Even if they were detected, due to their speed, they would be almost impossible to catch and eliminate.

Lee was impressed that they could fire a torpedo and be miles away from their firing position before the torpedo had hit its target. They could run circles around any cruiser sent to depth charge them. Any ship sent to hunt them became an immediate target. As well, being able to quickly descend to depths, miles below the surface, meant they would be miles below any depth charge designed to explode at the shallower depths that conventional submarines operated at.

Lee was told that after the Americans had abandoned magnetohydrodynamic propulsors, the Japanese had started their research on it. They eventually succeeded in building a small prototype submarine they called the Yamata. Chinese spies had then stolen this advanced technology from the Japanese. They had then spent the last two decades, perfecting the technology.

The propulsion system was described as being as close to a perpetual motion machine as man had ever achieved. The movement of saltwater over the drone's flexible, conductive skin generated an electrical charge that assisted the generator in keeping the batteries perpetually charged. The faster the boat moved the faster it recharged its batteries which generated the electric current which interacted with the magnetic field in the saltwater.

General Lee had been one of the advisers consulted on whether the submarines should be manned or whether they should be drones operated by naval pilots thousands of miles away from where the submarines might be operating. It soon became obvious in their research that drones would eliminate many of challenges that conventional submarines faced.

Having no humans aboard the drones, there was no reason to generate or store oxygen. Since there was no internal combustion engine, there was no need for oxygen or fuel storage. Without oxygen or crew, the conventional problem that submarines have of being crushed by water pressure at great depths did not exist. The interior of the submarines was flooded with a special oil. Unlike air, the more this oil was compressed while descending into the depths, the stronger the shell of the drone submarine would become. Its carbon-glass sheathing would become stronger and more rigid the greater the depth the submarine operated at. The more rigid it became, the more it was able to increase its hydrodynamic speed. With no air in the submarine, the submarine did not require ballast tanks to keep it from popping to the surface. It could move as if suspended in the weightless vacuum of deep space.

The normal human essentials, such as sleeping quarters, food storage, fresh water, entertainment, food service and a conning tower could also be eliminated. The drones never needed to surface. Since there were no sailors there were no personnel problems to contend with. Without humans on board, the long-pointed submarine could also be spun like a drill bit. This permitted a super-cavitation effect that helped it to bore through the water at great speed with a minimum of drag.

Controlling the drones had presented them with a challenge. While communication with the drones could have been achieved through their satellite system, satellites were considered to be too visible and thus vulnerable to attack. They had created an overlapping network of 200,000 transmitter buoys spread across the 139,000,000 square miles of the earth's oceans. A sophisticated computer system kept each buoy in its assigned position. The batteries in the communication buoys were kept charged by both solar power and wave action.

The buoys were about the size of beach balls. Sensors could temporarily sink the buoys several hundred feet into the depths if any unauthorized vessel approached them. While the buoys could receive and send signals for thousands of miles while on the surface, underwater they could only send communications a maximum one hundred and fifty miles. This had necessitated the great number of buoys. It had taken two years to secretly create this secret world-wide communication grid. The fishing boats they had used to place the buoys had never raised the suspicion of the Americans.

General Lee had been impressed with the fire power that had been incorporated into each drone. Each had two missiles armed with nuclear war heads. These missiles can reach targets a thousand miles away. In addition, they were also equipped with four torpedoes. Two can destroy the largest aircraft carrier and two were special torpedoes designed to launch a metal net that entangled propellers of ships rendering them dead in the water.

According to the latest report General Lee had received, over 1,000 of the drones had now been launched from a vast, hidden, sea cave on the China coast. Since the subs were smaller and technically easier to construct, five new submarines were being launched every week.

They had kept the ship yard secret by making the thousands of workers virtual prisoners for years. By Chinese standards, the workers were well paid and their housing was modern and comfortable. However, until the drone submarines secret status was removed the shipwrights building them were isolated from the world.

Knowing that 1,000 drone submarines were now dispersed around the world had given General Lee and the Chinese leaders a great feeling of power and self-confidence. They were now capable of instantly destroying the world's 2,000 most strategic targets.

The Chinese leaders had long ago recognized that the United States' dominance of the world was derived from its navy. The drone subs had effectively neutralized the power of the United States Navy within a few years instead of decades it would have taken if they had tried to build a conventional naval force.

The U.S. navy consisted of twelve aircraft carriers, twenty-five cruisers, sixty destroyers, sixty-one nuclear attack submarines and thirty amphibious assault vessels. It was a greater sea force than all of the other navies in the world combined. The Chinese now had a fleet of drone submarines constantly shadowing every U.S. Naval vessel.

American intelligence forces had been easily distracted from their secret building of the drones by openly building aircraft carriers. The Americans were convinced that the Chinese were intent on building a conventional naval force to match their own. This made the Americans feel safe because they believed that it would take fifty years for the Chinese to acquire the skills to effectively operate their aircraft carriers.

Since General Lee had studied for many years at American universities, he was in a position to compare the technical ascension that Chinese central planning had wrought. The Chinese were graduating 500,000 engineers each year. This was five times more than were being graduated from American universities. The Chinese leaders had read with great interest a U.S. National Academies report that had raised the alarm about the declining number of U.S. students enrolling in mathematics and science disciplines, when compared to the increasing numbers in China. They had not corrected the American academics that sidetracked the threat by arguing that China's engineering graduates were not up to the same standards. It took only a few years before the American academics realized that the Chinese standards were superior to those of the U.S. The newly minted Chinese engineers were busy making millions of Chinese workers more productive.

General Lee knew that these great technological advances were being quickly made in China because the People's Republic of China was a cohesive one-party state. The Chinese Communist Party, with 100,000,000 members, was the largest political party in the world. Unlike an American Congressional government where the winner takes all, the Chinese do not get into inter-party fractional politics.

While there are two competing ideologies in the party, neither faction had the ability, or the desire, to completely dominate the other. Neither would ever do anything that would threaten the continued rule of the Communist party. Each faction had its own areas of expertise. If anything, they had a complementary approach to establishing policies. Once every five years there was a National Congress where local communist party representatives gathered to hammer out direction and policies for the next five years. They also anointed the leadership who would implement the new objectives.

The National Congress of the Chinese Communist Party held the ultimate power. Its General Secretary was the nation's ultimate authority. As a member of The People's Liberation Army, General Lee fell under the control of the Central Military Commission that along with Central Committee reported through the Secretariat to the Politburo Standing Committee's nine members. These nine effectively administered and coordinated this vast nation of 1,300,000,000 people.

General Lee was a member of the communist party, as was every significant Chinese government official. His primary objective, as a young man, was getting accepted as a member into the party. It was the first step to success for the ambitious. It was not easy to get an invitation to join the party. He had been assisted by his father who was a senior party official.

The party was very careful who they selected as members. Doing a good job and giving unwavering support to the party was the only way to advance in both the private and public sectors. Both sectors were controlled by Secretariat of the Central Committee. Contrary to normal capitalist systems, Chinese manufacturers shared their technological advances with each other rather than using their advances for competitive advantage.

The party saw a naval base in the Western Hemisphere as one of the most important steps in China's ultimate ambition of controlling the world economy. Establishing the base in Saint Matts would be General Lee's springboard to reaching the highest level in the party.

General Lee's phone began to buzz. He tore himself away from the plans on the drafting table and went over to his desk to answer it. The embassy intelligent officer, Po Chang, was on the line asking if he could see him right away. Lee agreed. In a few minutes there was a tap at his door and Chang entered. They nodded to each other. Lee indicated that he should take a seat.

"What is it Comrade Chang?"

"I've been monitoring the media's response to our plans for the naval dockyard. It must be a dull news day. Rumors of our acquiring the naval dockyard are getting an incredible amount of attention in the press. I've also been monitoring the feed from Prime Minister Chumley's office. Chumley seems pleased with the hornet's nest he has stirred up. He also seems to be interested in a passenger who arrived on the American Airlines flight from Miami tonight, a Rob Lyons. We accessed the Saint Matts registry. Here is his passport photo. He is part of the Bishop clan but most importantly he appears to be an official in the US Secretary of State Department. Chumley seems to think that it is too coincidental for Lyons to appear on the same day that news breaks about our plans. He has ordered around the clock surveillance of Lyons and is going to try to arrange a meeting with him at his beach house tomorrow."

"Do we have the beach house wired?"

Yes, of course."

General Lee tilted his chair back and closed his eyes to think about this new development. He then turned to Chang. "I do not remember a Rob Lyons appearing in your profile of the power structure of the island."

"That is because he does not live on the island. He gets his Saint Matts citizenship from his mother, Monique Bishop. She is married to a Canadian, Colin Lyons, who worked for a large company in the United States. Rob Lyons was born in the US and has US citizenship."

"We do not want the United States to interfere with our plans. However, I am sure they will do what they can to stop us. It is important that we prepare for any threats to our plans. I think we can assume that Rob Lyons is their first probe to asses our capabilities and strength. Where is this Rob Lyons now?"

"Our monitoring picked him up at the Bishop compound. He was speaking to his father."

"We need to know who he sees, what he discusses and what his conclusions are. If he interferes with our plans, then he will need to be removed. We also need to control what he will be feeding back to Washington. Thus, we need to meet with him so that we can make Washington understand the fairness of our protecting our interests in the Western Hemisphere in the same way their bases in Korea, Japan and the Philippines protect their interests in the Eastern Hemisphere.

Chang nodded his agreement. General Lee continued, "Chumley needs to be replaced. He must be made an example of. How dare he play these stupid games with The People's Republic of China. That man will prostitute himself to whoever lines his pockets with the most gold. Has he forgotten who put him into power?

We must prepare a plan to put the leader of the official opposition into power. It should not be the difficult. In their ten-seat legislature, Chumley has a majority of only two seats. Let us see which Members of Parliament are ready to abandon Chumley and move over to the opposition party. Unlike Chumley, we will make sure the leader of his majesty`s opposition, understands that the power we give him is solely due to us and that if we can remove Chumley then we can do the same to him."

Chang continued, "We have also detected a U.S. drone. It is circling the island at 40,000 feet. We believe it is armed with missiles. It appeared shortly after Rob Lyons landed at the airport. I have instructed a squad to stand by on the embassy roof with ground-to-air missiles that could remove this threat within minutes, if you see it being necessary."

"Very well, Comrade Chang, it is good to be prepared. You should also immediately instruct Captain Wei at the construction camp to make combat ready half of our comrades who are working in the construction platoon. Put them on standby in case we quickly need them"

General Lee stood. He bowed slightly. Chang took his leave.

CHAPTER 7

China

"Hello, Mister Horsemont this is Florence, Secretary MacSween's administrative assistant. She wants you to meet with her in her office as quickly as possible."

"I'll be right up Florence."

Russel Horsemont wondered what this was all about. He could count on one hand the number of times he had been in her office. He did not like, not being in control and going into meetings unprepared. He walked briskly to the elevators that took him up to her floor. As soon as he arrived, Florence, knocked on Secretary MacSween's door and announced that he was here. She then held the door open for him to enter before quietly shutting it. MacSween indicated that he should take a seat across from her. She sat at her desk framed by the two stars and stripes on each side of her.

"Well, Russell has there been any developments yet in Saint Matts?"

"Not really, Doctor Lyons has just arrived. He went through customs and immigration with no problem. We did get a glimpse of people lined up at the airport trying to get off the island and got a good view of the Chinese construction camp."

"I'm trying to determine how this problem managed to creep up on us. It seems to have come out of left field. Wouldn't the Chinese's ever-increasing dominance of the Caribbean have been immediately noticeable?"

"Not necessarily. The Chinese have been a presence in the Caribbean for almost two hundred years. In islands like Jamaica 95% of the grocery stores are owned by Chinese. There are hundreds of thousands of West Indians who can trace their ancestry back to these early Chinese immigrants."

"What brought them to the Caribbean?"

"Slavery ended in the British Caribbean in 1834. The West Indian planters still needed cheap labor. From Hong Kong the British brought in hundreds of thousands of Chinese contract workers to cultivate the sugar cane fields. Another group immigrated after the United States passed the Chinese Exclusion Act in 1882. It forced many Chinese in the United States to flee to the Caribbean. The act had excluded Chinese from citizenship and prohibited the men from bringing their wives and children to America. To be reunited with their families they had to leave. Interestingly that act did not get repealed until 1943. Unfortunately, America has a long history of Chinese racial discrimination that goes all the way back to the California gold rush days in the mid eighteen hundred.

"That all seems a very long time ago. How have the Chinese managed to move from being poor contract workers to be the dominant foreign power in the Caribbean?

"Over the past two decades the People's Republic of China has invested more than five billion dollars in the Caribbean. The money was transferred to their Cayman bank accounts and then dispersed across the Caribbean. For example, hundreds of millions of dollars was invested in Bahamian hotels and casinos in Freeport."
"Freeport is only about sixty miles from Miami, Florida. "

"That's right. They are right on our doorstep. Further billions in foreign aid have been pumped into many of these small, desperately poor Caribbean countries. The objective was to secure them as allies and as safe, reliable sources of raw materials. Bauxite is being shipped from Jamaica and Grenada. Oil is being transported from Venezuela and Trinidad. Much of the nickel in Cuba is being used in the Chinese steel mills."
"Isn't that an awful long way to ship these raw materials?"

"Yes, it is. It is almost eight thousand miles. However, without these raw materials to transport many of their ships that are taking export goods to America and Europe would be returning to China empty. The cost of shipping these raw materials over such a long distance on a return voyage then becomes cost effective."

"Why isn't America importing these goods from the Caribbean nations?"

"Because America's manufacturing is being done in China."

"Were we asleep at the switch to have allowed the Chinese to win over the Caribbean?"

"No, we were preoccupied fighting unwinnable wars in the Middle East. You would think that we would have learned from Vietnam that we can't win ideological wars. Our wealth and technological superiority is no match against zealots who see dying in a holy war against infidels as the absolute pinnacle of human ambition?"

"It seems that St. Matts is sending us a message that we need to strengthen our ties with our neighbors and stop taking them for granted. They are a buffer on our immediate borders. Is there anything more we should be doing about Saint Matts?

"Not until Doctor Lyons can give us a better understanding as to what our options are."

CHAPTER 8

Chumley

Rob did not sleep well. Several times he awoke and had a hard time getting back to sleep. At daybreak he realized that he had forgotten to close the hurricane shutters on his bedroom window. They were a substitute for blinds in the Caribbean. They allowed air to circulate through their slanted slats while keeping the room dark for sleeping. As the sun had climbed into the sky, the intense tropical blue skies had shaken him awake. Without getting out of his bed, he could see out the window, across the sloping lawn and over the cliff into the harbor below. A brilliant white passenger liner was gracefully leaving its mooring in Georgetown. The lush greenery and the spikes of palm trees confirmed that he was not in Washington. The crow of a rooster from below the cliff doubly confirmed it.

He normally slept naked, comfortable under the single sheet. No blankets were needed in this climate and it cooled off enough at night that air conditioning was also not needed. The only thing he now wore was the ring that he had been told never to take off. He sat on the edge of the bed staring out the window.

"THAT IS A BEAUTIFUL SIGHT," control whispered in his ear.

Rob jumped. He still was not accustomed to hearing phantom voices

"Yes, it is," he quietly murmured assuming and hoping control was talking about the view through the window. It felt uncomfortable to be speaking to no one visible.

"WHILE YOU WERE SLEEPING, WE HAVE BEEN FOLLOWING THE DEVELOPING STORY OF CHINA ESTABLISHING A WESTERN HEMISPHERE NAVAL BASE. FOX NEWS SEES IT AS ANOTHER SIGN OF AMERICA'S WEAKENING POSITION IN THE WORLD. THE NEW YORK TIMES SEES IT AS AN OPPORTUNITY FOR THE PEOPLE OF SAINT MATTS TO IMPROVE THEIR ECONOMIC SITUATION WITHOUT HAVING TO BEG RICHER NATIONS FOR FOREIGN AID. SEVERAL ISLANDS IN THE CARIBBEAN, INCLUDING SAINT KITTS, ANTIGUA AND GRENADA ARE UNDER ATTACK BY THEIR OPPOSITION PARTIES FOR NOT HAVING DONE MORE TO ATTRACT CHINESE INVESTMENT INTO THEIR ISLANDS. VENEZUELAN NEWSPAPERS ARE HERALDING THEIR CLOSE TIES WITH CHINA AND PRAISING THE BUILDING OF THE SAINT MATTS NAVAL BASE AND VOWING TO COME TO THEIR DEFENSE IF THE UNITED STATES EVER ATTACKS THEM. THE BRITISH NEWSPAPERS ARE CALLING ON THEIR GOVERNMENT TO SEEK COMPENSATION FROM THE CHINESE GOVERNMENT FOR THE MILLIONS OF DOLLARS THEY HAVE SPENT OVER THE LAST HUNDRED YEARS TO DEVELOP THE SAINT MATTS ROYAL NAVAL BASE. THEY NOW CLAIM THAT THEY HAD ONLY TEMPORARILY ABANDONED IT. CHINESE NEWSPAPERS ARE NOT COMMENTING. SPOKESPEOPLE FOR THE CHINESE GOVERNMENT HAVE MADE THEMSELVES UNAVAILABLE. THE SECRETARY OF STATE IS BEING PRESSED BY THE PRESIDENT AND CONGRESS TO FORMULATE OUR OFFICIAL RESPONSE. SHE IS WAITING ON INFORMATION FROM YOU TO GIVE HER DIRECTION IN HOW TO PROCEED. SHE WANTS TO KNOW WHAT YOU ARE GOING TO DO ABOUT IT."

Rob thought to himself, "God damn, do I really need this at seven-thirty in the morning." He then whispered a response to control, "Thanks for the update. The first thing I want to do is drive around the island to get a feel for what changes have been made. That will take a couple of hours. It is a small island. During this reconnaissance I will visit the old naval base to see what changes have been made there. I will then approach some of the power brokers on the island to get their fix on the situation. You will see what I see and hear what I hear." He then got up, put on his robe and went down the hall to take his shower – with his ring recording everything.

As he was drying himself off, he could smell coffee brewing and ham being fried. He quickly got dressed in a short-sleeved shirt that he let hang over his shorts. He went barefoot down the hall to the kitchen.

He loved this house with its thick limestone walls. Caribbean houses were open all the way up to their dark wood stained roof. Thirty- foot peaked ceilings give a great sense of spaciousness to a house and helped keep them cool. The ceiling fans, the ceramic tiles and large windows, opening on to a wide, shaded porch that circled the entire building, kept them comfortable without air conditioning. The sea breeze blowing through the shaded porch kept the house remarkably comfortable.

His mother was standing at the stove making him his favorite, a New Zealand rat cheese omelet with thick slices of Virginian ham. He noticed the sliced tomato and avocado on the plate waiting for the omelet and ham. He reached around her to grab the coffee pot and pour himself a coffee. She smiled at him and said, "Did you sleep well?"

"Yes, thank you. You know, I'm a big boy now. I could have made my own breakfast."

"And mess up my kitchen."

Rob smiled. He knew his mother expressed her love by feeding people. He marveled that he had not been fifty pounds overweight, like his father, when he lived at home. His mother put his plate in front of him. He sat down at the kitchen table to eat. The kitchen was at the back of the house and he could look out the windows down the hill to the harbor. It was now just after eight o'clock.

He heard the bing-bong of the front doorbell.

"Who could that be at this hour of the day?" his mother said as she headed towards the front door.

"Good Morning, Mrs. Lyons."

"Good Morning, Winston. How is your mother?"

She's just fine Mrs. Lyons. Would your son be home?"

"Yes, he is having his breakfast. Have you eaten?"

"Oh, I have had my coffee," Austin said hopefully."

"A growing boy like you needs more than coffee."

"Oh, no... No, I'm fine"

"Nonsense, there is some ham already cooked and it will take just a minute to fry an egg."

"Oh well, if you insist Mrs. Lyons."

Winston Clark looked like he was far from starving. He could easily do with losing thirty pounds. Could it be that he had deliberately chosen to come at breakfast instead of just phoning? He could almost taste that ham that had been first baked with cloves and covered with pineapple. Monique led him down the hall to the kitchen. Rob looked up.

"Rob, I don't know if you remember Winston Clark, Mrs. Clark's youngest boy, from over on Apes Hill."

Rob stood up and shook Winston's hand and indicated a chair across from him. Winston would have been a few years younger than Rob. He did not really remember him. All those Clarks looked the same to him.

Control whispered in Rob's ear, "WINSTON CLARK IS PRIME MINISTER CHUMLEY'S CHIEF OF STAFF. HE IS THIRTY YEARS OLD, A GRADUATE OF THE LONDON SCHOOL OF ECONOMICS. HE WAS CALLED TO THE BAR IN LONDON FIVE YEARS AGO. SHORTLY, AFTER HE RETURNED TO SAINT MATTS TO SET UP HIS PRACTICE, HE GOT INVOLVED IN POLITICS AND CHUMLEY ENLISTED HIM AS HIS CHIEF AID TWO YEARS AGO. HE IS TRYING TO MAKE A NAME FOR HIMSELF."

His mother put on two eggs to fry.

"Good to see you again Robby. Welcome back, I had heard you were on the island."

Rob hated being called Robby. He had a good idea as to where this was going. "The word gets around fast, "Rob replied.

"I don't know if your mother told you but I'm now the Prime Minister's Chief of Staff."
No, I hadn't heard. Congratulations, I'm impressed"

"Well, the Prime Minister heard that you were now with the State Department and he wanted to me to come around and officially welcome you back to the island."
"That is very kind of him but I'm just a lowly analyst in the State Department and I'm just down here to visit with my parents."

"Well, none the less, the countries relationship with the United States is extremely important and we want to make sure that any employee of the State Department, especially one who is also a Saint Mattitian, is treated well and takes back to Washington a good impression of us."

"You don't need to worry about a good impression. Being a Saint Mattitian, I, of course, always do my best to promote my island."

"Oh, we are sure of that, but you can never take things for granted. The Prime Minister is actually wondering if you could join him today for lunch."

Control softly murmured in his ear, **"WE WOULD BE VERY INTERESTED IN HEARING WHAT HE WOULD HAVE TO SAY."**

Rob, took another forkful of his cheese omelet, smiled and replied, "I'm flattered that he would be interested in talking to me, although I'm not sure what he would gain from a lowly employee of the State Department. However, when a prime minister calls, you go. When and where would he like us to get together?"

"Around noon, he wants you to meet him at the Beach House. We can send a car for you.``

``That won't be necessary. I have a car.``

``Do you know where it is?"

Rob shook his head to indicate that he did not know.

"It is over on the North Shore. You drive past the Casino and it is the first road on the right. You will see a small sign with a red crown on it at the entrance."

The eggs were ready. Toast and ham were added to the plate. Winston Clark wolfed down the food like he had not eaten in several days. Monique poured him some orange juice and coffee. Let no one say that they ever left the Bishop compound hungry. Having completed his mission and thoroughly stuffed himself, he got up, shook Rob's hand, wiped a bit of egg yolk from his chin and left.

Monique looked at Rob and asked, "What was that all about?"

Rob replied, "You heard. I'm not sure but obviously they are reading something official into my visit to the island. I only arrived last night, and I have not been out of this compound. The government's monitoring of who is coming and going on this island is very impressive."

"You be careful now, I've known Victor Chumley since he was a little boy. He hasn't changed in sixty years. He was a hot headed, bully then and he is still an aggressive, hot headed bully, now. He always thought everyone was stupider and weaker than he was. I remember him complaining to the principal because I came first in the class. He said that it wasn't fair because I was taking an easy subject like home economics. Even then, he wasn't afraid of anybody. Becoming a doctor hasn't changed things. The other doctors knew what he was like and tried their best to stop him from coming back to practice in St.Matts."

"When did you see last see Chumley?"

"A few weeks ago, at a Chinese embassy cocktail party."

"How would he know I was with the Secretary of State?"

"I might have mentioned it to him when we were talking about our children. His son Reggie is now a doctor?"

Rob finished his breakfast.

"Well if I am going to be having lunch with the Prime Minister, I guess I better put on a nice shirt befitting the State Department."

He went down the hall, changed into a light summer suit, grabbed the car keys, that his father had given him, off the dresser and yelled out to his mother, "See you later today, I'm going to check out the island". His father, knowing his taste in cars had got him a Subaru WRX out of the car pool. This was a rugged, all-wheel drive, rally car. It was more than able to cope with the poor roads and had lots of power for climbing the mountains and going off road if that were ever necessary. He drove through the rock cut and down the hill to the main road. As he pulled out on to the main road, he noticed that the two cars that Control had warned him about had fallen discreetly in behind him. The numerous jitney buses, always in an insane hurry, tempted fate by speeding by all three of them on blind corners and brinks of hills as he made his way into Georgetown.

Control started to speak into his ear, "TWO CARS ARE NOW FOLLOWING YOU. IF THEY BECOME AGGRESSIVE, THEY WILL BE ELIMINATED. YOUR FIRST PRIORITY IS TO GIVE US A FEEL FOR THE HARBOR AND THE OLD BRITISH NAVAL DOCKYARD."

The Harbor Road went for miles all around the harbor. It was shaped like a horseshoe. The British naval base was at the East end. As he drove towards Harbor Road, he looked for changes. If anything, the tiny one story, weather beaten, wooden buildings looked shabbier than ever. Some looked like they had not seen paint in this century. Their rippled corrugated tin roofs were streaked brown with rust. To make them even uglier, when the tin roofs were replaced, the old rusty tin roofs were transformed into rusty brown fences around the property. In a place where the temperature never fell below 74 degrees Fahrenheit, all you really needed was somewhere to sleep out of the wind and rain. Thus, the slap dash, fragile, beaten down appearance of the houses was understandable. Other small, but well-maintained houses, were painted in Caribbean colors: bright pink, canary yellow, electric blue and lime green.

At most corners were small stone structures with a water pipe and tap. Many of the houses had no running water and this was their source of fresh water. During the day mothers and children would appear with buckets to carry water home. Rob had stood in awe the first time he had seen a mother carry a bucket of water balanced on her head, her back as straight as a runway model. As he got closer to the center of the town there were open ditches about a foot wide and a couple of feet deep. He had always had a concern about his front wheels falling into them if he was not careful navigating the narrow, poorly maintained roads.

Cars were parked on the right side and wrong side of the roads. Drivers double parked to talk to friends at the side of the road, totally oblivious to the traffic backed up behind them. Very carefully, traffic edged around these inconsiderate conferences. No one honked as that would have been rude and on a small island you could not be anonymously rude. Pedestrians lurched out from between cars without any apparent concern of being struck down. Everywhere there were young mothers, carrying children on their hips. Many of these mothers looked like children themselves. The palm trees and lush greenery, growing on every inch of soil, confirmed that you were in the Caribbean.

When he got to Harbor Road, he had reached the commercial hub of the island. Usually there would be two large cruise ships moored at the passenger ship dock. Each ship would be capable of hosting four thousand passengers. They would have vomited their multitudes into the port. Competing taxi drivers would normally have been frantically trying to net as many passengers for a tour of the island as they could. A string band sitting on a wall, with one musician ringing a bell, at oddly disconcerting times, would be soliciting tips. Blond haired tourists with naturally straight hair would be sitting getting their hair braided into rope like strands so they could have something tangible from their vacation to flaunt when they went to work on Monday morning. Sellers of T shirts and expensive jewelry would be trying to reap the bounty that the cruise ships had delivered on to them.

The docks were empty. The taxis had vanished. No string band was playing. No tourists were in sight. The threat of the island being bombed had scared away the cruise ships just like a loud noise in a fishing boat scares away the fish.

Rob would normally have been stopping every few feet to allow careless tourists to cross the street but not today. At the island's most important corner were the ultimate representatives of capitalism. On one corner was the Royal Bank of Canada, on another was the Bank of Nova Scotia, on another was the Canadian Imperial Bank of Commerce and on the fourth corner was the Saint Matts Commercial Bank. Rob had once wondered out loud why the Canadian banks dominated the Caribbean. He had been told it had to do with the centuries old export of salt cod fish from Canada to the West Indies with the ships then returning to Canada with Caribbean sugar and rum.

He slowed to a crawl. At the corner a few elderly ladies were seated hoping that someone would come to buy their local vegetables that they had neatly placed on plastic sheets on the sidewalk. Pedestrians had to carefully step around their display. A wiry hawker stood by his cart, loaded with green coconuts, hoping that some thirsty soul would appear, so he could show them how skilled he was in chopping small holes with his large machete in the top of the coconuts for inserting a sipping straw to suck up the cold refreshing coconut water. He sold them for five Eastern Caribbean dollars each but today there were no buyers at any price. The coconut water was allegedly good for your liver. Rob turned left and headed towards the abandoned Naval Dockyard which was a few miles away.

As he moved away from the center of town, all traffic disappeared. He passed the dock where the large Chinese hospital ship was still moored. A short distance from it was the three-story Chinese embassy, its clean, modern, urban design looked out of place next to the decayed, century old British colonial administration building and the scruffy wooden shacks. In a few minutes he came to the limestone walls of the old British naval base. The gate to the narrow, arched, entrance was open. He ignored the "No Trespassing" sign and drove through, past the boarded up, abandoned gate house, past all the empty stone warehouses, barracks, machine shops, dry docks, wharves, office buildings and fortifications. If he were to estimate it, he thought it covered at least a square mile. Much of it was overgrown. He drove across the main parade square and then towards a rock face at the extreme end.

Close to the caves in the rock face a large container ship was tied up at the old naval wharf. Its cranes were unloading long metal containers.

As he drove closer to the rock face he was surprised to come across several parked vehicles. He parked his car beside them and started walking towards a group of people a few hundred feet away. As he approached them, they turned and stared at him. They appeared to be engineers taking readings from instruments on tripods. As he climbed a small rise, he saw that their interest seemed to be centered on two large caverns cut into the rock face with channels leading into the harbor. All the engineers were Chinese, dressed in light tan cotton shirts and pants. In strongly accented English the tallest one who appeared to be in charge said, "Can help you?"

"No, I am just looking around?"

"This private property. You no allowed here."

"Who are you?

"We engineers."

"I can see that but for whom are you working?"

"We engineers."

They started to talk among themselves in Chinese. Rob stood looking them.

Control started to transmit a translation, **"THEY ARE DEBATING WHAT TO DO WITH YOU. IT APPEARS THAT THEY ARE SOLDIERS. ONE SUGGESTED SHOOTING YOU BUT IT APPEARS TO BE A JOKE. THEY ARE CONFUSED AS TO WHO YOU MIGHT BE. YOU DO NOT LOOK LIKE A LOCAL TO THEM. THEY THINK YOU LOOK LIKE A WELL-DRESSED TOURIST, BUT IF YOU ARE, WHAT ARE YOU DOING HERE. THEY HAVE CONCLUDED THAT YOU MAY BE SOMEONE IMPORTANT AND THEY DO NOT WANT TO GET INTO ANY TROUBLE WITH THE EMBASSY OR THE LOCAL GOVERNMENT. WE ARE RUNNING TRACES ON THEIR VOICE PRINTS AND FACE SCANS BUT SO FAR, WE ARE NOT ABLE TO IDENTIFY THEM. WE THINK IT BEST THAT YOU LEAVE. WE HAVE A GOOD UNDERSTANDING OF THE NAVAL BASE FROM THE IMAGES YOU ARE TRAMSMITTING AND WHAT WE HAVE PICKED UP FROM THE DRONE THAT IS CIRCLING OVERHEAD. THESE GUYS APPEAR TO BE JUST DOING SURVEY WORK AND WE ALREADY KNOW WHY. IT MAY TAKE YOU ALMOST AN HOUR TO GET UP TO THE NORTH COAST FOR YOUR MEETING WITH CHUMLEY."**

One of the soldiers took out a personal communication device and took a picture of Rob which he then seemed to transmit. Rob turned around and headed back to his car. He noticed as he approached his car that the two cars, which had been following him, were parked in the shade a hundred yards away. Watching but not interfering. He looked at his watch. Control was right. He had just enough time to get up to the North coast for his luncheon.

Back along the Harbor Road he went, through the town before he headed back up the North Road. The two cars continued to discreetly follow him. A few minutes past the airport he passed the casino. It was a typical six story American luxury resort hotel: seven hundred rooms and vacation time share apartment units, golf course, water sports, beach, gymnasium, spa, luxury retailers, with numerous restaurants and bars. It could have been anywhere: Florida, California, Arizona, and Puerto Rico or any of a dozen other islands in the Caribbean. Most of its clientele never left the security blanket of its walled grounds. The impressions of St. Matts these timid tourists formed were based on the short drive to and from the airport. The food they ate arrived from Miami by container and was prepared the way Americans liked it. They watched American television via cable in their rooms. The people they talked to were Americans. They were billed in American dollars and they paid in American dollars. Outside the resort, the shops and restaurants always provided bills in both Eastern Caribbean Dollars and American dollars. The exchange was $2.67 EC for every US dollar. The top management of the hotel were all white Americans and all the other employees were local blacks. This was the largest business and biggest employer on the island. The owners were assumed to be American mobsters who had been given a sweetheart deal by Chumley to build the resort on the island. They paid no taxes and the authorities apparently turned a blind eye to the bags of money being received from all over the world that was being laundered through the casino.

Chumley had been given a forgivable loan by the American owners to invest in the resort. He received a generous dividend check from the hotel every month. When they needed more land adjacent to the hotel for expansion, Chumley quickly made sure a law got passed through parliament to expropriate the land, at a fraction of its true value. The government then immediately sold it to the resort at that discounted price. The speculator who had owned the land for decades had to be content with the few hundred thousand he got for the land instead of the millions he had anticipated receiving on the open market.

Rob slowed down to a crawl after he passed the casino, looking for the sign that would direct him to the prime minister's beach house. One of the cars that had been following him, sped up, passed him and then slowed down, put its turn indicator on and led him into the road to the beach house. Rob saw the small discreet sign with the red crown. With one car behind him and another in front, they proceeded down the sand road towards the ocean. A thousand feet in, they came to a gate and a high chain link fence with razor wire on top that stretched off into the jungle on both sides. The car in front stopped. Rob stopped behind him. An armed guard came out talked to the car in front and waved them though the gate. They proceeded another six hundred feet before they emerged from the jungle of sea grape trees onto a wide beach. The beach house was a large, single story, white limestone building with a red terra cotta roof in a Spanish colonial style.

All three cars wheeled into the cobblestone court yard in front of the grand entrance. Rob could see through the open center of the house to the blue ocean and the white capped waves crashing on the beach. He got out and walked towards the entrance. Winston Clark appeared and waved to him as he approached.

"Hi Robby, sorry about this, but due to the high alert right now, we need to do a routine security check."

Two beefy men in colorful short sleeved shirts and black pants, from the car, that had been in front of him, approached. They asked Rob to raise his arms. They very thoroughly patted him down and then nodded to Winston, indicating he had no weapons or listening devices. They were totally oblivious of the innocuous ring on his finger which could have killed both instantly and was recording everything it saw and heard.

Winston led Rob through the open concept house to the wide patio facing the ocean. It circled a large swimming pool. Looking like a giant black bull frog, Prime Minister Chumley was on the telephone sitting at a round, white, cast iron table. He waved his big beefy hand to indicate that Rob should take a seat across from him. He gave Rob one of his famous, with teeth like tombstones, political smiles. He continued the greeting by reaching across the table to shake Rob's hand while still pressing the phone to his ear with his other hand. Winston Clark took a seat between them at the round table.

Control whispered in his ear," CHUMLEY HAS NO ONE ON THE PHONE. THERE ARE SEVERAL LISTENING DEVICES WITHIN TWENTY FEET OF YOU. ONE APPEARS TO BE BUILT INTO THE TABLE. A SECURITY SNIPER WITH A RIFLE IS LOCATED ONE HUNDRED AND TWENTY-FOUR FEET FROM YOU, BEHIND THE BUSHES ON THE WEST SIDE OF THE SWIMMING POOL. HE APPEARS TO BE AIMING AT YOUR HEAD. THE FOUR SECURITY PERSONNEL THAT WERE IN THE

TWO CARS, THAT ACCOMPANIED YOU, ARE WATCHING YOU FROM JUST INSIDE THE BUILDING. TWO SOLDIERS WITH MACHINE GUNS ARE PATROLLING THE BEACH IN FRONT OF THE BEACH HOUSE. A MAID IS APPROACHING TO YOUR LEFT WITH A TRAY OF FOOD FROM THE KITCHEN. THE SECRETARY OF STATE HAS BEEN LINKED INTO YOUR TRANSMISSION; SHE WANTS TO HEAR WHAT HE HAS TO SAY."

The prime minister with great flourish said goodbye and put down the phone and greeted Rob with, "Busy, busy, busy. Sorry about that Rob. It's been years; I haven't seen you since you were a kid. Now look at you, all grown up. It is so good to see you."
Rob smiled and responded, "Good to see you too Doctor Chumley."

" And how is your beautiful mother?"

"Fine, just fine, she sends you her greetings."

"I saw her just a few weeks ago. I believe that she said that you had left Harvard and were now working for the State Department in Washington."
"Yes, that's right - just a minor analyst's position."

"Well I was led to believe by her that you had a doctorate. So, I am sure it can't be that minor."

"Oh, they say at the State Department that even the janitors have doctorates."
"So, what brings you home to beautiful St. Matts?"

" A holiday, a chance to get out of the cold and an opportunity to see my parents and the rest of the clan."

"St. Matts was in the news yesterday."

"Really, what was the occasion?"

"Rumors, about our leasing the old British naval yard."

"That is a coincidence, I was out there this morning."

"Interesting, did you see anything unusual?"

Not really, just a team of what looked to be engineers surveying part of it and a ship that was unloading long metal containers."

"Did you recognize any of these engineers?
"

"No, they were all Chinese."

"Chinese! Well I must certainly ask our security personnel to investigate that. The base is supposed to be locked up so no one can get in and hurt themselves. Here comes our lunch"

The maid placed a bowl of conch chowder in front of each of them. Rob could see that this was going to be followed by a lobster salad. She opened a bottle of a rare Japanese white wine from a small, century old, winery North of Tokyo, which he knew retailed for well over $200 a bottle. She carefully filled their wine glasses. Chumley toasted Rob's health.

"Do you think you could possibly intervene on St. Matts' part with her if the need should ever arise?"

Control whispered in his ear," **THE SECRETARY OF STATE SAYS YES.**"

"I am sure I could, as you can imagine I have a soft spot in my heart for St. Matts and would assist it in any way I could."

"That's good to hear. There actually is a small issue right now that perhaps you could help us with."

"And what would that be?"

"St. Matts was in the news yesterday."

"Really, what was the occasion?"

"Apparently this lease has really stirred up Washington."

"It must have happened after I left."

"Have you ever met the Secretary of State?"

"Yes, I've met her."

"Do you think you could possibly intervene on St Matts part with her if the need should ever arise?"

Control whispered in Rob's ear, **"THE SECRETARY OF STATE SAYS YES."**

"I am sure I could. As I am sure you can imagine I have a soft spot in my heart for St Matts and would assist in any way I could."

"That's good to hear. There actually is a small issue right now that perhaps you could help us with."

"And what would that be?"

"Well, you see the government of St. Matts is under great pressure from the Republic of China to grant them a rather trivial concession which might be misinterpreted by the United States. For several years now, the Chinese have greatly assisted the island with financial and technical aid. The kind of aid we used to receive from the United State before the cold war ended and the threat of a Caribbean communist revolution evaporated. Unfortunately, since then the United States has been distracted, fighting wars overseas, and they seem to have forgotten their friends in the Caribbean. It would be a tremendous blow to St. Matts if the Chinese were to cease to assist us because they thought we were not appreciative of their aid. The electorate would be very displeased if things on the island started to deteriorate. Poor old Doctor Chumley would be out on his ass." He laughed at his rudeness.

The Secretary of State started to speak directly to Rob from the control center, **"TELL HIM THAT THIS INITIATIVE ON THE PART OF THE CHINESE IS HAPPENING AT THE WORST POSSIBLE TIME. THE PRESIDENT IS FACING RE-ELECTION IN THE FALL AND ANYTHING THAT DETRACTS FROM THE PRESIDENT'S IMAGE AS A POWERFUL STATESMAN IS NOT GOING TO BE TOLERATED. THE CHINESE MUST BACK DOWN FROM PURSUING THIS NAVAL BASE. ALSO TELL HIM THAT NOW IS A GOOD TIME TO SEEK AID FROM US BUT ONLY IF WE CAN BE ASSURED THAT THE CHINESE ARE NOT IN THE PICTURE."**

Rob took a few minutes to compose himself. He noticed Chumley staring at him as he replied, "From the meetings I have been involved in at State, I would suggest that this is not the right time for any foreign friend of the United States to be aligning themselves with the Chinese. The President is up for reelection and he will seize any opportunity to confront the Chinese and humiliate them so that he can appear as the powerful statesman. If you are suggesting that you are seeking financial assistance from the United States, then this is feasible however any funding would be contingent upon you not proceeding with an inflammatory relationship with the Chinese."

Chumley had anticipated the response and quickly replied. The charm had departed from his voice, "Let's cut to the chase. Are you speaking for yourself or the Secretary of State?"

"It isn't a coincidence that I am down here. I am speaking on behalf of the Secretary of State."

"Okay then. Let's get down to business. The Chinese are willing to lease the naval base for $40,000,000 a year for the next one hundred years with an adjustment for inflation every three years. The Chinese are still a developing nation. I am sure the world's only super power can do much better than that."

Rob picked away at his lobster salad as he waited for Control to give him guidance. Chumley thought Rob was being coy. He stared at him with his big, brown, bull frog eyes. Chumley was too good a salesman to break the silence and possibly say something that could queer the sale. The unbearable silence stretched on.

Finally, the Secretary of State responded, **"AN AMOUNT LARGER THAN $50,000,000 WILL REQUIRE SOME TIME TO PUT TOGETHER. TELL HIM YOU ARE SURE THAT THE UNITED STATES CAN FIND $50,000,000 IN IMMEDIATE AID TO DIRECT TOWARDS SAINT MATTS."**

Rob, put down his fork and stared at Chumley, "The United States should be able to come up with $50,000,000 in immediate aid."

Chumley, took a sip of his exquisite wine, patted his rubber tire lips with the fine linen napkin, "$50,000,000 is a nice start but what about next year and the next one hundred years?"

The Secretary of State, responded in Rob's ear, **"FAT, GREEDY, BASTARD, TELL HIM TO GIVE US A FEW DAYS AND WE WILL BE BACK TO HIM. I WONDER HOW MUCH OF IT WILL END UP IN HIS CAYMAN ISLAND BANK ACCOUNT'.**

Rob took a sip of his wine, and said quietly, "Give us a few days and let me see what we can do."

"You've got until nine tomorrow, back here. If you don't show up I will assume that you do not have a better deal than what the Chinese are offering."

Rob nodded and finished his lobster salad. They chit- chatted for a while about the island and mutual acquaintances as they waited for their dessert. Winston Clark suddenly got up and walked across the patio into the beach house. Rob could see through the open concept house to the parking area. A taxi had arrived. Clark came back and sat down and said quietly to Chumley, "The television team have arrived for the one-thirty interview." Chumley nodded, sipped his wine and looking like the cat that had swallowed the canary.

Rob finished his fruit salad of pineapple, passion fruit, soursop ice cream and star apples inside half of a small papaya. He put his fork down and said, "Well I guess I better get going." He stood, shook hands with Chumley and Clark and walked from the patio, through the Beach house on his way to the parking area. Clark accompanied him. The television team was two people, sitting in the luxurious reception area. Rob was distracted thinking of his conversation with Chumley. He was not paying the media people much attention. As he passed by, Rob felt a tug at his elbow, and a familiar voice said, "I thought you said that you were just on vacation." He turned and saw that it was Barbara Wall. His heart skipped a beat. She was as beautiful this morning as when he first saw her in the airport lounge in Miami. He had a great urge, like a teenage kid, to give into his impulses, reach out and hug her to his body and kiss her neck. He restrained himself not knowing whether the sign of affection he felt for her would queer their potential relationship. He was not willing to risk it.

"And I told you that it was a small island and we would be seeing each other."

"Yes, you did, but it isn't even 24 hours. Isn't it unusual for an accountant to be meeting with the Prime Minister?"

"Yes, I suppose it is, I was surprised when I was invited for lunch. I think he must have mistaken me for someone important. Now, I am being hustled out so the very important television people can do their interview. Are we still having dinner together tonight?"

"I was counting on it."

"My, my, my, that sounds very encouraging or someone is really hungry."

"I should be free after I finish editing and sending this interview."

"What time would you like me to pick you up at the hotel?"

"How about at seven o'clock?""

"Sounds good to me. See you then."

CHAPTER 9

Power

Rob left the prime minister's beach house and drove towards the gate. The two cars that had been shadowing him all morning, immediately moved in behind him. He turned left onto the main road and headed past the casino, the restaurants, the T-shirt shops and other related tourist traps. He then turned South on to The North Road. He soon passed the airport on his way back to the compound.

He drove, lost in thought, mulling over his meeting with Chumley. His reverie was broken by the Secretary of State. Once again, he had forgotten that he was totally wired for sound. He jumped, and the car swerved dangerously close to the edge of the road, which at this stage, was running along the rim of an extinct volcano with a thousand foot drop on either side – with no guard rails. Control could see on his biometric meters that they had startled him.

He had not realized the Secretary of State was still patched in, **"SORRY DOCTOR LYONS, I DIDN'T MEAN TO STARTLE YOU, BUT I WOULD LIKE YOUR INSIGHT INTO THE SITUATION AS AN ANALYST AND HISTORIAN. WHAT ARE YOUR THOUGHTS ON WHY ACQUIRING THIS NAVAL BASE IS SO IMPORTANT TO THE CHINESE?"**

"I believe that the Chinese are always very strategic and defensive in their objectives. First, they are traders, probably the greatest traders the world has ever seen. Their economy and strength are based on their ability to easily, cheaply and safely move their goods to distant markets. If the Americans control the seas, the Chinese do not have control over their economy nor over their future. No matter how rich and successful they become, they must always bow to the king of the castle who controls the waves. There is always a threat to their ability to trade, lying just below the surface, waiting to bite them. This worries and concerns them. Let me elaborate.

The problem is that the Chinese ports sit behind a natural barrier that blocks them from easily getting out of the China Sea. The borders of Vietnam, Malaysia, Brunei, Taiwan, Japan, Korea, the Philippines and Indonesia restrict China's access to the Pacific Ocean. The open seas can only be gained by the Chinese ships passing through a few very narrow channels. These channels can be very easily blockaded by the U.S. navy.

The naval bases the United States set up after the Spanish American war in 1898 and the Second World War in 1945 are still in place. After what happened at Pearl Harbor, the U.S., whether they admit it or not, are paranoid about a sneak attack from the Fa r East. Both the Chinese and the U.S. believe that within hours the U.S. could stop the flow of raw materials into China and th e flow of finished goods out of China. A third of the world's maritime shipping passes through these channels.

China produces about five times more than it needs for its domestic market. This means it must export if it is too survive. The irony is that China is the world's primary manufacturer of low-cost goods because the U.S. Navy now protects their trade routes. What happens if the U.S. can no longer protect their trade routes or chooses not to? Being good strategists, the Chinese must always prepare for the worse possible scenario. They face the dilemma of asserting a historic maritime claim to the waters between the Sea of Japan in the northeast to the Gulf of Tonkin in the south.

"While China cherishes access to American consumers, they actually have more trade with Europe and other nations than they do with the United States. The U.S. only has five percent of the world's population and while it is a wealthy, five percent, it is still only five percent.

"Creating a naval base in Saint Matt's is part of the Chinese contingency plan to take responsibility for the safety of their trade routes. It is an attempt to remove the threat of the United States or some other foreign power's future policies from impinging on their economic progress. Just as the United States does defense risk assessments of every country in the world, so do the Chinese."

"Preparing in a time of peace for an attack by an ally or trading partner is not as ridiculous as it might seem. I have seen our military threat assessments of a possible invasion by Canada. As if hordes of wild Canadian hockey players were going to turn into an invading army. Canada is so integrated into the United States economy and culture that a study has shown that 48% of Americans think Canada is part of the United States. However, good generals prepare for the implausible. It is no coincidence that Fort Drum in Upper New York State is within an easy two-hour drive of Canada's capital."

"WHY IS ACCESS TO THE SEAS SO IMPORTANT? THEY COULD SHIP TO EUROPE THROUGH RUSSIA VIA TRUCK OR TRAIN."

"Economics and a distrust of Russia rule out these transportation alternatives. Russia has been a traditional threat to China and land transportation can be 40 times more expensive than water. China produces for a world market, not just their domestic market. They would choke on their production if they could not easily and cheaply move their goods to a vast world market. As more and more manufacturing is transferred to China, there is less and less manufacturing being done in North America and Europe. What happens, if in the future new governments in the United States and Europe increase their tariffs to preserve manufacturing jobs or decide to create some incident to justify a blockade? China's success is built on a foundation of sand. They need to have some form of retaliation in place that would make the Americans and any other foreign government think twice before implementing a blockade."

"THEIR NAVY, ALTHOUGH SECOND IN STRENGTH TO THE UNITED STATES NAVY, IS STILL LESS THAN HALF ITS SIZE ACCORDING TO OUR INTELLIGENCE REPORTS. IT WILL BE DECADES BEFORE THEY CAN CHALLENGE OUR DOMINATION OF THE SEAS. WHY ARE THEY CHALLENGING US NOW?"

"Yes, that puzzles me as well. Why now? What don't we know? What are we missing? They would not be threatening America's domination of the Western Hemisphere unless they felt they had the power to do so. They could be bluffing but generally they methodically prepare their position and do not commit to a course of action unless they are sure they can win."

"I DO NOT UNDERSTAND WHY ST. MATTS IS THEIR APPARENT LINE IN THE SAND. WHAT IS THERE ABOUT THAT HARBOR THAT APPEALS TO THEM SO MUCH?"

"It is a remarkably good harbor. Its narrow entrance can be easily protected. Since it is the sunken bowl of an extinct volcano, it is remarkably deep. The high mountains that ring the bowl help protect it from hurricanes and from attack. I noticed that the Chinese engineers seemed to be very interested in the caves that are cut into the side of the mountain. This would protect anything in the caves from aerial bombardment. There is a thousand feet of solid rock above the caves. A submarine could move undetected into those caves from the deep-water harbor. As well, it is the most Eastern of the Caribbean islands, so it is in a good spot to protect their trade routes around Africa, South America and through the Panama Canal as well as up the East coast of the United States."

"IT CAN'T BE THAT - THE CHINESE HAVE ONLY A FEW NUCLEAR SUBMARINES AND A FEW MORE DIESEL-POWERED SUBS THAT WE CAN EASILY NEUTRALIZE."

"If it isn't submarines then there must be something else, they wish to hide in these caves.

Rob assumed that anyone who saw him driving and talking thought he was just talking to himself. He was getting close to the Chinese road camp. Cars were stopped in front of him. The two chase cars were right behind him. The traffic was snaking slowly forward. He could see a flag man waving the cars through. Several would go through and then the line would stop. Cars going in the opposite direction would then be directed over the one free lane before it was their turn again. He could not see around a bend as to what was holding up the two-way traffic. He finally got to the front of the line. The flag man got a message on his phone and waved Rob through. Rather than let the cars behind Rob go with him, the flag man immediately brought his flag down and prevented the chase cars from following Rob."

"What's the problem?"

Control answered, "WE AREN'T SURE. THERE IS SOME LARGE CONSTRUCTION EQUIPMENT ON THE ROAD AHEAD AROUND THE BEND, BUT THEY DO NOT SEEM TO BE DOING ANYTHING WITH IT."

As he rounded the bend, Rob could see the construction equipment and some workers close to it. As he approached these men another flag man stepped into the road to stop him. The worker closest to Rob's car turned quickly around drew a pistol, seemingly out of nowhere, and leaned into Rob's open passenger window pointing it at Rob's head."

Control immediately responded, "LASER ACTIVATED AND READY TO FIRE."

Rob instinctively pointed his finger at his assailant's chest and pressed his thumb against the side of the ring. The Chinese attacker never knew what hit him. He was dead before he hit the ground. Rob gunned the WRX; hit the flagman sending him flying on to his right fender where he then rolled off on to the road. The other work men, surprised, stared at their two dead companions in surprise and then began groping for their hidden weapons. Before they could aim at the rapidly moving car, an AGM – Hellfire air to surface missile, triggered by Control from the drone that had swooped down from 30,000 feet, at the first indication of trouble, obliterated the road crew and their machinery.

Travelling at ninety miles an hour, Rob saw the explosion in his rearview mirror. He came to the end of the construction and breezed by a flagman who looked confused. Smoke was rising in the distance behind him.

"Control, thanks for the assistance."

"NO PROBLEM, YOU CAN SLOW DOWN NOW. THERE IS NOTHING IN THE ROAD AHEAD TO BE CONCERNED ABOUT AND NO ONE IS FOLLOWING YOU. IT WILL TAKE THEM A WHILE TO REPAIR THAT ROAD AND GET TRAFFIC MOVING."

"What do you think that was all about?"

"IT APPEARS THE CHINESE ARE AWARE THAT YOU ARE ON THE ISLAND AND THAT YOU ARE A PERSON OF INTEREST. IT ALSO APPEARS THAT THEY HAVE UNDERESTIMATED YOUR RESOURCES. NOW, THAT THEY ARE AWARE OF YOUR RESOURCES, WE WILL HAVE TO BE EXTRA VIGILANT. WE ALSO SUSPECT THAT CHUMLEY'S RESIDENCES AND OFFICES ARE BEING MONITORED BY THE CHINESE. THUS, THEYARE AWARE OF CHUMLEY'S DOUBLE DEALING AND THAT YOU ARE TRYING TO STEAL THEIR NAVAL BASE AWAY FROM THEM. ELIMINATING YOU WOULD BE A GOOD STRATEGIC MOVE."

"Thanks", Rob said, "I really needed that last comment."

Rob slowed down to make the turn into the rock cut that led to the compound. Just before he got to it an ambulance and police car at great speed went screaming past with sirens screaming. He parked his car and went into the house. His mother was out. His father was busy in his study and looked up when he leaned into the room.

"Well, Rob was it a productive day."

"You could say that. Did you hear the ambulances go screaming by?"

"Yeah, what was that all about?"

"A piece of construction equipment exploded on the North Road, just before the Chinese construction camp."

"Really?"

"Just after one of the Chinese construction guys with a gun tried to hijack me."

Colin Lyons swung around and faced his son and gave him a long hard look. "Are we in danger?"

"Perhaps"

"Should we secure the compound?"

"It might not be a bad idea.".

"OK, let me go round up and arm the cousins and secure the perimeter."

Colin slowly rose from his swivel chair and moved as fast as his arthritic knees would permit him. He went out onto the porch that circled the house and began to hit a large metal triangle hanging from the ceiling with a steel bar. This triangle, over the two centuries that the family had lived in the compound, had only been rung when pirates had raided Georgetown or when a hurricane was approaching. Within minutes the extended family started to gather. Those that were not in the compound were summoned by their personal communication devices to return home from the Bishop's various enterprises throughout the island.

A large truck was pulled across the entrance to the rock cut, completely blocking it. Two cousins returned with rifles and side arms to stand guard at the truck and move it out of the way as the rest of the family returned. Other cousins climbed the steep hill on either side of the rock cut to cut off that approach if anyone dared to climb the mountain to reach them or foolishly entered the rock cut without first identifying themselves. Others set up a defensive perimeter at the low stone wall looking down the cliff into Georgetown.

The houses in the compound were on a flat, half-moon shaped plateau with impregnable mountains guarding it on three sides. Dynamite was quickly wired up under boulders high above the rock cut. If a heavily armed force tried to approach through the rock cut, they and would be buried under tons of rock. Dynamite was also wired up half way down the cliff above Georgetown to shower boulders down on anyone approach from below.

Colin returned to Rob in the study after he had confirmed that the compound was secure.

"Rob, what's going on?"

"I'm not really sure but I suspect that the Chinese could be threatening the security of this island."

"Well, we are ready for them if they try to attack us".

The telephone in the study rang. Colin picked it up He listened, turned and handed the phone to Rob.

"Hello, Rob Lyons here."

"Hello Doctor Lyons, this is Po Chang from the Chinese Embassy

Control interjected itself into the conversation, **"DON'T FORGET THAT THERE ARE LISTENING DEVICES IN THE ROOM YOU ARE IN. THEY WERE PROBABLY PUT THERE BY THE CHINESE WHO ARE AWARE OF EXACTLY WHERE YOU ARE AND WHAT YOU AND YOUR FATHER HAVE BEEN DISCUSSING. PO CHANG IS THE INTELLIGENCE OFFICER AT THE EMBASSY. WE ALSO SUSPECT THAT THEY HAVE WIRED CHUMLEY'S BEACH HOUSE AND ARE AWARE OF YOUR DISCUSSION WITH HIM."**

"Yes, Mister Chang what can I do for you."

"Our ambassador wondered if he could arrange an appointment with you?"
"Why would the ambassador be interested seeing me?"
"The ambassador was hoping that perhaps you could advise him on American foreign policy. He understood that you were an employee of the U.S. State Department."

Control responded to this request, **"MEET WITH THEM. LET'S SEE WHAT THEY HAVE TO SAY BUT MAKE THEM COME TO YOU. IT WILL BE SAFER FOR YOU AND WILL SEND THEM A MESSAGE THAT YOU ARE NOT ABOUT TO KOWTOW TO THEM. WE WILL PATCH THE SECRETARY OF STATE INTO THE FEED TO MONITOR THAT CONVERSATION."**

" I have a very minor position with the State Department. I am not sure whether I can provide you with relevant information or not"

Doctor Lyons, we will not know until we talk to you. Possibly this afternoon?"

"Yes, that is possible."

"Could you be here in half an hour?"

"I'm afraid that I am unable to travel at this time. Could we meet at my parent's home?"

"Just a minute, please." Chang switched into Chinese and carried on a conversation with a third party.

Control started to supply Rob with a simultaneous translation from Chinese into English, "**HE IS NOT ABLE TO COME TO THE EMBASSY. HE SAYS HE WILL MEET YOU AT HIS FATHER'S HOUSE IN THEIR COMPOUND UP ON THE RIDGE. THIS WILL MAKE IT DIFFICULT FOR US TO STOP ANY FURTHER COMMUNICATION BETWEEN CHUMLEY AND THE AMERICANS. WE HAVE BEEN MONITORING HIM CLOSELY. SO FAR, HE HAS NOT YET TOLD THE STATE DEPARTMENT WHAT CHUMLEY WANTS. NOR HAS HE TOLD THEM ABOUT OURATTEMPT TO ABDUCT HIM ON THE NORTH ROAD. PERHAPS WE HAD BETTER CUT OFF ALL PHONE AND INTERNET COMMUNICATION TO THE COMPOUND AFTER THIS CALL. I WILL TRY TO GET HIM TO COME TO THE EMBASSY BUT IF I CANNOT THEN WE WILL HAVE TO GO TO THE COMPOUND.**"

"Doctor Lyons, it would be very difficult for the ambassador to leave the embassy at this time, he would be very appreciative if you were able to meet him at the embassy."

"Mister Chang, I wish that I could go to the embassy but earlier this afternoon an incident occurred that makes my travel on the island very dangerous and I am not about to leave this compound."

There was a long pause as Mister Chang recognized that ridiculousness of their asking Rob to put himself at risk after they had just threatened his life.

"Very well, Doctor Lyons, the ambassador will come to the compound. He will be there in half an hour."

"Thank you, Mister Chang, I look forward to meeting the ambassador."
"Rob hung up the the phone. His father grabbed it to make a phone call and said, "The phone has gone dead.""

Somehow that doesn't surprise me. I think you will also find that your internet service is also out of commission. That goes for cellular service as well. I suspect that the Chinese have long ago gained control over all electronic communication on the island – or at least they think they have."

His father's voice, a couple of octaves higher with stress and excitement, said "We are cut off. What the hell do we do if we need to call for reinforcements?"

Don't worry about reinforcements. I have a few aces up my sleeve.""

"What are you talking about?"

"Don't worry Dad, everything will be O.K. I'll meet with the ambassador when he arrives."

CHAPTER 10

Ambassador

The Chinese ambassador's limousine turned off The North Road into the compound's rock cut. Small red, People's Republic of China flags were flying on both front fenders. General Lee looked at the impassable mountain rising above them on each side of the rock cut as they went slowly through it. As they rounded a corner the driver slammed on his brakes to avoid crashing into the truck that blocked the entire road. A tall, muscular black man with a rifle and a pistol on his belt approached the limousine while his partner covered him with his rifle from behind the truck.

"Who are you? State your business?"

"I am Ambassador Lee from the Chinese embassy. I have an appointment with Doctor Lyons"

Andy Bishop took out his walkie-talkie that was capable of transmitting a half mile and hit the send button, "Tell Rob that Ambassador Lee has arrived. Does he want me to send him through?"

There was a cracking and then Rob's voice came through, "Send them through but pat them down for weapons and check the vehicle for weapons."

Andy Bishop quietly said, "Ambassador Lee could you and your driver please step out of the vehicle?" They meekly complied, well aware of the rifles that were trained on them from the other side of the truck and from the mountain above them. Andy patted them down from their ankles to their chest. He checked the vehicle's glove compartment and trunk for weapons. None were found. Lee and the driver returned to the car. The truck backed up opening the road. They passed by the security point into the compound. The truck rolled back into place blocking the entrance to the rock cut.

Rob stood in the parking area at the front of his parent's house. He waved the limousine over. They parked it. Lee got out of the car and made his way to Rob. He was neatly dressed in a conservative blue suit. His Gucci loafers were buffed to a high sheen. The chauffeur stayed in the car. One of the armed cousins came over to guard the chauffeur.

Control whispered in his ear, "THIS IS NOT THE AMBASSADOR. THIS IS GENERAL LEE, THE MILITARY ADVISOR AT THE EMBASSY. IT IS OUR UNDERSTANDING THAT THE AMBASSADOR-IN-CHARGE AND ALL OTHER CHINESE OFFICIALS IN THE CARIBBEAN, REPORT TO HIM. THE SECRETARY OF STATE HAS BEEN PATCHED IN."

Rob strode over to shake General Lee's hand. The General shook hands and bowed. "Doctor Lyons it is a pleasure to meet you."

"It is a pleasure meeting you too, General Lee."

For an instant there was a flicker of surprise as General Lee noticed he was being addressed as General Lee instead of Ambassador Lee. The Americans were obviously more clued into what was going on than he had thought.
"Please come inside and we will talk."

Rob led Lee through the house into the study. He indicated that Lee should take one of the red leather wingback chairs while he took the other. An old antique coffee table was between them. On the table were a teapot and small, ornate, delicate china tea cups, without handles. Rob's wife had received them as a present shortly after they were married. When he had divorced, he had sent these and other items he was fond of, to his mother for safe keeping. The table also had a plate with some of his mother's home-made tea biscuits and small crocks of strawberry jam and whipped butter.
"Some tea, General?

The General nodded and smiled. Rob poured some green tea into the tea cups. General Lee smelled the sweet perfume the tea emitted. He tentatively sipped.
"Am excellent tea. I do not recognize it. Where does it come from?

"It comes from a small, ancient plantation in the Azores."

"The Portuguese islands eight hundred miles off the coast of Portugal?"

"Yes. They say its unique taste comes from the island's rich volcanic soil. I believe the tea bushes were brought to the island from China by the early Portuguese explorers."

"Ah yes, the Portuguese traders were the first Europeans to establish trade relationships with China."

They sipped their tea quietly, each contemplating how to begin, glancing at each other from time to time over the rim of their cups. Rob was not about show any rudeness to the older man. General Lee finished his cup of tea. Rob poured him more.

General Lee quietly began, "We understand that you are a representative of the State Department?"

"Officially, I am on vacation leave from the State Department, just visiting my family in Saint Matts. I am only a very minor analyst in their policy department."

"That is not our understanding. We understand that you have direct access to the Secretary of State and thus to the President."

The Secretary of State whispered in his ear, **"TELL HIM THAT HIS SOURCES ARE VERY GOOD AND THAT HE IS CORRECT. THEY OBVIOUSLY WERE LISTENING IN ON THE CONVERSATION AT THE CHUMLEY BEACH HOUSE."**

"Your sources are very well informed. Yes, it is correct that I have had, from time-to-time, direct access to the Secretary of State, as have many State Department employees."

The General sipped some more of his tea and looked intently at Rob. He decided that he would address Rob as if he were talking directly to the Secretary of State.

"Our two countries have developed close ties over the last few decades. This relationship has brought great prosperity to China and provided consumer goods to Americans at very low prices. American retailers and wholesalers have become very rich selling our goods."

He paused. Rob nodded his agreement with this statement. The General continued, "We would like to feel that the United States is our friend and understands that we can be trusted not to do any harm to the United States. It is one of our most important markets."

Rob nodded his head in agreement again.

"We do not understand why a friend would increase its already large military presence with our South China Sea neighbors or why such a good friend would want to threaten China's sovereignty and access to our trade routes. We do not appreciate your senators calling for your involvement in our disputes with our South China Sea neighbors. These are disputes between sovereign nations that should be of no concern to the United States. "

General Lee paused took a sip of his tea and tried to judge what effect his words were having on Rob. Rob kept his face and body as unresponsive as possible. The General continued, "We also object to the United States interfering with our development of the large oil deposits off our Spratlys Islands. Our objective, like that of the United States, is to wean our dependence off Arab oil, especially oil from Saudi Arabia. China has become the largest importer of fossil fuels in the world and needs to develop domestic sources. The presence of your Seventh Fleet's 50 warships, 350 aircraft and 60,000 navy and marine personnel, adjacent to our China Sea's key shipping lanes makes our neighbors very brave and disrespectful of the People's Republic of China. Pearl Harbor and the Korean War took place more than half a century ago. It is time for the United States to get over its paranoia and stop policing the countries of South West Asia."

The General stopped and waited for a response. Rob quietly responded, "The problems in the South West China sea are a long way from Saint Matts. They cannot be resolved at this time. What we wish to discuss are China's intent to establish a naval base in Saint Matts."

The General looked long and hard at Rob before responding, "China is a friend of the United States. The People's Republic of China has signed no agreement with the government of Saint Matts. However, if such an agreement between two sovereign nations was considered, why would the United States of America be consulted or have a vested interest in it?"

Rob waited to see if the Secretary of State would provide him with a response. She said nothing. The silence stretched. Colonel Lee stared hard at Rob. His eyes like two, hard, black rocks, not blinking. Rob decided to take the initiative and replied, "General, you seem to be a student of history. You, I am sure, have heard of the Monroe Doctrine. You know that the United States, being protected by two great oceans, the Atlantic and the Pacific, has never suffered an invasion. America has a long history of regarding the entire Western Hemisphere, and by that, I mean both North and South America, as extension of the United States. No competing world power has ever succeeded in challenging this right of influence over this area. The old communist Soviet Union almost brought the world to the edge of a nuclear war when they tried to establish a nuclear missile site in Cuba. They backed down, probably because only one nation in the world, the United States, has ever used nuclear weapons in combat."

"Yes, only one nation has had the inhumanity to drop atomic bombs on a defenseless oriental population, wiping out 200,000 civilians within seconds. Were they just expendable foreigners? Are you threatening the People's Republic of China with nuclear war? Do you forget that we too have nuclear weapons?"

"No, the United States is not threatening any one. I am just a historian relating the facts."

"Do you not recognize the obvious contradiction that it is OK for you to increasingly threaten our sovereignty with your bases surrounding the China Sea, but it is not OK for us to have one naval base in the Caribbean to protect our trade routes? What about the famous American principle of fair play."

"Of course, I recognize the contradiction but that is just the way things are in the real world. The United States became the primary political, economic and military super power in the world by default after the fall of the Soviet Union, not by plan. It is our opinion that it is in our best interest, and that of the world's, for the U.S. to maintain its dominant position in the world's power structure."

"Doctor Lyons, there is a new world order and it is time that the United States recognized it. China and the rest of the world are no longer prepared to allow a nation with only 5% of the world's population to interfere in sovereign issues which are beyond the borders of the United States. While U.S. intentions may be good, they are selfish, destructive, intentions. The United States, like a bull in a china shop, is making situations worse. Look at the wars in Vietnam, Iraq, Afghanistan and Syria. Too often, U.S. foreign interference is being used by its politicians to garner points with domestic voters to the exclusion of the best interests of citizens in foreign countries. The U.S. fails to understand that much of the rest of the world is appalled by U.S. insensitivity and ineptness. You have forced us into taking a stand to protect our sovereign rights. Unless the United States is prepared to remove the Seventh Fleet and its bases from the China Sea then China will be establishing bases in the Western Hemisphere, starting with Saint Matts."

Rob and General Lee stared at each other. The silence dragged on. Finally, Rob responded, "The United States does not want any new foreign presence in the Western Hemisphere, Chinese or otherwise. This policy goes all the way back to the Monroe Doctrine in 1823 which proclaimed that European powers would not be allowed to form new colonies in the Western Hemisphere and should they lose power in their existing colonies, America would use its power to prevent their re-entrance. Back then it was a reaction to Russian Expansion along the Pacific Coast. They had established a fort within a hundred miles of San Francisco. The People's Republic of China would be advised not to test the United States resolve to uphold the Munroe Doctrine."

General Lee again stared long and hard at Rob, before quietly and calmly saying, "I would not have expressed the displeasure of the People's Republic of China with the present status quo unless I had had permission to do so from the highest level of our government. We do not seek a confrontation, but I have been instructed to make it clear to the United States that we are no longer intimidated by America's show of power. We will develop a naval base in Saint Matts and we are prepared to defend our sovereign right to do so."

"General Lee, I am sure the United States will thank you for your frankness and the Secretary of State and the President will take your position under advisement."

Having no more to add, General Lee stood and bowed and murmured, "Doctor Lyons it has been a pleasure meeting you. I thank you for your hospitality. I would also like to apologize for the incident that took place on the North Road earlier today. It had not been our intention to harm you in any way. We had only wanted to talk to you but it appears mistakes were made in how we should be brought together. We are pleased that you were not injured in this unfortunate incident. I will also take into consideration our conversation. It will be reviewed at the highest level of the People's Republic of China."

The General returned to his car and left the compound. Rob wondered what would really have happened to him if they had kidnapped him. He wondered whether they would try again. He watched Lee go from the verandah. As the diplomat's car entered the rock cut, Rob turned around and went to his bedroom. He locked his door, so he would not be interrupted or be overheard. He kicked his shoes off and lay down on the bed. He then addressed the Secretary of State, still feeling foolish talking to an invisible entity, "Secretary, are you still patched in?"

"YES, I AM STILL HERE."

"Are we prepared to return the Seventh Fleet to the United States?"

"NOT IN AN ELECTION YEAR. IT WOULD BE POLITICAL SUICIDE. ESPECIALLY, IF IT EVER LEAKED OUT THAT WE HAD DONE IT TO AVOID A CONFRONTATION WITH THE COMMUNIST REGIME IN CHINA."

"What are you proposing to do?"

"THE MOST EXPEDIENT THING TO DO IS TO BUY OFF CHUMLEY...UP OUR OFFER TO $60,000,000 THE FIRST YEAR AND THEN $60,000,000 FOR EACH OF THE NEXT TEN YEARS."

"The Chinese have offered $40,000,000 for one hundred years?"

"TEN YEARS IS A LONG TIME. WHO KNOWS IF THE CHINESE WILL BE IN A POSITION OF BEING ABLE TO KEEP UP THEIR PAYMENTS FOR EVEN TEN YEARS? IF YOU WERE BETTING ON WHO WOULD STILL BE ABLE TO DO IT IN TEN YEARS, WHO WOULD YOU PUT YOUR BET ON? CHUMLEY HAS GOTTEN A CONCESSION FROM US. HE WILL FEEL HE IS A WINNER. IN TEN YEARS, HE WILL NOT BE IN POLITICS. TOMORROW MEET WITH HIM AND GIVE HIM THE GOOD NEWS. HOWEVER GENERAL LEE'S CONFIDENCE AND HIS IN-YOUR-FACE ATTITUDE DOES WORRY US. SOMETHING IS UP THAT WE ARE NOT AWARE OF IT. OUR INTELLIGENCE RESOURCES WILL BE INSTRUCTED TO GO ON HIGH ALERT TO FIND OUT WHAT SECRET IS LYING JUST BELOW THE SURFACE. THEY WILL BE INSTRUCTED TO USE WHATEVER MEANS THEY HAVE TO, TO BRING IT TO THE SURFACE."

"I will meet with Chumley tomorrow, but I suspect that he will only try to use our offer to hammer the Chinese for more money."

"WHEN YOU SUP WITH DEVIL, IT IS BEST TO USE A LONG SPOON. CHUMLEY MAY FIND HE HAS BITTEN OFF MORE THAN HE CAN CHEW. THE CHINESE DO NOT EASILY TOLERATE DECEIT. IF HE HAS MADE AN AGREEMENT WITH THEM, THEN THEY WILL MAKE SURE HE LIVES UP TO IT. IN PREPARING FOR THE

WORSE, I AM GOING TO ADVISE THE PRESIDENT TO COMMAND THE 22ND MARINE AMPHIBIOUS GROUP TO IMMEDIATELY START STEAMING TO THE EASTERN CARIBBEAN. WE WILL ALSO ARRANGE FOR THE AMBASSADOR IN BEIJING TO ARRANGE A MEETING WITH THE CHINESE PREMIER TO FIND OUT WHETHER GENERAL LEE IS TRULY SPEAKING FOR THE PEOPLE'S REPUBLIC OF CHINA AND WHETHER THEY ARE AWARE THAT HE HAS THREATENED THE UNITED STATES."

"Is the North Road now clear?"

"OH YES, I HAD FORGOTTEN. YOU HAVE A DATE TONIGHT. THE IMAGE FROM THE DRONE SHOWS THEY HAVE VERY QUICKLY CLEANED UP THE ROAD. WE SHALL BE VERY INTERESTED TO HEAR MISS WALL'S IMPRESSIONS OF PRIME MINISTER CHUMLEY. IN VIEW OF THE ATTEMPTED KIDNAPPING, I THINK IT MIGHT BE A GOOD IDEA FOR YOU TO BRING SOME BODYGUARDS ALONG WITH YOU. DO YOU WANT THE CIA AGENTS ON THE ISLAND TO ACCOMPANY YOU?"

"Not particularly, they don't know me, and I don't know them. People on the island who know me will wonder who they are and why they are with me. It will raise too many awkward questions. We can keep the CIA in reserve. I'll take a couple of my cousins with me."

Rob got up off the bed and went down the hall to see if his father was in his study. His father was at his computer. Although he was long retired, he kept in close contact with his commercial risk resources and former colleagues around the world.
He greeted Rob, as he came into the study," How did you and General Lee make out."

Rob sighed and replied, "Not at all well. I think we are headed towards a confrontation of some sort."

"As a historian Rob, you know that all empires are eventually challenged by those they see as barbarians and sooner or later all empires fall. To the Chinese, Americans are barbarians. When their culture was inventing paper and gun powder, our ancestors were primitive, ignorant savages."

"Yes, America has acquired an empire without having to formally colonize foreign countries, but America still wants to believe that they are God's chosen and that anyone who stands up to them will be struck down."

"Oh, you refer to the old "manifest destiny delusion', that Americans have lived under for the last two hundred years. Surely, you recognize that it was not God that made the United States the most powerful nation in the world. It was the United States unique geography that made it powerful."

"How so?"

"The Mississippi river and the large river systems that feed into it, and to a lesser extent the Atlantic Intracoastal Waterway, provides more miles of navigable internal waterways than anywhere else on earth. Added to this you have the American Midwest that is the largest area of fertile, well-watered, farmland in the world. This has not only resulted in food surpluses but the access to cheap water transportation to export this food surplus to foreign countries at affordable prices. The money from these exports provided the capital to invest in American technology and industry. In addition, the U.S. Atlantic coast has more natural, deep water, major seaports than all the Western Hemisphere combined. Since water transportation is 10 to 40 times less expensive than any form of overland transportation, this geographic reality gives the United States a greater competitive advantage than any other nation in the world. When you look back at history, you see that Britain, Japan, Germany and France, all established strong maritime transportation networks that allowed them to become major economic powerhouses. The Second World War left the United States with the most powerful navy in the world and they have never relinquished this advantage. It is the quiet, often ignored, primary reason for America's world dominance. "

Colin Lyon paused and sipped on the coffee that was almost always within his reach despite his wife's protests about the dangers of too much caffeine in his diet. He continued, "The other American geographic advantage is defensive isolation. It has been protected from the political turmoil and wars that have taken place elsewhere in the world because it has two enormous oceans sheltering both its West coast and its East coast. The Mexican deserts protect it on the South and the harsh Artic conditions, in relatively unpopulated Canada protect the U.S. on the North. With the economic collapse of the world-wide British Empire after World War II, Canada was abandoned by British sea power. Until then, the dominant British navy had historically constrained American economic expansion around the world and its annexation of Canada. Now because of late twentieth century trade agreements both Mexico and Canada have become so integrated into the U.S. economy that their interaction with the United States has become more like domestic states, like

California, than foreign governments. They have become the safe, easily protected, easily controlled, dependable suppliers of raw materials for America."

Rob smiled at his father and added, "I see what you mean. After the Second World War, the United States was the only nation whose industries were not in tatters. No battles had been fought on the main land in the United States and not one American factory had been bombed. The U.S. was the only world power that had thrived and prospered because of the war. While it had had a major navy before the war, after the war, it achieved naval domination by being the only navy, other than the British navy, that had not been destroyed. It might as well have been because a bankrupt Britain could no longer support its navy. America had always been a maritime merchant power but now it was able to join its economic advantage to total domination of the sea and all trade routes. It cemented this position by forming the International Monetary Fund and the World Bank to fund reconstruction of war damaged nations' infrastructure. This resulted in the U.S. dollar becoming the only viable global currency. The later formation of the World Trade Organization firmly established the American dominance of the seas and the global economic system. It uses funding and aid from these international organizations to make sure no alliances are formed to challenge its power and position. Just as it is cheaper to transport goods by water, it is also cheaper to transport military resources by water. The fleets the U.S. maintains around the world have the sole purpose of preserving a balance of power to the United States' advantage, especially in Eurasia where the U.S, has done all it could to prevent any process that would result in a single dominating power that could challenge it, until perhaps now."

Colin smiled, got up and put his arm around Rob's shoulder and said, "Who am I to lecture the great historian, Doctor Robert Lyons, on American history and strategy. You are living it and at this moment, in Saint Matts, it is very real. I wait with great interest to see how the United States government is going to bring Saint Matts into line with its historical strategies."

"Dad, my love of history was obviously inherited. We live in interesting times. Now, I am going to get two of the cousins to keep me company for the evening and protect my backside while I have dinner with a very interesting lady."

"Enjoy your date. I hope she is beautiful. Despite your peaceful meeting with General Lee, we will maintain a defensive perimeter at the compound until all this is resolved. I wonder if General Lee has reconnected our phone and internet service." Colin picked up the phone and heard a dial tone, "Ah, we have phone service."

CHAPTER 11

Interlude

At ten minutes to seven, Rob's WRX, with his cousin driving, pulled under the covered portico at the front of the Saint Matts Casino and Resort. Rob left the one cousin in the car, in case he needed a quick getaway, and took the other cousin with him into the hotel. Both cousins were tall, muscular and trained in martial arts - as were most of the Bishop clan. They were also crack shots and were each carrying hidden pistols. They first went to the main dining room and arranged two separate tables close to each other. The cousin's table gave him a clear view of anyone entering the restaurant.

Control interrupted his thoughts with **"YOU ARE ADVISED THAT THERE ARE LISTENING DEVICES INSTALLED IN EVERY TABLE IN THIS DINING ROOM AND CAMERAS COVERING EVERY INCH OF IT."**

Having picked his table, Rob went into the lobby and phoned the hotel switchboard on his cell phone. He asked for Barbara Wall. She answered the phone on the second ring. Rob said he was down in the lobby and would wait for her by the elevator. As he strode across the massive white Italian marble lobby towards the elevators, his cousin got up and shadowed him, searching for anyone who was paying Rob more attention than would be normal. The cousin sat down on a lobby couch and pretended to be reading a magazine that had been abandoned on the round marble coffee table. He watched Rob waiting by theelevators.

A large party of what appeared to be Chinese gamblers on holiday, noisily crossed the marble floor of the lobby and approached the door to the casino. Two of them, talking loudly to each other, separated from the main group and headed towards Rob and the elevators. The cousin quickly rose from the couch and rapidly crossed the lobby to the elevator. The elevator doors opened. The two loud Chinese entered without looking at Rob. The next elevator door opened, and Barbara stepped out. Rob approached her and gave her a brotherly kiss on her cheek. She looked stunning.

Prince was on duty at Control. He gave a loud wolf whistle in Rob's ear and said, *"YOU CAN SURE PICK 'EM."*

"My, my, my, don't you look beautiful tonight," he said.

She smiled and said, "I think to impress you, it takes more than beauty."

"Am I that easy to read?"

"Most definitely, you struck me as the kind of man who immediately assumes that a beautiful woman must be a bimbo or else, she would not be beautiful. You have no appreciation for the thought and technique that goes into creating the illusion of beauty, and it is an illusion that can be turned on and turned off, instantly."

"Now you have impressed me. I am now curious. Who is behind the mask?"

"Well, I shall be careful not to let my mask down during dinner. Where are we eating?"

"I thought we would eat right here at the hotel. The food here is as good American fine dining as you are going to find on the island. I have assumed you are looking for typical American fare."

"You mean the kind of food I am going to find in a typical Marriott or Fairmont hotel anywhere in the world?"

"Exactly."

"You mean no goat water with cornmeal dumplings or steamed red snapper with boiled green bananas or peas and rice?"

"Whoa, your mask is starting to slip."

"You know so little about me. The hotel dining room will be fine, maybe next time you can take me to the best West Indian restaurant on the island."

She took Rob's arm and he led her across the lobby to the main hotel dining room.

Control started to whisper in his ear, **"BARBARA WALL'S GREAT GRANDMOTHER WAS A JAMAICAN WHO SETTLED IN BERMUDA IN THE EARLY NINETEEN HUNDREDS. WALL'S GRANDMOTHER WAS A BERMUDIAN WHO MARRIED A SCOTSMAN. HER OWN MOTHER MET AND MARRIED AN AMERICAN EXECUTIVE WHO HAD BEEN SENT TO BERMUDA TO RUN THE OFFSHORE REINSURANCE OPERATION OF A LARGE NEW YORK BASED COMPANY. BARBARA WAS BORN IN BERMUDA AND SPENT HER EARLY CHILDHOOD THERE. HER FATHER'S CAREER THEN TOOK THEM TO OTHER FINANCIAL CENTERS AROUND THE WORLD. SHE CONTINUED TO RETURN TO BERMUDA ON EVERY SCHOOL HOLIDAY TO STAY WITH HER GRANDPARENTS. TO HER IT WAS HOME, THE ANCHOR IN HER LIFE. HER GRANDMOTHER TAUGHT HER HOW TO COOK WEST INDIAN FOOD."**

His cousin trailed them into the restaurant and took up his position at his table. A few minutes later two beefy, well-tanned, goon types came into the restaurant, nodded at the manager as if he were an old friend. They took the only table between Rob and his cousin. The both had to be close to 280 pounds and at least six feet four inches tall. Unlike the tourists who were all dressed casually in brightly colored tropical shirts, these two were dressed very formally in expensive dark suits, well fitted white shirts and expensive silk ties. They were working. They were not on a holiday or attending a conference. Rob wondered who they were.

Control had read his mind, **"THE TWO MEN WHO HAVE COME IN AND SAT BETWEEN YOU AND YOUR COUSIN ARE LOW LEVEL MAFIA SOLDIERS, BROTHERS, BRUNO AND GINO DELUCA, OF THE LEPARDO CRIME FAMILY FROM NEW YORK THAT CONTROLS THIS HOTEL. THEY PROVIDE SECURITY AND MUSCLE. THERE ARE OUTSTANDING WARRANTS FOR THEM IN NEW YORK STATE FOR EXTORTION, LOAN SHARKING AND ATTEMPTED MURDER. THEY ARE MOST LIKELY ARMED. YOU SEEM TO BE ON THEIR RADAR."**

Barbara leaned close to Rob and whispered, "The black guy at that table keeps looking at us. Do you know him?"

"Yes, I know him. He's my cousin."

"Why doesn't he join us? Why hasn't he come over to talk to you?"

"He drove up in the car with me and another one of my cousins."

"

"This isn't making a lot of sense."

"He is acting as my bodyguard."

"You need a bodyguard?"

"Probably, but let's just ignore him. Things are a bit strange in Saint Matts right now and some people think that I am involved in this Chinese naval base thing that you are down here investigating. That Senator has really stirred up some bad feelings here on the island towards Americans. The locals are not keen on being blasted to smithereens."

"You aren't an accountant, are you?"

"I never said I was an accountant. I said I was a civil servant, which I am, that did accounting type things. I am an analyst in the State Department and now is not a good time for a State Department employee to be visiting his parents in Saint Matts. Of the thousands of employees in the State Department, they think that, somehow or other, every employee has some direct link to Secretary of State and the President. Thus, my cousins are here to make sure no one bothers us."

Barbara laughed a real belly laugh. "You have got to be kidding. Is that why you were having lunch with the Prime Minister?" "Yep, even he thought that I was someone important."

"Wow, they really are a naïve bunch, aren't they?"

"Listen, on a small island where everyone knows everyone else, their only frame of reference is to believe that if I am in Washington then I must be connected to everyone in Washington."

"Yeah, I suppose I can see that. You know I spent my childhood on a small island."

A waiter approached their table with a silver ice bucket and bucket stand. He put the bucket stand down beside their table. Rob looked questionably at him. The waiter smiled and said, "With the compliments of the hotel manager."

He then pulled a bottle of very expensive champagne from under a linen tablecloth draped over the ice bucket and proceeded to carefully remove the gold foil around the cork to open it. A second waiter appeared with chilled champagne glasses and proceeded to put them on the table. The first waiter poured out the champagne, put the bottle back in the ice bucket, smiled, reached into his jacket pocket and handed Rob a small envelope. He then retreated.

Rob opened the expensive linen envelope with the hotel crest on it; Barbara was giving him a puzzled look. Rob read the message that was on a hotel card. It read, *"Dr. Lyons, we are honored that you have chosen to visit the Saint Matts Hotel and Casino and hope that you enjoy the champagne. Would it be possible for you to spend a few minutes with me before you leave the hotel tonight? Two of our employees have been assigned to provide security for you while you are at the hotel. When you are ready, they will bring you to me. Enjoy your evening. Roberto Bento, President, Saint Matts Hotel and Casino Limited."*

Control was scanning the letter as Rob was reading it and providing a running commentary, **"BENTO IS VERY SENIOR IN THE LEPARDO FAMILY. THE FAMILY HAS INVESTED CLOSE TO TWO HUNDRED MILLION DOLLARS IN THIS RESORT. THE CASINO IS BEING USED TO LAUNDER DRUG MONEY THAT IS BEING GATHERED AS DRUGS MOVE UP THE ISLAND CHAIN FROM COLUMBIA TO FLORIDA AND BEYOND. THEY ARE ALSO FINANCING A LARGE MARIJUANA GROWING OPERATIONS IN JAMAICA AND MOVING IT TO MARKET. THIS IS AN IMPORTANT AND PROFITABLE PART OF THEIR OPERATION. BENTO IS FIFTY-FIVE YEARS OLD. HE WAS BORN IN SICILY AND CAME TO THE U.S. WHEN HE WAS FIVE YEARS OLD. THE FAMILY SETTLED IN NEW JERSEY. HIS FATHER WAS A BAKER BY TRADE BUT WELL CONNECTED TO THE MAFIA STRUCTURE IN SICILY. THEY OPENED SEVERAL BAKERIES IN NEWARK AS A FRONT FOR THEIR ILLEGAL OPERATIONS. ROBERTO BENTO HAS A HARVARD M.B.A. IN FIVE STATES, HE HAS OUTSTANDING WARRANTS FOR HIS ARREST FOR RACKETEERING, EXTORTION, LOAN SHARKING, BRIBERY AND OBSTRUCTION OF JUSTICE. PRIME MINISTER CHUMLEY HAS BEEN SECRETLY GIVEN A PIECE OF THE RESORT WHICH IS REPORTED TO BE EARNING HIM A DIVIDEND OF OVER A MILLION DOLLARS A YEAR. CHUMLEY MAKES SURE THAT LOCAL AND FOREIGN LAW ENFORCEMENT AGENCIES STAY AWAY FROM THIS OPERATION. THE FACT THAT ROBERTO BENTO WANTS TO SEE YOU PROBABLY HAS TO DO WITH THE CONCERN THE LEPARDO FAMILY HAS FOR THEIR INVESTMENT IN THIS ISLAND. THE SENATOR HAS CAUGHT THE ATTENTION OF MANY INVESTORS IN SAINT MATTS."**

While this information was being fed to him, Rob had to remember what Barbara had just said. Fortunately, the reading of the note covered the long pause before he responded with, "Really, what Island was that?"

"Bermuda. My father was an executive there with an insurance company."

"I know Bermuda. It is a unique island, a tax haven and a major reinsurance center, more than a thousand miles north of the Caribbean. It sure isn't one of your typical poor starving Caribbean islands like Saint Matts. A lot of West Indians from islands like Saint Matts immigrated there in the early nineteen hundreds to build a Royal Navy Dockyard there. Does that explain how you know West Indian cooking?"

"In a roundabout sort of way, it does. My great grandmother migrated there, from Jamaica. She taught my grandmother and my mother how to cook West Indian food and they in turn taught me."

"So, you have a lick of the tar brush in your background, do you?

"Why do you presume that? There are white Jamaicans too, you know."

Rob stared at her and wondered if he had offended her with a racial insensitivity and assumption. Several seconds went by. She smiled and winked one of her blue eyes and said, "Got you. Yeah, I've got a lick of the tar brush and I see that you do to."

"Yeah, with me it is a bit more obvious. With your blond hair and blue eyes, I would have thought that you were another uptight Anglo, through and through."

"It makes for some interesting and uncomfortable situations for me. Bigotry lies just below the surface in America. When certain types think that they are with their own kind, it is interesting to hear the racial slurs and prejudicial hatred that comes out of their mouths."

"What do you do when you hear it?"

"I say nothing. I just store it away and make sure I never have anything more to do with them. I now know they are two faced and not the sort of people I want too close to me. Sometimes they find out about my background and are embarrassed at having revealed their prejudices. Often, they then try to apologize, which is stupid on their part. I am just glad that I learned what they were really like before I committed or did business with them."

"You really are more than just another pretty face."

"Funny, I have never thought of myself as being pretty and it concerns me that people think I am just another dumb blond and that they do not take me seriously. That too is a form of prejudice, especially, being in the media where you are reduced to being a talking head."

They scanned the menu. The waiter came and took their order. Rob's cousin also ordered his dinner. The two thugs just sat at their table delicately sipping Perrier like two gorillas. Their assignment was to make sure that Rob did not leave the hotel without seeing Roberto Bento.

The dining room was busy. The buzz of conversations, plates and silverware clinking and the soft back ground music was appropriate for an upscale hotel dining room. It was clothed in dark wood, fine white linen, softly lit, very romantic except for the bodyguard and the two goons.

The food came. Rob had ordered the surf and turf. It was a spiny Caribbean lobster without the large claws the lobsters have in New England. It was huge and obviously very fresh. The steak was imported corn fed beef from Texas. He enjoyed the meal and thought about whether he could put it on his expense account. This reminded him that this was a business dinner and that he better ask some probing questions for those who were listening in.

"How did your interview with Chumley go?"

"It was on the six o'clock news. He denied that there was any agreement with the Chinese and inferred that the senator was a madman. He also stated that the United States and Saint Matts were the best of friends. He is a real true two-faced politician. Then as I was leaving, he grabbed my behind so hard that he left bruises. He asked if I was available for dinner and I said that I had a prior engagement. I wonder what he will think when it gets back to him that my prior engagement was you."

"It will be kind of symbolic; you have dinner with the United States representative instead of the Prime Minister of Saint Matts. Hey, he might have been interesting."

"I'll pick who is going to maul me."

"Are you expecting me maul you?"

"No, I was not inferring that you were expected to maul me."

Oh, good. For my country, there is only so much I am willing to do."

"Spoken like a true patriot."

"Do you wish some coffee?"

"No. I've had enough.".."

"Ok, let's go upstairs. They have a nice bar on the roof."

Rob motioned to the waiter that he wanted the bill. The waiter came over and learned forward to quietly tell Rob that he was the hotel's guest and there would be no bill. Rob thanked the waiter and pulled out Barbara's chair. She took his arm and they left the dining room and took the elevator up to the penthouse bar. Rob's cousin and the two thugs joined them in the elevator. The two thugs were eyeing Rob's cousin with great suspicion. Rob, nodded at his cousin and said to the two thugs, "He's with me." They relaxed, a bit.

Barbara Wall looked at Rob quizzically. Rob responded, "These two gentlemen are with hotel security. They are here to make sure no one bothers us."

The two thugs enjoyed looking at a beautiful woman. They smiled and nodded at her. This was the first time Rob had seen them smile. The almost looked like warm friendly teddy bears. He wondered if being a thug was just a job to them - nothing personal, just business, or did you really have to have a passion for being a thug.

When they got to the roof, Rob's cousin got out first and did a quick scan of the bar. Part of it was open so they could look up and see the stars. Although it was too dark to see the ocean, they could hear the waves crashing on the beach. A soft, warm breeze was a nice change from the air conditioning in the dining room. A local three-man band, made up of a drummer, keyboard and electric guitar, was softly playing oldies-but-goldies. A few couples were dancing.

"Do you want to dance?"

She did not reply but took his hand and let him lead her onto the dance floor. He took her into his arms. They danced slowly. She smelled sweet and light. Her hair was soft against his cheek. He could feel her breasts pressing softly against his chest. She felt firm and athletic as they swayed in time to the music. She snuggled closely into him. She aroused him. He wondered if she too could feel it. His cousin was sitting on a stool in the far corner of the bar checking out everyone who came off the elevator. The two thugs sat at a table close to elevator where they would not be noticed by anyone entering the lounge but could surprise them from behind - if there was some reason to surprise them from behind

Rob and Barbara sat down at their table and had a couple of drinks. They danced some more. It was getting late. Rob looked down at her and whispered, "Can I walk you home?
"

"Sure."

They went over to the elevator. The two thugs and his cousin followed them into the elevator. Barbara put her universal ID card into the elevator scanner and it automatically took them down to her floor. They all got off and started down the carpeted, corridor. Rob's cousin stayed back about fifty feet. The two thugs stayed behind the cousin. When Barbara got to her door at room 409, she scanned her universal card and the door slid open. She was holding Rob's hand and she pulled him into the room. The door slid close. The entourage took their positions on either side of the door. The two thugs eyed the cousin with a professional interest and then dismissed him as a professional does any amateur.

Rob, on the other side of the door leaned forward and gave Barbara a long passionate kiss. His hands slid behind her and pulled her into him. She put her arms around him and thrust her body into him. Rob pulled back, looked at her and whispered, "As much as I am enjoying this, duty calls."

Control interrupted at this point and said, **"DON'T STOP ON ACCOUNT OF US. WE WERE ENJOYING IT. YOU SHOULD SEE YOUR PULSE RIGHT NOW. WOW!"**. Prince then started to laugh until he turned off his microphone.

That quickly evaporated any of Rob's burning passion. He had forgotten, for a few sweet moments that every breath and every beat of his heart was being monitored. Every word he said and everything he saw, they saw, they heard, and they recorded.

"Sorry, but I've got to go."

They passionately kissed again.

"Will I see you tomorrow?" she asked.

"I sure hope so. I'll phone you in the morning."

He gave her a long hungry look. Pushed the door button and it opened. He stepped out into the corridor and the door slid closed behind him. He looked at the two thugs and said, "Where do we find Mr. Bento?"

The bigger of the two brutes, with a raspy voice, that sounded like something out of a Godfather movie, said, "His office overlooks the lobby and the casino floor. We get into it from the second floor. We'll take you there now."

They started off down the corridor to the elevator. The cousin followed them.

When they got to the second floor Rob was led to the first door next to the elevator. The thug leading the way inserted his universal ID card. The door opened, and they entered a room with no windows and another door in front of them. Two security guards, in uniform were sitting at a table to the right of them. They were staring at a bank of dozens of monitors on the wall across from them. Rob glanced at the monitors and saw the lobby, the corridor they had just been in, the outside entrance to the hotel, the car park and many views that he did not recognize. The two guards got up and politely asked him to spread his legs and hold his hands up in the air. Rob noticed they were armed.

Control whispered in his ear. **"LASER ACTIVATED".**

Using a hand-held metal detector, they very carefully scanned his entire body. They never got as high as his ring. They put their detectors away and pushed a button on their desk. The door to the next room slid open. Rob walked into a darkened room that was like walking into the control center of a space ship. The two thugs stepped in front of the cousin which stopped him from entering. The door slid closed. Rob looked, through one way smoked mirrored glass over the casino floor at one end and at the other end the hotel lobby. On the back wall there was a wall of monitors following the action on each gaming table. One of the monitors had a flashing red light above it. A short elf of a man was standing in front of that monitor. A dozen other men were so intent upon looking for crooks in the busy casino that they did not appear to be aware that Rob had entered their sanctuary.

Control enlightened Rob. **"THE SHORT MAN IN FRONT OF THE FLASHING MONITOR IS ROBERTO BENTO. HE IS ARMED WITH A WEAPON ON HIS RIGHT ANKLE."**

Bento seeing the flash of light as the door opened, slowly turned and faced Rob. He was a compact man. No more than five feet- five inches tall, even with the two-inch lifts in his shoes. He was well dressed in an expensive suit. His curly dark brown hair was streaked with grey. He looked to be in his mid-forties. He smiled warmly at Rob and started towards him. He moved gracefully.

"Doctor Lyons, it is a pleasure to meet you. Enjoy your dinner?"

"Yes, we did. Thank you very much for your hospitality."

"Come over here, let us sit." He led Rob over to a reception like area with two leather love seats and a coffee table.

"Can I get you a drink? I have some excellent ancient single malt."

"No thanks," Rob replied. "I have had quite enough to drink tonight."

"How about a Perrier, then?"

"Sure, that would be great. Thanks."

Roberto Bento walked over to a cabinet. When he slid it open there was a small hidden refrigerator. He filled a glass with ice and slowly added the Perrier.

They sat down facing each other.

"This senator of yours wants to bomb Saint Matts into oblivion."

"You mustn't pay too much attention to senators who are up for election in November. Rick Wilcox sure isn't my Senator."

"My partners and I have invested hundreds of millions of dollars in Saint Matts and you know Doctor Lyons, there is nothing more nervous than millions of dollars. I don't believe in beating around the bush. We are looking for someone who can advise us and give us advance warning of anything coming down the track that could affect our investment here. Do you think you could be that person?

Rob didn't immediately reply. He wondered what to reply with. What was in the best interest of the State Department and the United States of America? The seconds dragged on like hours. Bento was staring at him, waiting for a reply, but was too smart to interject and possibly scare away a resource that could be worth millions of dollars to them.

Rob heard control's microphone click open. The voice of the Secretary of State came on and said, "**ROB, TELL HIM THAT YOU ARE HIS MAN. THEY COULD BE A USEFUL RESOURCE AND ALLY IF WE GET INTO A CONFRONTATION WITH THE CHINESE.**

Rob broke his silence, "Mister Bento I would be more than pleased to assist you and your partners."

Bento smiled, "Good. What do you think the States will do about this situation?"

"It is too early in the game to predict what my government will do. I am here to help them assess the situation and formulate a plan. You've been here for several years, what is your assessment of the situation?"

"When the Chinese came and started to fix the roads and other infrastructure, I thought this was going to be good for business. Anything that makes the island more attractive and user-friendly puts more tourists in our hotel and casino. Now, I suspect that right from the beginning the Chinese had their eye on the old British naval base. They were training Chumley to eat out of their hand. You know, we had made him a silent partner in the casino which has made him a very wealthy man. However, we noticed that more and more he was less forthcoming on what was going on in the island and less interested in protecting our revenues. They must have bought him off with a load of cash for him to lose interest in milking this cash cow. I think he is getting ready to sacrifice his involvement with us. The Chinese will do their best to discourage tourists coming to their island. It would only increase their security risk. I suspect they would do their best to get the native population off the island as well."

Rob asked, "Do you think he deliberately leaked the Chinese intentions to Senator Wilcox?"

"It would not surprise me. If the Chinese will pay a fortune to get in, how much will the Americans pay to keep them out?"

"Isn't that a dangerous game to play?"

"Doctor Chumley is one of most greedy men I have ever met and believe me, in my line of business, I have met a lot of greedy men. He also thinks that he is the smartest man in any room and that all rules and regulations are for other people. The way he looks at it, he can't lose. He thinks the Chinese will get into a bidding war, no matter what the Chinese have already paid for. The big question is what is America going to do to protect our investment? Do we get out before the shooting starts and kiss our operation here goodbye or do we wait for the Chinese to throw us off the island. My thinking is as long as you are alive and, on this island, not much is going to happen. If something happens to Chumley, I am not sure what that will do to the situation."

"At this stage I do not know how Washington will handle this, but I can see that it is in the Hotel's interest to support us."

"No doubt about that. What are your plans?"

"Tomorrow, I will again be meeting with Chumley."

"Where?"

"At his beach house."

"Next door to the hotel?"

"Yes."

"There isn't much point in you going back to the Bishop compound tonight. The sun will be up in a few hours. Why don't you be our guest and stay overnight in the hotel?"

"That is very generous of you. I am tempted to take you up on the offer."

"No, please do. Let me phone down and get you a room."

"Great could I get room 407 or 411".

"It was going to be the presidential suite."

"That won't be necessary. Could you swing a room for my two cousins across the hall from me?"

Roberto Bento talked quietly on the phone and then he hung up and turned to Rob, "It's all set up. You were lucky. I was able to get you into room 407 and your two cousins are across the hall in room 408. All you have to do is pass your universal ID card across the scanner for those rooms."

As they parted, Roberto opened a drawer and took out a credit card. He took out his personal communication device and appeared to enter in the credit card number.

"Doctor Lyons, do you like to gamble?"

"Oh, I've been known to."

"Well, I think you will find this card will bring you luck. Go down to the casino now and put it in any of the one-dollar slot machines."

Rob took the card and left. His cousin was still standing in the small ante-room with the two thugs and the two security guards. Rob explained that they were staying the night and told his cousin to get the other cousin out of the car and get some sleep in room 408.

Followed by the two thugs he took the elevator down to the lobby and went past the greeter at the door into the casino. It was a cacophony of sound – people excitedly laughing, talking, shouting, bells going off for the slot winners, the rattle of the balls on the roulette wheels, the squealing artificial sounds of the slot machines. It took him awhile to find the one-dollar slot machines. He put the credit card into one of them and hit the button that spun the wheels. He hit the jackpot. Why, was he not surprised? The lights flashed. The bell rang loudly. People crowded around him, congratulating him. He had won ten thousand dollars. He printed out the ticket and took it over to the cashier. She handed him ten thousand dollars in one hundred-dollar   bills. So, this is how they clean the dirty money and get it back in circulation, he thought to himself. Being able to insert a credit card into the slot machine made it easy for them to identify who was supposed to win.

He collected his entourage in the lobby and proceeded to room 407. The cousins went into 408. The two goons went back to whatever cave they had left. As soon as he got in the room, he immediately phoned room 409. He could hear the phone faintly ringing in her room.

Barbara Wall sleepily answered the phone, "Hello?"

"I told you I would phone you in the morning."

"It is still dark out. Where are you?"

"In the room, next to yours. There is an interconnecting door. I've unlocked my door."

"Just a minute."

Barbara went over to the interconnecting door and unlocked it and opened it. The lights were off as were Rob's clothes. He reached out and she went into his arms. His lips locked onto hers as he picked her up in her nightgown and carried her over to his king size bed. Her arms were locked tightly around his neck. They fell gently onto the bed. She helped him pull her night gown off over her head and then rolled over into his arms. She felt soft, warm and firm against his body. He leaned down to caress her with his tongue as he reached around her with the other arm to stroke her. Her pelvis thrust against him. She rolled onto her back and pulled him to her.

CHAPTER 12

Explosion

The sun rose on another beautiful day in Saint Matts. Barbara Wall slipped out of the bed and found her night gown on the carpet where she had dropped it. Rob was floating in that never-never land between sleep and wakening. He felt the lessening of the pressure on the mattress and sheets. Slowly he ascended from the depths. He opened his eyes just enough to see Barbara going through the interconnecting door to her own room. Looking at the angle of the light coming in around the edge of the curtains he figured it was about seven o'clock. He played a little game each morning to see how close his guess was to reality. 7:05, close, not bad at all, for some reason it made him feel good to have almost nailed it.

"GOOD MORNING, DOCTOR LYONS", Control whispered in his ear. **"JUST TO CLUE YOU IN, THE 22ND MARINE EXPEDITIONARY FORCE OUT OF LEJEUNE, NORTH CAROLINA, HAS BEEN DEPLOYED AS A STRIKE GROUP TO SAINT MATTS. IT IS COMPOSED OF THREE AMPHIBIOUS SHIPS THAT WILL DISEMBARK 2,200 MARINES AND THEIR EQUIPMENT. THEY ARE BEING ESCORTED BY A GUIDED MISSILE CRUISER, A GUIDED MISSILE DESTROYER AND A NUCLEAR ATTACK SUBMARINE. YOU SHOULD EXPECT THEM TO ARRIVE OFF THE NORTH COAST OF SAINT MATTS AT TWENTY-ONE HUNDRED HOURS TOMORROW. THE SECRETARY OF STATE WILL BE PATCHED INTO YOUR MEETING WITH PRIME MINISTER CHUMLEY AT NINE HUNDRED HOURS. THE SATELLITE AND THE DRONE SHOW ACTIVITY, TAKING PLACE AT THE OLD BRITISH NAVAL YARD. ENJOY YOUR BREAKFAST."**

Rob could hear Barbara taking a shower in her room. It was time to rise and shine. He slowly got out of bed. Unlike Barbara, he didn't have a night gown. He never wore anything to bed. He decided to give Barbara a surprise. He walked across his room into her room and into her steamy bathroom. He slipped into the shower with her. He reached around her from behind and pulled her in close to him. She felt soft and slippery. The hot water felt good. With the other hand he took the soap away from her and started to wash her. This aroused him. He dropped the soap.

"Rob I've got to go to work," she whispered.

"This won't take long," he replied with a smile in is voice.

After they dressed, they headed up to the buffet breakfast in the nightclub on the roof. It had been magically transformed into the hotel's breakfast room. A large buffet was laid out with separate stations on the side for making waffles and omelets. The morning sun skipped off the ocean waves. A gentle, warm, tropical breeze kept them comfortable as it blew through the open windows and across the room on its way to the island's mountains. The two cousins were a few tables away eating their breakfast. The two thugs from hotel security took up their usual position just inside the door.

"Beautiful view, it makes a snowy, cold Washington seem very far away and very unimportant." Barbara said, as she slowly sipped her coffee.

"Watch it, or you may get island fever and never leave. A lot of islanders think those who live in climates where the temperature falls below 78 degrees must be crazy. They also don't care what goes on in the stock market or who the United States is currently at war with or preparing to go to war with."

"You could live here. Why don't you?"

"Oh, I have thought about it, but I found that I need the stress and challenges of the real world to feel fully alive and get my creative juices flowing. I might live longer if I lived here or at least it would feel like I was living longer".

"What's your plan for today?"

"I am meeting with Chumley again. We have some unfinished business."

"Is it something I should know about?"

"Probably, but you will not hear about it from me."

"I could torture you and make you talk."

"You had your chance, but now I would have to bite the cyanide pill that they implanted."

"You're kidding, aren't you?"

"Of course, I am."

He gave her a big smile. She wondered if he was serious or not.

"With you I am never quite sure. I've got to go down and hook up with my cameraman in the lobby. We are off to interviewing students at the medical school – that is if there are any left. I understand that they've been leaving the island like rats from a sinking ship. Do you think Washington would ever drop a nuclear bomb on the island?"

"I cannot conceive under what logical circumstances it could ever be an option. To me, it would be a criminal, ridiculous, inhumane, un-American, stupid thing to do. I guess the simple answer is no."

"Am I going to see you later?"

"You can count on it. I'll give you a call later. I think once I tie up the loose ends this morning with Chumley that my assignment here is over."

Barbara left. His two cousins joined him at the table. He looked at his watch. It was 8:50 and time to get going. They rose and headed towards the elevator. The hotel's two thugs followed them down to the lobby but left them when they passed through the entrance and headed towards the hotel's parking lot.

It only took a few minutes to get to the turn off into the prime minister's beach house. As soon as they had turned out of the hotel's drive way they were picked up and followed by the same two cars that had followed them the day before. The two cars followed them up the sandy lane to the beach house and parked behind them. The two cousins stayed in the car, so they would not be searched, and their ankle holsters detected.

Rob got out and was thoroughly searched like the day before. He could see Winston Clark watching from his seat at the pool side table on the patio. Rob walked through the elegant reception areas. He admired the large bouquet of fresh flowers on a round table glass. As he walked, Control set the scene.

"SAME SECURITY AS YESTERDAY, THERE ARE TWO SECURITY PEOPLE PATROLLING THE BEACH BETWEEN THE PATIO AND THE OCEAN. THE SECURITY THAT WAS IN THE TWO CARS THAT FOLLOWED YOU IN IS WAITING IN THE RECEPTION AREA. THE SNIPER WITH THE RIFLE IS IN THE SAME BUSHES ON THE OTHER SIDE OF THE POOL."

Chumley was seated with his back to Rob reading some documents. His game was to show no respect to Rob, the representative of the United States of America. Winston shifted his weight as if he were going to get up to greet Rob. Chumley motioned with one hand for him to remain seated.

Rob reached the table. Chumley left him standing there, just long enough to make the point that he was not kowtowing to the United States. Ever so slowly he put down his papers. Winston knew this was his signal to leave. He left without greeting Rob. Not bothering to look at Rob or indicating he should take a seat, Chumley grunted, "What's your offer?"

Rob looked at his fat, beach ball, head and wanted to give it a quick couple of Karate chops to smarten Chumley up but he didn't.

"The United States will secretly transfer $60,000,000 into a private account in the Cayman Islands that only you have access to. How much of that you transfer into the Saint Matt's treasury is your business. Each year, for the next ten years, they will transfer a further $60,000,000."

"Chumley had now turned and looked up at Rob in response to the offer."

"Ten years?" " "

Rob responded, "Ten years."

"The Chinese offered one hundred years with a built-in inflation accelerator."

"Ten years is a long time. Ten years from now you will be seventy-six years old. When do you get to enjoy the fruits of your labor? Someone else will be prime minister. The Chinese will be long gone from Saint Matts. It is easy to offer payments for one hundred years, but it is another thing to deliver. You don't have a crystal ball and neither do I but if I were a betting man, I would place my bet on the United States."

Rob stood looking down at Chumley who still had not indicated he should take a seat. He stayed quiet, letting Chumley mull over his options. He could hear the waves crashing on the beach and the birds twittering in the bushes. A large bumble bee buzzed by as it headed towards the nectar in a bright red hibiscus. Finally, Chumley looked up at Rob. He stood up, turned and smiled his famous hippopotamus smile. He reached out for Rob's hand.

"You've got a deal".

In recalling it later, Rob remembers, at that moment, seeing Chumley's head explode like a watermelon that had been dropped from twenty feet. Blood and grey brain tissue sprayed out covering Rob. At the same instant Rob heard the crack of the high-powered rifle that had sealed Prime Minister Chumley's fate. To protect himself, Rob instinctively spun sideways and launched himself into the pool.

Control excitedly shouted, **"LASER ACTIVATED."**

He was deep in the pool when a mighty rushing sound filled the air and a rocket, from the C.I.A. drone, exploded where Chumley's security sniper had been positioned. Sand, dust, pieces of flesh and bits of coconut trees were thrown high into the air and began to fall into the pool.

The security people in the reception area had all ducked down behind the furniture. The two who were patrolling the beach had their machine guns in hand as they bravely charged from the beach towards the explosion. Rob's two cousins came running through the reception area onto the patio deck with their guns drawn. Rob surfaced, as debris were falling onto the surface of what had been a pristine pool. The pool was already pink with Chumley's blood. Shouting and screaming filled the air. He took a big breath and tread water. He felt his legs and arms, everything seemed to be functioning. His cousins shouted at him from the side of the pool.

"You okay Rob?"

"What the hell happened?"

"They got Chumley."

"So, I noticed. Who the hell is "They"?"

"Good question. We may never know. A rocket came in and wiped out whoever took the shot. I doubt if they will find enough of him to fill a thimble."

"His cousin tucked his weapon back into his ankle holster and held out his hand to Rob, "Give me your hand. Let's get you out of the pool."

"let's get you out of the pool."

Rob took his hand and was hauled dripping wet out of the pool. In the distance, security people were running, shouting excitedly and fanning out over the grounds - now that they had assumed that there was no real danger. Chumley's body lay sprawled on the ground next to his chair that had tipped over when he fell. A large puddle of blood was growing bigger as it continued to drain into the swimming pool. Rob heard the waves crashing on the beach and the birds twittering in the bushes.

They stood their stunned, absorbing the horror of it all. As if he had been waiting close by, a man Rob had never seen before, wearing just a bathing suit, stepped out from behind a bush and rapidly approached them from the direction of the water. As soon as he was within hailing distance, he cried out, "Doctor Lyons, I've got orders. You are to come with me, now. Washington does not want you at the scene of this assassination."

"Who the hell are you?"

"I am Ken Davis from the Central Intelligence Agency."

Rob's first reaction was one of wonderment. Why should he believe that this man was from the CIA? What was he doing here? Where did he come from? Who the hell shot Chumley?

Control interjected, **"CONFIRMED THAT IS KENNETH DAVIS, THE C.I.A. FIELD OPERATIVE ASSIGNED TO SAINT MATTS. YOU ARE TO GO WITH HIM IMMEDIATELY. YOU WILL BE SAFE."**

"What about my cousins."

Davis responded, "They are in no danger, you are. The police are on their way and are going to come down that lane from the main road in the next couple of minutes. We are only equipped to remove you from the beach. Your cousins will not have any problem with the police. They can simply say they had come to discuss family business with Chumley. Now, let's get the hell out of here."

"Rob said to his cousins, "OK, I'll see you guys later."

The cousins sat and waited for the police.

With his soggy shoes squishing loudly, Rob quickly followed Ken Davis towards the water. His wet pants made walking difficult. As he moved at a fast walk, he took his shirt off and wrung it dry as he could. When they got closer to where the surf was breaking on the beach, he could hear police sirens approaching.

Waiting on the beach was a powerful Seadoo. Davis took a key from a container on a necklace around his neck, inserted it in the machine and started to push the Seadoo down the sloping sandy beach into the surf. Rob helped him. Davis climbed on while Rob held the Seadoo from behind, stopping it from being washed back up on the beach by the surf. With a roar the engine started. Davis yelled at Rob, "OK, get on behind me and hold on tight." Rob got on the saddle behind him and held on to Ken's waist as they rapidly accelerated towards a fifty-foot white cabin cruiser, which, as he got closer, he could see was named the Sea Witch. It was about five hundred feet off the beach gently rocking on the waves. The exhilarating ride took only a few minutes. They bobbed up and down in the swells alongside the cruiser. Rob stretched for the ladder and missed it the first time. The next time the two vessels moved in harmony, Rob was able to grab the ladder and quickly swing his body onto it. He was helped up the ladder by a tough looking leggy blond in a bright red bikini who did not look like thecute and cuddly type.

"Welcome aboard Doctor Lyons. I'm agent Mandy Derk. Make yourself at home. Ken will get you one of his spare bathing suits as soon as we haul the Seadoo on board."
Ken had moved the Seadoo to the back of the vessel and gunned it up onto a ramp which then hoisted it out of the water. The twin diesel engines of the cruiser burbled away as the vessel rose and fell in the swells. As soon as Ken had the Seadoo stowed away, he came back and joined Rob. The crewman gunned the engine and the burbling turned into a thunderous roar as the cruiser accelerated away from the assassination.

Control came on, **"HOLD ON FOR THE SECRETARY.** "There was a change in background noise and suddenly the Secretary of State was patched in, '**DOCTOR LYONS, IT HAD NOT BEEN OUR INTENTION WHEN YOU TOOK THIS ASSIGNMENT TO PUT YOU IN ANY DANGER. WE ASSUMED THE SECURITY SNIPER WAS THE SAME SNIPER THAT HAD BEEN THERE THE DAY BEFORE PROTECTING**

CHUMLEY. THE C.I.A, SPECULATES THAT A CHINESE SNIPER KILLED CHUMLEY'S SNIPER AND THEN TOOK UP THE SAME POSITION. WE HAVE JUST REVIEWED A VIDEO. ON FURTHER SCRUTINY, JUST BEFORE THE SHOT, WE SEE WHAT APPEARS TO BE A BODY NEXT TO THE NEW SNIPER. IT DID NOT SHOW UP ON OUR EARLIER INFRARED SCAN THAT WE USED TO DETECT PEOPLE IN UNDERGROWTH. THE BODY COULD HAVE BEEN COLD. ASSASSINATING CHUMLEY CERTAINLY THROWS A NEW TWIST INTO THIS. WE ASSUME ANY AGREEMENT HE REACHED WITH CHINESE IS NOW NULL AND VOID. THE QUESTION IS, WHAT ARE THE CHINESE GOING TO DO NOW? THE C.I.A. WILL KEEP YOU SAFE AS WE WAIT TO SEE WHAT IS GOING DOWN."

Rob pondered what she had just said and all that had happened in the last few minutes. Something was not ringing true. Everything was just a bit too well coordinated. The very second Chumley agree to $60,000,000 over ten years, he was shot. Then, within another few seconds a rocket from a drone, probably controlled by the C.I.A, vaporized the assassin and made it impossible to identify who the assassin was and whether his allegiances were to the Chinese or not. How is it that there was a C.I.A. agent so conveniently close by, ready to immediately remove him from the assassination scene? Wasn't it a bit too fortuitous that there was a Seadoo and a cruiser standing by to whisk him from the murder scene and away from the investigation's prying questions? Assassinating Chumley not only saved the United States $600,000,000 over the next ten years but probably screwed up the deal Chumley had with the Chinese.

How much money would it have taken to get Chumley's security sniper to assassinate Chumley? Rob figured that on an island like Saint Matts where a good salary was $10,000 U.S. that it could have been easily done for about $100,000. Especially if the sniper thought he was going to be whisked off the island and given a new identity. If the sniper had seen the Seadoo and the cruiser, he would probably have concluded that they were part of his escape plan. Killing Chumley's sniper and substituting another sniper seemed farfetched.

This was an election year. To what extent would a president go to avoid a leak to the press that he had been responsible for the murder of the head of state of a friendly sovereign nation? The rocket made sure there were no loose ends that could come back and bite the president during the campaign. Rob wondered if he was just being cynical. There was probably a good explanation for everything and the United States was innocent of his wild conjecture.

Rob changed into a bathing suit that Ken loaned him and sat down in a deck chair to watch the East coast of the island slip by. Ken Davis asked him if he wanted a beer. He nodded that he did. Ken went below and came back with an ice-cold slippery can of Coors Lite. He popped the top and handed it to Rob who poured it down his throat. The sharp, ice cold, malty tartness felt good as it tingled his tongue and slipped down his throat.

"Where are we heading? he asked Ken.

"South, to the Georgetown Harbor Marina."
"How long will it take?"

"Depending on how much we want to get bounced around by the waves, it could take us two hours or more"

The boat seemed to Rob to be moving along at a good clip. Rising and falling on the swells. As Rob went over the trauma of the morning, he felt uneasy. He was no longer sure, beyond his family, whom he could trust or believe. In a society where it appears the ends always justify the means and where the law and public opinion could be bent to suit political agendas, an individual's life, including his own, did not seem to have much value. Would the President of the United States order the assassination of a Prime Minister of a sovereign foreign nation, to remove a possible threat to his reelection campaign? Would he order the CIA to eliminate him because perhaps he knew too much? Rob was glad that Control could not monitor his thoughts.

CHAPTER 13

Media

While Rob was on the cruiser, CNN was busy. Within two hours they were broadcasting Prime Minister Chumley's assassination to the world with vivid tasteless pictures of his body sprawled in a pool of blood. Since, the CNN team had already been on the island dramatizing Senator Rick Wilcox's proposal to drop a nuclear bomb on the island; they were now able to charge their travel costs to two stories instead of one. They were ready to milk the story for as many days as they could.

Peter King, the anchor in Atlanta, surrounded by dozens of T.V. monitors said, "We now go live to Jim Sandman in Saint Matt's with breaking news on the assassination of the Saint Matt's beloved Prime Minister, Doctor Victor Chumley".

Jim Sandman appeared on the screen looking suitably mournful, standing in front of the inevitable yellow police tape stretched between two palm trees, across the laneway leading to Chumley's beach house. In soft, modulated tones, reserved for funerals and natural disasters, he addressed millions of viewers in the U.S.A. and abroad, "The island of Saint Matts was rocked today by the assassination of their beloved Prime Minister, Victor Chumley. This is the second blow to the island this week. Earlier Senator Richard Wilcox threw the island into panic when he demanded that the United States destroy this Caribbean island paradise by dropping a nuclear bomb on it. He said this needed to be done to prevent the People's Republic of China from establishing a naval base on the island. He said the government of the United States should see such an installation as a direct threat to American security. So far, we have been unable to confirm that such an agreement for a naval base was ever concluded with the People's Republic of China. We were scheduled to meet with the Deputy Prime Minister today and confirm this allegation. Our subsequent investigation has still been unable to confirm that an agreement had ever been signed with the People's Republic of China. Unidentified government sources are now linking the assassination to China's displeasure with the leaking of the naval base agreement by Victor Chumley before it had been concluded."

"A spokesman for the St Matt's Police Department stated that Prime Minister had been slain by a single bullet from a high-powered rifle. They believe that the gunman then committed suicide by detonating a powerful bomb that made his identification impossible."

"Efforts to interview the ambassador at the Chinese embassy on the assassination have been unsuccessful. They did issue a release that said the People's Republic of China was saddened by the sudden death of this great statesman who had been a good friend of the Chinese people."

"A state funeral for the Prime Minister is scheduled for next Monday. Flags will be flying at half-mast until after the funeral. The Deputy Prime Minister, Wilson Dodge, immediately assumed the Prime Minister's duties. He has scheduled a press conference in an hour. It is rumored that he will declare martial law and seek armed force assistance from a yet to be named foreign country to bring calm to a population that has been thrown into panic. There are long line ups at the airport by those desperate to leave the island for any destination. A video clip of long line ups the airport was shown. The people were backed out through doors of the terminal into the parking lot. Another clip was shown of line ups at the harbor showing citizens with bags and boxes lined up to get into crowded decrepit boats that would take them to nearby islands in the Eastern Caribbean.

The reporter continued, "Over the last two days, it is estimated that ten thousand residents, out of a population of forty thousand, have departed the island of Saint Matts because of the irresponsible threat of nuclear annihilation instigated by Senator Richard Wilcox. Were these threats just an attempt to garner publicity for Senator Wilcox's campaign fund? Was Senator Wilcox provided with confidential information knowing that he would release it and that it would result in the assassination of the prime minister for revealing a secret agreement with a foreign power? The government of the United States will be keeping a close eye on the People's Republic of China's intentions for Saint Matts and other islands in the Caribbean. Back to you Peter."

Peter King stood in The Situation Room at CNN with a photograph of Senator Wilcox in the background. He peered at the camera and in his deepest baritone

126

voice said, "We now go live to the Russell Senate Building where Senator Richard Wilcox is about to begin a news conference".

The scene shifted to a conference room in the Senate Building. The camera did a quick pan of the room that was filled with dozens of reporters, cameramen and Senate staff. Smiling, nodding and waving to the crowd, Rick Wilcox entered from a side door and proceeded toward the podium that was on a small raised platform, framed on each side by the prerequisite two huge stars and stripes on poles with shiny brass eagles on top. Patriotism sells, and Rick wanted all the patriotic voters back in Texas to know there was no greater patriot in Washington. Elated, he moved like he had springs in his tall, lanky frame. After all, he was getting a million dollars' worth of free promotion. He dazzled the room with one more of his brilliant white smiles that had been beautifully enhanced by the best cosmetic dentist in Washington and began, "Ladies and gentlemen, I want to thank you for attending this brief but important news conference. I will answer questions at the end."

He coughed and paused for dramatic effect. The room became very quiet. The old Washington hands among the press corps wondered what this loose cannon was going to come up with.

"Two days ago, I brought to this great nation's attention a national security threat that the Democratic government was choosing to ignore. A country, with a billion more people than the population of the United States, has deliberately chosen to confront us. Since 1823, the United States has said that it would come to the protection of any nation in the Western Hemisphere whose independence was being subverted by a foreign nation. The army of the People's Republic of China has thousands of their troops on the island of Saint Matts in the Eastern Caribbean. Through subterfuge these military personnel were placed on the island as construction workers. Yesterday over a thousand of these Chinese workers dropped their shovels and picked up rifles with the intent of removing the democratically elected government of Saint Kitts.

It appears that because of this morning's tragedy that the Deputy Prime Minister of Saint Matts has been persuaded to, or possibly forced to; declare a state of emergency and to call upon the Chinese to provide security to the island."

He paused to let it sink in. Took a sip of water and continued, "This call to arms was delivered after the dastardly assassination of one of the world's greatest democratically elected leaders, Prime Minister, Victor Chumley, a true friend of the United States. Someone our government could depend upon for support. The

127

cowardly assassin, after fulfilling his master's bidding, committed suicide by igniting a bomb that has now made him impossible to identify. However, it does not take too much imagination to determine who was behind this assassination. Although his body could not be identified, the remains of the high-powered rifle he used, has been identified as being of Chinese manufacture. When is our nation going to wake up to this threat on our very borders and send the Chinese packing? Back in Texas we don't mess around with rattlesnakes. We get them before they get us. It is time to call in the marines and return the island of Saint Matts to its elected democratic government."

The room filled with an excited buzz.
"I'll take questions."

One of the silver haired stalwarts of the Washington press corps slowly rose. One of Wilcox's aids passed a microphone to him and the veteran newsman addressed the podium with a Connecticut Yankee accent.

"Senator Wilcox, two days ago you demanded that the United States immediately nuke Saint Matts into oblivion. Do you want them to do this before or after the marines storm their beaches?"

Rick Wilcox glared at the newsman and replied, "While a nuclear bomb would certainly have been the quickest and most cost-effective solution to this incursion, the Prime Minister's assassination has changed the game plan. The marines can certainly help evacuate the civilian population from this island so if it becomes necessary, we can take more extreme action to make this island unattractive to the Chinese."

Now thinking that giving the press the freedom of asking questions, was not such a good idea. Rick waved to the crowd and said, "Thank you all for coming." He quickly left the room, ignoring the reporters who hurled questions at him as he made his escape.
A
lthough Rick Wilcox was ignorant of the fact that the marines were in transit to Saint Matts, by calling for the marines to invade, he had effectively drawn attention to the President's initiative. Chinese intelligence forces watch CNN, they reviewed the position of all their submarine drones that shadowed every U.S. naval vessel. It took them seconds to pin point a marine fleet moving South off the coast of Florida. It was the only unusual naval traffic close to the Caribbean. The deduction was made that it must be heading to Saint Matts. When the Chinese politburo was

presented with this probability, they realized that the time had come to draw a line in the sand and show the world that a new super power had arrived.

CHAPTER 14

Confrontation

The C.I.A. cruiser rounded Pigs Head point. Rob squinted into the sun reflecting off the Caribbean Sea. He wished he had his sunglasses. It was now a straight run into Georgetown. The South side of the island was always calmer than the North side. He turned to Ken Davis who was sprawled in a blue canvas deck chair across from him.

"Ken, what's the game plan when we get into the marina?"

"My car is parked there. Mandy and I will drive you back to the compound. I think that is the safest place for you right now. If your family doesn't mind, we would like to stay there with you. We have been assigned to protect you."

Control suddenly interrupted, **"IF YOU GO INTO THE MARINA. YOU WILL BE DETAINED BY THE CHINESE SOLDIERS WHO HAVE BEEN POSTED THERE. A STATE OF EMERGENCY HAS BEEN CALLED BY THE DEPUTY PRIME MINISTER AND HE HAS CALLED UPON THE PEOPLE'S REPUBLIC OF CHINA FOR ASSISTANCE. ALL CITIZENS ARE BEING ASKED TO RETURN TO THEIR HOMES AND STAY THERE. ARMED CHINESE SOLDIERS ARE ENFORCING THIS PROCLAMATION. INSTEAD OF GOING INTO THE MARINA, YOU SHOULD IMMEDIATELY HEAD TO THE FISHERMAN'S DOCK AT DEEP HOLE AND LAND THERE. ON THE DRONE'S OBSERVATION CAMERAS, WE CAN SEE NO CHINESE TROOPS THERE. IF YOU TAKE THE OLD ABANDONED MINE ROAD, IT SHOULD TAKE YOU ABOUT AN HOUR TO GET BACK TO THE COMPOUND. THE CHINESE WILL BE LOOKING FOR YOU IN A VEHICLE, NOT ON FOOT."**

"Ken, if we go to the Marin, we are going to be seized."

"What the hell are you talking about?""

"While we were travelling the island has effectively been put under a control of the Chinese."

"How do you know this?"

"Let's just say a little bird told me. We should head into Deep Hole and hike overland to the Compound. You must have a satellite phone on board. Phone Langley and confirm what I've told you."

Ken looked at Rob strangely but ordered the boat to heave to. It wallowed in the water like a tired turtle, the exhaust making low guttural bubbling sounds as the exhaust pipes slipped in and out of the water. The vessel rolled to and fro with the waves. Ken was on the satellite phone for almost five minutes. When he finished, he told the crewman to head for Deep Hole. Rob gathered his, now, dry clothes and proceeded to put them on. His shoes were not fully dry, but they would have to do. They would have a hike of about three miles to the compound and much of that was uphill. It would be hot work. The shade of the rainforest would cool it a bit.

They entered the small cove through a narrow slit in the cliffs. On bright sunny days like this, the fishermen who used this port would have gone out early in the morning. They were fair weather fishermen. Any chance of inclement weather and they stayed ashore. It was still too early for them to have returned with their catch. There appeared to be no one around when they got off at the old stone dock. The fishermen's pickup trucks were parked haphazardly as close to the docks as they could get them, in anticipation of transferring the catch to the trucks. From here they would drive into the Fishermen's Co-op in Georgetown. The cruiser turned around and headed back through the slit on its way to the marina at Georgetown. Rob noticed that both Mandy and Ken were now armed with submachine guns.

Single file, with Rob in the lead, they started off up the rough unpaved road that led to the main North-South road. The old abandoned mine road was about five hundred feet ahead of them on the left. It would take them kitty corner through the bush. They would come out close to the rock cut that led into the compound. The mine road had been abandoned years ago. It was now more of a narrow trail than a road. As a boy, Rob and his cousins had roamed this green lush wilderness. Many times, on a steamy summer's day, they had followed the mine road down to Deep Hole to dive off the dock and swim in the sheltered cove.

Walking through the jungle it was like being in a mighty cathedral of green. The trees soared more than a hundred feet above their head. Other than the chorus of the birds in the trees, sounds were muffled.

The mine road met the main road about a hundred feet north of the rock cut that led into the compound. They left the path and using the jungle as cover approached the entrance. It was on the other side of the road. They would have to cross the road to get into it. They paused and scanned the entrance.

Control, with its all-seeing eyes, was able to advise them, **"THERE APPEARS TO BE TWO ARMED CHINESE GUARDS SITTING UNDER THE TREES JUST TO THE SOUTH OF THE ENTRANCE. WHILE WE COULD TAKE THEM OUT WITH A ROCKET, IT WOULD ATTRACT TOO MUCH ATTENTION AND BRING MORE TROOPS. THE SIMPLEST, QUIETIST THING IS FOR YOU TO TAKE THEM OUT WITH YOUR LASER. JUST WALK UP TO THEM AND WHEN THEY COME TO YOU, ZAP THEM. YOUR LASER IS NOW ACTIVATED."**

Rob turned to Ken and Mandy, "The two of you stay here, I am going to approach the entrance and take care of two guards who are hiding in the bushes. When I wave for you to come, you hoof it across the road double quick."

"It is our job to take out the enemy, not yours. Are you nuts, you aren't even armed? Leave it to the professionals."

"Don't worry I've got this under control and I am armed."

They looked at him as if he were crazy. They could not see any weapon. Ken held out his submachine gun and said, "At least take my weapon."

"I don't need your weapon. If I approach them with that weapon, I will only increase the possibility that they will get stressed and do something stupid, like shoot me. Besides it would make too much noise and bring more soldiers."

"OK, but we will have you covered."

Rob stepped out of the undergrowth and made his way slowly across the road towards the rock cut. As he approached the entrance, two Chinese soldiers in tan fatigues, who had been smoking and laughing, were surprised to see Rob approaching them. They stood up and stepped out from behind the bushes where they had been sitting in the shade. Rob approached them, smiling, with his arms outstretched showing that he was carrying no weapon. The two soldiers responded appropriately. They held their AK47s loosely with the barrels aimed towards the ground. Their orders, if Rob were to show up, were to immediately bring this civilian to General Lee. Under no circumstances were they to harm him. They had expected him to arrive in a car. They were surprised and relieved to see him walking alone towards them.

They chuckled and made comments about the praise they would receive for bringing in the Yankee. When he was twenty feet from the two soldiers, he swung his raised arms to the front, pointed his ring finger at the first one and pressed his ring. The silent laser flash was a thousandth of a second. If it were noticed, you would think that perhaps you had imagined it. As the first soldier crumpled, the second one turned in horror to look in wonderment at his comrade lying on the ground. Rob touched the ring again and the second soldier joined his fallen comrade.

Rob waved at Mandy and Ken to join him. They had been watching from their hiding spot across the road. They did not really understand what they had witnessed. They ran across the road and helped Rob pull the two bodies into the undergrowth. They then started the half mile walk into the rock cut.

As they walked along, Ken looked at Rob with new respect and asked, "How did you do that."

"Ask me no questions and I will tell you no lies." Rob replied. Ken laughed and replied, "Well it was impressive whatever you did. It takes a lot of balls to walk up to two armed soldiers and kill them."

As they walked quietly through the rock cut, they all jumped when from high above them in the mountain they heard one of the cousins suddenly shout out, "Rob's coming in on foot with two strangers." They heard this message repeated and echoing several times on the rock cut walls until it reached the compound. They went around the final bend and walked by the truck that was blocking the roadway. His mother and father, both armed with old .303 hunting rifles, were waiting for him along with a few dozen of the extended family, all of them armed.

"Thank God you're OK. Jeez, it is good to see you, son. Your mother and I have been worried sick about you."

He hugged his mother and father. Turning towards Mandy and Ken, Rob murmured, "These two are Mandy and Ken, there here to make sure I don't get into any more trouble. Can we find somewhere for them to stay? Rob's mother took charge of them like a mother hen who had found two abandoned chicks.

Rob asked his father, "Did the cousins make it back from Chumley's OK?"

"Yeah, they got in about an hour ago, but they were also worried about you. They weren't totally sure who you had run off with. General Lee has been phoning here every fifteen minutes. He says it is critical to the security of the United States that you talk to him. I am not sure if he believes me when I told him you were not here, and I had no idea where you were."
"I better get to a phone and see what he is talking about."

Rob headed towards the house with his father. The phone number was written on small piece of scrap paper that his father had probably extracted from his waste paper basket. He didn't believe in wasting money. As a kid Rob remembered him using old Christmas cards as scrap writing paper.

Rob phoned the number. It was answered on the second ring. Rob recognized Lee's soft voice when he said, "People's Republic of China's embassy."

"General Lee, this is Rob Lyons. I understand you wish to speak to me."

"Are you at your compound?

"Yes, I am."

"What I wish to discuss with you is so confidential that I must do it in person with you. I will be there within fifteen minutes" "Good, I will see you in fifteen minutes."

Rob put the phone down and wondered what Lee was going to tell him. This gave him enough time to freshen up and change his clothes. He was sure he would hear the usual lecture from his mother about not taking care of his things when she found them in the laundry hamper.
Fifteen minutes later, the truck blocking the rock cut was rolled back. Sitting on the porch facing the rock cut, Rob could see that General Lee was made to get out of the limousine and go through the search routine. He got back in and the limousine drove into the compound. It drove serenely with red fender flags flying, crunching along the crushed stone oval and stopped in front of Rob. Colonel Lee stepped out dressed in green camouflage fatigues. His paratroop boots were polished to a high

sheen. He no longer looked like a diplomat. He bowed slightly to Rob. Rob gave him a respectful bow. Rob ushered him into the house and led him to the study. Lee looked out the sliding screen doors to the garden and the gazebo.

"Would it be possible to go into the garden?" General Lee quietly asked.

"By all means," Rob replied. He slid the door open and followed Lee out. The sun streaming through the leaves of the trees that encircled the garden left a dappled effect on the thick Bermuda grass. Lee seemed deep in thought as they approached the gazebo. They both sat down facing each other.

Lee nervously coughed and began to speak, "The leaders in Beijing have asked me to outline the concerns that they have and how they intend to resolve these concerns. They think that you are in almost instant communication with the highest level of your government and that by working through you, informally, that they will achieve their objectives quicker with less chance for manipulation and misinterpretation."

Rob nodded to indicate he understood but he neither confirmed nor denied Lee's supposition. He waited for Lee to continue.

Control interjected at this point, **"THE SECRETARY OF STATE AND THE PRESIDENT HAVE BEEN PATCHED INTO THIS TRANSMISSION."**

Rob almost visibly flinched when he heard the president was also going to be part of this meeting.

Lee stared off over the cliff at the end of the garden towards the Caribbean Sea and continued in a flat monotone, "We have identified a U.S. marine invasion fleet heading towards Saint Matts. They are less than a day away. We believe that the intent of your government is to invade Saint Matts."

"I know nothing about a marine fleet approaching the island," Rob replied.

"What my government, with the greatest of respect asks, is for your government to order this fleet to immediately turn around and return to the port that it left two days ago."

Lee stared at Rob waiting for a reply. Rob waited to see if the President or the Secretary of State would provide guidance.

The president was his usual arrogant, obscene self when he exploded with, **"WHO DO THESE SONS-OF-BITCHES THINK THEY ARE DICTATING TO THE UNITED**

STATES OF AMERICA. RESPECT MY ASS. YOU TELL THEM THAT WE WILL SAIL OUR FLEETS ANYWHERE IN THIS WORLD THAT WE DAMN WELL CHOOSE."

The Secretary of State, interjected, "WE PROTECT THEIR TRADE ROUTES. IT IS VERY UNUSUAL FOR THEM TO INSTIGATE A CONFRONTATION. THERE IS SOMETHING GOING ON HERE THAT IS NOT BEING SAID. ROB, SEE IF YOU CAN FIND OUT WHERE THIS IS GOING".

Rob suspected that General Lee knew, that somehow or other, he was hot wired into the White House. He must look like a zombie or that he was in a trance when he sat there waiting for his inspiration to arrive from Washington. He spoke as calmly as Lee when he responded, "General Lee, with all due respect, the United States of America is till the world's only super power. For decades, we have provided protection to the People's Republic of China's trade routes, not only to North America but Europe and all your other major markets. Rank has privilege. One of those privileges is the unspoken agreement of nations that we have the freedom to deploy our resources where ever we feel that it would be most advantageous for world peace."

General Lee stared at Rob and very carefully worded his reply, "The People's Republic of China recognized that, until now." Here, he paused to let it sink in before continuing, "The United States of America had the most powerful navy in the world and it was in China's best interest to tolerate the United States imposing their policies and controls on sovereign nations, such as ourselves. However, as of this day, the United States Naval power has now been tethered. It now operates only with the consideration and consultation of the People's Republic of China."

"Sorry, I do not understand. Why does our Navy have to consult with the People's Republic of China"?

"Because, we now have the technology to immediately disable every vessel in your Navy."

The President could not hold back and shouted in Rob's ear, "WHAT THE HELL IS HE TALKING ABOUT. HE'S BLUFFING. TELL HIM TO SHOVE HIS TECHNOLOGY WHERE THE SUN DON'T SHINE. WE AREN'T BUYING THIS."

"We aren't aware of any technology that could disable even one of our vessels, never mind all of them. Could you describe this technology?"

Looking at his watch, Colonel Lee replied, "No, what I will do is demonstrate it. In thirty minutes, at 4:30 PM, we will start to disable your fleet around the world, one vessel at a time, at five-minute intervals until that marine force turns around and heads back to its home port. We will start with the lead vessel in the Marine invasion force. You can contact me at any time and we will discuss this new world order further". With that he stood, bowed, and started across the grass towards the side of the house and around it to his limousine.

Rob sat there stunned. Was this a declaration of war? Were they standing on the brink of Armageddon? China had the nuclear weapons and the long range intercontinental ballistic missiles to deliver them to any target in the United States. Two years ago, they had landed a man on the moon. Was it possible their technology had leaped ahead of the United States?

The Secretary of State broke the silence, **"THAT DID NOT SOUND LIKE A BLUFF TO ME. PERHAPS, MISTER PRESIDENT THE NAVY SHOULD BE PUT ON IMMEDIATE ALERT"**.

The President had already left the link. He was on the phone to the Secretary of the Navy demanding an immediate alert to all Navy vessels and to the vessels in the marine invasion force approaching Saint Matts. The puzzled Secretary of the Navy asked what the nature of the threat was and was rewarded with an expletive and admittance by the President that he did not know but to keep their eyes open for an attack which could come from anywhere.

Within five minutes, ever admiral and captain on every vessel around the world was handled a puzzling message to put their vessels on high alert. Some were woken up in the middle of the night. Crews ran to their battle stations. Fighter aircraft were launched from aircraft carriers to search for intruders. Submarines submerged. Nuclear missiles were readied for launch. Radar aircraft were deployed searching the skies for attack forces. Sonar listening posts were put on high alert.

The president looked at the grandfather clock in the corner of his office. It was 3:25 PM in Washington. They were an hour behind the time in Saint Matts. He really did not need this stress. In five minutes, he would know if the Chinese were bluffing or not. He tried, unsuccessfully, to read a report attacking the long established North American trade agreement for taking jobs away from Americans. He kept looking up at the clock. Surely this was all one big bluff. He wanted to get up and kick that grandfather clock to make it move faster.

The lead vessel in the Marine invasion force was the guided missile cruiser, the USS Rochester. The Chinese stealth drone submarine that was shadowing it was positioned three miles below it. At exactly 4:30 PM Atlantic Time, a drone operator in a bunker, twelve hundred feet below ground in an abandoned mine in China, sent an electronic command that tilted the drone from horizontal to a vertical angle. A port opened, and a torpedo exploded from the drone. A motion seeking sensor in the torpedo locked on the ships spinning propeller. Within a foot of the spinning propeller a powerful explosion from the torpedo propelled a gigantic stainless-steel net into the propeller. The spinning blades sucked it in like a magnet. Within seconds the net had so entangled the gigantic propeller that it stopped spinning. Inside the ship, the engine desperately tried to keep shaft moving until its bearings melted and the gears were noisily stripped. The Rochester's engine stopped. The vessel started to coast to a stop.

When the torpedo was launched, the sonar operator aboard the Rochester was using his active sonar. It was detecting no unusual maritime traffic close to them. The operator heard something which he later assumed must have been the torpedo exiting from a sub and a few seconds later, he heard an explosion when the stainless-steel net was deployed. He could not grasp what the first noise was because his instruments indicated it was coming from a location three miles below them and he knew that no U.S. Navy submarine had ever operated at more than a mile below the surface. As the Rochester's engines became silent, he listened for a submarine. There was only the usual noise of the ocean. No propellers were heard. The pinging of his sonar was not bouncing back off metal objects. All of this was reported to the Captain.

Sitting in his small private study in the White House apartment, the President smiled when the hands on the clock moved to 3:34 and no one had contacted him. He knew the Chinese had been bluffing.

At 3:35 an urgent call from the Secretary of the Navy was put through to him. He hesitated at picking up the phone and silently prayed that this was not the Secretary reporting that a vessel had been disabled.

"Mr. President, the missile cruiser Rochester, that was leading the expeditionary flotilla to Saint Matts, has just reported that they are dead in the water."
"Was anyone killed?"

"No there appear to be no casualties but the engine is beyond repair and a tug will have to tow them back to Norfolk. They are putting divers into the water to see how the damage was done."

"It must be a damn coincidence."

"Perhaps you are right, sir. Wait a minute, I have just been handed a note from the commander of the attack submarine, La Jolla. It reads that at a depth of seven hundred feet, their propulsion was stopped. They have blown their tanks and are now floating on the surface in the China Sea. This occurred at 3:35 Washington time."

"Oh, my God, turn that damn expeditionary force around."

"Yes sir, the command has been issued. Another vessel patrolling in the Red Sea has also been disabled at approximately 3:40."

"I want you and every admiral you can find for a meeting in two hours."

"Yes sir."

The President hung the phone up and cradled his bent head in his hands. "Why in the hell does this have to happen in an election year?" he screamed to an empty room. He then picked up the phone and asked the operator to set up an immediate conference call with the Secretary of the Army and the Secretary of the Air Force. They were both told to put their commands on full alert and to attend the meeting with the Secretary of the Navy and other cabinet staff.

The operators of the Chinese submarine drones immediately noted the change in course by the Marine expeditionary force and halted their disabling of American war ships. The Marine force reduced their speeds and reversed course. Moving very slowly north they waited further orders as to their deployment.

CHAPTER 15

Retribution

It was late afternoon and starting to get dark. Senator Rick Wilcox was in his $300,000 Mercedes Benz SLS AG sports car speeding along the Beltway when his cell phone rang. In Texas he drove a Chevrolet Silverado, a pimped up pickup truck. Other than his wife and a few senior aides no one had this very private number. Ignoring laws about driving and talking on a hand-held cellphone, he answered it. After all, he was a senator and it might be a rich lobbyist.

It was that same distorted electronic voice asking, "Do you know who this is?"

Rick wondered if he would recognize the voice if it had not been altered. He replied, "Yeah, I know who this is."

"Thought you would like to know; the Chinese have taken out the navy."

Rick stared at the phone with disbelief. He almost went off the road. There was a good reason why using hand held phones, while driving, was against the law.

"What do you mean by "taken out"? Whose navy?"

"The Chinese have disabled four ships at different locations around the globe within minutes of each other. They say they have the technology to disable every ship in the U.S. Navy within minutes. They would have disabled more ships if the Navy hadn't called off their invasion of Saint Matts"

"What invasion?"

"The President approved sending a strategic marine invasion group to Saint Matts yesterday."

"Really?"
Rick's mind was rapidly working out a strategy as to how he could maximize media attention with this revelation. "Senator, you still there?"

"Yeah, I'm here. Where are you getting this information?"

"Senator, I'm just a patriot who knows what is going on."

"Well patriot, I am in your debt."

The patriot clicked off without saying goodbye. Rick took the next exit and turned around and headed back to his office. As he drove, he worked the phone, calling in his aides to set up an immediate urgent press conference in his office. He then phoned his sources in the defense department to confirm what he had just heard. Most were reluctant to talk about what was going on. He really had to lean on some. He threatened to reveal all sorts of dirty little secrets that he had stored away for a rainy day. This was a rainy day. He got the confirmation he needed.

Some of his key staff members had already arrived by the time he arrived. The press conference was scheduled in half an hour. With his key staff assembled he shut the door of his office and started to outline the talking points. At the appointed time an aide opened his office door and the media charged in. They smelled blood. They were almost vibrating. They had managed to round up two camera crews and ten reporters. They busily got to work setting up microphones and positioning cameras. There was a bit of subtle pushing to get the best camera angles. Lights went on. You could smell the heat from the lights and the sweat from the media. It was not that big a room and some of the less aggressive were forced to stand just outside the door.

Rick put on his most serious face. All activity ceased. His audience waited expectantly. He nodded at them. They nodded back. He cleared his throat and began using his most presidential voice. It was almost devoid of its usual Texas twang and cowboyisms. He wondered if what he was to about to say would get the attention of the Republican Party brass. Perhaps he could even get a Draft-Richard-Wilcox- For-President movement going. Hell, he would even settle for vice president.

141

"Gentlemen, thank you for assembling on such short notice. I am sure that you will not be disappointed in what I have to say tonight. Our nation, the greatest most powerful nation in the history of mankind, teeters at the edge of an abyss. It has been brought to the edge of oblivion by the incompetence of our current government.

Today I learned that the United States Navy was made powerless by advanced technology of another nation. Earlier this week I had demanded that the United States of America obliterate the island nation of Saint Matt's for harboring our enemies. Within minutes the president could have cut the Chinese dragon's head off and sent a message to all those who dare to challenge our preeminent position in the world. Instead of acting quickly and decisively, he wavered. He ordered a marine invasion flotilla to take possession of this island, this pimple on our backside. Only hours away from the island, the Chinese disabled the lead ship. To further humiliate our great nation, they proceeded within the next fifteen minutes to disable three of our other vessels a round the world to prove that our nation was powerless to stop them. Defeated, the president ordered the flotilla to turn around and return to its base. He is now licking his wounds in the White House."

Rick paused and looked around the room full of reporters. This was obviously a scoop. Even the cynical, grey haired, veteran reporters registered surprise. He continued.

"Here we are, the richest, most powerful nation in the world, brought to our knees by a second-rate power. How is it possible with the billions of dollars that our military intelligence operations receive that they knew nothing of a Chinese technology that has rendered us powerless in protecting the citizens of this great nation? Leaving our international trade routes unprotected. They are threatening the very safety of our overseas military bases. Are we no longer able to protect our allies? I am calling upon the president of the United States to set an example and immediately vaporize that island. Show the Chinese that our great nation will not be humiliated in this way. We will show all nations in the world that if they are friends of the Chinese then they are enemies of the United States and they too run the risk of incurring our wrath.

Thank you all for coming to-night. I will now take your questions."

The most experienced and senior of the reporters, Larry Aliston, from the Washington Post got the nod to ask his question. "Senator Wilcox, could you please identify the source of your information?" "I'm afraid that the source of my information must remain confidential, but he is an extremely senior official in this Democratic administration with firsthand knowledge of the events that have taken place. I am sure you will not have any difficulty in getting either the Pentagon or the White House to confirm that this is the greatest humiliation the United States of America has ever experienced".

Another reporter who Ricky did not recognize got the next nod. A few reporters could not wait for the question and had quietly slipped out of the room to get a jump on reporting the story.

"Senator, surely you are not serious about, as you say it, vaporizing the island of Saint Matts. There are a significant number of American citizens on the island and the people of Saint Matts are an innocent party to whatever the Chinese may have done?"

Rick gave the reporter a condescending stare before he replied

"What this nation needs is strong decisive leadership. You can't make an omelet without breaking a few eggs. My concern is the safety of the three hundred and fifty million citizens in the United States of Americas. Yes, it would be unfortunate if a few American lives were lost but it would be sending a message to the Chinese, and their fellow travelers, that America acts decisively, is strong and will not be toyed with."

There was an audible gasp from the reporters. One of them, who must have been from the BBC, asked a follow up question in a clipped upper-class British accent.

"Saint Matts is a member of the British Commonwealth. Wouldn't this seriously alienate the British government and all the other nations in the Commonwealth like Canada, Australia and India, just to mention a few?"

"I doubt if the members of the British Commonwealth give a damn about what happens in Saint Matts and even if they did when they are forced to choose between this nothing country and maintaining a relationship with the richest market in the world for their exports, the choice will not be difficult. Since Suez in nineteen-fifty-six Britain has always done exactly what they thought America wanted them to do. The British Commonwealth is a joke, an excuse for a party. It is an old boys club. They do nothing. They accomplish nothing. It is astounding that in this twenty-first century that they still pretend that they have any relevancy. It is an anachronism that exists out of the laziness of Commonwealth countries to replace their governments with a republican system. Last question."

A lardy, tall, untidy reporter with the red veined nose of a serious drinker stood and was recognized.

"The Republican primaries are showing that there is no Presidential front runner who has captured the imagination of the voters. Rumors are circulating that you are considering, at this late date, in entering the race for the Republican nomination."

"The purpose of this meeting was not to discuss politics but to bring to the attention of the American people this serious breach of our safety and security. I love this nation and I feel honored that I have been allowed to serve it. If the nation were to call upon me in its hour of need to serve it in some other capacity, I would be honored to do so. I have never considered running for president but with our nation calling out for real leadership I want them to know that I would be willing to give them that leadership if that is what they want."

Rick paused looked around the room and once again thanked them for coming. Since he was in his own office, it was awkward for him to leave the clutch of reporters who wanted the meeting to go on. He managed to make it to the door by pretending he had received an important phone call on his personal communication device. He kept it pressed to his ear as he nodded and smiled his way out of his own office and out of his suite of offices. He then hurried to the elevators and took the elevator to the ground floor. He then went for a brisk walk, hoping by the time he circled the building that the media would be long gone.

The reporters rushed off to their news rooms, their home offices and their cars – and in some cases local bars to gather more information for their stories. CNN interjected the story into their programming minutes after the meeting ended. The president was informed that the story had broken a few minutes after it appeared on CCN. He switched on the television in the Oval Office to watch Ricky Coxwell's news conference. His chief of staff suggested that they have their pollsters run a quick poll to determine how American's would feel if they were to vaporize Saint Matts. It was an election year. He was prepared to do whatever he had to do to be reelected. It was a great job with lots of perks. He enjoyed being the center of attention. He even enjoyed the stupid silly game of politics. He was sure that he had the best team in politics and that they would show him how to get out of this mess.

The Chinese also watch CNN and they too watched Rick Wilcox's news conference. They smiled, the smug smile of the winner, when Rick mentioned their secret weapon. They did not appreciate Wilcox's suggestion that America vaporize Saint Matts. They had spent the last three decades building relationships with developing countries. Now, their carefully constructed image of developing countries always benefiting from a close working relationship with the People's

Republic of China was unraveling. America's knee jerk reaction to obliterate Saint Matts could scare developing countries from forming a close relationship with China. America, land of the free, was prepared to make it very clear that they would bend developing countries to their will with their military might. Faced with an apparent American willingness to drop nuclear bombs on small insignificant countries, what developing country would not bend to their will? This forced the Chinese leadership into a discussion on how to neutralize America's aggressive stance.

CHAPTER 16

Retaliation

As the president got off the elevator and approached the command center in the war room bunker, buried deep below the White House, he could hear angry, excited voices rising and falling. The president assumed from this that Navy had filled in the Army and Air Force on the situation and there were disagreements on how to react to it. As he walked into the room with his entourage, all discussion ceased as if he had turned off a tap. All eyes focused on him. Whatever strategy was going to be worked out in this room would only be enacted if he approved it. It all came down to one person's decision. In this room there was no democracy. There would be no vote on the options. A decision had to be made.

The room was a large rectangle. It could easily hold a hundred people. Large presentation screens filled three walls of the room. On one of the screens was a world map with four red explosion icons displayed on it. The President assumed that these marked where the four ships had been disabled. The room had been engineered to withstand a direct hit on the White House by a nuclear bomb. Like Hitler, buried deep in his bunker in Berlin in World War II, they too could hold out for months, even years if necessary.

The president took his designated seat at the head of the long walnut table. Flags for each service and Old Glory framed him. A brass plate that had his name engraved in it was screwed to the back of his chair. All the major power brokers who jockeyed for control of the president's decisions had designated seats at the table with brass plates screwed into their chairs. Their plates were smaller. When they retired, they could actually take these chairs with them. The chairs were carefully stationed around the table. If the President wanted to punish a Secretary, he would move their chair further away from him. Another Secretary would be rewarded by being moved closer to the president. It forced them each time they came into this room to check the nameplate on the back of each chair to see if they had risen or fallen in the pecking order. The Secretary of State was seated beside the President. She had patched Rob into the meeting just in case his input was needed.

Rob had climbed a mountain above the compound. Here he could sit and contemplate what was being discussed in the meeting while looking down over the compound, over the cliff to the town below and far out into the Caribbean Sea.
Lesser lights sat in a row behind their designated power broker. Close enough that they could whisper, what they hoped would be interpreted as intelligent insights and observations, into his ear. They looked forward to the day when they would be able to move up to the grown-ups table and have a small brass name tags on their chairs.

The president began quietly, "Whose bright idea was it to send a marine invasion team to Saint Matts". Everyone in the room stared straight ahead, down at the wooden table or at the perforations in the ceiling tiles. No one answered. The silence was like a thick, deadly, fart that no one would take ownership of.

"This screw up has already been picked up by the media. However, I guess in this world of instant communication with several thousand Republican seamen on four vessels, dead in the water, that it is little wonder the greatest set back in our proud military heritage is already front-page news. After nine-eleven the nation gave you guys billions of dollars to make sure that the United States of America would never again get caught with its pants down - especially in an election year. Now, it appears, the largest, most powerful navy in the world has been effectively turned into a pile of junk. Can anybody please explain to me what the hell is going on?"

All the eyes in the room focused on the Secretary of the Navy. He was looking down at the table. He raised his eyes as if their gaze was burning a hole in his head. He wondered why he had ever thought being Secretary of the Navy would look good on his resume when some day he would leave Washington and seek his fortune with a defense supplier. He cleared his throat and slowly responded, "We have not had much time to determine what happened, but a sonar operator believes that some kind of torpedo was launched from the bottom of the ocean at a depth that it is impossible for submarines to operate at. This torpedo exploded behind the ship and disabled it. Divers were sent overboard to determine what damage had been done. They found large, stainless steel cables wrapped around and around the props so tightly that it seized the propeller shaft and burned out the engine. We have never previously encountered such a weapon, nor have we ever even anticipated a weapon whose intent was to disable but not destroy a vessel. As I speak, our most experienced staff is determining a defense against such an attack"

The president glared at him and asked a question he knew the Secretary could not be expected to answer, with any confidence, but he knew he would, "And how long will it be before our vessels will be safe from such attacks?"

"Mr. President, our best naval minds are working on this problem. I am sure that within a day or, so they will come up with a defense. We would then apply the defense to our vessels according to their strategic priority."

The President paused for a moment and then responded, "Mister Secretary, those who launched this new weapon against us must be extremely proficient if they can deliver a torpedo that can deliberately disable a vessel. Why didn't they just destroy the vessel?"

"Our intelligence network is on the full hunt for the perpetrators of this attack and I am sure within hours it will be revealed. We had always assumed that no one had the technical ability to destroy our vessels."

"You can be assured that they had the ability to destroy the vessels. This attack was done by the People's Republic of China. Did you not wonder why I told you to alert all vessels to be on the alert for an attack - just minutes before it happened? I was party to a meeting with the Chinese where they stated that in half an hour, they would disable one naval vessel and keep on disabling vessels every five minutes until the marine invasion force being sent to Saint Matts was turned around and started to head back to its base." The president paused, to let it sink in. He then looked sadly around the room before he said, "We, gentlemen, have a situation here."

The president continued, "If they had been Americans instead of Chinese, they probably would have blown our ships to smithereens and killed thousands of the crew, but they are not Americans. They do not want to destroy us. After all, after Europe, we are their second largest export market. They only want to control us, just as they have been controlled by us, and the British before us, for the last couple of hundred years. What we have received is a warning. Not one American life has been lost but they have made their point and now we have to respond to it."

The Secretary of the Air Force interjected, "Perhaps an immediate nuclear strike on Saint Matts would send the message that we will not be toyed with."

"We aren't dealing with some Middle East terrorists who might use underwear bombs against us. We are dealing with a nation who has just demonstrated that they have advanced technologies that we are not even aware of. The Korean War was a lesson to the Chinese. It showed them they needed nuclear weapons and the rockets to deliver them if they wanted our respect. For decades, they have had nuclear weapons and the means to wipe out every city in America. Their rockets put a man on the moon two years ago. How many minutes do you think it would take for their rockets to destroy every city in America. Do you really want to get involved in a war with a nation who, if we wiped out 300,000,000 of them would still have a billion people left to carry on the fight?"

"A blockade to stop their importing of materials and exporting of manufactured goods might bring them to their knees."

"I see, and how do we implement this blockade if they can disable every vessel in our navy. In twenty minutes at four different sectors of the earth they have just disabled four different vessels even though we were expecting an attack. We do not even know how they did it but they did it and we have to assume that they can disable any vessel we have at will."

An aide whispered in the Secretary of the Air Force's ear. The Secretary nodded. The eyes in the room settled on him. He started to speak firmly, "Whatever technology the Chinese used to deploy their torpedoes around the world, it obviously required instant communication, and this could only be possible through their satellites. If we destroy their satellites, we can stop their technology dead in the water."

All the grey heads in the room nodded their head at this wisdom and insight. The President looked almost hopeful as if he had just seen the road to the Promised Land. "Do we have the capability of doing it?" he asked excitedly.

"Hell yes, we've been tracking their satellites for decades. Our missiles were ready to blast them out of the sky as soon as they had established their orbits."

"I like it. No casualties, no victims, just pieces of intrusive technology removed from their arsenal. How quickly can this be done?"

"Almost instantly Mr. President"

"How many satellites?"

"Approximately 300.".

"What do you think they are using these satellites for?"

"As far as we knew they were using them for global positioning, eye-in-the-sky spy satellites and global communications. Global positioning satellites allow missiles to be aimed when you can't use laser technology."

"

You are sure this will put whatever technology they are using, to neutralize our navy, out of commission?"

"Absolutely Mr. President, what else could it possibly be?"

"Well, that's what worries me. You don't really know how they tracked our ships, disabled them or escaped detection and quite frankly that worries the hell out of me."
"Perhaps what we do is tit for tat. They disabled four of our ships let's disable four of their satellites. Let's see if that makes them back off."

From half way down the table a general cleared his throat to get the President's attention.

"You got something to say, Bill?"

The white haired general nodded, "Mister President, the way I see it this is not the time to screw around. It seems our only hope of getting out of this mess is to shut the Chinese down and the only way we can see to do it, is to destroy their satellite communication system. If it was me and you knocked out four of my satellites, I would retaliate with everything I had. We won't get a chance to knock out the other two hundred and ninety-six satellites. Our only hope is that by removing these satellites, we will have leveled the playing field and made it difficult for them to retaliate.

"Thanks Bill. I see your point. I had hoped there was some way that we could have negotiated our way out of this situation, but I think you are probably right. It's moved a bit beyond what the diplomat's in the State Department can resolve. Has anyone else got anything to add?'
Eyes shifted around the room. Otherwise all sat mute and still.

"OK, I guess it's my decision."

He looked down at the table and looked over some notes he had made. He looked around the room. No one interrupted his thought process. He cleared his throat and said, "We are going to blast their three hundred satellites out of the sky. Let's get it done as soon as possible."

He stood up slowly, gathered his papers together and left the war room with his entourage trailing behind him. The meeting was adjourned. They all quickly headed for the exits.

Within two hours from U.S. missile bases all around the world, in one coordinated effort, three hundred missiles, valued at $150,000,000 roared into the sky. On the dark side of the earth the night sky was lit up with massive explosions as the missiles connected with the Chinese satellites.

Chapter 17
PAYBACK

The first representative of a world power to meet with Wilson Dodge, the new acting Prime Minister of Saint Matts, was General Lee. He warned of chaos and lawlessness that was about to descended upon the island. Wilson Dodge was warned by General Lee that he might be the next target of whoever was behind Victor Chumley's assassination. It was suggested that even the island's small security force could be part of a conspiracy.

General Lee's recommendation was for Dodge to declare a state of emergency with an immediate night time curfew until the threat was removed. He offered to secure the island with an armed force of five hundred soldiers. Lee explained to the acting Prime Minister that the Chinese construction crews were all professional soldiers who were assigned after their basic training to the construction division of the army.

Frightened, it took only a few seconds for Wilson Dodge to accept General Lee's offer. Within an hour, he had read a proclamation of martial law on the two radio stations and the one television station. The citizens of the island were sub ject to martial law and to a curfew that would be in effect from sunset until sunrise. Dodge publicly thanked the Chinese government for coming to Saint Matts' assistance in their hour of need.

The Chinese troops were swiftly deployed across the island. Roadblocks were set up at all major intersections. Vehicle traffic ground to a halt. The Chinese soldiers were supposedly seeking a mysterious assassin. The roadblocks made travel around the island almost impossible.

At the airport and the harbor, the long lines of desperate people trying to escape the island stopped growing. The curfew and numerous road blocks forced Mattitians to remain in their homes. Many of them saw Rick Wilcox's press conference where he again called upon the United States government to destroy the island. This further increased their anxiety and their desire to escape the possibility of a fiery death.

Surrounded by family and friends, Rob felt safe in the almost impregnable family compound. However, he was anxious about Barbara Wall's safety at the hotel. Unable to retrieve her from the hotel because of the travel restrictions, he decided his only option was to phone General Lee and seek his assistance. Put on hold for several minutes, he was finally put through to General Lee. Before he could make his request, General Lee took the opportunity to pass on a message from his government, "Your country, in its futile attempt to delay the inevitable, have destroyed our satellite system. These satellites cost the citizens of the People's Republic of China billions of dollars. Their destruction will not be ignored. Your government's foolish action has not diminished our capabilities."

At this point, Control inserted itself into the conversation, "**THE SECRETARY OF STATE HAS BEEN PATCHED INTO THIS CONVERSATION.** A few seconds later, the Secretary spoke, "**DOCTOR LYONS, IF SHOOTING DOWN THE CHINESE SATELLITES HAS FAILED TO FREE OUR NAVY FROM BEING ATTACKED THEN WE HAVE A SERIOUS PROBLEM. ASK THE GENERAL IF HE WILL AGAIN DEMONSTRATE THAT THEIR TECHNOLOGY. WE WOULD LIKE HIM TO RENDER POWERLESS THE MISSILE CRUISER, THE ATLANTA. IT IS ON MANEUVERS OFF ICELAND.**"

"Rob incredulously replied, "Nothing changed?"

"The satellites were irrelevant to our neutralizing your navy."

"You can still render powerless any vessel in our navy?"

"Yes"

"Can you render powerless our missile cruiser Atlanta?"

"One minute, please."

The connection went dead. Rob waited apprehensively. The line clicked on live again and General Lee said, "The missile cruiser has been rendered powerless."

The Secretary of State responded, "**DAMN, THE COMMANDER OF THE ATLANTA HAS JUST REPORTED TO THE SECRETARY OF THE NAVY THAT THEY ARE DEAD IN THE WATER.**"

Rob felt a dread and insecurity that made it difficult for him to continue. General Lee waited. Finally, Rob replied, "Thank you for that demonstration."

"It appears that your government has great difficulty in accepting the People's Republic of China's new status in the world. We will not be trifled with. Let your government know that I will come to your compound tomorrow at noon to further demonstrate our capabilities. We were obviously wrong in believing that disabling your naval vessels would be enough proof of our technical superiority. We are growing impatient with your obtuseness. We want your troops withdrawn from your bases surrounding the South China Sea."

"General Lee your concerns have been made known to my government and they will be prepared to further discuss your concerns tomorrow at noon. However, that was not the reason for my phone call. I had phoned to ask for your assistance. It is almost impossible because of your road blocks for us to travel around the island. I have a friend at the Saint Matts Hotel and Casino who I wish transferred to the Bishop family compound."

"Who is this friend?"

"A Miss Barbara Wall."

"Let me see what I can do.

Rob was put on hold. In a few minutes General Lee returned to say, "I have instructed one of our officers to bring Miss Wall to you at the compound."

"Thank you, General Lee."

General Lee terminated the phone call abruptly.

The Secretary of State was shaken by the ease in which the cruiser Atlanta had been left powerless. The United States had gambled and lost. The destruction of the Chinese communication satellites had not leveled the playing field. Without having fired a shot or losing one sailor, the greatest navy in the history of mankind had been defeated. She dreaded having to relay their status to the president. They were being backed into a corner. What was China going to demonstrate tomorrow that could be even more devastating? She knew she would not sleep well that night.

An hour after Rob had hung up with General Lee, he heard the clatter of a helicopter approaching. He went out on the porch and peered up into the sky. The white helicopter from the Chinese hospital ship with its flood lights illuminating the compound, started to descend beside the swimming pool. A dozen rifles in the compound were immediately aimed at it. It slowly settled, throwing up dust, leaves and dried grass. The blades gradually slowed. A door slid open on the side. A soldier got out, turned around and held out his hand. He helped Barbara Wall descend from the helicopter. Next to come out was her camera man. Their luggage was handed down. Rob stepped off the porch and headed to the helicopter to retrieve Barbara and her luggage. She smiled when she saw him. Rob thought she looked a bit shell shocked. He led her back to the porch. The soldier climbed back into the helicopter. Slowly the blades accelerated and with a mighty roar the helicopter climbed into the sky.

"Where am I," Barbara asked?

"You're in my family's compound."
"
How did you arrange this?"

"It's a long story but I'm just glad that you are here and safe. You know about the assassination and the state of emergency?"

"Of course, about an hour after it, Chinese troops had surrounded the hotel. Guests are now only being allowed to leave to go to the airport, under armed escort, to catch the planes that have been chartered to remove them. An hour ago, a Chinese officer showed up at my door with two armed soldiers and told me to pack. He said that they had been ordered to bring me to you. I refused to leave without my cameraman. I couldn't abandon him. The officer contacted someone and then came back and said he could come. We were escorted through the hotel to the large beach patio just as the helicopter landed. I had no idea what was going on or where they were taking me. You have no idea how glad I was to see you."

Rob's mother and father had taken up an expectant position behind Rob. Cousins, aunts and uncles had also encircled them. Rob turned and introduced Barbara to his mother.

"Mom. I would like you to meet my friend Barbara Wall."

His mother gave her a hug.

"Barbara, you must be hungry. Let's go on into the house. This good-looking man beside me is Rob's father, Colin."

Colin thrust out his hand. She shook it. Colin wasn't into hugging. His mother took Barbara's arm and guided her through the crowd of cousins towards the house. The cousins picked up their bags and carried them on to the porch.

His mother said, "We will arrange for you to sleep at my sister Mia's house on the other side of the compound. Your cameraman can stay with us."

Rob was amused. Old Victorian moralities lingered in Saint Matt's. His mother was protecting Barbara's reputation by making sure she did not sleep under the same roof with him. Barbara was led into the dining room. Monique Lyons scurried around setting the table, getting bowls of fish chowder that was always simmering away on the back of the stove. It was so thick that it was really a stew with corn meal dumplings and vegetables complimenting the large chunks of fish.

Rob listened to the rave reviews of his mother's chowder. Monique smiled and insisted that they all have seconds. She enjoyed entertaining and meeting new people. After being stuffed, they waddled out to the porch to take in the fresh breeze off the Caribbean. Later, under a night sky with a billion stars, Rob walked Barbara over to his aunt Mia's. Her son had already brought over her suitcase.

In the middle of the dark compound, he stopped and took her in his arms. Her lips were hungry for his lips. She thrust her breasts into his chest. Her hips rubbed against his. He kissed her long and hard. Finally, they pulled themselves apart.

"Maybe it wasn't such a great idea bringing you here. Maybe I should have gone back to the hotel."

"Yeah, well it's too late now. I got to meet your mother. There will be other nights."

"You're right. I guess, I will just have sleep all alone in my big bed."

"Poor boy, you'll survive."

"Speaking of survival, something big is coming down tomorrow."

"What?" "

"I'm not sure. The top honcho at the Chinese embassy has arranged some kind of demonstration to show the American government that they are no longer the marshal in Dodge City."

"Am I invited?"

"I do not see why not. Sleep tight. Don't let the bed bugs bite."

I haven't heard that saying in a long time. Do you know its history?"

"No, it's just an expression."

"Actually, it goes back several centuries to when beds had a network of ropes running across them that the mattress was placed on. Over time the ropes would loosen and must be tightened to stop the mattress from sagging. As well, back then bed bugs were a real problem."

"Thanks for the history lesson. You should get together with my father. Don't worry there are no bedbugs in Saint Matts".

"Well, maybe tomorrow, history will be made. See you in the morning."

Rob gave her another long lingering kiss and slipped his hand under her blouse.
"Down boy." "

OK. I'll see you in the morning. Come over for breakfast around 8:30"

"OK, see you then."

She gave him another long, lingering, soul churning kiss.

"Have I told you I love you?" she said.

Rob looked down at her; He had never wanted to be part of anyone's life like he wanted to be part of hers. "No," he said, "You have not told me you loved me. I just assumed it."

Barbara laughed and said, "You arrogant bastard."
"True, but this arrogant bastard loves you and wants to spend the rest of his life with you."."

"Are you asking me to marry you?"

"Yeah, but you think about it overnight. I love you."

Rob reluctantly let her go. He turned and walked back across the compound. Barbara opened the screen door and went into his aunt's house. A television was playing somewhere in the house. Rob knew his aunt would take good care of her. As he walked across the compound, he wondered what surprise the Chinese had in store for them at noon.

CHAPTER 18

Change

After breakfast, Barbara got together with her cameraman. Before breakfast, she had been on her satellite phone with her editor. She had told him that there were rumors that something big was going to happen early in the afternoon. He told her he would be ready for any new developments that she could bring him but first she should to do an update from the compound on the current situation in Saint Matts. So, under a bright blue Caribbean sky, with the Caribbean Sea and the shacks of Georgetown at the bottom of the cliff behind her, she recorded her report.

"Barbara Hall, reporting from the Caribbean island of Saint Matts, it was peaceful on the island last night after the turmoil caused by the assassination of Prime Minister Victor Chumley. The Deputy Prime Minister, Wilson Dodge, immediately assumed the Prime Minister's duties. His first official act was to declare martial law and to order a dusk to dawn curfew. He called upon soldiers of the People's Republic of China, who are currently involved in infrastructure development on the island, to assist in securing the island. This was a temporary measure until the assassination was fully investigated and the possibility of a conspiracy to overthrow the government had been ruled out. Here on this cliff overlooking the capital of Georgetown everything appears to be peaceful. We will be providing updates throughout the day."

Barbara and the cameraman did a quick on the spot editing job and then transmitted their report via the satellite phone to the editor, so he could have it on the early morning newscast.

After breakfast Barbara and Rob lounged around the compound's community swimming pool. Just before noon, they changed out of their bathing suits into more suitable clothes for the meeting with General Lee. At five to twelve, the embassy limousine, in its entire splendor, rolled into the compound. General Lee got out, dressed in military camouflage fatigues. His brown paratrooper boots gleamed in the sun. He glanced at his watch and then at Rob and Barbara Wall as he walked towards them. They were standing on the porch that encircled the ancestral home. Lee carried a shiny brown leather briefcase that matched his boots.

"Doctor Lyons. Miss Wall. Good Morning." He bowed politely to them both.

Barbara was surprised that he knew who she was. She wondered what else he knew.

Rob respectfully returned the bow and said, "General Lee can I get you a cold drink?"

"Only some water, please." "

Barbara went off to get glasses and a pitcher of water with slices of lemon and ice cubes in it. Rob gestured to a chair across from him. The Colonel put out his open hand indicating a problem.

"What I must discuss, I believe your government would want only you to hear. I would suggest that for security reasons that we retire to the gazebo on the back lawn. I would have suggested the study but if we have it bugged, then others may also have it bugged."

When Barbara returned with pitcher of water, Rob took it from her and told her that the Colonel wished to meet alone with him in the gazebo. She raised a curious eye, but being a guest, she was not about to protest.

Rob and the Colonel stepped down from the porch and walked around the house to the back gazebo. Rob placed the pitcher and glasses down and gestured towards a seat. The Colonel sat down gracefully. He neither looked sad nor happy. He rested his briefcase on the low table between them, snapped it open and took out a personal communication pad.

"This pad is hooked up to your satellites. For some reason our satellites are not functioning."

He smiled at his irony and looked at Rob intently before continuing, "I have activated the pad's microphone, so our translators can translate for the politburo. They in turn can respond in writing on my screen and ask me questions. Are you in contact with your people?"

Control instantly responded. **"THE SECRETARY OF STATE, SECRETARY OF DEFENSE AND THE PRESIDENT HAVE BEEN PATCHED INTO THIS TRANSMISSION."**

"Yes, the President and select members of his cabinet have joined us."

"As I told you yesterday, we are going to give you a demonstration of our technical capabilities, to make it very clear why we Chinese are no longer going to march to an American drum beat. Is the Secretary of Defense part of this communication?"
"Yes, he is."

"Please, ask him to make immediate contact with the commander of the cruiser Honolulu in San Diego harbor."

Control confirmed, **"WE HAVE LINKED THE SECRETARY OF DEFENSE TO THE COMMANDER OF THE CRUISER HONOLULU."**

Rob passed this on to General Lee, "We have linked in the commander."

"Is the commander on the bridge?"

"He is on the bridge." "

"Ask him what he sees about three hundred feet off the starboard bow."

Through the link with control, Rob could hear the commander exclaim, **"HOLY SHIT, WHAT THE HELL IS THAT?"** THE PRESIDENT EXCITEDLY INTERJECTED, **"WHAT DO YOU SEE?"** THE COMMANDER SAID, **"I THINK IT IS A SUBMARINE. IT IS A POINTED CYLINDER IN A VERTICAL POSITION POINTED AT THE SKY. HOW IN THE HELL COULD IT HAVE GOT INTO THE HARBOR WITHOUT BEING DETECTED?"**

"He thinks he sees a submarine and it isn't one of ours."

General Lee looked deep into Rob's eyes before he replied, "It is a submarine. An unmanned, drone submarine armed with two nuclear missiles that can travel at a speed of 15,000 miles per hour for 1,200 miles. It is also armed with two torpedoes capable of immobilizing the largest ships in the United States Navy, as we have already demonstrated, plus four conventional missiles, each capable of carrying a half ton of conventional explosives. Ask the commander what he now sees."

Rob could hear the commander respond, **"A HATCH ON THE SUBMARINE HAS OPENED. GOOD GOD, THEY HAVE LAUNCHED A MISSILE."** Rob heard the roar of it taking off as it climbed rapidly into the sky with its deadly cargo.

Rob stared at General Lee with shock and disbelief choked out, "You've launched a missile against the United States of America?"

"Yes, we have. Not just any missile but a nuclear missile, one that could have wiped out all of Washington, D.C. if that had been its intended target. However, this is merely a demonstration of our potential. We are not like America who in August of 1945 murdered several hundred thousand Japanese civilians at Hiroshima and Nagasaki in order to demonstrate their new weaponry.

Our missile's target is the nuclear testing site at the White Sands Proving Grounds in New Mexico. Except for a little radioactive fallout no one should be harmed. It is one of our smaller nuclear bombs. We made it the same size as America's first nuclear bomb, equivalent to 20 kilotons of TNT. The same size as your scientists detonated at White Sands on July 16th in 1945 when they tested their first nuclear bomb.

At 15,000 miles per hour, in approximately three minutes, this missile will have reached its target and exploded in an empty desert. Your Secretary of Defense should immediately contact the commander at White Sands. This is just one, of more than one thousand drone submarines, that we have deployed around the world. Each one is shadowing a United States naval vessel. We have the capability of leveling every major city in the United States and eliminating the lives of most Americans within minutes. However, we Chinese are a practical people. The United States is out second largest market after Europe. We need you and quite frankly you need our manufacturing capacity to supply your citizens with cheap goods. A war between our two nations would be stupid and self-defeating."

General Lee paused and looked at his watch. He then directed a question at Rob, "Ask the commander at San Diego what is going on."

The commander of the Honolulu who was now plugged into the communication quietly answered, **"THE SUBMARINE HAS DISAPPEARED AS IF IT HAD NEVER BEEN HERE."**

Rob said, "The commander says the submarine is gone."

"It is now miles away and miles below the surface, totally undetectable by your technology. These drones are capable of moving at a tremendous speed. You have no defense against them."

"What do you want?"

"You ask what the People's Republic of China wants. We want our territorial security. We had thought that back in the nineteen- seventies when we first proved that our missiles can deliver our nuclear bombs to any target in the world that America would back off. Instead, you expanded your bases in Australia, South Korea, Taiwan, Vietnam, Cambodia, Malaysia, Brunei, Philippines and Japan. You hemmed us in even more. We have bided our time and patiently developed weapons that we knew you would have no defense for. It is time for the United States to withdraw to North America. Neither we, nor any of the South East Asia countries need your protection of our trade routes nor do we need you undermining China's interests and jurisdictional rights."

Control interrupted, **"THE COMMANDER OF THE MISSILE PROVING GROUNDS AT WHITE SANDS NEW MEXICO REPORTS THAT THERE HAS BEEN A LARGE UNSCHEDULED EXPLOSION ON THE MISSILE RANGE."**

"MY GOD, WHAT HAVE THEY DONE?" the president cried out. **"OH MY GOD. OH MY GOD. GOD DAMN IT. THEY REALLY DID IT. WE ARE UNDER ATTACK. THIS IS WAR. I WANT THE FORCES ON FULL ALERT."**
The Secretary of Defense responded, **"THEY HAVE BEEN ON FULL ALERT ALL DAY."**
"WHAT DO WE DO? WHAT DO WE DO?" The president moaned quietly and lowered his head into his hands in despair.

The Secretary of Defense, almost in a whisper said, **"MISTER PRESIDENT, MY RECOMMENDATION IS THAT WE BUY TIME. IF THEY HAVE A THOUSAND MISSILES READY TO BE FIRED WITHIN SECONDS FROM SUBMARINE DRONES AND WE DO NOT HAVE SLIGHTEST CLUE WHERE THEY ARE, THEN WE HAVE NO**

DEFENSE AGAINST THEM. OUR WHOLE DEFENSIVE STRATEGY WAS TO TAKE OUT THEIR INTERCONTINENTAL MISSILES FROM THEIR LAND BASED SITES BEFORE THEY COULD BE LAUNCHED. NEGOTIATE WITH THEM. GIVE THEM WHAT THEY WANT. WE NEED TIME TO WORK OUT A SOLUTION TO THIS CHALLENGE."

The president was motionless for a few minutes before raising his head and in a resigned voice saying, "DOCTOR LYONS, TELL THEM THAT WE WILL LAY OUT PLANS FOR AN ORDERLY WITHDRAW FROM THE SOUTH CHINA SEA."

Rob had sat quietly listening to the discourse. Colonel Lee looked intently at Rob who appeared to be almost in a trance as he waited for a response. Rob finally responded, "Colonel Lee, the United States is prepared to withdraw its forces from the bas es surrounding the South China Sea."

"When will this start and be completed?"

"As soon as they arrange it."

"That answer is unacceptable to our leaders. Ninety days. You have ninety days to close these bases down."

The president snorted with derision, "NINETY DAYS. HOW THE HELL CAN WE BE OUT OF THERE IN NINETY DAYS? TELL HIM WE NEED A YEAR. ALSO, WE NEED TO BE ABLE TO EXPLAIN ALL THIS TO THE ELECTORATE. FOR CHRIST'S SAKE THIS IS AN ELECTION YEAR. THE MISSILE AND THE NUCLEAR EXPLOSION CAN BE EXPLAINED AS A NEW SECRET WEAPON WE ARE WORKING ON. OUR WITHDRAWAL FROM THESE BASES CAN BE EXPLAINED AS A COST CUTTING MEASURE TO LOWER TAXES."

The Commander of the Honolulu quickly interjected, "THAT MISSILE WAS PROBABLY SEEN NOT ONLY BY THREE HUNDRED SEAMEN ON THIS SHIP BUT HALF THE POPULATION OF SAN DIEGO. IT BROKE THE DAMN SOUND BARRIER AS IT ACCELERATED AWAY FROM THE SUBMARINE. A HARBOR TOUR BOAT WAS AS CLOSE TO THE SUBMARINE AS WE WERE. TOURISTS PROBABLY TOOK PICTURES OF IT. WE HAVE NEVER LAUNCHED A MISSILE FROM THIS NAVAL BASE. I AM NOT SURE HOW THE HELL WE COME UP WITH A LOGICAL EXPLANATION FOR WHAT THESE PEOPLE SAW."

The president responded angrily, "YOU JUST TELL ANY SON-OF-A-BITCH THAT ASKS THAT FOR NATIONAL SECURITY REASONS WE FELT IT NECESSARY

TO LAUNCH A MISSILE TO TEST OUR WEST COAST DEFENSES AND FOR NATIONAL SECURITY REASONS YOU ARE NOT AT LIBERTY TO DISCUSS IT ANY FURTHER. YOU TELL THOSE SEAMEN UNDER YOUR COMMAND THAT THE GODDAMN PRESIDENT OF THE UNITED STATES OF AMERICA HAS SAID THAT IT IS VITAL TO THE SAFETY OF THIS GREAT NATION THAT THEY NOT DISCUSS WHAT THEY SAW AND SO HELP ME IF THEY GET CAUGHT DOING IT I WILL SEE THAT THEY ARE TOSSED INTO THE BRIG FOR THE REST OF THEIR MISERABLE LIVES. GOT IT?"

The Commander of the White Sands Proving Grounds took this inopportune time to add his two cents. "WE HAVEN'T EXPLODED AN ABOVE GROUND NUCLEAR DEVICE SINCE THE NINETEEN SEVENTIES. HOW DO I EXPLAIN THAT? WHAT ABOUT THE RADIATION CLOUD THAT IS GOING TO DRIFT ACROSS NEW MEXICO INTO TEXAS AND THE GULF OF MEXICO?"

The president had worked himself up to full steam, "YOU TELL THE PRESS THAT FOR NATIONAL SECURITY REASONS IT WAS NECESSARY TO DETONATE A SMALL NUCLEAR DEVICE IN THE PROVING GROUNDS AND THAT ANY FALL OUT FROM IT WILL BE NEGLIGIBLE AND HARMLESS. ONCE AGAIN, YOU TELL THEM FOR NATIONAL SECURITY REASONS YOU ARE NOT AT LIBERTY TO DISCUSS IT ANY FURTHER. HAS EVERYONE NOW GOT IT?"

Rob appeared to have gone back into his trance like state as he followed the exchange that was taking place inside his head. When it ended, he told General Lee, "We cannot withdraw in 90 days. It will take a year."

General Lee quickly responded, "Korea in 90 days and Japan in 180 days and the others within a year."

"We will work towards those dates. It must appear to be our initiative. The missile and nuclear explosion can be explained as new weapons we are testing. The withdrawals can be explained as cost cutting measures.

"Really Doctor Lyons, your political strategies are of little interest to us as long as you meet the withdrawal targets. I suppose that if there were a change of president in the fall election, we would have to start our demonstration all over again. That would be a waste time, so we will go along with your spin on it. I would suggest that there are already too many people in your camp aware that the People's Republic of China launched a missile and exploded it within the United

States. Our embassy and ambassadors will deny that this demonstration took place."

The president took the opportunity to interject, **"IF ANYONE ON THIS COMMUNICATION LEAKS ANYTHING ABOUT THIS INCIDENT, I WILL CUT THEIR BALLS OFF AND FEED THEM TO MY PET ALLIGATOR. I'VE GOT A GODDAMN ELECTION TO WIN AND I NEED THIS CRAP LIKE I NEED A HOLE IN THE HEAD. LET'S GET ROLLING ON THE PLAN TO SHUT THOSE BASES DOWN AND WORK IT INTO MY ELECTION PLATFORM AS A TAX CUT. DOCTOR LYONS IS THERE ANYTHING FURTHER THEIR REPRESENTATIVE WISHES TO IMPART TO US?"**

"General Lee is there anything further?"

"No but I will be in contact."

General Lee stood, bowed slightly, smiled smugly and left the gazebo. He strode with dignity across the neatly cut green lawn and disappeared around the corner of the house.

Rob could see Barbara wall peering out through the screened door to the study. He waved at her as he stood up and walked towards her.

"What was that all about?", she asked.

"Unfortunately, my dear, as far as national security is concerned that meeting did not take place."

"Saying that to a reporter is like throwing gasoline on a fire. You can tell me. I never reveal my sources."

"I can assure you that if I told you the president and the cabinet would immediately know I had told you. It might then mean that you and I would not live to see the sun rise tomorrow."

CHAPTER 19

Leak

Behind closed doors, Rick Wilcox was doing the Times crossword puzzle when his private cell phone rang.

"Good afternoon Senator, you know who this is?"

Rick was startled to hear that metallic distorted voice once again. He replied, "No, I don't know who it is, but I do recognize the voice. What can I do for you?"

"Oh, it's not what you can do for me Senator. Do you love your family?"

"Of course, I love my family. Are you threatening me>"

"No Senator but get them out of Amarillo immediately."

"Why would I get them out of Amarillo?"

"Because young children are very susceptible to radiation poisoning."

"What the hell are you talking about?"

"Two hours ago, a nuclear bomb was detonated in the desert at the White Sands Proving Ground in New Mexico. That is less than three hundred miles from Amarillo. Depending on the wind and the weather, radioactive particles could be falling in Amarillo within hours or a couple of days. As I am sure you are aware the prevailing winds tend to be from the West."

"They haven't tested any nuclear weapons above ground in decades. You're talking about an underground explosion."

"Oh no, this was above ground and the "they" you refer to did not detonate it."

"

What are you saying? Terrorists detonated a bomb in the White Sands Proving Ground?"

"No, the missile, with the nuclear bomb was launched from a submarine in San Diego."

"Was it some kind of accident?"

"The submarine was Chinese."

"Holy shit are we at war?" "

Rick leaped out of his chair as if he had been hit by a lightning bolt. Leaning one hand on his desk and holding the phone to his ear.

"No, the president is covering it up and caving in to the demands of the Chinese."

"I don't believe it."

"Have I ever lied to you before?"

"No."

There was a click and then a dial tone. The call was ended. Senator Wilcox stood holding a dead phone to his ear. He slowly sank back into his fine Italian leather clad chair. He hit the speed dial to his wife's phone. She answered on the first ring.

"Sweet heart get the kids and get out to Tradewind Airport - now. I am arranging a charter to fly you to Washington."

"Rick, the kids are in school and daycare. I've got an appointment to get my nails done in an hour. What is it, life or death?" She gave a little laugh at the end.

"Yes, it's a life or death situation. Get out to the Airsky charter terminal at the airport. Don't pack and don't stop to talk to anyone about it."

"What is it?" Now, she sounded frightened.

"I can't tell you and I have to verify it, but the source of the information has always been right on the money, so I am not going to take any chances. If you stay in Amarillo you may be in danger in the next few hours, so get out of there now. GO! Let me set up the Charter." Rick hung up the phone, opened his business card holder and looked for the jet charter company he had used in the past. He dialed the number. A woman answered.

"This is Senator Wilcox. I need to charter a plane to immediately bring my family to Washington?"

"We book flights twenty-hours in advance, so it would be approximately this time tomorrow."

"No, I need my family flown out of there within an hour."

"Oh, sir, that would be impossible. Our pilots are all engaged."

"How much would you normally charge for such a charter"

"Forty thousand dollars.""

"Get a plane and pilot ready in an hour and I will pay eighty thousand dollars."

"Senator Wilcox let me see what we can do. Can you give me your phone number and I will phone you right back?"

Rick gave her the number. Then he got up and started to pace back and forth in his office. His boots left a noticeable foot print trail on the thick carpet. The phone rang five minutes later.

"Senator Wilcox? This is Trudy. The president of Airsky Charters is personally going to fly your family to Washington."

Rick smiled and thought, money conquers all obstacles. Now, he had to verify that the Chinese had really detonated a nuclear bomb. His mind switched into high gear. Who would know if a bomb had been detonated in New Mexico? It would have been heard and felt within a hundred miles. Constituents would be concerned. Some would be phoning their congressman. Which of the three congressmen for New

Mexico would be getting these phone calls? He went to a directory and saw that the White Sands Proving Grounds would be part of New Mexico's Second District. The congressman was Stuart Leadbetter. He dialed his number in the Rayburn House Office Building. An aide answered the phone.

"Could you tell Congressman Leadbetter that Senator Rick Wilcox is on the line."

"He's on another call right now, Senator. Let me slip him a note. He should just be a minute."

In less than a minute, Leadbetter was on the line, "Senator Wilcox, what can a humble New Mexican do for the junior senator of the mighty state of Texas"

"This could be a social call." Rick replied.

"I doubt it but I'm all ears."

"Have you been getting any calls this afternoon about an explosion in your district?"

"Yeah, my phone's been ringing off the hook. One of the old timers said it was so strong that it reminded him of the nuclear tests they used to do back in the fifties. It seems to have come from the direction of White Sands. Why? Was it felt in Texas too?"

"No, but I had a phone call about it and I thought if anyone knew what was going on you would."

"Well I phoned the base commander at White Sands and he confirmed they were doing some testing but that is all he said about it. He assured me that it was nothing to worry about."

"OK, thanks. Take it easy."

Rick hung up. He started to look at the maps of the congressional districts in San Diego. The 51st district looked like it was right down in the harbor. The congressman's office was only a few blocks from the water. He phoned the congressman's office.

A staffer answered the phone. "The congressman is out of town. Can I help you?"

"This is Senator Wilcox, are you from San Diego?"

"Born and bred."

"Has the congressman been getting any phone calls about a submarine and missile launching from San Diego harbor?"

"Yeah, funny you should ask that. The hotels on Coronado have been raising all hell about a missile launch that took place about two hours ago. It scared their guests. Apparently, a submarine nosed its way out of the water and launched the missile. Some of their guests were on a harbor tour and saw it. Our office in Chula Vista said something loud broke the sound barrier over the city."

"Has the Navy ever done this before?"

"Jeez, No, I've lived here all my life. I have never heard of such a thing. Launching a missile, from the middle of the city sounds dangerous as hell to me. What if the missile malfunctioned?"

"OK thanks a lot. I was asked if I knew anything about it."

Rick hung up, leaned way back in his swivel chair and propped his thousand-dollar black leather cowboy boots with their fancy tooling on his large and imposing desk. For a few minutes he lay back, almost horizontal, pondering what to do. His mysterious informant seemed to be very well informed. While his family should be out of any danger within the next few minutes, what about his constituents and his extended family? Would they be harmed by the radioactive fallout? How could he turn this event to his benefit? Had the time come for another press conference? Was this one more opportunity to increase his profile before the Republican convention blessed a presidential candidate? Why couldn't that candidate be him?

He brought himself back to vertical with a bang as his boots hit the floor. Grabbing the phone, he punched in his chief of staff's extension.

"Yes, Boss."

"I need you to set up another press conference. This is a big one, a matter of life and death. The United States of America has been attacked by a foreign country and the president's response has been to hide it. We need a really big room. See what you can round up on short notice. We need to be quick about it before someone else beats us to it. Get on it."

Rick smiled and slammed down the phone. He was pumped up. How many opportunities do you get like this in your life?

The staffer was able to get the congressional auditorium in the Capital Visitor Center. It could hold up to four hundred and fifty journalists. He then got the word out to the press by phone and electronic communication that something big was coming down at six o'clock. They were told that they would kick themselves if they missed it.

At five minutes to six, Rick Wilcox approached the rear entrance of the auditorium. He peeked through the curtains at the side of the stage. The glare of the television flood lights was blinding. The rumble of excited voices, raised in speculation of what new bomb Senator Wilcox was going to drop upon the nation, was deafening. The room felt like it was alive and vibrating.

Slowly, Rick crossed the floor of the stage. He was wearing his best western cut, charcoal grey suit. His pointed boots with their fancy stitching shone like mirrors. He stood quietly behind the podium. The room jammed with journalists instantly became so quiet that the silence felt thick and pressing on your ears. All eyes focused on Wilcox who quietly began to speak.

"I want to thank you all for coming on such short notice. This date will be remembered in the same way as generations before us remember that Pearl Harbor was attacked on December 7, 1941 and that the World Trade Center fell on September 11, 2001.

Today, a missile was fired from the middle of San Diego harbor by the People's Republic of China. The nuclear bomb it delivered exploded on United States soil in the state of New Mexico at approximately 12:05 P.M. The explosion was seen and heard by thousands of New Mexicans. Radioactive fallout from this bomb is now being spread across the state by the prevailing winds. It will increase atmospheric radioactivity all around the world – harming children and generations of children yet to be born. It has been decades since our atmosphere has been poisoned with radioactive fallout.

Prior to today, there had been only two other atomic bombs used aggressively in the entire history of mankind. In 1945 two bombs were dropped, one on Nagasaki and the other on Hiroshima. The justification by the United States for the using a weapon of mass destruction on Japan was to bring World War II to a speedy end. It was considered to be a justified payback for the sneak attack on Pearl Harbor.

Our government vowed that after Pearl Harbor never again would the United States be caught unprepared. Never again would innocent Americans die because we let our guard down. Never again would we have to use a nuclear weapon to right a wrong. Billions of dollars have been spent over the last half century to make sure that we could never be the victim of an unprovoked surprise attack.

Your current government has let you down. They have failed you miserably. Have they retaliated to today's unprovoked attack? No. Have they warned the citizens in the South West of the danger they face from radiation poisoning? Are they able to protect us from further unwarranted attacks? Who knows? They have not seen fit to even inform the citizens of the United States of the attack.

Why? Why is the greatest military force in the world frozen, waiting to be attacked? Are we cowards? Is our commander-in-chief scared to fight back? I say that I would rather fight to the death than roll over and play dead. I would rather be feared than be seen as a timid coward. If the commander-in-chief, of the greatest military machine the world has ever known, is not up to the job then he needs to be replaced – now. If he will not step down, then he needs to be impeached.

There is a microphone set up for questions. I will now take questions."

"Senator Wilcox - Jim Brown, El Paso Times, when our newspaper contacted the authorities' about the explosion that rocked New Mexico today we were told that they were doing necessary testing at White Sands for National Security. Who do we believe you or the authorities?"

"Has your newspaper checked for radioactivity?"

"Not to the best of my knowledge."

"I would suggest that you do that and when they do see that the radioactivity level has dramatically increased, you might want to ask these authorities why United States citizens are being put in mortal danger for national security."

Other reporters quickly lined up behind the mike. The next in line stepped up the mike.

"Pete Smith - Washington Chronicle, where did this bomb come from? How was it delivered?"

"It was delivered by a missile launched from a Chinese submarine in San Diego Harbor, just a few minutes before it exploded in New Mexico. Thousands of

Californians heard and saw this missile being launched right from the middle of our largest military base on the Pacific coast."

"How do we know it wasn't one of our own missiles fired from one of our own submarines?"

"That may well be what this administration will want to sell you, but don't you buy it. This missile was launched by a Chines submarine. The interesting question is why did the Chinese choose to detonate the bomb in a remote empty desert in New Mexico? Why was it not detonated where hundreds of thousands of casualties would have been the result? Is America being held for ransom? Why were we not able to protect ourselves from this attack which will be just as devastating to us as 9/11 was."

With that, Rick Wilcox looked around the room full of hundreds of reporters anxious to get on to the story. Some of them were already slipping out the rear to get a jump on the laggards. Rick could see it was time to bring the news conference to an end before he was left talking to an empty room. "That will be all folks. I am counting on you to bring the truth to your fellow Americans. God bless America and protect it in this time of great danger."

Their excited voices were raised to a high deafening pitch. Their fingers were busy transmitting the story and the video that they had all taken, on their personal communication devices, back to their editors. A security camera in the ceiling of the cavernous room had transmitted Rick Wilcox's greatest moment direct to the White House. The hotel microphones had also been patched in. The president was overwhelmed. His futile attempt to disguise the attack on the United States was being revealed like a stripper in a cheap gin joint. You had to go back in history to War of 1812 to find any other attack that had ever been made upon the continental United States. That one was by the British who burned down the White House.

There was no precedent to guide a president in how best to handle this situation. Attacks by Intercontinental ballistic missiles had been imagined and defenses had been constructed, but a thousand missiles being launched at once in a coordinated attack had never been considered. To now launch American intercontinental ballistic missiles and transport China into the stone ages was futile. Before the first missile had reached China, America would be reduced to ashes.

The president scanned the faces of his advisers. They avoided his gaze, staring off into space, at the table, at the ceiling, everywhere but him. Obviously, they were as drained of strategies as he was. They sat in silence. Finally, the Secretary of Defense feeling a greater responsibility for their predicament than the others, cleared his throat and threw out a possibility, "I would like to take out Wilcox and shoot him."

"Well, it is a little too late for that now. The genie is out of the bottle and it isn't going back in. Wilcox obviously has his eye focused on getting the Republican nomination," the president replied.

The Secretary of Defense, continued, "We all thought he was a nut bar when he suggested bombing that island in the Caribbean where the Chinese were intent upon establishing a naval base. However, we formed a strategy committee to study it as a possibility. You know what we need now is a distraction, a whipping boy."

One of the junior aids in the room interjected, "Whipping boy?"

The Secretary of Defense continued, "Yeah, whipping boy. Back in medieval times, if a young prince misbehaved and had to be punished, a whipping boy was called upon to take the beating that the young prince should have taken. Hopefully the prince was not a sadist and felt badly at seeing someone taking his punishment. It was a logical solution since the prince was a future king with a long memory and supposedly God's chosen, no one was prepared to punish him directly. We're kind of in the same boat. Rick Wilcox is going to put so much pressure on our administration that we are going to have to respond to the Chinese attack. It seems clear that we sure are not going to attack China. So, we are going to have to find a good substitute to attack. I can't think of any better whipping boy than the island of Saint Matts."

The president took this in and leaned back in his leather swivel chair, rocked back and forth a few times, made a couple of humming noises and then said, "Wouldn't the Chinese see an attack on Saint Matts as an attack upon themselves?"

"It all depends on how it is done. We tell the Chinese what we plan to do and get them to go along with it. What they want is for us to get the hell out of the South China Sea, so they can have their way with their neighbors without our interference. I don't think that they really care about Saint Matts. If we give them time to get their people off the island, they will understand that this is a face-saving strategy on our part. They have more or less said that they would prefer that your get elected so they do not have to break in a new president. They will sacrifice Saint Matts in a heartbeat to get their real objectives which are those huge oil reserves off the coast of the Philippines. Without the USA to come to their aid the Filipinos are going to be out of luck."

"Who might object?"

"Well, obviously the people of Saint Matts but we can buy them off. What the hell, the people on those islands are as poor as church mice. If we move in, transport them to Puerto Rico, give them the same citizen rights as Puerto Ricans, plus a check for $100,000 US dollars and compensation for any assets they are leaving behind, they will be out of there pronto. $10,000 is a typical annual salary for someone in Saint Matts. A hundred thousand in cash would be real money to them. There are only 40,000 on the island. We should be able to do it for less than five billion dollars. We spent more than that on researching that miserable Bradley armored personnel carrier."

"Why not just drop the bomb on the island today and save the five billion?" the President's Chief of Staff enquired.

The President's Campaign Manager quickly interjected, "Because we have a goddamn election to win. While bombing them today might get some Republican, red neck, conservative votes, our Democrat, bleeding heart bases in New York, Florida and Chicago would not be at all pleased. Since this is a Democrat administration, I think we have to take that into consideration. Any way, it's not your damn money. With what we are going to save by abandoning those China Sea bases, we won't even notice the five billion."

The president slouched down in his chair and stared at the ceiling for several minutes before replying, "OK, we have our whipping boy. Nuking the island will show the world that we are not standing idly by while we appear to be under attack. How do we spin today's attack?"

The president's chief speech writer saw this as his signal to respond, "Any responses, so far, have come at a very low level. What I would suggest is an immediate press conferences where you confirm that a nuclear bomb was detonated at the White Sands Proving Grounds and that our scientists have said it was a relatively small bomb and that there will be minimal radiation fall out. Almost all of it will be confined to the Proving Grounds. You then explain that it was a missile fired prematurely as a test by a visiting Chinese vessel on a technology exchange visit and that they have apologized for their misunderstanding of our testing procedures. We then explain that they had been asked to assist us in finding weaknesses in our west coast defenses because they were concerned that their merchant ships might be attacked by terrorists."

The spin doctor looked around the table to see if they were buying it. Several were nodding their head in agreement. He continued, "While we can accept that a missile was fired in error, America cannot ignore that an explosive device has been detonated on our soil by a foreign government. To ensure that the Chinese never again make such a mistake, we are going to demonstrate to them, and to the rest of the world, what they would face if such an error should ever happen again. On Sunday at noon we are going detonate a nuclear weapon on the island of Saint Matts in the Caribbean."

That got their attention. Several eyes popped open and they straightened up in their chairs. The speech writer then added the motivation for this aggressive stance and a sweetener for the bleeding hearts, "This is the island that China had planned to invest several hundred million dollars in building a Western Hemisphere naval base that threatened our national security. Prior to Sunday, the entire population of this remote island is going to be moved and comfortably settled in Puerto Rico. Anybody got questions or something to add."

The Secretary of State asked, "What about the monkeys? There are 80,000 wild monkeys on the island."

"Excuse me Madam Secretary, but the monkeys are expendable. They don't vote, and they don't pay taxes. Anybody else got anything they want to suggest or have another approach?"

The Chief Speech Maker and the President looked around the room. It was wall of blank faces. The president then said, "Ok, let's set this up. We need to get hold of the Chinese to immediately get them on side. Do we do this through Doctor Lyons?"

The Secretary of State said, "Let me patch him into this meeting but shouldn't we be contacting the new Prime Minister of the island first?"

The Chief Speech Maker replied, "Hell no, we'll contact him after we have informed the world. We don't want him screwing things up. It will be presented to him as a fait accompli. That way he won't have much choice but to support our plan. All we must do is figure out how little we have to pay him to get his full co-operation. After all what is he going to do about it? Declare war on the United States?" He smiled at that last bit of reality.

CHAPTER 20

Choices

W hat happened? Has the United States retaliated to the nuclear bomb detonated by the Chinese? Has war been declared? Is the world on the brink of incineration? These were the questions that kept rolling back and forth in Rob Lyons head throughout the afternoon after General Lee had left the compound. Since he was under constant surveillance by Control in Washington, he could not discuss his knowledge of the Chinese attack with Barbara Wall, his father or anyone.

He nervously paced around the compound, visited an aunt, talked to his father and climbed the mountain to talk to the cousins who were guarding the rock cut. They had planted dynamite in the heights that could cause a rock slide into the cut if the Chinese should attempt to enter the compound. He got Barbara to go for a swim with him in the pool and then watched while she and the cameraman recorded and sent a report back to the network that nothing was going on in Saint Matts. He tried to read but couldn't. Every few minutes he would check his computer and television to see if there was any news about the explosion.

The sun sets early as you get closer to the equator. By six p.m. it was already dark. He was eating his dessert when Control finally contacted him.

"DON'T RESPOND DOCTOR LYONS, THE PRESIDENT WISHES TO MAKE IMMEDIATE CONTACT WITH THE CHINESE LEADERS, CAN YOU SET IT UP. WE SEE THAT YOU ARE AT DINNER IF YOU CAN SET IT UP TAP THE RING TWICE."

Rob tapped the ring twice and then excused himself from the table. He went to the phone in his father's study and looked at the small screen on the phone for the last call he had received from the Chinese embassy. He hit the speed dial. The phone was answered by an aide. Rob identified himself and asked to speak to General Lee. It took a few minutes for Lee to come to the phone.

"Good evening General Lee, I've received a request from the White House. They wish to make immediate contact through me to your leaders. Can that be set up?"

"Yes, Doctor Lyons. While you are on your way to the embassy, I will set it up. I will have one of the guards, stationed at the road into your compound, escort you to the embassy."

"It will take me about fifteen minutes."

Rob came out of the study and told his parents and Barbara that he was on his way to the Chinese Embassy. His father asked if he thought that was a good idea considering the circumstances. Rob hesitated for a minute and responded that he felt he could trust General Lee and that really, he had no choice; it was part of his job. He left the house and drove the Subaru WRX through the dark rock cut, conscious of the tons of rocks that could hurtle down on the car if his cousins had an accident and detonated the dynamite. As he emerged from the cut, a soldier, with a flashlight, was in the middle of the road flagging him down. The soldier leaned in the window and shone the light on Rob's face.
"
Doctor Lyons, I go with you."

"OK, get in,"

The soldier got in beside Rob. They took off down the dark road. Rob noticed several soldiers loitering around the entrance to the rock cut. Driving through Georgetown Rob found it unusual but not surprising to find the streets empty. The curfew was obviously effective. They pulled up to a gate in front of the embassy. The soldier in the car with him opened his door and stood with one leg in the car and one outside as he told the guard in Chinese to open the gate. The gate rolled back. Rob drove into the Chinese courtyard and stopped by the massive main door. His companion got out and led Rob up the steps into the embassy. They walked down a wide hall way with marble floors, their footsteps echoing in what appeared to be a deserted building. They came to a door which the soldier held open for Rob and then closed it behind Rob after he entered. The soldier then stood at attention in the hallway, waiting to accompany Rob back to the compound.

General Lee was sitting at his desk smoking a cigarette. He gestured imperiously for Rob to take a seat across from him. "Doctor Lyons, I have an open communication line to my leaders. How can we assist you?"

Control responded in Rob's ear, **"THE PRESIDENT AND HIS ADVISORS HAVE BEEN PATCHED IN. THE PRESIDENT WANTS YOU TO COMMUNICATE THE FOLLOWING TO THE CHINESE."**
The president then began to speak, and Rob transmitted it exactly as he heard it.

"THE PRESIDENT OF THE UNITED STATES OF AMERICA WOULD LIKE TO THANK YOU FOR ARRANGING THIS MEETING ON SUCH SHORT NOTICE. THE INCIDENT TODAY HAS CREATED CHALLENGES THAT REQUIRES THE AGREEMENT OF THE PEOPLE'S REPUBLIC OF CHINA TO RESOLVE. WE HAVE BEGUN TO EVACUATE OUR BASES AND FORCES FROM THE SOUTH CHINA SEA. WE IN TURN WOULD REQUEST THAT YOU WITHDRAW YOUR PERSONNEL FROM THE ISLAND OF SAINT MATT'S WITHIN THE NEXT TWO DAYS. WHILE THIS IS BEING DONE WE WILL BE EVACUATING ALL THE CITIZENS FROM THE ISLAND. THEY WILL BE TRANSFERRED TO PUERTO RICO, BE GIVEN AMERICAN CITIZENSHIP, A HUNDRED THOUSAND DOLLARS AND BE COMPENSATED FOR THE LOSS OF ANY ASSETS THEY HAD ON THE ISLAND. ONCE THE EVACUATION IS COMPLETED, WE WILL THEN BE DETONATING A NUCLEAR BOMB ON THE ISLAND AT NOON ON SUNDAY. WE FEEL THAT THIS COURSE OF ACTION IS NECESSARY IN ORDER FOR OUR CITIZENS TO BELIEVE THAT THE BOMB THAT WAS DROPPED ON THE UNITED STATES WAS NOT DONE WITHOUT RETALIATION."

Rob almost choked on what he had just transmitted for the president. He could not believe it. His beautiful island, his beloved ancestral home, wiped off the face of the earth. A weak sovereign nation that had made no aggression towards the United States was now being made a scape goat by a powerful nation rendered toothless by a foreign power.

The General's eyes opened wide with surprise, but he said nothing as he scanned the computer screen in front of him waiting for a response from Beijing. Time stood still. Finally, General Lee responded.

"The People's Republic of China recognizes that while our actions today were necessary that we feel that it is not in our best interest of our economy to cause panic and fear in the United States of America. We agree that it is important for Americans to believe that they are still citizens of the most powerful nation in the world. We will commence our evacuation from the island of Saint Matts immediately."

The president responded, and Rob transmitted.

"WE THANK YOU FOR YOUR UNDERSTANDING AND LOOK FORWARD TO COOPERATION BETWEEN OUR TWO GREAT NATIONS "

General Lee stood, Rob stood, and they bowed to each other. General Lee escorted Rob to the door and opened it. The guard accompanied Rob back to the compound.

When he stopped the car, Control interrupted his thoughts. **"DOCTOR LYONS, THE PRESIDENT SAYS TO TELL YOU THAT HE WILL BE GOING ON TELEVISION TO ADDRESS THE NATION IN TWO HOURS. WE REMIND YOU THAT YOU ARE SWORN TO SECRECY AND AS FAR AS THIS MEETING IS CONCERNED, IT NEVER TOOK PLACE."**

Rob stepped into the house. His father and Barbara were in his father's study. Barbara was laughing at some story his father was telling. Colin looked up when Rob came into the room. He did not like the look he saw on Rob's face. "How did the meeting go?" he asked.
"There was no meeting."

"I thought you had left to go the Chinese embassy."

Rob sadly repeated what he had just said." "There was no meeting."

Colin then understood." "Would you like to join me and Barbara in a drink? She is sampling some of my best twenty-five-year-old Scotch."

"I think I would like that very much."

Colin got some ice out of his ice bucket and poured a good stiff shot. "Drink up my boy, it will cure what ails you."

"It will take much more than this."

"What's wrong?"

"I can't discuss it, at least not right now, but I will in two hours. The president will be addressing the nation."

He took a sip of his whiskey, the ice cubes tinkled against the side of the heavy crystal classes. He leaned back closed his eyes for a few seconds, opened them and sat up straight and said, "I can no longer work for the United States government. As of this moment, I am resigning my position in the State Department."

Barbara and his father stared at him as if he had lost his mind. Rob started to laugh. He took another sip

.

The disembodied voice of Control took this moment to interject, "**DOCTOR LYONS, ARE YOU SERIOUS? ARE YOU SURE YOU WANT TO DO THIS? IT MEANS THAT YOU ARE ON YOUR OWN. YOUR INCOME WILL CEASE. ANY FURTHER EXPENSES YOU INCUR WILL BE NOT PAID BY THE DEPARTMENT, INCLUDING YOUR AIRFARE BACK TO WASHINGTON. WE ALSO REMIND YOU THAT YOU SOLEMNLY SWORE THAT YOU WOULD SUPPORT AND DEFEND THE CONSTITUTION OF THE UNITED STATES AGAINST ALL ENEMIES, FOREIGN AND DOMESTIC: THAT YOU WOULD BEAR TRUE FAITH AND ALLEGIANCE TO THE SAME, AND THAT YOU WOULD FAITHFULLY DISCHARGE THE DUTIES OF YOUR OFFICE.**"

Rob ignored the voice in his ear and turned to his father and Barbara and said, "If you have not guessed already, I am linked in electronically by satellite to the State Department. They can hear and see everything that I hear and see. I have a device implanted in my ear that they use to communicate with me. This ring transmits images. Interestingly it is also a very dangerous weapon. They have just responded to my resignation by telling me that I am on my own and they will not pay my way back to Washington. I am now informing them that my intentions, now, are to never leave this island. They have also reminded me that I have sworn to support and defend the Constitution of the United States. I am now informing them that the United States is in violation of the fundamental principles of international law and treaties. I am also pointing out to them that if they continue with their proposed plan that they are guilty of offenses for which the Nuremberg defendants, at the end of the Second World War, were convicted and sentenced - some to death by hanging. Unlike those Nazi participants, I will not be put in a position of defending my participation by pleading that I was only following orders."

Colin and Barbara stared at Rob as if he had lost his mind. Barbara was reminded of the crazies, who were off their meds, who wandered the downtown streets loudly shouting obscenities at people that only they could see

The Secretary of State was patched in by control, **"DOCTOR LYONS, WHAT ARE YOU DOING? THIS IS NEITHER THE TIME NOR PLACE FOR YOUR PERSONAL VIEWS, WHATEVER THEY ARE; YOU ARE NOT TO INTERFERE WITH THE POLICIES OF YOUR GOVERNMENT. YOU ARE A REPRESENTATIVE OF THE UNITED STATES OF AMERICA. YOU ARE AN EMPLOYEE OF THIS GOVERNMENT. I WILL HAVE YOU ARRESTED FOR TREASON AND BROUGHT BACK TO THE UNITED STATES IN CHAINS. IF YOU DID NOT KNOW IT, LET ME INFORM YOU THAT TRAITORS ARE EXECUTED. WHATEVER YOUR PROBLEM IS, IT CAN WAIT UNTIL WE ARE THROUGH THIS CRISIS."**

"It cannot wait, and I will do all I can to stop the United States of America from destroying this island."

Colin looked beseechingly at Rob and said, "Who in the hell are you talking to?"

Rob turned to his father and said, "In about an hour, the president is going to address the nation and you will understand then what my resignation is all about. You won't want to miss it."

He left the room and walked over to the wall at the edge of the cliff. He looked down into Georgetown and the harbor. He couldn't believe it. It had only been an hour. The harbor was a hive of activity. Flood lights lit up the three Chinese transportation ships. The cranes on the ships were swinging over to the wharf and picking up vehicles and other equipment, lifting them high into the air and slowly depositing them inside the cargo holds of the ships. From this distance the vehicles looked like toys. He could also see a line of people snaking up the gangway into the ship. He sat down on the wall facing the harbor, his feet dangling over the edge. His ring broadcast the scene back to Washington. Barbara left the house and came over to the wall to join him.

"What's going on with those ships?"

"The Chinese are leaving the island."

"Why?"

"When the president gives his speech, all will be revealed. You are going to be in the middle of one of the hottest stories in the world."

"You have got to be kidding."

"No, I am not kidding. The interesting question is whether you will stick around to report on it or not."

She reached out and put her arm around Rob. He stared down at the ships being loaded. They sat that way for a long time. They were too far away to hear the sound in the busy harbor. A sea breeze rattled the palm fronds above them. Finally, Rob said, "We better get in or we are going to miss the big show." He held her hand as they walked back across the lawn. He could hear the TV blaring as soon as they got in the house. It was loud. A sign that someone's hearing was not what it used to be. His father rarely wore his hearing aid because he found it to be irritating.

The president was ready. This communication with the electorate was going to be short with no chance for the reporters to ask questions. He had run through it six times with his aides. It was almost memorized, but he had stopped short of memorizing it because he wanted it to sound fresh and unrehearsed. He could hear the ebb and flow of the crowd on the other side of the curtain. They were speculating on what he was going to say. The whole idea was to beat the media to the punch on the reporting of the dropping of the bomb.

The senators and congressmen had been given priority seating. Richard Wilcox was in the first row. The cabinet and the civil servant department heads were seated behind them. The rest of the mob was made up of the media. Some were forced to stand at the back. A wall of security surrounded the building.

In the glare of the media's flood lights, the press secretary slowly crossed the stage and took the podium. The room immediately became quiet. He thanked them for coming on such short notice, introduced the president and then left the stage.

The president walked briskly out to the podium. He wanted to appear strong and vital, a leader, a man in charge, not the leader of a second-tier country.

"Mr. Vice President, Mr. Speaker, members of the Senate and the House of Representatives:

Today is a remarkable day in our history. In error, a foreign power has detonated a nuclear device within the continental United States. While launched with good intentions, the logic and severity of their act are questioned. The intent of the People's Republic of China was to prove to us that our defense of the trade routes between our two countries were not as secure as we had believed them to be. We had refused to accept this reality before, but it has now been proven to us. We thank the People's Republic of China for enlightening us.

Fortunately, not one American has been harmed by their explosion. They deliberately exploded their device over the White Sands Proving grounds in New Mexico. This remote desert location is where we first tested our own nuclear devices in 1945. The historical significance of their test target has been noted.

While I stress that China remains a close friend and our greatest trading partner, the United a States of America is unable to ignore what could have been a tragic act if there had been a miscalculation on their part. It has forced us to send them a message that such dangerous tests must not be repeated. We will send this message be detonating a nuclear device in a territory that China covets.

As Commander-and-chief, I have directed that on Sunday at noon, a nuclear device is to be exploded and destroy the naval base that the People's Republic of China was establishing on the Caribbean island of Saint Matt's. This will render this island uninhabitable for the next five hundred years.

As I speak, the first waves of our largest military transport planes are on their way to this island to evacuate its few thousand inhabitants. They will be transported to the island nation of Puerto Rico. The Chinese troops who were on the island of Saint Matts have already commenced their departure. A marine expeditionary force will immediately set up a permanent blockade around the island to prevent any ships from travelling within 50 miles of the island. Our air force will turn away all unauthorized aircraft flying within 50 miles of the island.

I believe that I interpret the will of Congress and the people of the United States of America when I assert that we are required to send this strong message to the People's Republic of China. It is not wise to test the military might of the United States of America - no matter how good the intentions are.

With our confidence in our armed forces, with the determination of our people, we remain strong. So, help us God. I ask that the Congress and the people of the

United States to stand firm with me in the face of these challenges. God bless America and all Americans."

The president looked up from his teleprompter. His cabinet and political appointees had been told to loudly cheer at this point; the choir owed their next meal to this man. They stood and cheered for team America. The sheep in the room joined in. They stood up clapping and cheering. Hearing which way, the wind was blowing, the Congress seated at the front of the room, as a whole, got their feet and cheered like the true patriots they were. Only the reporters at the back of the room held back. They were trained to look behind the magician's curtain. The president's speech raised more questions with them than it answered.

In Saint Matts, due to the curfew, most of the population would be watching a speech by the president of a foreign nation. However, within minutes almost every citizens of the island wanted to know what the hell was going on. They loved and were proud of their island just as much as Americans love and are proud of the United States. While the rest of the world might see Saint Matts as an insignificant dot on the World's map, they saw their nation as the center of their universe. They were proud to be an independent sovereign nation with representation at the United Nations and a proud member of the British Commonwealth of Nations. When they sang their national anthem, they did it with enthusiasm, dignity and pride. For hundreds of years their ancestors had inhabited this island. It was their home. It was their identity. It was their anchor. It was their refuge from a cruel, harsh world.

Colin sat stupefied as the president's address came to an end. His Saint Mattitian passport was an accident of history. If he had not met and fallen in love with Monique, he would never have learned to love Saint Matts. Being a Canadian by birth, he had never really felt totally comfortable living in the United States. The annoying racial slights that Monique had encountered almost every day that they had lived in the United States were his slights too. The polarization of the races in the United States made it a stressful place to live. The fact that he was often the only one in the room who did not buy into the United States being the best country in the world also made him uncomfortable. He often felt like an impostor.

He looked like a typical, fat, white, American executive. He even sounded like one from maybe Michigan or upper New York State, but on the inside, he never felt wholly part of team America. The American arrogance, of assuming that the American way was the only way, was not well received by the foreign executives that came in contact with Bull & Goring. As the head of their international operations, Colin had been sensitive to this blind spot in the American character and as a fellow foreigner he had done his best to counter act it. He turned to Rob, who was now sitting beside him, "You knew this was coming down?"

"I did."

"You couldn't tell me?"

"I had sworn an oath."

"You are resigning?"

"I don't have a choice. I have resigned."

"Are you going to evacuate?"

"No, I am not."

"What if they forcibly evacuate you?"

"If it comes to that, then they had better be prepared for a fight. I would rather die fighting for the preservation of Saint Matts than be executed in the United States for treason."

"So, by Sunday the bomb will have been dropped and we will all be dead."

"Perhaps, but in my heart, I cannot accept that a civilized powerful country would do this to a small weak nation. Obliterating the island of Saint Matts is unjust. It is evil. I can't believe that the world will just stand by, do nothing and allow this to happen. Saint Matts is a sovereign nation, just like two hundred other big and small nations in the world. If America can destroy Saint Matts so cavalierly then it can destroy those other countries too."

"Yes, it is evil, and it is wrong, but it is not without precedence. The United States of America has the most powerful armed force in the world. If you stand up against them, they will do their best to destroy you. Look at the embargo on the island of Cuba. It went on, decade after decade."

"Yes, but Fidel Castro never backed down. They could never assassinate him. God knows, they tried. He lived to be a very old man and died in his bed. It was tough but the Cuban's survived. What about you Dad? Are you going to leave?"

"Not without you and not without your mother. Son, I am an old man. I've done everything I ever dreamed of doing and achieved far more than I ever dreamed of achieving. What better way to die than as a martyr for a cause. You are still young. You can live to fight another day. Being my son, I am protective of you and I would rather you leave this fight for Saint Matts to me. If someone needs to be sacrificed let it be me."

"My age and stage in life has nothing to do with it. I intend to stay right here to the bitter end."

"OK, now that we know where we are going, it is time for me to find out how the rest of the family feels. The Bishop family roots are deep in this island. We have a fortune invested here. It is an ancient trust that our ancestors left us to protect and grow."

Colin pointed to Rob's ear and his ring.

"They have heard all this haven't they?'

"They have heard it, recorded it and passed it on to the highest levels."

"Well, we have but one life to give. Give me liberty or give me death."

"I think I heard that one before. Was it George Washington?"

"Yeah, you did, Washington was at the meeting, but it was Patrick Henry at the Virginia Conference in 1775, in his call to arms against the British navy, the most powerful military force in the world at that time."

With that bit of history, Colin limped off to gather consensus. Rob turned to Barbara, who had sat quietly through their discussion, and said to her, "This is not your fight."

"Oh, you are very wrong. You think that just because I am an American that I can't see the injustice? I understand your love of these lush green mountains, beautiful beaches, clear waters and its kind, generous people. I am ashamed that my country chooses to be so blind that they are going to destroy this Eden. As a reporter it is my duty to change their mind."

Rob held up his hand to indicate that Barbara should pause in the vehement declaration of her intentions. He pointed at his finger and said, "We are not alone here." He proceeded to take off the ring. He held it in his hand wondering what to do with it.

Control responded, "**DOCTOR LYONS PLEASE DON'T DO THIS. WE WILL NOT BE ABLE TO ASSIST YOU IF YOU CUT OFF THIS LINK.**"

"No, you don't understand. I don't want you to assist me. I am no longer a State Department employee. As a matter of fact, the Secretary of State considers me a traitor and I am sure orders will go out to have me shot on sight. I also want this goddamn thing out of my ear."

"**SORRY, BUT WE HAVE BEEN INSTRUCTED THAT IF YOU MADE SUCH A REQUEST THAT WE WOULD NOT BE ABLE TO COMPLY WITH IT.**"

"Who issued that instruction?"

"**WE ARE NOT AT LIBERTY TO DISCUSS IT.**"

Rob was still standing, holding the ring, then he remembered that his father had a small safe inside one of the cupboards of his study. He went over to it. He twirled the dials and then entered his birth-date, his father's and his mother's birth-dates. The safe clicked open. He placed the ring in it and shut the door. It left the ring blind, deaf and in the dark.

What was that all about?" Barbara asked. She found Rob's conversations with someone she could not see or hear unnerving.

"State is not happy that I have severed their eyes and ears. Unfortunately, they will not remove their speaker from my ear. So, they can still talk to me. This could be a problem until I can figure out how to get it out of there but at least we can talk freely without them eavesdropping on us by means of the ring. Which reminds me, this room is bugged? Let's go for a walk. You were about to tell me how you were going to save Saint Matts."

They stepped out onto the grass and walked towards the wall at the edge of the cliff. Rob put his arms around her and they kissed. There was a refreshing sea breeze. He felt like he could hold her forever.

"Rob, I want to record a video with you tonight, edit and send it to the network."

"Will they broadcast it? The government will lean on your executives to stop it.".

"If they don't, there are several internet publishing sites where it can be posted. Millions of people will be searching the internet for information about Saint Matts."

"OK, let's do it."

Barbara tracked down her cameraman. He quickly set up his equipment in Colin's study. Barbara put Rob in a very tropical, white wicker, winged back chair and sat across from him in another. A round mahogany table on a small rich Persian carpet was between them. She began slowly, "This evening we are coming to you from the Eastern Caribbean island of Saint Matts where we are interviewing Doctor Robert Lyons. He has just resigned his position as an analyst with the State Department. Why have you resigned your position with the State Department Doctor Lyons?"

"Four days ago, I was sent to Saint Matts by the State Department to investigate rumors that the People's Republic of China was intent upon establishing a naval base on the island. I confirmed that this was their intention. Even though this is no longer their intention, the United States of America has said that they will be dropping a nuclear bomb on the island of Saint Matts on Sunday at Noon. My conscience does not allow me to be associated with a government that would initiate an unprovoked attack act upon a defenseless sovereign nation. "

Rob paused here to let it sink in before he continued, "It is a direct violation of the United Nations charter which binds nations to seek the resolution of disputes by peaceful means and requires the authorization of the United Nations before a nation may initiate any use of force against another, beyond the inherent right of self-defense against an armed attack. One hundred and eighty-three countries, including the United States, have signed this charter. Saint Matts is a tiny independent sovereign nation of 40,000 citizens with a defense force of only a few hundred. Saint Matts has certainly not attacked the United States, yet the United

States is effectively going to violate Article 15 of the United Nations Charter which states that everyone has the right to a nationality and no one shall be arbitrarily deprived of his nationality nor denied the right to change his nationality. By destroying this island, the United States will thoughtlessly and arbitrarily deprive every citizen of this worldly paradise of their nationality. I cannot be part of such a travesty."

Barbara then asked, "Why would the United States, a nation of 350,000,000 people, with an armed force of several million, want to annihilate what would be the population of a small American town?"

"Politics! It is all about politics. The People's Republic of China earlier today dropped a nuclear bomb on the United States. They were provoked in to doing it when the United States destroyed every one of their three hundred communication satellites last night; satellites that had taken them years and billions of dollars to launch. The United States made a horrible strategic mistake in destroying these satellites. They had thought that their destruction would disable a new technology the Chinese had developed that effectively removed the super power status of the United States. This aggressive attack on their satellites had no effect upon their new technology.

The reality is that the United States is now as defenseless as any other country in the world. Interestingly the Chinese carefully dropped the nuclear bomb in such a way that that no one was physically harmed. It was meant to be a warning. However, it has been a blow to the prestige of a president who is seeking a second term in November. In a selfish, callous disregard for the citizens of the sovereign state of Saint Matts he is attempting to regain prestige with the electorate by destroying a country that had a rather remote connection to the People's Republic of China. Saint Matt's, has done nothing to provoke this destruction."

"Is it not true that the Prime Minister of Saint Matts had signed an agreement for the establishment of a Chinese naval base on the island of Saint Matts in direct violation of the Monroe Doctrine"

"The prime minister you are talking about was assassinated yesterday. No agreement was ever signed by him nor could it have been until it was debated and passed by Saint Matts' democratically elected parliament. The Monroe Doctrine which was a statement made by a president two centuries ago has never had any justification or acceptance under international law. It was meant to stop the European nations from regaining their colonies in the Americas. These days, what two sovereign nations agree between themselves is none of the business of a third nation.

The days of the United States feeling free to invade such countries as Grenada and Panama have come to an end. Thanks to the Chinese, a new balance of power has been born and the world is now safer because of it. No longer can the United States make arbitrary decisions that destructively impact the other ninety-five percent of the world's population who are not Americans. No longer can America disregard the impact of their aggressive behavior on innocent populations beyond their borders."

"What if that the entire populations of Saint Matts were to be safely removed by the United States prior to the dropping of the bomb and compensated for any financial loss that this exile will cause. Would this not be sufficient recompense to permit the destruction of the island?"

"Not everything in this world can be bought. The entire population of Saint Matts is not going to leave the island. I, for one, am not going to leave nor are my immediate and extended family. What are they going to do? Forcibly remove us? Is the army going to hunt us down like the 80,000 monkeys on the island? Put us and them in cages for removal? If that is their plan, then American soldiers will die trying to do it. This island is my ancestral home. I love it as much as any American loves the United States. We refuse to be dismissed and treated as if our existence does not matter.

I am calling upon the citizens of all free sovereign nations in the world to express their horror over the intended act of the United States of America to destroy every living thing on this island. I am calling upon the governments of the world to protect Saint Matts because if the United States can destroy Saint Matts, they can destroy their nation as well. I am also calling upon the People's Republic of China to cease withdrawing their workers from Saint Matts. I am calling upon China to stay and prevent the UnitedStates from destroying this beautiful island."

Barbara signaled to the cameraman that she was finished. He started to pack up his equipment. She turned to Rob, "That was really good. I am going to send it to the network but at the same time I am going to put it on the internet as quickly as I can. It is too important to depend upon the network to decide whether they have the balls to show it or not. Time is running out. The network will probably fire me as soon as they find out I pre-empted them on the internet. So, I guess you are going to be stuck with me staying with you in Saint Matts."

Rob smiled and put his arms around Barbara. Within An hour the interview was posted on numerous sites on the internet. An hour after that, hundreds of other sites had picked it up. By the time the sun came up in the morning, millions of people around the world had seen and heard Rob's impassioned plea. Numerous networks had picked it up and broadcast it along with videos showing Saint Matt's natural beauty – the lush, beautiful green jungles, the mountains soaring thousands of feet into the blue skies, the pristine beaches, the crystal-clear flowing river waters, the quaint villages and most of all the happy, gentle people. The editors and directors especially focused in on Barbara's pictures of baby monkeys being nurtured by their mothers, as their fathers stood on guard, protecting their families from dangerous prey.

The irony was not lost on the Society for the Prevention of Cruelty to Animals. They were flooded with messages from chapters of the SPCA in every town and city in America demanding that not only the monkeys, but all the innocent dogs, cats and other animals be saved from slaughter by the dropping of a nuclear bomb on the island of Saint Matts. Every pet owner in the United States was urged to contract not only the president but their local congressman and senator. Foreign animal rights urged their politicians to get involved in saving the animals of Saint Matts. Saving the people of Saint Matts became of secondary importance.

CHAPTER 21

Fight

Before Rob's interview appeared on the internet, the Secretary of State was phoning Wilson Dodge, the new beleaguered prime minister of Saint Matts. He was busy planning a state funeral for Victor Chumley. Protection of the island, from whatever mysterious forces were loose, had been abdicated to the Chinese troops. No one had yet made him aware that the Chinese troops had started to withdraw from the island. He was also not aware that the island was scheduled for destruction. Optimistically, he was imagining the bribe money that would now be flowing into his pockets instead of the dear departed, Chumley's. One of the first phone calls he had fielded after the assassination was from Chumley's banker in the Cayman Islands selling him on immediately opening a U.S. dollar bank account. Prime ministers may change but the bankers go on forever.

When the Secretary of State finally got through to Wilson Dodge, she first gave the condolences of the United States for the loss of that great statesman, "Wilbert Chumby". Prime Minister Dodge ignored the Secretary's mistake in the Victor Chumley's name. It was close enough. "Madame Secretary, what can Saint Matts fo for the United States?"

"I gather you are not aware of the President's address earlier to-night?"

"No, as you can imagine, I have been distracted by the fallout from the assassination."

The Secretary of State paused for a long time. How do you break the news to a Prime Minister that you are going to obliterate his country? She decided to just plunge in, "Well during the speech the president said that on Sunday we would be dropping a nuclear bomb on the island of Saint Matts."

"What? I think we have a bad connection. Could you please repeat that?"

"This Sunday we will be dropping a nuclear bomb on the island of Saint Matts."

"Why in the hell would you be doing that?"

"Because the Chinese have dropped a nuclear bomb on the United States."

"Well, why don't you drop a nuclear bomb on China?'

"Because they are able to drop a a nuclear bomb on us."

"And we can't."

"Exactly, and since Saint Matts dared to negotiate a naval base treaty with the Chinese, we have to show the Chinese that their meddling in the Western Hemisphere cannot go unpunished."

"Let me get this straight, you are going to destroy my country because we didn't attack you, because we are not able to defend ourselves and because we tried to strengthen our economy by inviting another country to invest in our useless real estate so we would not have to renege on the loans we have to pay American bankers?"

"Yes, but we are going to reward the people of Saint Matts for withdrawing from the island."

That got Wilson Dodge's attention.
"Really, go on, I'm listening."

"We need for you to immediately declare a state of emergency on the island and that you have requested that the United States provide immediate protection for the island."

Wilson Dodge quickly interjected, "That is going to be a bit difficult to do since we have just made the same request of the People's Republic of China and they have accepted it."

"Oh, don't worry about them. They are withdrawing from the island as we speak.""

"They are?"

"Yes, they are. Now let me continue. We have a fleet of planes in the air, right now, heading to Saint Matts. In two hours, they will be landing. We want our military personnel to then take over air traffic control and policing functions for the island. These same planes will be used to ferry your citizens to our closest facility, the Coast Guard Air Station Borinquen in Puerto Rico. As each of your citizens is processed through this base, they will be given a check for $100,000 and be transported to hotels that we have leased. We will be housing and feeding them. When they first board the flight in Saint Matts, they will all be hired as employees of the United States government. This then allows us under existing statutes to immediately grant them, as our employees, U.S. citizenship on disembarking in Puerto Rico. U.S. Passports will then be supplied to them within a week. After that, they will then free to travel wherever they wish to in the world."

"You mean everyone, the rich, the poor, children, babies, prisoners, the sick, old people, everyone."

"Yes, everyone"

"What about the assets that they are leaving behind on the island? "

"They will be allowed to make a claim for abandoned assets. If it is under $100,000, which will be the vast majority, it will be granted it automatically over and above the blanket $100,000 they will receive on embarking in Puerto Rico. Over $100,000, documentation will be reviewed to establish their restitution claim."

"What about patients in our hospital?"

"They, the foreign medical students and any tourists will be among the first to be transported off the island. The patients will get full and complete medical attention in Puerto Rico until they are well enough to be discharged. We will need a list of these special categories as quickly as possible, so we can round them up."

"What about me?"

You and the eight members of Parliament will receive $500,000 for your special efforts in assisting the United States of America in facilitating this evacuation. In addition, as Prime Minister you will have five million dollars deposited in that new Cayman bank account you opened two hours ago."

Wilson Dodge's mind was racing. He was not even surprised that the United States was already aware of his secret Cayman account. His thoughts turned to how, each year, a thousand or more of Saint Matts' citizens immigrated to the United States. It was incredibly difficult for a Mattitian to legally get into the United States. Thousands who wanted to emigrate were never successful. Some resorted to shipping their very pregnant wives to hospitals in the United States so their child could be born in that country and be able to legally apply for American passport when they became adults. Once these American born Mattitians had then taken up residence in the United States, they could then bring in their aged parents. This would then complete the processes that takes most of a life time.

Dodge also knew that $10,000 U.S. a year, in Saint Matts, was a good salary. $200,000 for a couple and $100,000 for each of their children was a fortune. Dodge's five million dollars bribe, to him, was like winning the Power Ball Lottery.

"Madam Secretary you will have my fullest co-operation. I will be at the airport to greet your first arrivals. Before I leave for the airport, I will have convened parliament and a state of emergency will have been passed into law. It will call for the immediate evacuation of the island. We will then arrange for all those first evacuees to be identified and contacted tonight, even if our civil servants have to stay up all night. Mattitians will be readied for an organized evacuation of the island."

"Good, we had hoped that we could count on your co-operation. Now, you realize that we must get every single person off that island. Our public relations consultants do not want any Mattitians dying Sunday night in the bomb blast."

"I am sure, with the assistance of your troops, that we will have no problem in evacuating everyone from the island."

"Well, one group does concern us. There is a Bishop family on the island that may be a problem. I understand, from one of their members, a Doctor Robert Lyons, that they will not withdraw. Apparently, they will resort to armed resistance to stay on the island. We are counting on you to change their mind."

The acting prime minister was not overjoyed to hear that there could be an obstacle in his acquisition of sudden wealth. The Bishops were the richest family on the island. They were not intimidated by anyone. That family compound was a virtual fortress and he had no doubt they were armed to the teeth. Being a good politician, he told the Secretary what she wanted to hear, "I am sure we will be able to persuade the Bishops to co-operate".

In his hearts of hearts, he knew he was mouthing nonsense. He would see that he was on the first flight off the island and leave it to the Americans sort it all out. After all, they were the ones who had sent Rob Lyons to the island and had created the problem.

"General Horatio Douglas has been given command of our expeditionary forces. He will be on the first plane to land. I am sure he will be pleased to hear that you will be there to greet him. Thank you once again.

" The Secretary of State abruptly hung up. She had done her job. It was now in the hands of General Douglas to execute the plan.

Wilson sat holding the telephone wondering what protocol required him to do next. He punched in the number of the Governor- General, the king's representative on the island. He felt sure that protocol demanded that the titular head of government be informed first. Under the British parliamentary system, the monarch in England is the titular head of government of the former colonies, such as Canada, Australia, Antigua, Saint Kitts and Saint Matts. Even though the local prime minister would have chosen who the king would appoint to be Governor-General, the illusion still existed that the Governor-Generals in each country were selected by the British monarch. While the Governor-General's role is mainly ceremonial, there are situations where a governor-general can impact political decisions.

The Governor-General, Harry Trott, was seventy-one years old. He liked the quiet, unhurried pace of Saint Matts. Whenever he did think of the future, it did not include leaving the island. He had been born here and he intended to die here. He had only reluctantly left the island to go to university and medical school in England. At his age, money was rather irrelevant, other than the security and comfort it seemed to give him. He had been a successful doctor with little time to spend the money he had accumulated and invested. He enjoyed his ceremonial role.

He could not share the Prime Minister's enthusiasm for evacuating the island. After listening to Dodge's enthusiastic selling of the evacuation, he wondered how much the Americans had paid for his co-operation. He was too diplomatic to suggest that Wilson Dodge had more than the welfare of Saint Matts' citizens at heart.

He also sat there holding the telephone receiver and puzzling over what the evacuation meant and what he was expected to do about it. He finally concluded that the last thing he wanted, was to be the last Governor-General of Saint Matts. He punched in an unlisted phone number for the British Home Office. The duty office answered the phone. Harry identified himself. It was the wee hours of the morning in London.

"I need to speak to the Minister."

"Your Excellency, it is the middle of the night, here."

"I am well aware of that. It is an emergency."

The duty officer was thinking what in the hell could be important coming from a fly speck of an island like Saint Matts. "Please hold your Excellency."

He put the Governor- General on hold and dialed the minister. He let the phone ring. Finally, on the tenth ring, the minister groggily answered, just as the duty officer was about to hang up.

"Yes?"

"Sorry Minister, but I have the Governor General of Saint Matt's on the line. Shall I put him through?"

"What does he want? It's the middle of the goddamn night."

"I am not sure Minister, but he did say it was an emergency."

Duty officers do not question the queen's representatives.

199

"Put him through. What's his name?"

"Harry Trott."

There was a click and the Governor General of Saint Matts was put through. "Your Excellency, how good it is to hear from you."

"Sorry to bother you in the middle of the night Charley but I have a bit of a situation here, that I want to enquire if the Home Office is aware of, and to seek your advice on protocol."

"And, what would that be Harry?"

"Are you aware that the U.S. is planning on dropping a nuclear bomb on Saint Matt's on Sunday?"

"What? Would you please repeat that? We must have a bad line."

"Are you aware that the United States is planning on dropping a nuclear bomb on Saint Matt's.?"

"Harry, is this a joke? Have you been drinking?

"No, I am not joking, and I have not been drinking."

"Surely, this must be a misunderstanding. Is the source of this information credible?

"Yes, it is the acting Prime Minister. He seems rather pleased about it."

"Really?"

"Quite so."

"Why would the prime minister be pleased? He's the new one who took over from Chumley, after that unfortunate assassination?"

"The Americans are buying off the entire population and evacuating them. I assume that Wilson will do quite well out of it, at least, in a monetary way."

"Really?"

"I am not at all pleased. I will refuse to leave this island. "

"Well, well, well, this is certainly a situation, isn't it? I am afraid that I will have to ring you back after I have had a chance to look into it."

"You have my number."

"Oh yes, I will be back to you as soon as I am able."

The Minister of Foreign Affairs hung up. Governor-General Harry Trott sat there for a few minutes considering his brave words about not leaving. He had not yet discussed it with his wife and wondered whether his position would change when he was faced with her hard-nosed practicality. Suddenly he felt very old. He was getting too old for this kind of nonsense.

After he hung up, the Minister, in London, also thought about this late-night turn of events. Surely there was some way that he could turn it to his advantage. Why should a Prime Minister in some god-awful little island be rewarded and not him. He tossed and turned for the rest of the night as he created and rejected schemes on how he could benefit from this turn of events.

CHAPTER 22

Rescue

Just after midnight, as the Chinese were busily loading their ships in the harbor, the first of twenty giant transportation planes set down. The local air traffic control was still in place. General Horatio Douglas, his administrative command staff and several army air traffic controllers were on board the first plane. The giant camouflage painted plane waddled like a giant duck towards the terminal.

One after another, they landed and line up side by side down the air strip. Each plane was capable of transporting five hundred soldiers or the equivalent amount of equipment.

Prime Minister, Wilson Dodge had the official government Rolls Royce drive out on the tarmac as soon as the plane had come to a standstill. The rear cargo door of the plane slowly opened, and a ramp unfolded. A military green Humvee rolled down it on to the pavement. It circled around and came to rest beside the Rolls Royce. A tall lanky soldier, dressed in camouflage fatigues, got out of the Humvee. Dodge noticed the single star on his helmet as the soldier strolled over to the Rolls Royce.

Dodge lowered his rear window. The soldier came over to the open window and peered in.
"Prime Minister Dodge?
"General Douglas?""
Wilson pushed opened the rear door and General Douglas joined him on the fine brown leather seats. "Welcome to Saint Matts."
"Thank you."

The two men shook hands and grinned at each other as if only they knew what the joke was.

"According to the maps I reviewed there is enough vacant land around the airport for us to set up our base camp and field command right here. I've brought a thousand soldiers with me. That chain link fence all around the airport give us an established, defense perimeter. The air controllers I brought with me will take over air traffic control immediately. As I understand it, this is the only air strip on the island?"

Wilson nodded his head and replied, "Yes, this is it."

"Good, I've divided the island into grids."

"Grids?"

"Thousand-meter squares. We will systematically deploy troops and transportation to move the civilians to the airport in an orderly fashion, starting with those grids furthest from the airport and working their way back to the airport. Twenty rotating teams will be deployed in 12-hour shifts. As they move through each grid and they will mark each building as it is cleared."

Having spent the last 24 hours developing the evacuation plan, General Douglas finally had someone to impress with its detail and his cleverness. He continued, "When the civilians arrive at the airport for deployment, our field clerks will assign each a unique number and tag them with a blue bracelet containing a microchip that can be remotely scanned and activated. It will identify them and retain all information we acquire on them. With it, they will be able to access hotel accommodation, our field kitchens, and emergency medical care. Our computer system will assign them to a flight and when it is ready to be boarded; their bracelet will vibrate and turn green. The bracelet will be removed when they are handed their United States passports within 10 days. We expect flights to be taking off every fifteen minutes, once we get rolling. I have requisitioned enough planes that I anticipate it should take us no more than two days to clear the island, maybe less, because thousands have already left."

Wilson Dodge was not really listening. His mind had already left behind the island and his responsibilities as Prime Minister. He was now mentally spending his wealth.

General Douglas interpreted his silence as a keen interest in the details, so he elaborated, "In addition to the teams deploying the civilians, we have specialized military police teams who will be transporting the 250 prisoners in your prisons plus collecting, processing and documenting all confidential government records. They will also be assisting your five banks in the safe transfer of their assets and records. A medical team will be concentrating on the transfer of the two hundred patients in your hospital and any other civilians with health problems. Your business owners will be required to transfer their own records. We will assist them. They are being compensated for all the assets that they are leaving behind."

The General finally concluded by saying, "I understand that you have a news conference scheduled at the television station for 09:00, where we will lay out the evacuation plan. That will give us time to get everything in place. A message has gone out to all traffic controllers around the world that all scheduled flights into Saint Matts are now cancelled and the United States Army is now in control of the island."

Wilson Dodge winced when he heard the reality that he was no longer in control of his island. For a moment a bubble of rebellion almost burst, until the five million dollars that had just been deposited in his bank account bought his silence. He wanted to leap to his feet, dance around and sing, "I'm in the money". At this juncture, he really didn't care how the General was planning on carrying out his assignment. He just wanted to get off the island as quickly as possible.

The general took out a very detailed map of the small island and asked, "Could you show me where on the map the television station is."

Wilson pointed to where in Georgetown it was. The general took out a pen and made an X on the map to mark the spot. "How long will it take me to get there?"
"It shouldn't take much more than half an hour. The road is quite good."

"I understand that you will have the eight members of parliament at the conference to show that the evacuation is a democratically arrived at decision?"

"Yes, they will all be there."

"I would propose that they and their families be the ones to leave on the first plane out which will mean going from the television station directly to the airport and flying out as soon as they reach it. Can you arrange that? You and your family should leave at that time plus any other members of parliament, senior civil servants and anyone else that you want to go with you.

"How many should I include on this first flight?"
"Up to five hundred.""

"I am particularly fond of this Rolls Royce. Would I be able to take it with me?"

"Of course, you can, we should have no trouble in air lifting it out of here before Sunday."

"Well, it seems that I am going to be rather busy tonight rounding up these 500 people. I better get going."

The general climbed out of the Rolls Royce and stood by the door. He took the map out of his pocket again.

"Would you show me where I could find the Bishop compound?"

Wilson Dodge pointed to where the road though the rock cut terminated at the edge of the cliff overlooking Georgetown. The general thanked him and then strode toward his airplane's ramp. It was now a hive of activity as troops and trucks were being offloaded. The army air controllers had already made their way over to the control tower. The first large khaki tent had been erected and was being turned into a command post.

The rest of the island slept peacefully. Unbeknownst to them, the airport was being rapidly transformed into an American military base

Rob Lyons was jerked out of his dream world by control. "DOCTOR LYONS. DOCTOR LYONS. WE NEED TO COMMUNICATE WITH YOU. IT IS IMPORTANT. CAN YOU PLEASE PUT ON YOUR RING?"

Rob thought he was still dreaming. Half awake, he looked at the clock in the nightstand beside his bed. It read 12:45. He groaned, rolled over onto his right side and prepared to go back to sleep. "DOCTOR LYONS, PLEASE PUT ON THE RING WE NEED TO COMMUNICATE WITH YOU."

This time he knew it was no dream. He lay there thinking do I really want to communicate with these people? I severed my connection with them. They are threatening my life and my loved one's lives. **"DOCTOR LYONS, WE WISH TO TALK ABOUT THE SAFETY OF THE CITIZENS OF SAINT MATTS."**

Rob got out of his bed and went down the hall to his father's study. He turned the light on and then waited for his eyes to adjust. Carefully he dialed the combination on the safe. The safe opened and he took out the ring and put it on his finger. He then said the password, "Robert Lyons Thursday Les Prince."

Control immediately responded. **"THANK YOU, DOCTOR LYONS."**

Rob sat down in his father's swivel chair and leaned forward his elbows on the desk. He peered off into space and replied to Control in a flat unemotional voice, "What do you want to talk about?"

"OUR TROOPS STARTED LANDING ON THE ISLAND AT MIDNIGHT. THEY ARE UNDER THE COMMAND OF GENERAL HORATIO DOUGLAS. HE HAS TAKEN OVER CONTROL OF THE ISLAND ON BEHALF OF THE UNITED STATES OF AMERICA FROM ACTING PRIME MINISTER WILSON DODGE."

"How the hell did he do that? This is a democratic country. Who elected him?"

"THE DEMOCRATICALLY ELECTED MEMBERS OF PARLIAMENT MET EARLIER THIS MORNING AND TOOK A UNANIMOUS VOTE THAT THEY AND THE ENTIRE POPULATION OF THE ISLAND, WOULD IMMEDIATELY EVACUATE THE ISLAND. THEY REQUESTED THAT THE UNITED STATES OF AMERICA ASSIST THEM IN THIS EVACUATION. UPON LEAVING THE ISLAND, ALL CITIZENS OF SAINT MATTS WILL BE GRANTED AMERICAN CITIZENSHIP AND BE PAID $100,000 PLUS BE COMPENSATED IN FULL FOR ANY ASSETS THAT THEY ARE ABANDONING. THE ISLAND WILL THEN BECOME AN OFFICIAL NUCLEAR BOMB TEST SITE. EVERYONE IS TO BE OFF THE ISLAND BY SATURDAY IN PREPARATION FOR THE BOMB BEING DROPPED ON SUNDAY."

"Are you people nuts? What you are doing is in violation of the United Nations charter. You can't do this. My family and I will not leave the island."

"GENERAL DOUGLAS WANTS TO MEET WITH YOU AS SOON AS POSSIBLE. HE WOULD LIKE TO MEET WITH YOU AND YOUR FAMILY AT THE COMPOUND AT 7:00 AM."

"Why?"

"I DON'T KNOW, YOU WILL HAVE TO TALK TO HIM TO FIND OUT."

"Okay, tell him to walk in alone from the main road, unarmed. We will meet with him at eight."

"WE WOULD LIKE YOU TO KEEP THE RING ON. THE SECRETARY OF STATE WOULD LIKE TO PARTICIPATE IN THE MEETING."

"I make no promises. I will keep the ring on as long as I feel it is to my benefit."

Rob turned the light off in the study and went back to his room. He couldn't sleep. He lay there contemplating the shortness of his life. He thought of how much he had to live for. How much more out of life he wanted – a wife, children and grandchildren.

He knew he had slept because he suddenly jerked himself awake and saw that it was just after seven. He could hear the house stirring. His mother was already in the kitchen. He got up and quickly showered.

His father was already sitting at the kitchen table reading a book and drinking his coffee. Rob sat down beside his father. Colin looked at him and smiled. The smile slowly disappeared as Rob related his late-night conversation with control. His father looked sad when Rob told him how the island had been abandoned by its democratically elected government.

He stood up and said, "Well I'd better go out and make sure everyone is up. I'll let the family know what is going on. Eight o'clock is awfully early in the morning.

Couldn't it have waited until at least nine? I think it might be a good idea to double the guard on the rock cut." Colin limped off.

Rob crossed the compound to his aunt's house where Barbara Wall was staying. She was talking to his aunt in the kitchen when he arrived. He filled them in on what had taken place. He and Barbara then walked over to the cliff edge. A glorious sun was rising from the sea. It drenched everything in the harbor in a golden glow. The air was fresh and clear. A gentle breeze carried the sweet smells of the flowers, the musky scent of the trees and the tang of the ocean. The Chinese were still loading their ships.

They looked down on Georgetown. It was coming awake. Rob put his arm around her waist and pulled her tight to him. He whispered in her ear, "You know I love you?"

She turned and smiled. They kissed. He held her close.
"Barbara, I want you to leave before Sunday."."
"Why?"
"Because the situation is becoming dangerous and I do not know how it is all going to end up. If something happened to you, I could not live with myself."

"Nor I, if something happened to you."

"."You know why I have to stay."

"Yes, I understand, and I hope you know why I have to stay with you."

This could be our last few days on this earth. They are so goddamn stupid that they may actually drop the bomb on this island on Sunday, whether we are here or not. After all, why should the most powerful force in the world today, representing the will of hundreds of millions of people, care what happens to a handful of people on an island that no one can even find on a map. Mattitians are not Americans and it seems when Americans kill non-Americans, it never seems to register with them that are killing people, who are just like them, with children they love, hopes, dreams and ambitions. They could be mosquitoes for all they seem to care."

"Rob, all you can do is stand up for what you think is right and be prepared to die for it, if that is your fate."

"You're right. Destroying this island, as a strategy to win points in a presidential election competition, is grotesque. Are you going to film this meeting with their general?"

"Yes, I am but I want my cameraman off the island as soon as possible. He doesn't have the emotional and moral commitment, that I have, to keep him here. Are any of your cousins' photographers?"

"I've got a lot of cousins. I am sure I can find one who thinks he is a photographer."

They held hands as they walked back to the house and sat on the veranda to wait for the general. Slowly the extended family joined them on the veranda. Others brought lawn chairs and sat out on the lawn under a tree. They waited, talking quietly. The cameraman appeared with his equipment. He set up his tripod and did a sound check. An empty lawn chair was put on the lawn for the general to sit in when he arrived.

Just before eight, the cousins who were closest to where the rock cut opened onto the main road saw a small convoy of military vehicles approaching from the North. They came to halt at the entrance to the rock cut. The convoy pulled into a defensive herringbone formation. Armed soldiers took up positions on the side of the vehicles away from the rock cut. They nervously scanned the jungle and the cliffs on either side of the cut. The drone circling high overhead knew exactly where each cousin was deployed. They also knew that the cousins were armed with high velocity hunting rifles that were aimed at the soldiers. An officer got out of the second vehicle and made a show of removing his sidearm and handing it to an aide. The officer then started to walk into the rock cut. Shouts echoed from the Bishop sentries on each side of the rock cut, as the officer moved through it

"He's coming."

The shouts got louder as he approached the compound. Precisely at eight General Horatio Douglas strode, at an easy pace, into the compound. He looked around, saw the assembly and headed towards them.

"That is one brave son-of-a-bitch," Rob whispered to Barbara.

Rob got up from his seat on the veranda and made his way towards the General. He stopped about a hundred feet out and waited. "Doctor Lyons, what a pleasure it is to meet you. I'm Horatio Douglas."

"Glad to meet you General."

Rob looked him over. He saw the West Point ring on one hand and on the other hand he saw a ring that was a duplicate of the ring that Control had asked him to put back on.

"I had requested that you come unarmed?"

The General's eyes narrowed. Rob wondered if he was about to be executed in the family compound by the same kind of ring that he had used to kill the two Chinese sentries. The General responded, "I am unarmed."

Rob pointed with one hand towards the ring on the finger of his other hand. The General bent forward and looked at Rob's ring. He realized it was a duplicate of his own. He gave a nervous laugh and said, "Sorry, I had forgotten I had it on. The weaponry is not activated."

"That is fine, but I would like you to take it off and give it to me."

The General complied. Rob held out his hand and took the ring from the General. He put it in his pocket and then turned, motioned like a good host, for the General to accompany him back to the family gathering. They were sitting silently in the shade by his parent's house. Some monkeys were chattering in the trees to the north of the compound. He indicated the chair that the General should take, across from his own chair. Barbara signaled for the cameraman to begin recording the meeting.

"Are you here to arrest me for treason, General?"

"Hardly. I am here to seek your assistance?"

"Seek my assistance?"

Rob was surprised, and he showed it. This was not what he had expected.

"Yes. There is a long tradition of sea captains going down with their sinking ship. I see you and your family as captains of the good ship Saint Matts. I respect you for your bravery and admire you for having the guts to go down with your ship. However, I think I'm right in saying that you do not expect, nor do you want the whole population of the island to go down with you."

The General paused and looked Rob in the eye. Rob quickly responded, "You are absolutely right. While there are some among us who are prepared to die for a cause, I would not want anyone to suffer our fate, if they wished to be evacuated before Sunday. What do you have in mind?"

"Well, on the first airplane out of here, as expected, you are going to find all the politicians and senior civil servants. This mass exodus of the island's leaders will create a real problem for me. I need you and your family to assist me in making sure that everyone who wants off this island gets off. Your family is respected and looked on as the unelected leaders of the island. The people trust you. You can give us credibility when we assure them that they will be handsomely rewarded by leaving the island. Things will go much quicker and easier with your help. For example, I recognize that the locals on the island are speaking English, but my troops are having a hell of a hard time understanding them. We could sure use your help."

Rob recognized that he had been backed into a corner. If he cared about the citizens of this island, and he did, only one response was possible.

"Can you leave us alone for a few minutes, so we can discuss your proposition?"

Far enough away to give the illusion of privacy to the family. However, since Rob was once again wearing his ring which was broadcasting the meeting, it was entirely possible that the General was being patched by Control into what he was saying.

Rob stood up and faced his uncles, aunts, cousins and parents and quietly started to speak, "I was prepared to go into a battle to the death with these Yankee invaders. I had not expected that we would be asked to assist them in evacuating the island. However, he is right. I do not want to see even one person who is not willing to die for the cause on Sunday, remain on this island. I believe this goes for rest of you too. While I can't believe that the United States is really going to drop a nuclear bomb on this island, in the past, they have justified doing some horrible things that resulted in thousands of innocent foreign women and children being killed.

To Americans, the ends justify the means and we, who may die on this island on Sunday, will just be written off as collateral damage. To them we are foreigners. As foreigners, we have no rights under their constitution. Even though my parents and I have American citizenship, I am quite sure they will have no problem presenting me, and my parents, as traitors who deserved to die. Despite that, I feel obligated to assist this general in the evacuation of our people. How do the rest of you feel?

His Uncle Frank stood up and addressed the family.

"I was born on this island and I intend to die on this island. I am going to stay but I insist that my wife, my children and my grandchildren be moved out of harm's way. For those adult males that stay, I agree that we have no option but to assist these Yankees in getting those who want to leave safely off the island."

There was a murmuring in the group, heads nodded in agreement. Rob interjected after things had become quiet, "Does anyone disagree with Uncle Frank?"

He looked at each person in turn. No one hesitated in looking him straight in the eye. No one voiced an objection.

Rob waved at General Douglas to join them. The general who had been sitting on the wall rose and walked quickly across the lawn. As he approached, Rob put out his hand. The general smiled and grasped it.

"We will help you clear the island. How many of the family do you need to assist you?"
"That's good news. Can you supply us with twenty?" They'll each get a thousand dollars for helping us and be classified as official U.S. army scouts."

He hesitated and then continued, "I am wondering if you can accompany me to the television station where at nine hundred hours, we will be addressing the citizens of the island and filling them in on the evacuation plan. I would like them to see that locals, they know, will be assisting us in the evacuation after the politicians and civil servants are gone."

"Yeah, I can. Meanwhile my father will put together the twenty from the family who will be your scouts. It sounds like something out of an old Western movie before they move into Apache country. Can you leave one of the trucks, to transport them up to your base at the airport?"

The assembly broke up. The general and Rob walked through the rock cut to the convoy. As they walked along, Rob reached into his pocket and pulled out the General's ring. The General laughed and said, "Yeah, I better get that back or they will take it out of my pay."

When they got to the army vehicles at the entrance to the rock cut, the general explained to his second in command what was going on. One of the trucks drove into the rock cut to transport the scouts up to the base. The General and Rob climbed into the lead Humvee and led the patrol down the highway towards Georgetown. A short distance down the road, the general cried out, "Monkeys."

On the side of the road was a troop of about a dozen monkeys consisting of mothers, fathers and infants. The driver slowed down so the General could get a good look at them.

"So, these are the famous vervet monkeys I read about."

"Yes, and there are more of them on the island then there are people. They are damn pests. They eat the farmer's crops. If you have any fruit in your garden, you almost have to have a guard sit there, twenty-four hours a day, to protect your trees from them. At one time there was a call for the government to poison them, but the tourist industry fought that. The tourists like seeing them."

"Some animal rights people have already been lobbying the White House demanding that all the monkeys be safely removed before the bomb is dropped."

Rob started to laugh before he replied, "How would you go about capturing eighty thousand wild monkeys in a few days. Impossible, in the rain forest they are up in the trees."

The General smiled as he imagined soldiers trying to get monkeys out of trees. "Don't laugh I've been asked to submit a report to the President's chief of staff on a solution to the monkey problem."

The monkey's crossed the road and disappeared into the jungle. The driver sped up. Few people were stirring on the streets of Georgetown. They saw that the Prime Minister's Rolls Royce parked in front of the television station along with several other expensive vehicles. The convoy ground to a halt behind them. The troops embarked and formed a defensive perimeter around their vehicles. Rob and the General headed into the television station. It was in an old converted movie theater. The little glassed in ticket kiosk still stood abandoned in front of the entrance.

They were greeted by the station manager and led to the studio where the island's government had gathered. The politicians were shouting with excitement, describing how they were going to spend their Yankee dollars once they got to Puerto Rico.

When the General strode, with authority, into the studio, the noise stopped like it had been cut with a knife. All the members of parliament were seated in the room. They had been busy all night preparing to leave with their families on the first plane out. When the bank opened at ten, they would be converting their Eastern Caribbean dollars into Yankee dollars and stuffing them into their suitcases. They were anxious to get going.

The General stopped in the middle of the room. All eyes were on him. He addressed the group. He was the only man with real power left in the room.

"Good Morning, ladies and gentlemen, thank you for coming. The Prime Minister will be the first one to address the nation. He will explain that, you, the government of the island, have passed a law that calls for the island to be evacuated over the next two days with the assistance of the United States Army. The camera will then pan the room to show that all members of Parliament are present. He will then go on to explain why the evacuation is necessary and then he will explain the generous compensation that every citizen will receive from the U.S. government. He will then describe how we have enlisted many military aircraft to run a shuttle to move everyone swiftly to Puerto Rico.

Most importantly, he will explain how they will be immediately granted all the rights and privileges of American citizenship. Finally, he will turn the meeting over to me and I will explain how we will be transporting citizens in military trucks from their homes, parish by parish, to the airport. We will be starting with those parishes furthest from the airport. I will also explain that no one is going to be removed by force from the island and that some, like the Bishop family for example, have made a conscious decision to remain on the island despite the impending explosion of the nuclear device on the island on Sunday. Members of the Bishop family, who are staying, have agreed to assist our troops in the evacuation. Their familiarity with the island will help insure that this evacuation will go off without a hitch."

The General had nodded to Rob Lyons when he mentioned the Bishop family. The politicians hardly bothered glancing at him. They were already in another world, a richer more interesting place, a long way from Saint Matts.

The General stopped, looked at his watch and motioned for the Prime Minister to take the podium as he then stood to one side. The studio lights were hot. The room was feeling stuffy. The camera man wheeled in closer to the podium. Radio mikes, from the islands two radio stations, were also sprouting from the podium. Reporters for the five weekly newspapers, that represented all shades of the island's political spectrum, were seated off to the side on cheap metal stacking chairs. Why they were here was questionable, since it was unlikely that another newspaper would ever be published on this island.

The presentation to the citizens of Saint Matts went off smoothly. There was no rioting in the streets. No denunciations of American imperialism. Rob imagined how these poor island people, who had probably never touched more than a few hundred
U.S. dollars in their lives, reacted when they heard their politicians tell them that they would be receiving a check for a hundred thousand dollars on embarking from an airplane in Puerto Rico plus additional compensation for any additional assets they were leaving behind. They would all be mentally converting it into Eastern Caribbean Dollars. A hundred thousand dollars converted into Two Hundred and Seventy Thousand Eastern Caribbean Dollars. It seemed like a lot of money on an island where you did not need much money to live well.

Rob wondered how long they would be able to hold on to their newfound wealth once they were in the United States and, if they did hold onto it, how long it would bring them happiness. The vultures would quickly descend looking for easy pickings. While in their mind the streets of the United States were paved with gold, they would soon learn that life in United States was not easy for anyone, especially a black West Indian. Even American blacks resented the enterprising West Indians
. Having grown up on an island that was ninety-five percent black where the rich, the middle and the poor classes were black, for the first time they would encounter in-your- face racism of a predominately white society. Every time they went into a store and the minimum wage, white, clerk ignored them, they would wonder if it was because of the color of their skin or just poor service. Every time they applied for a job that they knew they were qualified for but didn't get, they would wonder if it was racism. Landlords would tell them that the apartment they wanted to rent was vacant until they arrived to look at it and were then told it was

rented. Nothing overt, but they would soon feel a subtle level of insecurity and frustration that pained their soul.

On the island of Saint Matts, they were surrounded by old friends, a loving extended family, a warm ocean, bountiful trees laden with fruit free for the picking, colorful birds, crystal clean air with a salty tang and bright daily sunshine. There were no strangers on the island. Those they did not know were related to someone they did know.

In a large American city, they would be in an alien environment. Surrounded by millions of people, who did not care whether they lived or died. Birds would be rare. The cold ocean would be far away. The sky, when they could see it between the tall buildings, would be dull and grey. The air would be polluted and the never-ending sound of the cars, trucks, buses, fire engines, police cars and ambulances would offend their ears.

After the presentation, the Members of Parliament quickly dispersed in preparation for their imminent departure from the island. The General asked Rob to accompany him back to the command post at the airport.

Prime Minister Wilson hurried off. It isn't that he had completely forgotten about the funeral preparations for Chumley. It was more a matter that that was yesterday's news. These were exciting times and really, he wasn't a Prime Minister any more. His family, getting off this island and collecting his just reward were his priority now.

A company of American soldiers would be assigned to bury all those abandoned in the funeral homes. They would dig mass graves with a backhoe and rapidly lower the coffins into their final resting places, if they had coffins. It wasn't as if anyone was ever going to visit these graves. A Caterpillar tractor would then efficiently push the dirt over the caskets.

These foreign soldiers would have no idea that they were burying the assassinated prime minister, nor would they have cared if they had known. Chumley's wife and children would have left on the first flight out. They would have their future and survival on their mind rather than mourning the nation's recently assassinated leader, husband and father.

CHAPTER 23

Plans

After four years of this nonsense, President Willie Brown wondered if he had inherited a masochistic streak. As his grandmother used to say to him, "Be careful what you wish for, as you may regret it if you get it." He had always wanted to be president. He had only thought it was possible when he easily won his first election to a nothing city councilman job. His dream only grew as he got elected to state senator and then eventually governor of the state. Being honest with himself, he knew he would have thrown his dear old grandma down the steps if that would have helped him become president.

Fortunately, Willie had not had to murder anyone to become president, but he had sold his soul in so many ways to achieve it. Now, here he was, selling himself, all over again, for another four years of fear, stress and an overwhelming feeling of inadequacy. To Willie Brown, being president was like being lashed to a wagon, without brakes, hurtling down a never-ending hill, never knowing what was at the bottom and desperately trying to steer by shifting his weight from one side to another, while an army of enemies took turns shooting at him.

He often thought back to his university professor days, before politics, when his biggest worry had been whether one learned paper would be accepted for publication in some prestigious scholarly journal or another. In his early teaching days, his biggest worry had been whether he would get tenure or not. Time had given those memories a golden glow. He thought of how much he had enjoyed the interaction with the students in his lectures and seminars. How he had had the freedom to leisurely read the morning newspaper while he sipped his first coffee of the day. In the middle of day, he had been free to go play squash at the athletic club, if a court and a colleague were available. Those regular Friday afternoon pub crawls with the other professors were looked forward to. There he could debate passionately the hot issues of the day without fearing any repercussions for his candor. On Saturday morning he could wake up with a hangover and have no fear that Friday night's passions would be flaunted in the next morning's newspaper.

Yes, after winning the presidential race in 2016, initially, the adulation of millions of people had made him feel super strong, in control, even smart. However, the euphoria had been short lived. Within a month, he realized that he was not the messiah that he, and his constituents, had thought he was. He realized just how inadequately he had been prepared for this responsibility, while realizing, at the same time, how impossible it was to prepare anyone for such a responsibility.

He had stumbled through the last four years making decisions as best as he could. He had failed to achieve any earth-shaking improvements in the lives of Americans. The harsh reality of how little real power the president had to make changes was depressing. He tried to avoid thinking about the powers lined up against him. Potentially, at any time, there could be one hundred senators, governors and legislators of fifty states, the heads of two hundred foreign countries, 435 members of the House of Representatives plus an army of civil servant mandarins opposing him. These were just the ones who had some reasonable access to him. In addition to them were millions of people around the world sitting in judgment of every action he took and having no hesitation in criticizing his efforts no matter which side of an argument he supported.

Wealthy lobbyists, much cleverer than he, with decades more of Washington experience than he had, were so much more skilled in pulling the levers in Washington than him. They sometimes chose to support his initiatives and at other times to stop him dead in his tracks. Other than foreign affairs and command of the military, the only real power he had was the negative ability to veto bills sent to him by Congress. Even this, supposedly supreme symbol of power, could be overcome by Congress. As he saw it, he functioned as a speed bump in the democratic process. The only semblance of democracy was that there were lobbying groups funding both sides of almost every issue. With all these forces aligned against him, it seemed very unfair to him that he was viewed as being omnipotent.

These thoughts skipped through his mind as he shaved. While the face that stared back at him was familiar, he was disturbed by: how grey his hair was becoming, those large purple bags under his eyes seemed to be growing and the crow's feet reminded him of a road map. He was naked. He looked down. His belly was in the way. He could no longer see his penis. He could feel it so he knew it had not deserted him. Where was that dynamic, handsome, athletic leader of the

Western world? He was turning into a flabby, middle aged, shadow of the man who had grabbed the brass ring and won the biggest lottery in the world.

All this fuss over dropping one stinking bomb on a nothing island in the Caribbean was a pain in the ass. Wasn't he taking care of the citizens of the island? Wasn't he going to make all of them richer than they had ever dreamed of being? Wasn't he giving them citizenship in the best country in the world? Damn, these were people who deliberately travelled to the United States, when they were pregnant, so their babies would be born here so they would be able to eventually claim American citizenship. Now he was giving citizenship away.

That Bishop family were really getting to him with their stupid death wish. So be it, if they wanted to make a political statement by defying the will of the President of the United States then they would learn that when he said he was going to do something he did it. Didn't they understand that they were defying the most powerful military force in the history of the world? It was strategically imperative for world peace that the United States be seen as the most powerful force in the world or all hell could break lose. Otherwise countries would just do what they wanted without checking first to see how it would impact America. The Bishops incineration would be quickly forgotten, and lord knows, over time, how many peoples' lives would be spared because the United States was still there making sure the world was safe.

You would have thought that now that he was committed to dropping the bomb that it would have shut up Rick Wilcox who had dared him to do it. That would have been a side benefit along with the improving his leadership image with voters. But no, Wilcox was still riding the issue for all it was worth, saying that he would chicken out at the last minute. He would show Wilcox that he was a man of resolve. This bomb was going to be dropped.

The president finished shaving. He gave the mirror that million-dollar smile that melted the hearts of voters, men and women alike. It was amazing what $50,000 in tooth implants could do. He was ready to face the world.

As the President was shaving Rick Wilcox was on the computer, next to his bed, checking out the National Radiation Network's website. This was a worldwide organization of individuals with Geiger counters hooked up to personal computers. The network monitored background radiation levels and reported it every minute. The volunteer in Amarillo Texas was now reporting a radiation count per minute of 110. The warning level was 100. Prior to the bomb being dropped, they had been reporting a reading of 38. Prior to the Chinese dropping the bomb in New Mexico you never saw a reading over 54 in the entire United States.

While he had got his family away from the radiation fallout that was carried on the prevailing West winds, there were still hundreds of thousands of his constituents that were going to be exposed to more radiation than was healthy. Not that they were going to keel over dead any time soon, but the chances were that they would eventually suffer higher incidents of cancer and other health problems than those who had not had such an exposure. His extended family, his neighbors, his colleagues were unaware that their lives had been shortened.

Up until he had looked at the radiation counts per minute, dropping a nuclear bomb had not been real. It had been just another stupid political talking point to be used to achieve his political agenda. The epiphany he now came to was that the dropping of a nuclear bomb anywhere in the world was equivalent to soiling your own nest. He realized that he had influenced the decision that backed the Chinese into the corner that had resulted in them dropping the nuclear bomb in the New Mexico desert. The second sobering thought was that he had now compounded the situation by pushing the president to drop a nuclear bomb on the island of St Matts. The president really was going to blast that island into oblivion. An island, that neither he, nor the president, had ever visited, wanted to visit or planned to visit. He was not the irresponsible cowboy halfwit that he was portrayed to be. The dropping of this bomb had to be stopped and there was not much time left to stop what he had started.

He tilted back his brown leather, executive chair; expensive tooled cowboy boots thudded onto the desk. He mulled over all that had been written and reported on Saint Matts in the last few days. Surely there must be a lever there that he could pull to stop this train wreck. It was just another island in the Caribbean full of black people. No one who could stop this insanity cared about black people on an obscure Caribbean island. The only unique thing about this island that had stuck in his mind was that there were twice as many monkeys on the island as there were people. As well, in the pictures, the monkeys had stared back in round eyed wonderment. Rick had thought that, as monkeys went, these were good looking monkeys.

That's it; the monkeys were the lever that he needed. No one cared about the people but saving God's innocent creatures in a tropical island Eden was something he could sell and make political hay out of. The cowboy boots thumped down from the desk. His personal communication device was fired up and he started to search through his contacts looking for someone who would be a sucker for big brown monkey eyes.

He had not gone far before he landed on PAP, which was short for Protect All Primates. They had donated millions of dollars to each party over the years, which was millions more than any other wildlife organization had ever done. They would be his first choice of a target to go after. Surely, they would have leverage with the President.

Rick Wilcox realized that having set up the destruction of Saint Matts that he could not now be seen as its savior. No one must know about his involvement in trying to stop the dropping of the bomb, except for one person, Albert White III. Albert White was the managing partner of the largest law firm in Washington, White & White. They employed an army of 635, up tight, buttoned down, lawyers who served in the best interest of their corporate masters. They influenced proposed legislation, adjusted existing legislation to meet their clients' best interests, fought penalties, reached out of court settlements, arbitrated and did any other task that would pay their thousand dollars an hour fee.

Albert White was a fat, red faced man who favored four thousand-dollar, dark blue suits with vests and a watch chain. His white moustache twitched, and his cold, hard blue eyes narrowed when he smelled money. One more million more would not change his life style. It was all about the game. It was all about accumulating the biggest pile.

Lawyer client privilege means that a lawyer can never be forced to disclose in a court of law whatever communication has passed between them and a client. Rick Wilcox knew that Albert White III would do his bidding without ever revealing Rick's involvement. He dialed White's most private line.

White's caller ID immediately identified that it was the junior senator from Texas. In his most honey voice, White answered, "Rick, what a pleasure it is to find Texas's most hard working, dynamic senator on the line so early in the morning."

"Morning Albert, I need your help. Can I come over to see you?"

"Of course, you can my boy. When would you like us to get together?" "

"It will take me about fifteen minutes to get over there."

"Oh my, this is urgent. Let me clear the deck and I will see you as soon as you get here."

Albert hung up, rubbed his hands with glee and buzzed for his administrative assistant, a bright young woman. He could smell a seven-figure billing.

"What appointments do I have this morning? Set them all back two hours."

Albert had never been fooled by Rick Wilcox's public good old boy persona. He recognized that Rick was a political animal with superb instincts. He had the everyman populist touch that appealed to Texans and the razor-sharp mind of a champion chess player. He wondered what Rick was about to drop on him. Whatever it was, he knew it would be lucrative.

Rick arrived within the fifteen minutes. Albert had decided to meet him in the small conference room beside his office. The room had been sufficiently tarted-up to easily justify his one thousand dollar an hour fee.

"Albert, as I am sure you know, I have maneuvered the president into dropping a nuclear bomb on the Caribbean island of Saint Matts this Sunday."

"Yes, so I had heard."

"Well, it was a mistake. The last goddamn thing this world needs is another dose of radiation. I've got to get the president to stop this insanity."

"Insanity?"

"Yes, insanity. The Chinese have just dropped a nuclear device in New Mexico. Radiation counts have climbed dramatically. All I seemed to have succeeded in doing is poisoning me, my family, my friends and my fellow Americans. I have to stop Sunday's explosion."

"Have you contacted the president and pleaded your case?"

"I didn't think that I had suggested that I had suddenly become stupid. Admitting I have made a mistake would be political suicide. Furthermore, I have zero credibility with the president. He would just think it was some kind of Republican trick. That is where you come into the picture. I need you and your army to solve this problem."

Albert White III, pausing for dramatic effect before he responded, calculated in his mind how much the market, or in this case Senator Wilcox, would swallow. He tested the water. "It would be expensive."

"Albert, everything you do is expensive. I need you on it, now. Look on it as being in your own selfish interest. As far as I know you still live on this planet. Breathing its radiated air. Drinking its radiated water. All your money is not going to do you any good if you die from radiation poisoning."

"I would need an advance of a million dollars. We will have to put a lot of cases on the back burner."

Rick snapped open his digital device. In a minute he had transferred a million dollars to White and White. Albert looked at him as he processed the payment. His mind was already churning out plans.

"Done." Rick said with a flourish, waving his arms like a magician.

"Any preference on where you want us to start, Senator?

"Yes, as a matter of fact, there is a foundation, P.A.P. It stands for Protect All Primates. My sources tell me that they have donated millions of dollars to each party. They are reported to be big time animal lovers who get involved in all kinds of wildlife projects. I suspect that once they see those big brown monkey eyes and realize that 80,000 poor defenseless monkeys on the island of Saint Matts are about to be destroyed that they will move heaven and earth to save them. We are down to a few days. You need people on this now. Let me get out of your way so you can save the monkeys."

Albert White smiled at the absurdity of it all. When he woke up this morning, monkeys had been the farthest thing from his mind. Now, to save the world, he was being paid to save a bunch of damn monkeys. Rick got up and left. Albert asked his assistant to find out which juniors could be temporarily sprung lose from their assignments to work on an urgent project. He wanted to meet with the best three within the hour.

The three young associates gathered around the big boss's table in his private conference room. Jay, the cockiest of the three, often wondered what he, was doing working in a bureaucracy like White and White. Even though he had never met Albert White III, and this was as close to the center of power that he had been in the last year, he was not intimidated by the room. The other two juniors, who were several years younger than him, were nervously shuffling papers and twitching in the fine leather seats, as if they were about to be tested.

Jay had landed in law more by circumstance then by a burning passion to be a lawyer. Unlike his fellow juniors, he had graduated without any student loans because he had found when he was very young that he had a special gift for collecting money and closing sales.

At sixteen, his parents had told him that he had enough education and it was time for him to make his own way in life. They had wished him all the best, bid him goodbye and left the hovel they were renting in the Betsy Layne coal camp in Fulton County, Kentucky. His father had been a coal miner until the underground mines shut down and strip mining took over. His parents headed West with his younger siblings. He had never heard from them again.

He had not thought that being discarded at sixteen was particularly harsh or unreasonable. He was the oldest child, big for his age and smart. He knew his father had left home to work in the mines when he was sixteen, so it was not as if there had not been a precedent. Even his grandfather with only a few years of schooling had left Poland as a young teenager and made his way to the coal fields of Kentucky. Jay knew that life was hard. He had no great expectations. When you are poor, you either adjust to your circumstances or you die.

Being on his own, Jay had felt liberated and grown up. Being resourceful, he had taken whatever menial employment he could find to survive. He was always able to just barely keep the wolf away from the door. Sometimes he had miscalculated his cash flow and had fallen behind in repaying short term, pay-day loans. This had brought him in contact with debt collectors. He had found their scripted, hard ass approaches, crude and amusing. I could do better than that, he had said to himself.

He sought out a small collection agency and said that he would work for nothing to prove that he could collect money. His deep bass voice and quick mind had made him a natural for the job. It took him only a few hours to prove that he had been born to collect money. Rapidly, he advanced from collecting small balances to collecting the agency's largest claims. His collection skills brought him to the attention of the largest collection agency in the region. They offered him an opportunity to immediately double his salary. With this new salary and a generous incentive commission, he was soon making more money than he had ever dreamed of making.

He was only twenty when his driving ambition again demanded more of him. He was told he could only make more money, if he went from collecting money to selling collection services. Collections had taught him how to motivate hard-nosed deadbeats to do something they really did not want to do. Jay quickly found it to be many times easier, than collecting, to convince credit managers to give his agency their bad accounts. As far as the credit managers were concerned, they were garbage accounts receivable that they had already written off to bad debt. They really did not expect them to be collected. If too many claims were collected by a collection agency, it could be interpreted to mean that a credit manager had not been as aggressive about collecting the receivable as they should have been.

Soon Jay was making more in sales commission than many of the collection agency's salaried managers, who were twice his age. Once again, his ambition hit a brick wall. His limited education was stopping him from moving into the executive ranks of a major collection agency. To him, this was only a hurdle to be overcome. He got accepted as a mature student at the University of Kentucky and started the daily grind. His life consisted of work during the day, classes and study at night, year after year. After his undergraduate degree, he had gone after a law degree because collecting money required total familiarization with court procedures, insolvency laws, garnishees and criminal laws. About five percent of the millions of collection claims processed each year ended up being litigated. That five percent employed thousands of lawyers. Jay knew, the better his grasp of the legal process, the more successful he would be running a collection agency.

Due to his knowledge of applied law and his analytical, creative mind, it was no surprise that he always stood at the top of his law class. While his initial ambition had been focused on obtaining a senior executive slot with a collection agency, when White and White contacted him, and offered a position, at what seemed to him to be an outrageous salary, he had accepted and moved to Washington. Now, he was not so sure he had made the right decision. The stuffy, slow, conservative atmosphere of White and White, sometimes made him feel that he was slowly drowning. The prestige of working as a lawyer for the largest law firm in Washington was wearing thin. He missed the intense daily action and quick results of a collection agency. He also found big city living too crowded, too noisy and too artificial.

The conference room door from Albert White's private office suddenly banged open, startling the two nervous juniors but not Jay. Jay wondered if Albert had done it deliberately and whether he enjoyed doing it. Albert looked at the three juniors.

Two of them looked nervous and petrified. The tall, big blond one stared at him calmly, making Albert White, senior managing partner, feel insecure as if he had suddenly come across a rattle snake and had no place to hide. ·

"Names?" White barked out as he stared down at them.

The tall, blond one did not hesitate in responding, "Jay Wasnewski" in a deep voice that came through like the steady beat of a bass drum. Jay did not relax his eye contact on Albert White.

The pretty girl to Jay's right said, "Mary Wright" in her high pitched, nervous giggle, glancing quickly away and gulping.

The dark eyed, intense junior, who looked like a deer about to flee from hunters, responded, "Michael Hunt". He had ever so slight a tremble in his voice.

"The three of you are going to assist me in a project. Whatever commitments you have over the next four days, cancel them." Mary Wright raised her hand like a student in ninth grade.

"Yes Mary?"

"Does this include the weekend?"

"Yes, it includes the weekend. If we are successful, we will be saving the lives of several brave people."
The three juniors' eyes opened with surprise and wonder.

"Have you been following the crisis going on in the Caribbean island of Saint Matts?

Jay nodded to indicate he knew the story. He was an incessant reader (several newspapers each day, magazines, cereal boxes - everything and anything).

The other two gave each other a puzzled look. Geography had not been one of their strengths. They only had a vague idea where the Caribbean was. They had never heard of Saint Matts. Albert White was not surprised.

"Mister Wasnewski, would you please enlighten your associates with what is happening with Saint Matt's."

Albert White gave Jay a hard look. He was curious as to how Jay would handle being put on the spot. Jay shrugged and replied in his quiet way.

"Sure. No problem. The island of Saint Matt's is about to be nuked into oblivion for aiding the Chinese in establishing a naval base on the island. This bombing is in retaliation for the Chinese having dropped an unauthorized nuclear bomb in our New Mexico nuclear test site the other day. That was thought to be in response to an American attack on their satellites"

"Is Saint Matts a sovereign nation Mister Wasnewski?"

"Yes, it is.""

"What right does the United States have for dropping a nuclear bomb on a sovereign nation?"

"None. It is an act of war on a defenseless nation who had every legal right to lease an abandoned British naval base to the Chinese. However, the Monroe Doctrine established in 1823 implied that the Western Hemisphere, which includes the Caribbean, Central and South America, was America's private lake and foreign nations were to stay out of it. Back then, the Monroe Doctrine was directed at the Europeans who had colonized the Americas. China had never even been considered as someday being able to intrude into the Western Hemisphere."

Albert White was impressed by Jay's snap analysis and grasp of the situation.

"Mister Wasnewski you will be the team leader. Our objective is to stop the United States from dropping that bomb on Sunday at noon. It is now 9:30 AM on Friday. As soon as possible, I want your team's best ideas on how we will stop the government from following through on their stated intent to destroy this island. At the same time, our client, who shall remain nameless, has given us one intriguing suggestion that has to be immediately worked on."

Albert had their rapt attention. He continued, "The island of Saint Matt's has a human population of 40,000. Most of these people will be evacuated in the next two days. It also has a population 80,000 wild vervet monkeys. The island is a lush, green, mountainous jungle from one end to the other. It is a paradise for these

227

monkeys. Our client suggests that while no one really cares that some stubborn humans are refusing to leave the island, and will perish in the nuclear blast, they will care if the population of innocent, defenseless, adorable monkeys perish in the blast. It seems that there is a Foundation, called Protect All Primates, who has made major contributions to the President's election campaign. The client wants us to immediately contact the powers at P.A.P and get them to lean on the president. Is this enough to get you going?

The three junior nodded that it was.

"Good I will do a progress check later this morning."

Albert White banged his door loudly behind him as he made his departure. The three lawyers looked intently at each other as they opened their laptops.

Jay immediately assumed command, "Mary can you research on vervet monkeys. Mike, can you compile a list of other organizations that would have any interest in what happens to monkeys in Saint Matts. I'm going to research P.A.P. and determine who we have to contact there."

The three of them got busy. Mary learned about how the monkeys had been transported as pets by French settlers from Africa to the Eastern Caribbean islands of Saint Matts, Saint Kitts, Barbados and Nevis. The monkeys had been studied by researchers at several universities and there were hundreds of research papers available on vervet monkeys.

Mike was amazed to find that there were dozens of organizations around the world dedicated to protecting primates. He got names, locations and phone numbers.

Jay quickly identified that a Marigold DuPont was the one who would be able to lean on the president. According to filings, she had directed five million dollars of P.A.P's funds to the president's last campaign. She apparently lived on the P.A.P's thousand-acre reserve in Florida just east of Port Charlotte. It reportedly sheltered several thousand vervet monkeys who had been used and then discarded by pharmaceutical companies' research operations. Monkeys were a significant export from the Caribbean islands.

When he phoned the foundation's number, Jay ended up talking to an answering machine. He left a message and started to search for a private number for Marigold DuPont. He found she had an unlisted number. This brought him back to his collection days when he used to skip trace. He opened his wallet and found the slip of paper with his important, secret phone numbers. It was for a supervisor at the phone company who made cash money on the side selling unlisted phone numbers to a few select clients.

"Hi Joan, you know who this is?"

"I sure do. I thought you were out of the game."

"You're never out of the game, just playing in a new arena. I need your help, an unlisted phone number for a Marigold DuPont in Arcadia, Florida."

"Hold on a minute."

Jay could hear her clicking away on her keyboard as she accessed the computer.

"I got it." She gave him the number

"Same fee?"

"Yep."

"I'll mail the cash today."

"Good doing business with you."

"Thanks Joan"

Jay checked out the fastest way to get to Arcadia, Florida. The local municipal airport in Arcadia was not able to handle jets. The closest airport that could handle jets was at Punta Gorda, eighteen miles away. He booked a corporate jet to fly him down at noon. He knew he had big balls reserving it under the name of White and White, but the clock was ticking, and White had said this was of the highest priority. He then settled down to learning all he could about Marigold DuPont.

At seventy-four, she was the oldest grandchild of Gabriele DuPont who had established the foundation. She had never married. She had had control of the foundation for thirty years.

Decades ago, Gabriele DuPont had bequeathed over a hundred million dollars to a foundation to protect monkeys, apes, chimpanzees, gorillas and all other near human animals from the most human animals. His original initiative of shipping the primates back to Africa, their natural habitat, proved to be a disaster when the first shipload full of primates got butchered sold for a fine profit in the African market as bush meat. Fortunately, this unfortunate repatriation's results got little publicity in the United States. The Foundation was now much more circumspect in their good works. Primate refuges in Florida and California were well funded and got good publicity. Post graduate grants were generously doled out to the deserving, and not so deserving, zoologists to study primates.

The foundation was professionally administered but one of the stipulations built into its charter was that the oldest direct descendent of Gabriele DuPont controlled the purse strings and set direction for the foundation. Although they liked the outside world to think that they were the DuPonts of the Delaware DuPonts who created a fortune in the Chemical industry, their links went back to a French-Canadian plumber who generated a fortune smuggling liquor across the Saint Clair River to Michigan during U.S. prohibition.

Gabriele DuPont had been an unsuccessful plumber but was a gifted smuggler. He had surreptitiously built a nine-hundred-foot pipeline under the St. Clair River, between wet Canada and the dry United States. Delivery was fast, efficient and virtually undetectable. Tanker trucks full of fine Canadian whiskey entered the mob's distribution network from this secret riverside depot in a small town just north of Detroit. Prohibition proved to be not only remarkably profitable for the Canadian distillers and the American mobsters but also for the clever smugglers like Gabriele Dupont who linked manufacturing with distribution.

One of the first luxuries Gabriele had bought with his new-found wealth was a vervet monkey. It was his constant companion and best friend. Unfortunately, the monkey was not only ill tempered, but not completely house broken. This made Gabriele a social outcast. His family hated that stinking monkey. When Gabriele died, the first thing the family did was to take that monkey out and execute it with a bullet from a twenty-two-caliber rifle.

It was only after the lawyer read out Gabriele's last will and testament that the family learned that Gabriele had left his entire fortune to the monkey and upon the monkey's death it was to go to a foundation that he had established prior to his death. The only saving grace, for the family, was that Gabriele's oldest surviving direct descendant was to always control the foundation.

His granddaughter, Marigold DuPont, was now the oldest surviving relative. She loved all animals, especially monkeys, and took their protection very seriously. She had contributed millions to both political parties to make sure that any proposed laws effecting primates always had the foundation's stamp of approval. For decades she had supported efforts to stop researchers from using primates in their experiments. While she had had little success in stopping primates being used in research, she had been successful in providing a sanctuary for the primates after the scientists had wasted them and cast them aside. Marigold was a proud compassionate woman who had learned to hate and distrust the powers that failed to see horror and destruction they had wrought on those who could not protect themselves.

Jay got the same feeling he used to get when he finally found where the supposedly insolvent debtor had hidden his money. He had found the lever that would give him a fighting chance to reach his goal. He dialed the unlisted number he had been given for Marigold DuPont. The telephone was answered with a simple, unpretentious, "Hello?"

"May I speak to Miss Marigold Dupont?"

"Speaking.".

"Miss DuPont, this is Jay Wasnewski, I am a lawyer with the law firm of White & White in Washington."

"I don't know you. How did you get this private unlisted number?"

"Miss DuPont, I recognize that this is an invasion of your privacy and I would only do it if it were an urgent matter of life and death. I am trying to save the lives of eighty thousand vervet monkeys who will be destroyed on Sunday morning."

"Eighty thousand monkeys? What eighty thousand monkeys?"

With that response Jay knew he had got her. He reeled her in a bit more, "It is such an urgent, horrific matter that I want to fly down to see you this afternoon, so I can explain in person why these monkeys need your intervention. Would you be available at three o'clock?"

"Well, I don't know. This is all rather sudden."

Jay shut up and said nothing. He let silence work for him. There was a long pause, which to Jay, felt like hours but, was only twenty seconds. He could almost hear the cogs in Marigold's brain spinning. Finally, she continued, "I suppose it will be all right. I will ask the foundation's lawyer to join me at the Foundation's office. Could you please give me your name again and the law firms phone number?"

Jay gave her his contact details and thanked her for agreeing to see him.

At ten thirty, the door from Albert White III's office banged open and startled them.

"Well Jay, have you got good news for our client?"

"Yes."

"Yes, what?"

"I've got an appointment set up with the Chairman of P.A.P. at three.""

"Where?"

"Arcadia, Florida."

How are you going to get down there by three o'clock?"

"I've booked a corporate jet."

"You must be rich."

"No, but White and White is, and it is a legitimate client expense. We wouldn't be working on this unless you had an advance to cover every possible expense that could be incurred."

"You're right. You better get your ass out to the airport. My chauffeur will drive you home, so you can pack an overnight bag."

"I had thought I would keep the plane waiting and return after the meeting."

"That makes sense, but it is also wise to prepare for the unexpected. Your plans may change so pack an extra suit, just in case. Phone me when you land and after your meeting. Now get going. Tom will be waiting for you in front of the office."

Jay got out and headed out the door. Albert White III turned to other two lawyers and asked them what gold they had found in their research.

CHAPTER 24

Attack

Western Florida, around Punta Gorda is probably where the myth of selling worthless swamp land to ignorant Northerners originated. Jay looked down on the area around Port Charlotte as the jet descended rapidly towards the airport. Manmade ditches were cut through the swamp to drain the swamps and allow the developers to charge an extra hundred thousand for water access lots to potential home owners. They weren't called ditches. They were called canals and they connected the home owners to the Gulf of Mexico. They were also a major breeding ground for mosquitoes and alligators. If you dug a hole more than three feet deep in these developments, it would immediately fill with water.

This had been Jay's first ride in a corporate jet. He had no problem adjusting to the benefits of not having to run the gauntlet of normal commercial security. As soon as he had sat down the plane had started to taxi for takeoff. The plane had taken off like a rocket. The captain had come back to talk to him after they had reached cruising speed. He learned that the pilot had been a navy fighter pilot.

The rental car he had booked was waiting for him at the Charlotte County Airport terminal when he disembarked. He had told the captain that he would probably be gone for about four hours. They had exchanged wireless phone numbers with each other, just in case the plans changed.

Jay set the GPS and followed the directions out of Punta Gorda, north, on I-75 until he got to highway 35. He turned east and followed it through scrubby bush and farmland into Arcadia. The GPS led him through the town and few miles east he turned down a private laneway. A thousand feet from where he turned off, he stopped in front of a 12-foot-high chain link fence. A small sign on the gate simply stated, " P.A.P.". A security guard stepped out of a shack beside the gate and approached.

"Mr. Wasnewski?"
"Yes, that's right."

"Could I please see photo ID."

Jay took his driver's license out of his wallet and handed it to the security guard. The guard glanced at it and handed it back. "You go down the road about five hundred feet and you will come to the office. Miss DuPont will be waiting for you there."

The guard went back to the shack. The gate rolled back. Jay drove through and stopped in front of a second gate and another 12-foot chain link fence. A sign with red skull and cross bones on it was prominently displayed on the fence. It read "DANGER ELECTRICALLY CHARGED FENCE – DO NOT TOUCH". The gate behind him rolled shut as the second gate opened. A grass strip, fifty feet wide, on the other side of this fence made sure there were no tree limbs overhanging the fence. A sign on this side of the fence read, "DANGER. KEEP WINDOWS CLOSED AT ALL TIMES". Jay pondered what danger there could be and how he was going to get from his car to his meeting with Miss Dupont.

He continued down the road until he came to a long one-story concrete building with a red adobe roof. The parking lot was deserted. He pulled into a parking spot in front of what appeared to be the main entrance. Carefully, he got out of his car quickly, shutting and locking the car door behind him. You cannot be too careful when you have been warned of danger. He apprehensively proceeded to the office entrance, while looking over his shoulder for imaginary dangers. He could hear the hum of an air conditioner and took this to be a sign that there were humans inside. He opened the door and entered into a drab but functional, reception area. An elderly woman was sitting behind the receptionist desk. She looked up from a document she was reading.

"Mister Wasnewski, you are early."

She said it the way Jay's fifth grade teacher used to say, "No talking." He concluded that this was no ordinary receptionist. He played his hunch by asking, "Miss DuPont?"

"Yes."

She stood leaning on the desk for support. Her right arm came up. Jay shook her hand and said, "It is a pleasure meeting you, Miss Dupont,"

She nodded and with a hoarse whisper said, "Come, let's go into the boardroom. Roger, my lawyer, should be here in a few minutes."

She walked slowly and deliberately as if her knees hurt her. Down the hall, they came to double doors. They went through them into what appeared to be a private art gallery. The theme of the original oil paintings all seemed to be primates: monkeys, chimpanzees, gorillas and orangutans. She walked through this room to another double door that opened into a boardroom with seating for twenty people around a beautiful wooden table. The soft, suede, swivel chairs looked comfortable. Marigold DuPont took her accustomed seat at the head of the table and motioned for Jay to sit in the first seat to her left.

Jay looked at her. She was a tiny woman. No more than five feet tall. Her high cheek bones and piercing bright blue eyes gave her a fierce demeanor. Other than the obvious intelligence that shone in those eyes, if he had passed her on the street he would have paid her no attention. She looked neither rich nor poor, no gold earrings nor necklaces. In Walmart she would have been just another old, white haired, pensioner in Florida. The millions that she controlled had had little outward effect on her. When doing his research, no pictures of Marigold Dupont had been retrieved. She wore a khaki short sleeved blouse that had a military cut to it as did her olive-green slacks. She was wearing beaded deer skin moccasins.

It was quiet as a tomb. An antique grandfather clock emitted thunderous tick-tocks. Marigold's bright blue eyes scanned him from head to toe. It made him feel uncomfortable. He felt like an impostor in his Armani suit.

"You are younger than I expected. Usually, Washington only sends down silver haired foxes to shake me down for money."

Jay laughed. Marigold laughed. At that moment the double doors opened, and a tall, silver haired fox entered the room. He stopped, taken aback by the laughter. Marigold indicated that he should take the seat on the other side of the table across from Jay.
"This is the Foundation's Lawyer, Roger Belanger. Roger, this young fellow is Mister Jay Wasnewski of the eminent Washington law firm of White and White."

Belanger nodded at Jay in a condescending almost hostile gesture. Jay nodded back at him, being careful to keep his face as neutral as possible. Jay recognized that Belanger was the hired gun who was there to protect the foundation from being ripped off by smooth talking bandits from Washington. He was a big man, an easy two hundred and forty pounds on a six-foot frame. He was not the sort of person who would be blown over in a high wind. Jay suspected that he probably packed a hidden gun and would only resort to using it if he couldn't beat you to death with his fists which looked to be the size of catcher's mitt. Jay's hand disappeared into the mitt when they shook hands. Belanger made sure that he crushed Jay's hand. Jay tried not to wince.

Miss Dupont got right down to business, "Well, Mister Wasnewski what do you want from the foundation if you don't want money."

"We don't need money."

"Good. What do you want?"

"What we need is your help and your influence."

"Mister Wasnewski I'm just a little old lady in Florida who runs a boarding house for a bunch of monkeys. Who could I possibly influence?"

"The president of the United States."

Marigold, laughed with disbelief and with a chuckle in her voice said, "What makes you think that I could possibly influence the president of the United States."

"A five million donation to his last re-election campaign."

"You must have made a mistake; government records will show that our donation to the president's re-election campaign was a small fraction of that amount."

"I'm sure the government records do show a much smaller amount, but my research shows five million"

Marigold gave him a long hard stare which if she had had super hero powers might have turned him into a cinder. She smiled and said, "The amount is not

237

important. Suppose I could influence the president, why in the world do you think I would do it for you?"

"It isn't for me. It is for the eighty thousand monkeys I told you about on the phone. It has been on the news for the last two days."

"I don't watch the news. It depresses me. Go on."

Jay then related to Marigold DuPont the situation in Saint Matts with the president's intention to drop a retaliatory nuclear bomb on the island and obliterate it from the face of the earth along with the poor defenseless eighty thousand monkeys.

Marigold's eyes widened in disbelief and then very loudly exclaimed in frustration, "You have got to be kidding me. Surely that moron isn't that stupid!"

"Can you help," Jay implored?"

"Is that jet you few down on waiting?"

"Yes, it is."

"Good, because you are going to fly me back with you. Give me half an hour to get an overnight bag together. I'll be right back."

Marigold quickly left the room. Jay looked at Roger Belanger. Belanger smiled and said, "Obviously my presence here was not necessary. I leave Mademoiselle DuPont in your good hands. Make sure nothing happens to her."

With that, Roger Belanger left leaving Jay alone in the boardroom. Marigold arrived a few minutes later with her overnight bag. She had changed into a severe white pant suit, had put on lip stick and pulled her hair back into a bun. She had put earrings on and a matching necklace of black pearls. Her six-inch white high heels made her a power to be reckoned with. She looked like a million dollars, maybe several hundred million dollars. She also looked about fifteen years younger.

"Let's go."

Why is it that the road back always seems shorter than the road there? Is it because the stress of finding your destination makes it seem longer? They were back to the plane in no time. Once she got on the plane, Marigold got busy on the phone. She had a limousine waiting for her when they landed. Turning to Jay, as she got off the plane, and she said, "Mister Wasnewski, I am going to save those monkeys or die trying."

With that parting comment she strode determinedly towards the limousine like Robocop ready to kick some ass in Washington.

Jay was pleased with himself. He thought to himself, "mission accomplished". He had not yet learned that the opera isn't over until the fat lady sings.

CHAPTER 25

Evacuation

The U.S. Army base camp at the Saint Matt's airport was a hive of activity. Trucks, that had been unloaded from the airplanes, supplemented with island trucks that had been purchased from the departing islanders, were roaring away from the dispatch office. Advance field teams already in the first parish were driving systematically down each street, knocking on doors and pinpointing where to send each truck.

The advance teams each had a member of the Bishop family in their Humvees. Each truck had a soldier driver and helper. They were all equipped with two-way radios to coordinate the effort.

A helicopter with one of the Bishop's on a megaphone system was flying over each sector asking those in the sector to stand outside their dwelling with their luggage ready to be picked up. A second helicopter flew into the remote desolate areas, broadcasting a message that the island was being evacuated and everyone should return to a main street or intersection to be picked up. There was a fear that there might be hermits and illegal marijuana growers living high in the mountains, totally cut off from any contact with civilization, oblivious to the imminent destruction of their island.

Rob Lyons sat in the control tower at the airport with the general. It had become the central control headquarter. Army air traffic controllers had taken over the airport. Trucks were roaring up to the departure area and discharging their passengers with all their attendant baggage: cheap cardboard suitcases, duffel bags, dark green garbage bags and cardboard boxes. Since there were no plane tickets or security checks, the luggage was loaded onto carts and trucked for departure on the next airplane. The passengers joined the line that snaked through the terminal and then out on to the tarmac. They were orderly. Everyone was smiling and joking. It was a carnival atmosphere. They were all rich. As a plane landed and taxied up to the terminal, five hundred passengers at a time would be quickly loaded on board. The plane, within a matter of minutes, would roar off down the strip. Rob and Horatio Roberts would scan the sky for the next plane.

A clerk in the corner was posting the number of landings and the number of passengers loaded. A map of the island was being colored in street by street as it was emptied.

A field kitchen had been set up in a tent complex just outside the terminal. Soldiers and anyone else who was hungry or thirsty could go in and get food and drink. Some of the Mattitians left the departure line to get nourishment.

Horatio turned to Rob, "Hey Buddy, let's go down and get something to eat, I'm hungry".
They took the steps down from the control tower and walked across the tarmac to the cafeteria. Soldiers eat well. A steak, cob of corn, mashed potatoes and broccoli were loaded onto Rob's plate. He grabbed a slice of apple pie with ice cream as he made his way to one of the long folding tables. They sat across from each other.

Horatio's military training was evident in the neat mechanical way he ate, as if ever conscious that he was setting an example for the troops. His fork would come down like a crane picking up the food and carefully bringing it to his mouth, always keeping his back ramrod straight. It had become noticeably quieter as soon as he had entered the tent. The laughter and horsing around had ceased. Rob felt like an unsophisticated slob as he slouched over his tray eating in a very unmilitary manner.

"Rob, I am pleased with the way the evacuation is going, I think we will be finished by early Saturday morning. More people must have left the island before we got here than I had thought. I gather most of the American students got out on Wednesday on planes chartered by their parents."

"There is that and I suppose you have given those that were still here every incentive to leave and fully co-operate. It is the ultimate old carrot and the stick school of management. The sooner they leave, the sooner they will be rich, by staying; they will be dead on Sunday at noon, very persuasive".

"Rob, if you left you would be rich too."

"General, richness is a state of mind. I love this country. I will do anything I can to stop its destruction. What America is going to do is wrong. Saint Matt's has done nothing to warrant the extreme retaliation for an event that never took place. You strike me as an intelligent, sensitive man. I wonder how in good conscience you can carry out your orders to destroy this island."

"It is very simple actually. I am a soldier. I follow orders. These orders come direct from the Commander-in-Chief. Mine is not to wonder why. Mine is but to do and die." Rob looked at the General with disbelief. The General took a sip of his coffer and continued, "Even after giving you the company line, I do have an understanding as to why the island has to be destroyed. We have to preserve our identity as the most powerful nation in the world. We must respond to the Chinese who have challenged our dominance. We must make it absolutely clear that we are prepared to fight a nuclear war to the death. The battle starts here."

The general got up and got a coffee. He continued where he had left off, "You are right, what we are doing isn't right. It isn't fair. It is the ultimate violation of an independent country's sovereign rights. It deserves condemnation from the United Nations and every country in the world. It is crazy, but its very craziness is what is required to send a message to the world that we are going to preserve what and who we are. An example of our resolve must be made, and Saint Matt's just happens to be the easy, convenient scapegoat. The rest of the world doesn't really care what happens on some remote Caribbean island they have never heard of. They will piss and moan about how terrible it is but that is all they will do. No one is going to threaten us over what we are doing to Saint Matts."

"You really do believe that they are going to bomb the hell out of this island on Sunday?"

"Rob, you and your family are being very naive if you think they won't. I am only surprised at the compassion of the United States in evacuating and rewarding the population. It is obviously an election year. The message would have been stronger if they had just bombed the island immediately."

"Christ, you really are cold, heartless bastard."
"No Rob, I am a pragmatist. I look at the big picture. It is important for world peace that someone step up and prevent world chaos. That is what the United States did after World War II and while we may have made lots of mistakes, I

believe billions of people are alive because of the peace and technology that we have brought to the world."

"General, all empires come to an end. What if the United States is a sinking ship and the Chinese have launched a new world order."

"Then Rob, we go down in flames, fighting for our domination of the world. While I recognize that you intend to go down with this island at noon on Sunday, it is an empty, wasted gesture. Some people may comment on your bravery, but it will change nothing and will be old news by Monday. Please reconsider your position and get off this damn island."

Rob looked at General Horatio Douglas and realized that what the General had said was the truth, at least as far as the General saw it, and the General was much more experienced than he was in predicting military behavior. He wondered whether he was just being stupid and stubborn with his intention to remain on the island after it was evacuated by all those who were intent on leaving. He then wondered if he really wanted to live in a world where nations could be destroyed at will. This then made him wonder if he had a death wish and if Sunday was just a convenient form of suicide. He didn't think he was suicidal.

"General, I think, and I hope you are wrong. I have to do everything I can to save this island and I am willing to die trying."

"Rob, I understand bravery and dying for a cause. I salute you. We better get back to that command post. We've still got to get a hell of a lot of people to lift off this island by tomorrow and I need your help,
Buddy."

CHAPTER 26

The Hotel

As they walked back to the command post, both the General and Rob were patched into Control.

"ROB YOU MET WITH ROBERTO BENTO THREE DAYS AGO. BENTO HAS MADE CONTACTS WITH SENIOR POLITICIANS IN WASHINGTON WHO WANT YOU TO GRANT HIM SPECIAL PRIVILEGES IN GETTING OFF THE ISLAND. THE WORD HAS COME DOWN FROM THE PRESIDENT THAT WE SHOULD DO EVERYTHING WE CAN TO HELP. HE COULD BE ARRESTED AS SOON AS HE STEPS ON U.S. SOIL. THUS, HE DOES NOT WANT TO BE TRANSFERRED TO PUERTO RICO. CAN YOU AND GENERAL DOUGLAS, PLEASE MEET WITH HIM AS SOON AS POSSIBLE.

Rob and Horatio looked at each other to confirm they had both got the same message. Rob pointed at his ear with a questioning look. Horatio nodded his head to indicate he had also got it. He then said to Rob, "Let's go over there right now."

The General found his driver and a Humvee. They piled in for the ten-minute drive over to the hotel. Rob found it strange to drive up to the hotel, it was normally bustling with travelers coming and going, now it was deserted – no doormen, no bell boys, no taxi drivers waiting for fares, no tourists waiting to go on tours, no guests going for walks, no one. They parked right in front of the main entrance. Since this was the Caribbean, the entrance was wide open with no doors. The trade winds blew from the ocean right through the immense lobby and out the entrance.

They walked up the marble steps into the main lobby which was like a morgue with scattered pastel flowered sofas spotted across it instead of tombstones. Sitting in a comfortable armchair just inside the lobby was Bruno DeLuca, one of the thuggish brothers that provided muscle for Roberto Bento. Bruno was as formally dressed as he had been on Tuesday night. He had on a black Hugo Boss suit and expensive black alligator skin shoes. He got up and approached them as they came up the steps. He smiled at Rob as if Rob were a long-lost friend.

"Mr. Bento told me to come down and wait until you arrived, so I could escort you up to his office."

Control warned Rob and the General, **"BRUNO DELUCA IS ARMED. HE HAS A SHOULDER HOLSTER ON HIS LEFT SIDE AND WHAT APPEARS TO BE SWITCHBLADE IN THE FRONT RIGHT POCKET OF HIS PANTS. YOUR RINGS HAVE BEEN ACTIVATED.**

Their footsteps echoed as they crossed the lobby to the bank of elevators. They didn't have to wait for an elevator. They got off on the second floor and followed Bruno to the viewing room. This time when Rob entered the security screening room, there were no security guards. The door to the inner sanctum was propped wide open with a chair. When they crossed into it, the only person in the viewing room was Roberto Bento who was sitting in the small reception area. The bank of monitors, for the casino, was turned off. When Rob looked through the window into the casino, he saw the garish bright lights had also been turned off. The casino was in darkness. The monitors for the lobby and entrance were still activated. He could see their Humvee drawn up to the entrance.

Roberto did not get up to greet them. He waved them over to the reception area and motioned for them to sit across from him. "Doctor Lyons, I didn't get a phone call before we were invaded."

Rob thought to himself, what the hell is this greeting about but he replied, "I was as surprised as you were to find we had been invaded. I would like you to meet General Horatio Douglas who oversees the evacuation, or should I say invasion".

Horatio leaned across the table and shook Bento's hand. Roberto Bento did not look like a happy camper. He looked stressed.

Rob decided to get to the chase, "We understand that you have a problem that we have been told to resolve for you. How can we assist you?"

Bento looked at the two of them for about ten seconds before he replied. Ten seconds can seem like an eternity in certain situations.

"This is a very sad day. In ten years, we built this Casino into one of the most successful businesses in the Caribbean. We employed over a thousand people. Now it is all gone. Not wiped out by a hurricane, which I could accept, but wiped out by politicians playing games. These same politicians have promised us that we will be fully compensated for our loss but I don't trust politicians. They seem to have convenient memories. A lot of our business is done on a cash basis and I am anticipating having to fight for the $500,000,000 that the United States Government now owes us. That is a future battle. The initial problem I need help with is in safely getting almost a hundred million dollars in cash safely off this island. I would like some of your soldiers to provide us with an armed escort to the airport."

Roberto Bento paused and looked at General Douglas, who replied,
"That's no problem when do you need this escort?"

"In two hours."

"Do you need them to accompany you all the way to Puerto Rico?"

"Oh, I am not going to Puerto Rico. I am flying to Cuba. Cuba has no extradition or diplomatic agreements with the United States. I am sure you are aware of the outstanding U.S. warrants against me."

General Horatio registered his surprise, "Cuba, you have got to be kidding. I can see us being shot down as soon as we enter Cuban airspace."

For the first time Roberto Bento smiled, "When you have a hundred million in cash and a potential for another $500,000,000 to invest in a country, they supply the transportation. A Cuban air force jet, without markings, will be coming to pick me up. I just want to make sure there are no screw ups when they come in."

Control interjected at this point, **"GENERAL DOUGLAS THIS HAS BEEN CLEARED ALL THE WAY UP TO THE PRESIDENT. IT IS NOT ROBERTO BENTO'S**

246

FAULT THAT HE HAS TO LEAVE THE ISLAND. HE HAS TO GO SOMEWHERE, AND IT IS FULLY UNDERSTANDABLE WHY HE DOES NOT WANT TO GO TO THE UNITED STATES. CUBA IS THE CLOSEST COUNTRY WITHOUT AN EXTRADITION TREATY WITH THE USA. WHILE. WE DO WANT HIM TO STAND TRIAL FOR HIS CRIMES, NOW IS NOT THE TIME TO MUDDY THE WATER. WE ARE GETTING ENOUGH NEGATIVE PRESS WITHOUT ADDING TO IT."

"Don't worry Mister Bento, the Cuban jet will have no problem landing in Saint Matts."

"Good, now I have a present for you."

"A present?

Yes, a fully stocked hotel. I can take the cash, but I can't take the steaks, lobsters, wine, beer, scotch and all the other odds and ends that make up a first-class hotel. On Sunday it will probably all be reduced to ashes which would be a hell of a shame. I want you and your men to enjoy the hotel for the next two days. This master key opens every locked door in this hotel. Enjoy yourself. If they shut the electricity off, our generators will automatically kick in and they have enough fuel to keep this hotel running for long past Sunday at noon."

Bento tossed the plastic card, which was his personal master key, to General Douglas, who caught it with a big smile.

"Thanks, that is great. Much appreciated. I have to be careful about inviting our troops over here as we still have a lot of people to transfer off this island, but I think by about noon on Saturday we will pretty well be finished, and I am sure the troops would enjoy a party before we evacuate them. Is there anything else we can do for you Mister Bento?"

"No getting me and my two aides safely on the plane is all I want."

"Great, let me leave and get things organized for your departure.""

They shook Bento's hand and left. As Rob and Horatio were walking through the lobby, Horatio tossed Rob the master key and said, "I will not be able to take advantage of this until tomorrow. Why don't you and your family take advantage of it now? I'll know where you are if I need you. You can take the Humvee and go back to your compound."

Rob said, "Are you sure?"

"Yeah, I am sure. You and your family have made this job a lot easier than it could have been. Look on it as the last supper the prisoner gets before his execution."

"Christ, that's morbid downer."

"Hey, you're the one who made this choice. I just want to see you happy for the next twenty-four hours."

"Okay, I guess you're right. You go through life holding back because you do not know how much time you've got left. I know how much time I've got left and no reason to hold back."

"You got it."

They climbed into the Humvee. The driver dropped the General off at the airport and then proceeded out to the North Road. When they got to the Rock cut, with the thought of the dynamite that could send tons of rock down on them, Rob got out of the Humvee and waved up at the cliffs. He yelled, "It's me I'm coming in." One of the cousins yelled back, "Okay." He could then hear a warning that he was coming in echoing down the rock cut from cousin to cousin.

They wheeled into the compound. His mother and Barbara came running of the house. Barbara beat his mother to him. He gave her a kiss and a hug and then gave his waiting mother a hug. Holding Barbara's hand, they walked back to the porch where his father was watching the return of his one and only son. Rob sat down beside his father and squeezed his shoulder while his mother went off to get him and his father a beer.

He looked at his father and said, "Are you ready for a holiday?"

"Holiday?"

"Yep, I've got the keys to the Saint Matts Hotel and Casino. The Bishop family has been invited to go in and eat their food, drink their booze, sleep in their beds, swim in their pool. The hotel has been abandoned."

His father smiled and said, "Why the hell not. It will take our mind off Sunday. I say we go." His mother nodded in agreement. Barbara didn't nod her agreement. Rob looked at her and said, "What's wrong Barbara?"

"Could it be some kind of trap?"

"In what way?"

"Inside the compound, I feel safe. You were originally prepared to fight the U.S. army. Maybe this is their attempt to get us out from behind our castle walls. I don't trust them."

"The majority of the Mattitians have been evacuated. Things will be winding down over the next 12 hours. The cousins have worked hard. Some of them will be among the last to evacuate. It will be our last chance to see them before they leave. The hotel is next to the airport. Why not have a party? It may be the last one we ever have."

After he said that, Rob felt bad. It kind of put a damper on the initial enthusiasm for the party. Barbara now felt badly that she had not enthusiastically embraced the idea of the party. She said in a low firm voice, "You're right Rob. Let's eat drink and be merry." She smiled. Rob knew that she had left off the ending of the quotation which was, "Let's eat drink and be merry for tomorrow we die."

"Okay, let's round up everyone in the compound and head for the hotel. The cousins will be able to join us at the hotel as they finish with their scouting job with the troops." Rob set off to call at each house in the compound to inform them of the party. Then he climbed the mountain to get the cousins down from guarding the rock cut.

In half an hour, everyone had piled into cars. Rob led the convoy out of the compound, through the rock cut and up the North Road to the hotel. They encountered only one evacuation truck on the drive up. It was too early in the afternoon to encounter any monkeys by the road.

The holiday atmosphere rapidly deserts a large, hotel without guests and staff. When they convoy pulled up at the impressive entrance of brass, glass and marble, they all sat in stunned silence for a few minutes. Having been isolated inside their compound, the emptying of the island had been a fleeting nebulous thing but now they were faced with reality that everyone was gone. They had all frequently visited this hotel. They knew the doormen, the bell boys, the receptionists, the concierge team, the waiters, the store keepers, cooks, the security staff and housekeeping staff. They were all gone. The hotel was open to thieves and mayhem. There were no thieves left to steal anything and the Bishops were not good at mayhem.

Rob was the first to get out. He stood on the wide steps leading into the hotel and shouted for them to get out and join him. They left their vehicles as they were on the long driveway which would not have been allowed, if there had been doormen. They trooped into the hotel with their overnight bags. If these are your last two days, you don't have to worry about packing a lot of clothes.

The family gathered around Rob in the lobby. He said, "I think we all need a drink." They followed him over to the lobby lounge. He went behind the bar and liberated a bottle of premium scotch from the display. He poured himself a Scotch, neat no ice. The others followed his lead and started to help themselves.

One of the cousins, who had sold and helped install the reservation and room management system at the hotel, volunteered to assign the best rooms in the hotel to the group. Some followed him over to get their room.

There were five restaurants in the hotel. After he had finished his drink, Rob and his mother decided to tour each of the kitchens to see what food supplies were available. The steak restaurant had thousands of pounds of steak; the seafood restaurant had thousands of pounds of seafood. Unfortunately, if they were going to eat, then they would have to cook it themselves. With much grumbling about a woman's work never being done, Monique Bishop, her sisters and nieces began to gather food for a barbeque.

Barbara had stuck close to Rob. She followed him over to the reception area. The cousin who was behind the counter smiled when he saw them.

"For you I have booked you into the Presidential suite. It is suite 610 on the top floor. All you have to do is swipe the sensor with your personal ID card."

Rob smiled and said great. He and Barbara headed to the elevators. For once, there was no waiting. As soon as the elevator door closed, he put his arms around Barbara and drew her to him. They kissed long and hard. His tongue stroked her tongue. His hands went up under her dress. The elevator door opened. He picked her up and carried her to the room's door. He had to put her down to open the door. As soon as they were inside, and the door was shut, he proceeded to unbutton her dress and unhook her brassiere. Barbara at the same time was unbuttoning his shirt, undoing his belt and pulling the fly down on his pants. They stumbled into the bedroom of the suite and fell naked onto the bed. They had not said a word since they left the lobby. They made love like neither of them had made love before, slowly, tenderly, sensitively, trying to fulfill each other's inner desires.

After, they lay still, holding each other in their arms. Feeling cool from the air conditioning, Rob pulled the bed spread over them. Barbara kissed him gently and said, "I love you."

Rob hugged her and kissed her and said, "I want to spend the rest of my life with you. Will you marry me?"

Barbara's eyes opened wide and she gave him a hard look, "Are you kidding?" she said.

"No, I am serious. Time is relative. Minutes can seem like days. Days can feel like years. Although I can't believe that we have only two days left, I want to make it the best two days of your and my life. That means committing myself to you until death do us part. In my last dying moment, I want to be holding my wife's hand."

"Rob are you serious?"

Yes, I'm serious."

"Who is going to marry us? There are no clergy left on the island."

"Ahhh that means you accept my proposal."

"Of course, I do."

"Well, I understand there is always a chaplain attached to the troops. He could probably do it for us."

Control interjected at this point, **"THERE IS A CHAPLAIN WITH THE TROOPS, A CAPTAIN PAYNE. WE WILL CONTACT HIM AND SEE IF HE CAN DO IT."**

Rob started to laugh. Barbara looked at him and said, "Why are you laughing."

Rob pointed at the ring on his finger, "I had forgotten all about this ring on my finger. They have been listening in and recording everything. They have just now volunteered to contact the chaplain. I guess you have to take the good along with the bad. I thank them for their assistance and compassion."

Barbara instinctively pulled the bed spread around her as if to protect herself from prying eyes.

Control came back into their sanctuary, Rob held up his hand to show Barbara he was receiving a communication, **"CAPTAIN PAYNE SAYS HE IS BOTH WILLING AND ABLE TO MARRY YOU AND SUGGESTS SATURDAY AFTERNOON AT FOUR O'CLOCK. HE SAYS BY THEN ALL THE MATTITIANS EXCEPT YOUR FAMILY SHOULD HAVE BEEN EVACUATED AND THEY WILL HAVE STARTED TO REMOVE SOLDIERS AND EQUIPMENT."**

Rob responded to control, "Thank you for your assistance we look forward to our marriage."

As he held his hand up and looked at his watch. It was almost seven o'clock. He asked, "Are you hungry?"

"Yes, I could eat."

"Well, I guess we had better get dressed and go down stairs and join the others. After all we have to invite them to a wedding tomorrow."

Barbara leaped out of bed and into his arms. He pressed her naked body close to his. She leaned back and moaned and said, "We're never going to get down stairs at this rate." Rob laughed and let her go.

When they got down to the lobby, they could hear loud reggae music playing over the speaker but could not see the family. They followed the music and found that the party had moved out onto the huge tiled patio between the hotel and the beach. The patio barbeques were smoking, and he could smell steak and lobster. The round tables were loaded down with potato salad, cobs of corn, salads, corn bread and bottles of wine. He grabbed a spoon and an empty bottle of wine. Holding it high in the air, he rapped the spoon against it. The clanging soon got everyone's attention. Someone turned off the music.

"I would like to make an announcement."

"Everyone quit talking, expecting bad news."

"Barbara and I are getting married here tomorrow at four P.M. and you are all invited to the wedding."

A cheer went up and his parents, aunts and uncles all came to congratulate them. His mother asked him whether he was giving Barbara a ring. He said he had not even thought about a ring. His mother took her own wedding ring and engagement ring off and gave it to him. She said, "You can use mine, I won't need it much longer."

Looking deep into Barbara's eyes, he took her left hand and inserted her finger into the engagement ring. It fit. Tears started to well in her eyes. She smiled at Rob as the tears slid down her cheeks. Rob hugged her to him. He said nothing. He didn't need to.

CHAPTER 27

Condemnation.

On Friday morning the United Nations News Centre had released the following breaking news bulletin –

"The United Nations Secretary-General Ram Singh today issued his condemnation of the United States military operation on the Caribbean nation of Saint Matt's. The statement was delivered at the Economic Commission Conference for Latin America and the Caribbean in Nassau, Bahamas.

The UN chief called for an immediate end to the Unites States evacuation operations that were removing the population of Saint Matts in anticipation of the United States detonating a nuclear device on the island this coming Sunday. The detonation of such a device will result in radioactive fallout across much of the Southern Hemisphere, potentially causing untold health problems to millions of people in the Caribbean, Latin America, South America and Africa for years to come.

The General Secretary stated that, "I remain deeply concerned about this forced, massive displacement of all 40,000 citizens of Saint Matts, a sovereign, independent nation and member of the United Nations.

Mr. Singh said this in the message, which was delivered on his behalf, by Kim Sung Boon, his Special Representative and head of the UN Regional Office for Latin America and the Caribbean.

He related how the democratically elected prime minister of Saint Matts had been assassinated on Wednesday by parties unknown and how the assassination was believed to be a result of lawful discussions between Saint Matts and the People's Republic of China concerning the lease of land on the island. No aggressive action had been initiated or even been proposed against the United States of America by either Saint Matts or the People's Republic of China.

The United States invasion is in violation of international law and the terms and conditions of the United Nation's charter of which the United States is a founding member.

This aggressive action by the United States of America poses a threat to the world's stability. The Secretary- General demanded their "immediate and complete cessation of all destabilizing activities and for the immediate removal of all the American troops from the island. "I condemn this assault upon a peaceful, sovereign country's very existence. The matter requires thorough investigation by relevant institutions and the perpetrators of the sovereign violation must be held accountable," he said.

He further pledged the readiness of the United Nations to provide appropriate support to Saint Matts, in cooperation with other regional and international partners.

He further stated, "I strongly encourage continued and strengthened high-level dialogue at the bilateral and regional level aimed at finding a durable solution to this charter violation, this would include the thorough addressing of the underlying causes of this intervention,"
He further called for an immediate high-level meeting of the General Assembly."

All the government of the United States heard was "blah, blah, blah". It was only one of many news releases by world governments. The United Kingdom released the following,

"British Government Seeks Commonwealth Condemnation of the United States

Foreign Affairs Minister, Sir Percival Peach said that the United Kingdom would be seeking British Commonwealth condemnation of the United States intention to explode a nuclear device on the Caribbean Island of commonwealth member, Saint Matts, and also for the forced evacuation of this commonwealth member's citizens.

Sir Percival said that he would be raising the issue in New York with the Commonwealth Ministerial Action Group. It investigates all human rights abuses in the 54-nation group. He added "that the Action Group provides a much broader sense of condemnation.

At a later summit, he said "the United Kingdom would agitate for a much greater commitment to sovereign nation freedom and self-determination for all Commonwealth members."

Where American's did sit up and take note was when the following full-page advertisement appeared in major newspapers around the world. It was allegedly written by Marigold Dupont, Chief Executive of the Protect All Primates foundation. The advertisement had pictures of a vervet monkey family, happy and free in the wild. It contained the following headline:

"The question is not, can monkey's reason? Nor, can they talk? But, can monkeys suffer?"

80,000 primates will be unlawfully destroyed by the United States government this Sunday on the Caribbean Island of Saint Matts. The Foundation for the Protect All Primates condemns this reprehensible, unnecessary act of terrorism.

For decades, Protect All Primates has led marches and demonstrations against drug and cosmetic companies who were using primates in their harmful testing of commercial

products. While the foundation has brought the agony and disfigurement of these test primates to the world audience, never has it faced the magnitude of unjustified slaughter of primates that the United States is intent upon committing.

In the past, dedicated sympathizers of the foundation have resorted to illegal acts. Laboratories were broken into and the primates were rescued. The importers of the primates, who sold them to drug testing facilities, were attacked. To disobey a law, in order to disrupt an action to make it possible for the intended victim to escape, is not morally wrong, if that pending action is morally wrong.

The President of the United States on Sunday is prepared to murder 80,000 vervet monkeys on the island of Saint Matts without giving the foundation an opportunity to launch a legal action to have the legality of the action argued in a court of law. There is no justification for the destruction of this population.

While national security reasons are being cited for this planned destruction, this is a sham. The island of Saint Matts is no threat to the United States of America. It is believed that these monkeys will be destroyed simply to demonstrate American military superiority by a president seeking re-election later this year.

While, the 40,000 human beings, who share this island with the monkeys, are being evacuated, no consideration is being given to the rescue of the much larger monkey population. The monkeys are being treated like stones. Like things that do not exist.

The Foundation maintains that it is a capacity for suffering that is the vital characteristic that gives lower creatures the right to equal consideration. The monkeys of Saint Matts are fellow beings who can feel pain and can suffer.

The foundation proposes that rather than destroy every living thing on the island of Saint Matts, that the island be quarantined and allowed to return to its natural state. It would then be a safe haven for the monkeys for time eternal.

The United States has the military power to easily enforce such quarantine if it is their intent to prevent human beings from visiting it. The island does not need to be destroyed with a nuclear bomb whose radiation fall out will haunt us for decades to come.

Only hours are left to stop this despicable act. It is time for not only Americans but the people of the world to let the President of the United States know that his immorality is being recorded for all time. Phone your local politicians. Join us in our picketing of the White House. Support Protect All Primates."

This advertisement triggered a massive fire storm of publicity about the evacuation of Saint Matts' citizens and the impending explosion of a nuclear bomb on the island. The television and internet news casts showed the video that Barbara Wall had taken of the monkeys at the pool in the pristine jungle of Saint Matt's. Members of the Senate and House of Representatives received hundreds of thousands of e-mails from outraged citizens, intent upon saving the monkeys. They in turn passed the angst of their constituents on to the commander in chief in the White House whose intent had been to use the situation to improve his chance of re-election. The white house was surrounded by a mob of unruly citizens who were shouting, "SAVE THE MONKEYS, SAVE THE MONKEYS, SAVE THE MONKEYS."

The president was flooded with requests by the media to face the nation and explain why it was necessary to obliterate the island of Saint Matts. This was the last thing he wanted to do. He called a meeting of his top advisers. They suggested that he should meet with Marigold DuPont and persuade her of the necessity to bomb the island. The bagmen, among the advisers, hoped that this meeting could salvage the millions of dollars that Protect All Primates had routinely donated to the Republican Party in the past. They had quotas to reach and had been counting on this money.

Marigold, as soon as she had arrived in Washington Thursday evening, had attempted to arrange a meeting with the president through the fawning bagmen that had always danced to her tune. She quickly learned that a president, who does not want to be reached, is not going to be reached. Her pleas to meet with the president were politely listened to. She was assured, with the greatest of sincerity, that her request for a meeting would be immediately brought to his attention.

Recognizing that she was getting the run around, she immediately moved to plan B which was to put pressure on the president through the media. It took her only a few hours to arrange, at great expense to the foundation, for the full-page ads to appear in all next morning's major newspapers in the world that she could reach that night. The ad agency who handled the creative work and the media placements made sure that they were well recompensed for working long into the night and early morning.

Marigold fell into bed in her suite at the Four Seasons Hotel at 2:30 that Friday morning. At 10:00 she was woken by her phone ringing, even though she had requested that no phone calls be put through. Annoyed she answered the phone. It was one of the unctuous bagmen asking if she could be available to have lunch with the president at the White House. She sleepily replied that she would be. He said that he would personally pick her up at the hotel at 11:30.

When she was taking her shower a few minutes later, she wondered how they knew which hotel she was at. She had only left her personal communication device number when she had been trying to get a meeting with the president and she had turned it off when she had gone to bed. "Politicians" she thought to herself, "are such a scummy bunch that you couldn't believe anything that came out of their mouth". You always had to count your fingers after shaking hands with them.

After she had finished dressing, she took the elevator down to the lobby to see the concierge. He was a handsome, elderly gentleman with a mass of pure white, neatly cut hair, very distinguished. The kind of man she liked. She told him she needed a small, unobtrusive, recording device by 11:25 A.M. and that money was no objection. He said no problem and that he would have one brought to her room. At 11:15 there was a knock at her door. A bell boy was there with a package. He handed it to her. She tipped him, and he left.

She opened the package it contained a small dictation machine which connected to a small remote microphone the size of a dime that she clipped to the inside her brassiere. The instructions said the machine would record 3 hours of conversation. She turned it on and put it in her purse.

She was ready sitting in the lobby, not at the door. She did not want to appear to be too eager. Precisely at 11:30 Matt Dunning, the chief Republican bag man, burst into the lobby. He looked expectantly around and then finally spotted her, a harmless, little old lady sitting on a hotel couch. He came over with his big toothy grin and hail-fellow-well-met demeanor. She shook his hand and followed him quietly out to the drive way at the side of the lobby that runs down to the

Pennsylvania Avenue North West. A very official looking limousine was waiting for her.

They headed East, around Washington Circle Park, past the US Post Office, turned onto 17 Street South West which would take them down to the entrance that would put them at the South Lawn entrance. As they got close to the White House, the streets were crowded with thousands of people shouting. Marigold could not hear what they were shouting. She lowered her window and heard, "SAVE THE MONKEYS. SAVE THE MONKEYS".

She smiled. She couldn't believe it. She looked with wonder at Matt Dunning. He avoided her eyes. He did not look happy to see the demonstrators. She started to laugh and was still laughing as the way was cleared so they could get into the driveway.

When they arrived at the South entrance to the White House, she was led through the Diplomatic Reception Room and upstairs to the private family dining room on the second floor. When she entered the dining room, the president rose and greeted her like she was a long-lost sister. He kissed her on her cheek, hugged her and insisted that she sit next to him. Matt Dunning sat across from her. She was handed a menu with her name on it.

There was a choice of vegetarian fare. Someone had done their homework. All three items were favorites. She chose the mushroom risotto with a California salad. A glass of a good white California wine was poured.

"Well Marigold, what brings you to Washington?"

"Willie, let's cut the crap.""

President Willie Brown winced as if he had been slapped in the face. This was not going to be the walk in the park he had hoped for. He had decided to treat her like a little old lady (which she was) but this was a mistake.

"Now, now Marigold I am sure that we can find a solution to this little problem."

Marigold exploded, her voice rising, "Little problem, you are about to murder 80,000 vervet monkeys and wipe an island off the face of the earth and you call it a little problem?"

Backed into a corner, the president became defensive, "Marigold, I love animals just as much as you do. We have looked at various solutions to saving the monkeys but there are just too many of them. This is a large, very mountainous island covered in dense jungle. It would take years to capture them."

"Then don't capture them. Leave them alone. By taking the humans off the island you've removed their only natural predator. They will get along just fine. If you don't want the damn Chinese on the island, then just embargo the island."

Trying to buy time, he decided to placate her, "Well Marigold we could certainly take that into consideration. It would require a change of plans. I will take it up with my advisors."

"You do that."

Marigold wondered if she had at least delayed the dropping of the nuclear bomb. Their first course of turtle soup arrived. She couldn't believe it. "What a bunch of insensitive clods they were," she thought to herself. An endangered turtle species had probably been slaughtered to provide the soup to a vegetarian. She put down her spoon, not having touched it, and signaled for the waiter to take it away. Willie Brown slurped his soup and seemed to enjoy it and didn't notice Marigold's disapproval. The risotto arrived. Matt Dunning thought that this was the ideal time to float by her what was foremost in his mind.

"Miss DuPont can the party count on Preserve All Primates for their usual generous donation?"

Marigold looked at him and replied, "I tell you what Matt, if your party saves my monkeys, I'll write a check right now that is double the five million, I gave them two years ago - ten million dollars, how does that sound."

That seemed to get both Matt's and the President's attention. The two men looked at each other almost drooling. Matt responded, "Well Marigold, I am sure if we had that check, you could stop worrying about those monkeys"

"Fine, money talks, bullshit walks, "she said as she reached for her purse. She opened it up and took out her check book. She opened it knowing that politicians had very short, selective; memories and that once they had her money that they might well "forget" that they had agreed to save the monkeys. There were no written contracts between them. It was all based on trust and the greed of getting repeat funding from her in the future. Whether Willie Brown got re-elected or lost the November election, he knew, and so did she, that he would never be running again, wouldn't need her donations again and could safely toss Marigold DuPont to the side of the road.

Fighting her premonitions, she went ahead and wrote out the check for ten million and handed it to Matt Dunning. She had said she would do whatever she had to do to rescue these monkeys and if a ten-million-dollar check would do it then it was worth it. As well, it was just money, not even hers. Ten million dollars is just a number when you are seventy-four years old. Of course, she had her insurance quietly recording the conversation in her purse. She would crucify him if he tried to screw her.

Dunning received the check with a big silly smile on his face. The president also had a big smile. He thought he was pretty damn smart and effective. He had averted a confrontation with Marigold Dupont and received a donation that would help get him elected in November. Now she could call off the damn demonstrators that he could faintly hear chanting outside, "Save the monkeys. Save the monkeys."

They played nice with each other as they had their dessert and coffee. The president again gave her hugs and kisses as she was leaving. As she was walking down the steps to the waiting limousine, the president turned to Matt and said, "See that the check gets certified this afternoon, we don't want any stop payments screwing things up."

Willie looked closely at the check. It was drawn on a New York bank. It was Friday afternoon. The banks closed in a few hours. He was going to have to use all the resources at the disposal of a president to get to the bank it was drawn on today. He left the president at a run. Getting to New York was just a negligible cost of doing business.

CHAPTER 28

Decision

Saturday morning, dawned cold and grey in Washington, snow was in the forecast. After all, it was February, Willie Brown thought to himself. The monkey demonstrators had all gone home. The only demonstrator out in the cold, damp winter morning was one who was there every Saturday morning, carrying his placard that read "USA TAXING CIGARETTES UNFAIRLY". Willie Brown wondered every time he drove past this demonstrator who he was: could he be a tobacco executive who picketed on his day off or maybe a really hooked smoker or, depending on how paranoid he felt that day, perhaps a foreign spy or presidential assassin who had assumed a disguise that essentially made him invisible to White House security.

Willie's resolve kept fluctuating back and forth. Was he or was he not going to bomb Saint Matts? Today was decision time. It had all seemed so very straightforward. Bomb the island and send a message to the voters that Willie Brown was their fearless leader who would protect them from terrorists and all their other boogeymen. The grateful electorate would then re-elect him for another four years. It was a simple concept. Why did it seem to be coming off the rails?

Monkeys! Who gives a shit about monkeys? Obviously, it seems the electorate did. Letters, petitions, phone calls, e-mails, twitters, just about everything but skywriting, had been blasted at him. That damn monkey woman with her full-page ad yesterday had certainly stirred things up. Pundits and politicians all around the world had jumped on the band wagon. Even that hypocrite Senator Rick Wilcox was condemning the extinction of the monkeys on Saint Matts and it had been his damn idea.

Yes, he knew that he had accepted the $10,000,000 from the monkey lady on the condition that he not kill her monkeys on Sunday, but he could always say that he had understood that it was just her usual donation to the Republican party and didn't remember that her concerns about monkeys even came up. She would squawk but what was she going to do about it. He chuckled to himself about fools and their money soon being parted. Well, he was backed into a corner. He had told the Chinese that he was going to bomb the island and close the American bases in South East Asia. If he closed the China Sea bases and did not bomb the island, then he would be accused of bending to the Chinese and there would go his re-election. The bomb was intended to be his sleight of hand distraction that all good magicians used, to take the audience's attention away from the real game being played.

The United States was in a serious predicament. The Chinese were now in control. He and the Chinese did not want this new world order to be evident to Americans. The Chinese did not want to shoot themselves in the foot. They wanted nothing to interfere with their exports to the United States.

The only good thing about the monkeys was that it had distracted the public away from any concern about that stubborn Doctor Lyons and his family being wiped out along with the monkeys on Sunday. It is too bad. Rob Lyons seemed like a very capable individual. He could have made a major contribution to the State Department.

The buck stopped here. It was his job to make the big decisions. His decision had not been swayed by all the correspondence that called for him to be impeached for destroying Saint Matts or had suggested he was going straight to hell or that he was an inhuman monster who should be assassinated. The pleading, weeping, wailing and bribing had all failed to move him. You had to be strong to be president and he was strong.

The bomb was going to be dropped, as he had ordered at noon on Sunday. He had an election to win. His back was against the wall and when you are backed into a corner you have to do what you have to do.

CHAPTER 29

Marriage

Rob woke up with Barbara curled deliciously around him. He smelled her perfume. For a moment, he was not sure where he was. Then he remembered he was in the presidential suite at the Saint Matts Hotel and Casino.

He looked at the slit of sunlight squeezing in through a crack in curtains. He figured it was close to nine o'clock. He raised his head, so he could see the clock on the night table. It read 8:48. He was pleased that he was so close.

Late into the night he had been accepting the congratulations from his cousins, aunts and uncles on today's marriage. Many toasts were drunk, and many memories savored. There would be hangovers this morning.

Today, he would get married. Tomorrow, he would die. He still had a hard time accepting the possibility that the United States of America would thoughtlessly and arbitrarily execute him, Barbara and the others in his family, without a legal trial and without any legal justification. Impossible, he could not believe that the country he knew and loved could commit such an illegal, immoral act. Surely, he had decades to love and enjoy a life with Barbara.

He kissed Barbara's hand. It was draped over him. He savored her heat in the air-conditioned room which gave him no great incentive to get out of bed. Barbara moaned softly, and he could feel her gradually came awake. She hugged him closer to her. They made love. After, sated, they lay holding each other, wishing that the warm glow could last forever.

Hunger finally overcame inertia. They got up, showered and made their way down stairs to forage for food in the hotel's larder. There was no one else around.

An empty hotel is eerie. They found a refrigerator that contained thousands of egg containers. Rob took enough to make a gigantic omelet. He found some cheese and tomatoes to add to it. He toasted some rye bread he found. They took their food out to the wide balcony to eat at one of wrought iron tables. It overlooked the beach. They listened to the surf roaring in and receding. The tropical sun was warm and lush. As they slowly ate, his mother and father came out and joined them on the balcony. Rob could tell that his mother had been crying. He got up and put his arms around her and hugged her.

"Oh Rob", she said, "I am so scared. You are our hope. You have so much to contribute."

"Mum, I am still here and I'm sure I will be here tomorrow and for many days after that and so will you, to enjoy your future grandchildren and all the other good things yet to come. They are not going to drop that bomb. It is all just their usual posturing and bluster."

She looked up at him and gave him a half smile. Rob didn't know what else to say to her. He patted her on her back. His father came along and sat down beside her. He held her hand.

"Barbara and I are going to go for a walk along the beach," Rob said. He needed some time to think, to walk slowly, fill his nose with the smell the ocean, feel the surf roll up the slope and gently kiss his bare feet as he trod on the hard-wet sand it left behind as it retreated.

They walked across the immense tiled patio to the sea wall. He took off his sandals and left them on the wall. There wasn't anyone to steal them. When he stepped down onto the hot sand, heated by the blow torch of a mid-day sun, it burned his feet. It felt like he was stepping on a thousand little needle points. They hurried across to the relief of the wet cool sand close to the water. The steady, strong trade wind kept them cool.

Hand in hand, they walked up the shimmering beach for a mile or more before turning around and heading back.

They didn't say much. He found it unnerving to find the beach and all the villas along it deserted. Usually you would encounter three or four other couples whenever you walked the beach. As they walked, Rob kept on thinking, if this is my last day of life what I want to do to squeeze as much out of it as I can. What would I rather be doing than walking on a beach beside the ocean in the sunshine with Barbara? He realized that that is exactly what he would want to do.

As they got closer to the hotel, he saw a tall figure in army fatigues walking toward them. As they got closer, they realized it was General Horatio Douglas. He had taken off his boots and socks and then rolled up his pants to his knees. He stopped waited for Barbara and Rob to come to him.

"How did you find us," Rob asked?

Horatio pointed to the ring on his finger. Rob looked down at his matching ring. It had become so much a part of him that he forgot about it. He had forgot that everything he saw, they saw and everything he heard, they heard.

"I wanted to check something out with both of you. The last plane full of Mattitians is leaving just about now. We are running ahead of schedule," as he said this Horatio looked at his watch. "We've started to dismantle our equipment and will commence our embarkation process with the next planes that come in. We should be out of here by midnight. I've got a bunch of cooks and others hanging around here for another eleven hours. I was wondering if you would object to them preparing your wedding feast," he smiled as he said that.

"That would be wonderful," Barbara said.

"Oh Yeah, I forgot to mention that I had them fly in a wedding cake from Puerto Rico." Rob shook his head and said, "You're kidding?"

Horatio had a big smile on his face when he replied, "Listen, you and your whole family have been a big help to us on this assignment and I wanted to do something for you."

Rob shook his hands.

"One other thing, I have to bring up. I recognize that you feel strongly about the president's decision in regard to Saint Matts and feel that even if it costs you your lives that you have to do everything you can to protect the country you love. I respect that, but I am asking you not to put your lives in jeopardy. The bomb is going to be dropped. Your willingness to sacrifice your lives will unfortunately not stop it. The power structure feels that they have much greater things at stake than a few lives lost in Saint Matts. I think you would be far more effective if you lived and made sure that no one forgot Saint Matts and what happened here. Can you please let me fly you and your whole family out of here tonight?"

Rob looked at Horatio, decision time, again. Do I go, or do I stay? Finally, he replied, "Horatio, I thank you for trying. I don't want to die but sometimes you've got to do what you've got to do, despite the consequences. I am not sure I could live with myself if I just turned and ran away."

"Okay, I had to ask. I can't say that I am happy with your reply. If you change your mind, we will get you out of here. Now, I've got a wedding to organize."

The three of them walked back to the hotel. Horatio had left his boots where Rob and Barbara had left their sandals. They went back to their room, changed into bathing suits and joined all the Bishops who had gathered around the giant swimming pool. The pool bar was manned by one of the cousins who was quickly depleting the bottles that had been left behind. They spent the rest of the afternoon talking, laughing, drinking and remembering happier times. At 3:00 they returned to their room to shower and dress for the wedding in matching new white shorts and cotton knit short sleeved shirts that they had liberated from the clothing store in the hotel lobby.

They noticed on their way back into the hotel that there was suddenly a large military presence scurrying around the hotel. They were wheeling big round tables into the lobby and covering them in white table clothes and laying out plates and cutlery. Chairs for the tables were also being covered in white. A head table had also been set up. In another corner of the large lobby, a separate area had been set up for the wedding ceremony. Stacking chairs had been laid out in a theatre arrangement with a central aisle. In the lobby bar area, a sergeant who looked like he knew what he was doing was busily polishing glasses.

At four o'clock the two of them stepped out of the elevator to applause and cheers from the family and soldiers. Horatio came over and said to Rob, "Can I give the bride away."
"Sure, thanks Horatio."

Rob walked over, to where he saw an army chaplain standing, to wait for Horatio to escort Barbara to him. The family and the soldiers quickly took their seats. An army private who had wheeled in an organ from somewhere in the hotel, started to play, "Here Comes the Bride". Horatio led Barbara, on his arm, down the aisle between the rows of chairs.

As Rob looked down the row at Barbara approaching, he was surprised to see CIA agents Ken Davis and Mandy Derk. They smiled at him and gave him thumbs up. He smiled back. He wondered why he had not seen them earlier with the others from the compound. Barbara looked radiant on Horatio's arm. Rob felt in his pocket to make sure he still had the wedding ring his mother had given him. Finally, she was standing beside him. The army chaplain performed a religious wedding service that was really no different than the typical non-army wedding ceremony. Rob placed the ring on Barbara's finger.

The minister's final words were, "Therefore, it is my joyful responsibility to officially acknowledge your union as "Husband and Wife." You may now seal your marriage with a kiss."

They kissed. To Rob, standing in the soaring lobby of the Saint Matt's Hotel in Casino, it seemed like something out of a movie. The chaplain continued, "May the glory which rests upon all who love you, bless you and keep you, fill you with happiness and a gracious spirit. Despite all changes of fortune and time, may that which is noble and lovely and true remain abundantly in your hearts, giving you strength for all that lies ahead." He finished with the traditional, "Ladies and Gentlemen, it is my privilege to present to you for the very first time, Mr. and Mrs. Robert and Barbara Lyons!

The witnesses clapped and cheered. Rob walked her back down the aisle. They walked over towards the bar. A reception line quickly formed. Soldiers and family proceeded down the line, congratulating the newly married couple. There were now many more soldiers in the lobby than family. A soldier working as a waiter came by with a glass of champagne for Barbara and Rob. They toasted each other, talked and laughed. The crowd kept the bar tender busy. Glasses of ice-cold champagne on silver trays went by carried by the soldiers acting as waiters. Eventually the new couple proceeded to the head table. Rob's parents and Horatio joined them there. The center piece for the table was a three-layer wedding cake.

The first course was a delicious spring salad, followed by a seafood risotto, next was steak and lobster. A dessert table was set up on the side. Barbara got up and cut the cake and served it. A finer "last meal" could not be imagined

CIA agent, Ken Davis holding a full glass of champagne in one hand and an open bottle of champagne in the other, insisted on filling Barbara's and Rob's champagne glasses. He seemed to be a bit drunk. He then insisted on drinking a toast to them. Rob and Barbara stood up and willingly complied. They drank it all down. Rob thought the champagne had a rather unusual metal taste to it, but he did not think too much about it until suddenly he felt very dizzy and tired. He had to sit down. As the room started to spin and turn black, he wondered if he had been poisoned. His head slumped down on the table. Barbara alsocollapsed.

There was a gasp from the crowd. Colin started to get to his feet to go assist them. Horatio put his arm on his shoulder to indicate he should stay seated. With his other hand he made a motion for someone to approach. Soldiers with two stretchers suddenly appeared moving rapidly towards the head table.

There was as a shift in the room. Each member of the Bishop family was flanked by three soldiers. Horatio then called," Do not be alarmed. Everything is under control. Rob and Barbara are going to be just fine, and we will be taking good care of them. Unfortunately, the party is now over. The soldiers went to the compound this afternoon and packed your personal belongings and transported them to the airport. Trucks are now waiting in front of the hotel to take you to the airport where you will be immediately processed and transported to Puerto Rico. These soldiers will be escorting you. I regret that your evacuation had to be done this way."

A shout went up from the crowd, "You lying, son-of-a-bitch, we trusted you."

Horatio looked at them and said, "Never trust a soldier who has taken an oath to obey his commander-in-chief. My orders, direct from the president of the United States, was to remove every human being from the island of Saint Matts and that is exactly what I am doing as painlessly, for you, as I could engineer. Tomorrow you will be alive. Believe me, that bomb is going to be dropped. Your protest has not worked. I am saving your lives and someday you, or maybe your grandchildren, will thank me for it. The government of the United States will see that you are fairly compensated for the assets you leave behind. Tomorrow, you will start a new life."

A lot of loud angry voices were heard for a few minutes and then gradually the shock of their changed circumstances sunk in. There was a sullen rumbling undertone and then silence. The soldiers made no aggressive moves towards them. They just stood silently beside the Bishop family members, but it was obvious to the Mattitians that they were outnumbered and that the US army was in control.

The inert bodies of Rob and Barbara had also unnerved them. They were not sure if the army had killed them with poison or not. It seemed obvious that the army was prepared to do whatever was necessary, including physical force, to get them to off the island. The fight went out of them. Secretly, they hid their relief that they would no longer be facing death tomorrow. Now, that the decision had been taken out their hands, they just wanted to get off the island. They were told that they would be accompanied back to their rooms to pack anything that they had brought to the hotel and that they would disembark for the airport in half an hour.

General Douglas followed the two stretchers out to the ambulance where the two unconscious newlyweds were placed side by side. Ken Davis and Mandy Derk joined them in the ambulance. Horatio had motioned for Colin and Monique, to join him in following the stretchers out of the hotel. He now motioned for them to also get in the ambulance. It pulled out, around the army trucks on the long horseshoe shaped driveway that were waiting to transport the Bishops and the soldiers to the airport.

The ambulance didn't need to turn on its siren, there was no one left on the island to slow their progress. At the airport, they pulled right out onto the tarmac and headed towards a small, black corporate jet with its two engines idling. The stretchers were taken out of the ambulance and carried on board. Rob and Barbara were put on cots across from each other. A paramedic appeared. He took the two unconscious newlywed's pulse and strapped them in to their cots.

Mandy, Ken, Colin and Monique followed them onto the plane and took comfortable leather seats. They fastened their seat belts. As soon as the paramedic closed the cabin door, the plane started to roll. It roared down the runway and, in a few minutes, they left the doomed island of Saint Matts far behind. From the time they left the hotel only twenty minutes had passed. Colin looked a bit disorientated by the rapid turn of events.

"Where are we headed? Puerto Rico?" Colin asked Ken.

"No much further than that. Our destination is the Canadian Air Force Base at Trenton about an hour and a half east of Toronto."

"We don't have our passports."

"I got them for you."

271

"You broke into my safe?"

"I did. I put everything that was in it, into a lock box that I have with me along with your clothes and anything else I thought you would need."

Colin glared at him. He did not appreciate this invasion of his privacy. After a few minutes, he finally accepted that the deed was done, there was no one to complain to and their future life was in the hands of this CIA agent.

"Why aren't we flying to the U.S.?"

"Until the presidential election is over in November the current administration does not want you around. If the Republicans get in, you can probably return but, until then, you will not be allowed into the States."

"But I'm an American citizen?"

"That you are, and I'm sure that you can initiate a lawsuit that would be successful in getting this presidential order rescinded. That should take several years before it gets to court."

"How are we going to live?"

"First of all, you, your wife and Rob all have Canadian citizenship and Canadian passports, so you are legally entitled to all the rights of Canadian citizens, although it will take you six months to re-establish your universal health care. Since Barbara is now married to a Canadian citizen, we have got a special ministerial order that gives her immediate landed immigrant status which will grant her all the rights of Canadian citizen. You are far from penniless. You, your wife, Barbara and Rob will receive $100,000 checks when you disembark."

"Where are we going to live?"

"That will be up to you but initially we have rented a very nice furnished two-bedroom condo for the four of you in Toronto. The first and last month's rent has been paid. We will be transferring you to that apartment as soon as we touch down. It is currently minus twenty degrees Celsius in Toronto. We have warm clothes on board that you will change into before we land. The flight is going to take about five hours, so you might as well sit back and relax. The paramedic will keep a close eye on Rob and Barbara."

"General Douglas said that the US government would be compensating us for the assets that they have taken away from us in Saint Matts. How is that going to work?"

There is a claim form that you will complete to fully compensate you for all the assets left behind. The US government has acquired all Saint Matts government records and bank records. They are being digitized and within a few weeks they should be able to process your claim. In your case, I expect it will be a considerable sum".

Colin sat back and thought about it. His mind started working out the options. He and Monique were not keen on cold Canadian winters. They would have to find another Caribbean island for the Bishop clan to settle and invest in. Perhaps Saint Kitts would be a good option or maybe Dominica. He would start his research tomorrow as soon as he could. Life was not over. It had just begun. He relaxed and eventually fell asleep.

After they had been in the air for an hour, Rob suddenly awoke from a dreamless sleep. It was if one second, he had been sitting at the head table in the lobby of the hotel and the next second his body was transferred to another environment. He opened his eyes and did not recognize where he was. His arms and legs were strapped down. He didn't like this. He cleared his throat and coughed. This brought him to the attention of the paramedic who gave him an injection of dantrolene sodium. He tried to avoid the needle but being strapped down he couldn't. In a few seconds he felt like he had lost control over his body. He was paralyzed. He had been put in a chemical straight jacket. He couldn't even move his head. He lay there motionless staring at the ceiling the cabin until he eventually fell asleep.

Barbara came awake fifteen minutes later and was also injected by the paramedic.

Colin saw them give the injections. He asked Ken why they had to do it, recognizing that there was no way he could stop them. Ken replied, "Our orders are to keep the two of them sedated until the bomb goes off at noon. They have said that they were prepared to do whatever it took to stop the bomb being dropped, even sacrificing their own lives. The president wants this to go off smoothly and this is the simplest way of guaranteeing that they do not contact the media or do something else that could interfere with the process."

When they got within half an hour of CFB Trenton, Ken and Mandy took out the cold weather clothes out of storage for all of them to change into. They undressed and then dressed the inert bodies of Barbara and Rob in the warm clothes. As they descended, Colin looked out the window. He saw nothing, it was pitch black. He figured they must be over Lake Ontario. The Trenton Air Force Base is on the north shore of the lake.

 Their jet landed smoothly. There was a thick blanket of snow at the edge of the runway. Canada looked cold, bleak and deserted. The jet rolled to a stop in an isolated area, far from any buildings or prying eyes. The pilot left the engines idling. This was not going to take long. He was anxious to get back into U.S. air space. They were only about ten miles from the US border that ran down the middle of Lake Ontario.

A large passenger van, capable of hauling a dozen people, and an ambulance pulled up next to the jet. A hatch opened on the plane and by the headlights of the van, boxes and luggage were transferred to the van. The door to the cabin opened and they all carefully shuffled down the airplane's small ladder steps in their bulky clothes. The van was about twenty feet away. A strong, ice cold, wind was blowing from the north across the open landing field. The cold brought tears to their eyes. Quickly, they got into the shelter of the van and shut the sliding doors. In a few minutes they were warm and started to unzip their jackets. Ken Davis then got into the front seat of the van with the driver. He introduced the driver as a member of the Canadian Security and Intelligence Service.

They waited until the stretchers took Rob and Barbara off the plane and put them in the ambulance. The van started off across the field with the ambulance following. It went past a guard house and out onto a main street. Every now and then they would hit an icy stretch and the wheels would spin and the van would swerve. In about fifteen minutes they were on the 401 Expressway heading west towards Toronto and a new life.

At ten o'clock on Saturday evening the White House released a statement that they had successfully removed all of Saint Matt's citizens from the island and that the army had now deployed its resources back to Florida and were landing at the MacDill Air Force Base in Tampa. The press wanted to know what had happened to Barbara Wall and Rob Lyons who had done so much to publicize the US invasion of the island and the pending destruction of the 80,000 vervet monkeys. The White

House spokesmen said that they had no idea where they were but thought they might be among the Mattitian refugees being processed in Puerto Rico.

When the Bishop family members arrived in Puerto Rico, they were only able to say they had last seen Barbara and Rob being loaded into an ambulance in Saint Matts. They had thought they had landed in Puerto Rico ahead of them. The US army spokesman was able to truthfully say that the army had not had anything to do with the removal of Rob and Barbara and that they had no idea where they were at this time.

When the van and the ambulance arrived at the condominium apartment building on Islington Avenue in Toronto it was two thirty in the morning. Other than the doorman at the upscale apartment building no other tenants were around to see their new neighbors move in. Within half an hour the van and the ambulance had left.

The paramedic made sure that Rob and Barbara were comfortable in their beds. He then relaxed in a comfortable chair and stood guard over them. The plan was that a CIA car from the U.S. consulate office in Toronto would be waiting at noon to take the two CIA agents and the paramedic to Pearson International Airport; it was only five minutes away, so that they could return home to the USA.

Ken Davis and Mandy Derk were joined in the apartment by two local CIA agents. Ken and Mandy crashed on the couch in the living room while the two local agents made sure that Colin and Monique had no external communication and remained in their bedroom.

CHAPTER 30

Salvation

On Sunday, the sun rose over the Atlantic Ocean and shone on the lush green mountains of Saint Matts. It awoke, as it did every morning, vervet monkeys who foraged for fruit, chattering excitedly in the tree tops. Colorful birds sang loudly and flitted from palm tree to palm tree. Cows and goats plodded freely along the dusty, empty roads eating the prickly scrub brush that always threatened to over grow the roadways. Hungry dogs barked, and lonely cats meowed. Roosters crowed. Hens clucked. The surf rolled in thunderously and retreated with a sighing whisper as it had for a million years and would for a million more.

The island's departing engineers had seen no point in shutting down the electric power generators. After all, what difference would it make? Thus, alarm clocks went off in empty houses. Air conditioners hummed away, cooling no one. Telephones rang from overseas callers without being answered. Televisions that had been left on blared loudly. The clock in the central square kept perfect time for no one to see.

No one coughed or sang or mumbled to themselves or cursed angrily or groaned in agony or laughed with pleasure. No one was on their way to work, opening their store or noisily slurping a cup of coffee. No cars travelled on the roads. No boat left a white wake to scar the blue harbor. The last man had left and hadn't bothered to turn off the lights. Fifty miles off the coast a flotilla of U.S. naval ships made sure no one disturbed the island.

The live satellite image on CNN showed a deserted island. The network talking heads, with their perfect hair, at CNN, burbled excitedly about the coming show. A digital clock in a corner of the TV screen was doing the countdown, displaying the hours and minutes to show time. Retired generals and ineffective politicians were called upon to assure the viewers, repeatedly, what a wonderful country America was, how brave its military was, how smart their politicians were and how the Chinese had forced them into this unholy act of destruction.

The plane with the bomb had left MacDill Air Force Base in Florida at nine. It had flown swiftly south. A full colonel was the pilot. He had pulled rank, so he would go down in history as the pilot of the third plane to ever drop a nuclear bomb as an act of aggression. He was excited.

At two minutes to twelve the bomber approached Saint Matts. It circled at a height of five miles above the island. On the command of the pilot, the bombardier released the bomb. As it fell, the airplane sped away. At exactly two minutes after noon, as planned, it exploded two miles above the island. At that height, they had calculated that it would create the maximum damage. The massive flash from the explosion was golden, purple, violet and gray. It was so intense that a blind lady in Antigua, eighty miles away, asked what was that flash. It was as hot as the sun - thousands of degrees hot. The sailors, on the ships fifty miles away, said it felt like someone had opened an oven door. It melted or vaporized everything within a mile of the epicenter.

The pilot had been warned not to look back at the flash because it could cause blindness. Winds of over 300 miles per hour, released by explosion, flattened all trees and buildings over the entire island. Tremors could be felt through all the Eastern Caribbean. It unleashed a fire ball that ignited all combustible material on the island. Within a few minutes the island became an ash pit.

The explosion sucked dirt and dust ten miles up into the sky. The black mushroom cloud could be seen a hundred miles away. Radioactive dust floated with the prevailing south east wind towards the North Atlantic and Europe. The sand on the beaches below the blast melted into a mildly radioactive, light green glass, called trinitite.

Fish were boiled in the waters close to the shores. Cows, goats, horses, dogs and cats were vaporized or burned to a crisp. Eighty thousand wild monkeys – males, females, juveniles and infants disappeared in and instant.

Hundreds of millions around the world watched the explosion, some in horror. Patriotic Americans cheered and applauded to see such a magnificent display of their countries raw power. They were encouraged to join with those shown on the

277

television chanting "USA NUMBER ONE", "USA NUMBER ONE". Being thousands of miles away, watching it on television, the destruction was as real to the viewers as watching the coyote being demolished in a Roadrunner cartoon – and just as empty and meaningless.

Watching with the critical eye of a seasoned politician, Willie Brown sat with his top aides in the oval office. He saw what he believed was his greatest triumph. One of the senior aids excitedly murmured, "Willey that puts the election in the bag, get ready for a second term."

Willie smiled happily to hear these encouraging words. He motioned to the steward hovering in the background and announced loudly, "Get the champagne; it's time for a toast."

The ships running picket duty far off the coast of Saint Matts had been flooded with requests by American and Foreign scientists who wanted, this once in a lifetime chance, to view an actual detonation of a nuclear bomb. They had seen the flash, had felt the heat and had seen the large black mushroom cloud rise above the horizon. They were now excitedly lining up to board one of three naval helicopters assigned to take them in close to the island, so they could record and measure the extent of the destruction. This was seen as very useful intelligence gathering for future aggressions.

Colin and Monique had slept late. They had woken shortly before noon just in time to watch the destruction of Saint Matts on the television in the bedroom that they had been confined to. They wept, at the travesty, not only for the senseless destruction of their beloved island but for their loss of innocence. No one wants to face the reality that they are irrelevant, that democracy is just a word and that your freedom and home can be taken away from you on a whim. From their bedroom Colin and Monique could hear the television in the living room. The CIA agents were also watching the bombing. After the bomb dropped, they heard the apartment door slam loudly shut and they could no longer hear the television. They turned off their TV set and listened. They heard nothing.

After a few minutes they tried their door. It was no longer locked from the outside. Colin cracked open the door and peered down the hall. All was quiet. It seemed the agents had gone. They hurried down the hall. The agents had departed. Immediately they went to the bedroom where Barbara and Rob had been deposited. They were surprised to find Rob sitting on the side of his bed holding his head and looking groggily across at Barbara. She too was coming awake.

Rob looked up at his parents in wonder and asked, "Where the hell are we? What happened?"

"Colin warily responded, "How are you feeling?"

"I feel fine, a bit of a headache but that is all. Where are we?"

"We are in an apartment in Toronto."

"Toronto? How in the hell did we get to Toronto?"

"What do you last remember?"

"We were at the reception. Ken Davis filled my champagne glass and he was toasting us."

"The champagne was spiked. You were drugged. Unconscious, you were then loaded on a plane and transported to Canada.

"Why Canada? Why not Puerto Rico like everyone else?"

"They wanted us out of the way until after they dropped the bomb."

"It has been dropped?"

"Oh yes, it most definitely has been dropped."

"It's gone?"

"It's totally and utterly...destroyed", Colin said this with a sob catching in his throat. He paused, a tear rolled down his cheeks. Rob reached up pulled him down to sit on the bed beside him. He put his arm around his father.

"Dad, I loved Saint Matt's too but most of all I love you and Mom, more. You brought me up to be a survivor just like you. We still have each other. We will survive."

Colin sighed and said, "Thanks Rob, you're right. We are a family and we are strong."

Rob slowly stood up. He was a bit shaky on his feet. He caught his balance and crossed the room to sit on Barbara's bed. Her eyes were open, and she appeared confused. "Welcome to Canada," he said.

"Canada?" she croaked then cleared her throat and coughed. "What happened

Rob explained what happened with the occasional interjection from Colin and Monique. Barbara looked frightened.

"Hey Barbara, everything's OK. We're safe. We've got shelter. We're not alone. I've got money in the bank. However, I have got to admit I am hungry." Rob smiled

Barbara looked at him, sat up and then slowly stood up. Her husband stood up beside her and pulled her to him in an embrace. They kissed. She looked up at him with love in her eyes. She had been prepared to die for Saint Matts. Saint Matts was no more, but she had a strong passionate man she loved who she knew loved her and would lay down his life to protect her.

Rob brought things back to reality, "Let's check out this apartment and see if they left us anything to eat."

Holding his hand, Barbara followed Rob down the hall into the kitchen, living room, dining room, and den. She was surprised how large the apartment was. There was a counter between the kitchen and the living room with stools. On the counter were four piles of documents. They immediately sorted through their piles. On the top of each pile was an official looking envelope addressed to each of them. When they opened it, they each found a check for $100,000. Barbara was surprised.

"This is freer cash than I have had in my entire life. Why did they give it to me? I'm not a Mattitian.

Rob laughed and said, "No, you aren't but you are married to one and it could be argued that if your life had not been disrupted you would have become one. Not only that, but they have destroyed your previous life. You are in a good position to sue their asses off. If you did, then they can now argue that you were compensated for any hardship and would show this payment. Take it. Spend it. They owe you."

Rob was pleased to see his Canadian, American and Mattitian passports were all there in his pile. He was not surprised to see that his passport had an official Canadian customs and immigration stamp in it with today's date. His wallet, with all his credit cards, was also there.

"What is this in my passport, Rob?" Barbara asked waving her passport under his nose?

Rob looked at the slip of paper. "My, my, my, aren't they thorough. You have been given landed immigrant status to Canada. It would allow you to work in Canada. They must have got the Minister of Immigration in Ottawa to approve this. Dad do you and Mom have everything."

Yeah, we do. There is a lease agreement here for this apartment in my pile with your name on it. The first and last month has been paid. It even looks like your signature."

"What is the address?"

"2200 Islington Avenue. At least we know where we are."

"I know that condo complex. It's a nice one. We are only about five minutes from Pearson International Airport. What's in the fridge?"

Monique opened the fridge and looked in, "Not much here," she said, "some eggs, bacon, orange juice, milk, six cans of Coke and some apples." She paused and opened the freezer, "Oh and we have some frozen pepperoni pizzas and some ice cream".

Rob said, "I don't know about the rest of you, but I am starving. How about heating up the pizza in the microwave?" They all agreed.

Rob was suddenly yanked out of his current reality when Control suddenly interjected, **"DOCTOR LYONS, THE SECRETARY OF STATE WOULD LIKE TO TALK TO YOU. ARE YOU FREE TO DO SO?"**

"Son-of-a-bitch! Rob shouted with anguish as he looked down at his ring and held his head with his two hands. He had forgotten all about it. Did they still think they had him on a leash, ready to jump to their bidding?

Concerned, his father said, "What's the matter Rob?"

Rob pointed to his ring, "The Secretary of State is trying to contact me."
He walked over to the large window that looked out onto the monogram of a Canadian winter landscape with its black filigree of tree trunks and branches stripped of leaves, harshly set against a background of glistening white snow, bisected by roads full of grey slush, bordered by mountainous snow banks. He wanted to make sure that the Secretary of State could see his changed circumstances. It was far different from their last conversation on a lush, warm tropical island.

Coleen MacSween did indeed see the frigid winter scene.

"DOCTOR LYONS," she said, "I DID ALL I COULD TO PROTECT YOU AND YOUR FAMILY. IT IS UNFORTUNATE THAT YOU GOT CAUGHT IN THE CROSS FIRE. I WANT YOU TO KNOW THAT THE STATE DEPARTMENT NEVER ACCEPTED YOUR RESIGNATION. TECHNICALLY, A RESIGNATION CAN ONLY BE OFFICIAL IF IT HAS BEEN SUBMITTED ON THE PROPER FORM WITH YOUR SIGNATURE ON IT. AS FAR AS THE STATE DEPARTMENT IS CONCERNED, YOU ARE STILL ON ASSIGNMENT AND ON OUR PAYROLL. I CAN WELL UNDERSTAND YOUR WISH TO RESIGN. WE HAVE CERTAINLY PUT YOU THROUGH THE WRINGER AND YOU CERTAINLY OWE US NOTHING. HOWEVER, WE WOULD REALLY LIKE IT IF YOU COULD CONSIDER HELPING US WITH A PROBLEM THAT WE HAVE WITH CHINA."

"Are you nuts, why would I want to help the State Department with anything, especially China?"

"BECAUSE, THE CHINESE TRUST ONLY YOU," she paused before continuing, to let it sink in, "GENERAL KWAN LEE INSISTED THIS MORNING IN A CONFERENCE CALL WITH THE PRESIDENT THAT YOU BE THEIR LIAISON. HE WANTS TO MAKE SURE THE UNITED STATES FOLLOWS THROUGH WITH THEIR AGREEMENT TO CLOSE ALL THEIR BASES AROUND THE SOUTH CHINA SEA -

OTHERWISE HE HAS THREATENED TO FOLLOW THROUGH WITH TOTALLY DESTROYING OUR NAVY."

Rob started to laugh and replied, "I bet the president was pleased that he had not succeeded in burying me. This is rich. I wouldn't miss the opportunity to be the designated liaison for, as my mother would say, all the tea in China, but I do have a couple of stipulations."

"WHAT WOULD THEY BE?"

"My wife joins me immediately on the State Department payroll as my assistant, at the same salary I'm making. I need someone I can trust to protect my back and give me honest feedback and observations."

"DOCTOR LYONS, I HAVE BEEN TOLD TO OFFER YOU WHATEVER IT TAKES TO GET YOU TO TAKE THIS ASSIGNMENT. IF THAT IS ALL IT TAKES, CONSIDER IT DONE. WHAT ELSE."

"My parents need to be immediately reinstated with all their U.S. rights and privileges. Then they need to be flown to Puerto Rico to rejoin the rest of our family. I also want the State Department to assist the family in finding a Caribbean island for them to settle and invest in."

"A CORPORATE JET WILL BE DISPATCHED WITHIN THE HOUR. IT WILL COLLECT YOU AND BARBARA AND RETURN YOU TO WASHINGTON FOR A MEETING IN FOUR HOURS WITH THE PRESIDENT AND THE JOINT CHIEFS OF STAFF. THEY WILL BE PREPARING YOU FOR A MEETING IN BEJING IN THREE DAYS. THE SAME JET WILL CONTINUE ON TO PUERTO RICO WITH YOUR PARENTS. WHEN THEY ARRIVE THERE, STATE DEPARTMENT STAFF WILL BE READY TO PRESENT THEM WITH SOME POSSIBLE CARIBBEAN NATIONS THEY MIGHT CONSIDER SETTLING IN. SINCE YOUR FAMILY WILL BE INVESTING SIGNIFICANTLY IN THESE ISLANDS, YOU CAN BE ASSURED THAT THEY WILL RECEIVE A VERY POSITIVE RECEPTION FROM THESE ISLAND GOVERNMENTS. WE WILL PAVE THE WAY FOR THEM."

Rob didn't say thank you. This was fixing a mess that they had created. He wondered if he could ever feel that burning pride of being an American ever again. Could he ever again put his blind faith in its leadership? He wondered what adventures and challenges he and Barbara would next encounter.

CHAPTER 31

Epilogue

In Florida, alone in her palatial house on the Foundation's estate, Marigold Dupont had watched the destruction of Saint Matts. Tears had rolled down her cheeks; she was saddened to see the blatantly destructive, cruel nature of mankind. She had sobbed loudly, and then got very angry. She had shouted out, "You lying son-of-a-bitch, I am going to destroy you." No one heard her, but Willie Brown's days were numbered.

Marigold reached into her purse, took out the small recording device and played back her meeting with the president. She distinctly heard "Well Marigold, I am sure if we had that check, you could stop worrying about those monkeys". First thing on Monday morning she would be contacting her banker to put a stop payment on that check. In the meantime, she would contact the Republicans to see what hornet's nest she could stir up with her recording of a Democratic president on the take.

In Washington, at home surrounded by his family, Senator Rick Wilcox, had shaken his head in disbelief to see that the fruits of his irresponsible political posturing had resulted in the President ordering the destruction of the island of Saint Matts. He wondered how many children around the world would be born with birth defects because of the release of radiation from this nuclear bomb. How many millions would have their life shortened by this increased dose of radiation? How many of those torn from the island would never be able to adjust to their new lives in the United States and would regret the day they accepted the $100,000 bribe?

Rick Wilcox feared for the future. For almost one hundred years the lid had been kept on nuclear weapons. Now, the lid was off. Twice, in less than a week, nuclear devices had been triggered by political egos for strategic objectives. What if other nations no longer restrained themselves in using this ultimate hammer for political gain?

When scientists had exploded Trinity, the first nuclear bomb on July 16, 1945 thirty-five miles southeast of Socorro, New Mexico, some of them had been concerned that it could set off a chain reaction that would not stop until everything in the world had been reduced to molecules. What, if each time a nuclear bomb exploded, it was increasing the odds that such a chain reaction could be triggered. Not only would he have killed his own children, and his children's children, but all mankind.

Watching the senseless destruction of Saint Matts, Senator Rick Wilcox had an epiphany. He was a changed, sober man. Politics could no longer be that silly game that he used to play. He suddenly realized it was a sacred responsibility. With this realization, a feeling of great guilt and shame descended on him like a shroud. He vowed that he would do everything he could to right the wrong that he had initiated. His new attitude was reflected in his speeches and actions in the months that followed. He gained a respect among his fellow politicians that had not been there before. In August, he accepted the nomination to run as Vice President on the Republican ticket with the hope that he could move the world from the brink of extinction.

Rick Wilcox's success had been aided by Marigold Dupont. Shortly after the destruction of Saint Matt's, Marigold DuPont had met with him and handed over the recording of the President accepting her $10,000,000. Having such a political weapon had been the key to his winning the Vice President nomination. He had taken great joy in playing the tape at every opportunity to show the Democrats as Machiavellian opportunists with no conscience or principles.

While the objective of bombing Saint Matt's was supposed to have sent a message to the electorate that Willie Brown was a strong decisive leader who had only done what he thought was necessary to protect Americans, it had backfired. Once the electorate understood that dropping the nuclear bomb had been a re-election gimmick by a man, without a moral conscience, he became the most despised politician in American history.

To further add to his woes, Marigold DuPont's Protect All Primates Foundation early in the campaign had merged with America's Green Party, the Foundation to Ban Nuclear Weapons and the International Organization For Displaced People to form the World Preservation Society (W.P.S.). As soon as Rick Wilcox had injected Marigold's recording into the election campaign, the Democrats had quickly returned the $10,000,000 to Protect All Primates. Marigold immediately chose to fund the W.P.S. with it. The W.P.S. chose as their emblem (with prodding from

Marigold) a curved yellow banana on a green background with a monkey perched in the curve. Some Republicans thought it looked too much like the old hammer and sickle symbol of the Communist party.

The W.P.S. membership quickly grew to several hundred thousand members. They took advantage of every opportunity to disrupt Democratic Presidential campaign rallies. Their favorite tactic was throwing rotten bananas on the stage before Willie Brown was introduced. The Secret Service brought in sniffer dogs to stop bananas from being brought into the rallies. The W.P.S. members then progressed to wearing yellow T shirts (with the W.P.S. symbol) under their regular clothing, so they could take off their outer shirts and drown support for Willie with a sea of yellow. This display was accompanied by their vocal protest as they shouted out "Remember the Monkeys, Remember the Monkeys".

The Republicans had won the November election in a landslide. Willie had left office with the chant of "Vote for the Clown, Willie Brown, vote for the Clown, Willie Brown" still ringing in his ears. While he could justify the destruction of Saint Matts to himself, he was unable to handle the disrespect by the voters and his shunning by his old colleagues.

Isolated and depressed, he had retired to the anonymity of a remote French Polynesian island not far from Tahiti. Within a month of his self-imposed exile he suddenly came down with a severe headache and a rash. This illness quickly evolved into a high fever, diarrhea and finally excruciating muscle pain. He died in agony in ten days from a spontaneous hemorrhage. His body was flown back to the United States for a funeral appropriate for an ex-president. The autopsy, back in the United States, revealed that he had died of the Green Monkey disease, Filovirida, a close relative of the Ebola virus.

Filovirida viruses are among the deadliest organisms known to infect humans. They are spread by encountering the saliva from infected monkeys. This was a puzzle to the forensic team investigating Willie's death because there were no monkeys on that island.

Upon her return from a South Pacific holiday, cruising among the French Polynesian Islands, Marigold DuPont had been questioned by the Secret Service. No evidence was ever found to link her to Willie Brown's infection or to her even being on the same Polynesian island as Willie Brown.

General Horatio Douglas was a professional. He too had watched the destruction of Saint Matt on his television. The senseless destruction of that paradise had made him very sad. He accepted that he did things for his country, with apparent enthusiasm, that he would never have chosen to do if the choice were his. To him the total and complete destruction of the sovereign country of Saint Matts was immoral and unnecessary. He had felt betrayed. He had sworn to protect his country from harm, not to commit narcissistic, selfish acts so politicians could get re-elected to second terms. He was tired of it all.

Central Command Headquarters in Florida received his retirement documents the day following the bombing. He had immediately started to make plans to settle in Panama. He had served there at the beginning of his career when it was critical for the United States to protect the canal. He had liked the people and the climate. Perhaps he would marry again for the fifth time and finally find peace and contentment.

General Kwan Lee's status in the Communist Party had taken a giant jump forward when he returned home with a commitment from the United States to abandon their military bases surrounding the South China Sea. He was placed in charge of taking advantage of this strategic victory. His concerns about having to solidify their position with the newly elected U.S. president were minimized when Doctor Rob Lyons was put in charge of fully briefing the new president's transition team. The military bases were abandoned. The troops were returned to the United States. The world did not fall into chaos.

With Willie Brown losing the election, Secretary of State, Coleen MacSween, was out of a job. It was disconcerting for her to go from carrying all the cares of the world on her shoulders to only worrying about whether there was milk in the refrigerator for breakfast in the morning. The civil servants in the State Department had quickly filled the void she left. They had set about to indoctrinate a new Secretary of State in the hidden perils of diplomacy.

Coleen was approached by the Democratic Party to run for Senator in Massachusetts a few months after she had left the State Department. Her husband said if she accepted, he would leave her. He wanted to retire and enjoy what time he had left. She accepted the nomination to run for the Senate. Her husband left her. She lost the election. The consensus was that she had been too closely associated with that clown, Willie Brown.

THE END

If you enjoyed this novel, then you will enjoy reading **USING DROUGHT USA**. It is the second action packed novel in Ian MacDonald's Rob Lyon's series.

Rob Lyon's mission this time is to convince separatists in Canada's Western Provinces and in Quebec to support a US plan to invade the Province of Ontario. In exchange the US will support their formation of independent republics.

The invasion intent is to relieve the American South West drought. This will be achieved by damming Canadian rivers that flow North into the sub-Arctic barren lands and re-direct that flow South, to the head waters of the Colorado River. This would bring desperately needed water to California, New Mexico, Nevada and Arizona. The plan is expected to win votes in November's Presidential election. It would eliminate the fast-approaching economic disaster caused by the shortage of water.

A Washington lobbyist becomes a casualty when he sells the President's secret water plan to the Canadian ambassador. Learning of the plan, native people, in the effected region and in the Washington area, make plans to assassinate the president. Rob becomes a fugitive hunted across Canada. The Canadian Federal Government prepares to repel the invasion. Rob partners with a beautiful State Department agent who shares the dangers......

For more information on purchasing your copy of the novel **"USING DROUGHT USA"** go to:

www.informus.ca/DROUGHT_USA.html

You can also read the novel for **FREE**. Segments of the book will be serialized in **"USING DROUGHT USA E-MAGAZINE"**at the same above email address. You may also request that these free segments be emailed to you, as they are released, by sending a request to **drought@informus.ca**.

****

You may also enjoy reading **BEWARE THE ABANDONED**, the first book in Ian MacDonald's new John Cross series.

John Cross was an abandoned child fighting for survival on the mean streets of Los Angeles, when The Sanctuary, a capitalist sect, that searches the world for the most intelligent, resourceful of abandoned street children found him. Recognizing his potential, they selected him to be trained to accumulate great wealth. His financial success allows them to recruit more children to further enrich The Sanctuary. How he accumulates his wealth is of no concern to The Sanctuary. What is critical is protecting their money maker and keeping him ahead of his pursuers, the FBI and the mob. The trail of bodies that John Cross leaves behind in Paris, Las Vegas and Delaware are just obstacles that had to be eliminated in his quest for wealth.

Can the murder of a wealthy socialite be justified if her money saves a thousand, abandoned, orphaned street children? What fate awaits his latest romantic interest? If you like suspense, action and a thoughtful story, you will like, Beware The Abandoned.

For more information on purchasing your copy of **BEWARE THE ABANDONED** go to

http://informus.ca/THE_EXPLOITED.html

You can also read it for **FREE** It will be serialized at the same above internet address in a "**BEWARE THE ABANDONED E-MAGAZINE**". You can also request that issues of this e-magazine be emailed to you as they are released. Send your request to **beware@informus.ca**.